MY FAIR LORD

ELISABETH HOBBES

One More Chapter
a division of HarperCollins*Publishers* Ltd
1 London Bridge Street
London SE1 9GF
www.harpercollins.co.uk
HarperCollins*Publishers*
Macken House, 39/40 Mayor Street Upper,
Dublin 1, D01 C9W8, Ireland

This paperback edition 2024

1

First published in Great Britain in ebook format
by HarperCollins*Publishers* 2023
Copyright © Elisabeth Hobbes 2024

Elisabeth Hobbes asserts the moral right to
be identified as the author of this work

A catalogue record of this book
is available from the British Library

ISBN: 978-0-00-863722-4

This novel is entirely a work of fiction. The names, characters and incidents portrayed in it are the work of the author's imagination. Any resemblance to actual persons, living or dead, events or localities is entirely coincidental.
Printed and bound in the UK using 100% Renewable Electricity
by CPI Group (UK) Ltd
All rights reserved. No part of this publication may be reproduced, stored in a retrieval system, or transmitted, in any form or by any means, electronic, mechanical, photocopying, recording or otherwise, without the prior permission of the publishers.

Elisabeth's writing career began when she finished third in Harlequin's *So You Think You Can Write* contest in 2013 and she hasn't looked back. She teaches Primary school but would rather write full time because, unlike five-year-olds, her characters generally do what she tells them. She spends most of her spare time reading and is a pro at cooking one-handed while holding a book.

She lives in Cheshire because the car broke down there in 1999 and she never left.

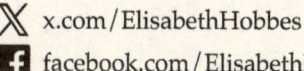

elisabethhobbes.co.uk

X x.com/ElisabethHobbes
f facebook.com/ElisabethHobbes

Also by Elisabeth Hobbes

The Secret Agent

Daughters of Paris

Writing as Elisabeth J Hobbes

Daughter of the Sea

The Promise Tree

To my son AW who has succeeded in becoming a fine young man despite my parental input!

Chapter One

"Would you risk your reputation to save a man's life?"

Florence Wakechild blinked at the man who had slid in front of her with such an unexpected question. She responded instinctively. "I think that very much depends on the worthiness of the life."

The man gave a warm laugh, as if this was the most amusing retort the world had ever seen. "You're an American! Well, madam, how worthy my life is remains to be seen, but I am rather attached to it and if you would help me keep it, I would be in your debt."

Florence bristled at "madam". Twenty-four was hardly deserving of that title. She wondered if he was intoxicated. He didn't reek of rum or gin like so many of the dock workers or sailors who walked Liverpool's streets, but Florence could think of no other explanation for his astonishing words.

She stared at him. He stared back from beneath the slightly shapeless brim of a tweed hat. Bright blue eyes, bordering on violet, held her gaze fiercely. Not pleading or desperate. Instead, they held a level of challenge that stopped Florence from sweeping past him where he stood. As she hesitated, his eyes flickered away, looking beyond her. He frowned then jerked his head around and looked behind him. Florence could see nothing that indicated danger, but she did not really know what she should be looking for.

Since arriving, Florence had discovered that Liverpool was a city of all races and religions. That very morning she'd bought pastries from a bakery run by an elderly Belgian woman, which stood beside a laundry run by two Chinese sisters. Men and women with skin in hues that ranged from the darkest mahogany to Florence's pale porcelain filled the streets. She had no idea where the source of his anxiety might be.

"If it is money you need, I'm afraid I have none at my disposal," she said cautiously. It was a lie. She did have a purse containing some of her allowance, but she wasn't yet sure enough about the relative values of dollars and pounds to know how much to give him.

"No money, just a small deception. All you have to do is act as my sweetheart for the next ten minutes."

The man held out an arm as if he expected Florence to join him for a promenade along the Mersey waterfront.

"I'll do no such thing!" she exclaimed.

The light in his eyes hardened to flint. He lowered his

arm and pulled up the collar of his coat, hunching his shoulders.

"Then you have answered my question and I shall bid you good day." He gave Florence a slightly condescending smile before turning away.

It was the smile that did it.

Florence had always believed she possessed a daring nature that would stand her in good stead for anything. A modern woman, worthy of being granted suffrage, of making her way in the world. Of being equal to men. Now the opportunity to prove it had come her way and she had been found wanting.

"Wait!"

She caught hold of his sleeve at the elbow. The man turned back in surprise. Florence looked him over once again. His outer coat was slightly baggy and a little faded, suggesting to Florence's practised eyes that it was a ready-made item using cheap dye, rather than tailored. He wore serviceable dark moleskin trousers but they were accompanied by a waistcoat of the most garish green and yellow tartan Florence had ever seen. His cap was of good tweed and his clothing was cleaner than other working men she had seen walking around the city streets. He spoke well enough. At least, no worse than many of the men Florence's father did business with back home. He might come from a home no less respectable than Florence's own father had been born and brought up in before he made the family a fortune by manufacturing dyes.

"What exactly would you need of me?" she asked

cautiously. "It's just that I don't have a maid with me to chaperone us."

Triumph rippled over his face. "You won't need a chaperone. I'm not suggesting we vanish into an hotel. All you need do is walk along the street with me, and if necessary, pretend to be absorbed in shop windows so our backs are to any passers-by. Just like that gaggle of hens are over there."

Florence glanced to where her sister, Cordelia, or as she was known since marriage, Lady Griggs, Baroness of Goreswarth, was currently peering through the window of Lewis' department store among a huddle of women captivated by the new hats on display. Her mother-in-law, Violet, Lady Griggs – so called for being the mother of Lord Griggs, fifth Baron of Goreswarth, and part of the reason Florence was certain she would never understand the British aristocracy – was gesturing to the window with extensive hand flourishes and almost knocking the hats off other women in the crowd. Neither of them had noticed Florence had been accosted by a stranger. As she watched, they simply upped and vanished into the store without even alerting her to the fact.

"Well, that's charming!" she exclaimed.

She was filled with exasperation at being forgotten so easily, but it would give her the opportunity to slip away. The Griggs women were highly unlikely to emerge before an hour was up so her absence would not be noticed.

Hats be darned! The morning had been dull as they had traipsed from shop to teashop to yet another shop. The afternoon promised to be more of the same. Florence drew herself up to her full height, little though that was, and lifted her chin.

"I'll do it." As his face lit, she held a hand up in warning. "But I won't kiss you or let you put your hand about my waist. And I won't go into any private rooms with you."

He laughed, revealing a set of even white teeth that were nicer than she would expect from a man of his station. Small lines appeared at the side of his mouth and at the corner of each eye, and Florence found herself smiling back in response.

"Those are acceptable terms," he said. "An arm though is perfectly respectable. If we stride along side by side, we'll look like we're having a lovers' quarrel."

He offered his arm again and this time Florence slipped her hand through it, resting her fingers lightly on his forearm.

"You recited your mamma's lessons in how to guard your reputation perfectly," the man murmured as they strolled through the crowds of Market Street and turned into Ranelagh Street. "She will be proud at how well you absorbed them."

Florence's muscles clenched, stomach tightening. Her companion must have sensed the change in her demeanour, or perhaps her hand had inadvertently clutched his sleeve tighter, because he looked at her earnestly.

"Did I say something wrong?"

"My mother has been beyond the cares of this world for the past eighteen years," Florence told him quietly.

The look of abject contrition that passed across his face was enough for her to forgive his blunder instantly.

"My apologies and condolences," he murmured. He covered her hand briefly with his, then removed it hastily as the indiscretion presumably struck him.

"It's been so long I barely remember her presence."

"I lost mine when I was eight. The pain diminishes but never departs entirely."

Touched at the sudden transformation from teasing to sincere, Florence acknowledged the apology with a tilt of the head. He had been mocking her in the first place, but there had been no malice in it even so. More irritatingly, he was partially correct.

"It was my aunt," she admitted with a small smile. "She took it upon herself to bring my sister and I up as she thought my mother would have wanted." She doubted Aunt Patricia would ever have anticipated a man such as this to be the recipient of Florence's attention. Additionally, from what she knew of her late mother from the tales Cordelia and their father told, Lavinia would have seen Florence's decision as a huge adventure.

She cast a surreptitious look at her companion. He was tall and slender; sharp-faced with good cheekbones and a straight nose that would have done a marble bust proud. His jaw was peppered with light stubble, suggesting he took little care over his appearance or hadn't had the opportunity to shave that day. His startling blue eyes roved constantly from side to side, animating his face. He walked with long strides and Florence's feet raced to keep up with him. She was glad of the sensible low-heeled shoes she was wearing and that summer in England was cool enough that she wasn't likely to overheat.

"Can we slow down a little?" she begged. "If you are trying to appear unobtrusive, you're going about it all in the wrong way. We hardly look like a pair of sweethearts out for a stroll."

"Good point." He slowed his pace. "I picked well."

"Why did you pick me?" Florence asked shyly.

"You didn't look busy, but you did look bored," he said. He gave her a sidelong grin. "Am I right?"

"Yes on both counts," Florence admitted.

Just beyond Central Station, her companion changed direction sharply and they crossed the road, dodging between the lanes of coaches and carriages. They turned into a street that was narrower and quieter than the main thoroughfare with its rows of storefronts. Now they were in the territory of warehouses and factories. The men and women they passed were working, or if they were shopping, they were buying food not fripperies.

Florence glanced back over her shoulder. Leaving behind the bustle of Ranelagh Street meant that if anything were to happen to her, there would be fewer people to come to her aid. No one knew where she was and she realised now how stupid she was being. She could be helping a criminal evade police capture.

"Where are we going?" She should have asked before,

really. Acting impulsively was a dreadful habit that she did try to be aware of, but somehow it was hard.

"To the waterfront. I need to deliver something to an office at the docks before three. Hold this please."

The man removed his coat and held it out to Florence. Taken aback, she took it without even questioning what he was doing. He removed his waistcoat and turned it inside out so that the hideous tartan disappeared and was replaced with a plain, dark grey cloth of much more respectable appearance. He took the coat back from Florence, took the tweed cap off his head, revealing light brown waves cut short on the side and long on top, and produced a slightly battered derby from inside his coat. His outfit now marked him out as a man of the working class, but probably a clerk or a secretary rather than a factory labourer.

"Are you a spy?" Florence asked, astonished at the change in his appearance.

"Of course I'm not a spy," he exclaimed.

He sounded incredulous and his face became a picture of innocence, leading her to immediately suspect there was more to him than he was revealing.

She narrowed her eyes. "That sounds exactly like the sort of thing a spy would say."

"It's also the exact thing someone who isn't a spy would say," he pointed out.

"I suppose so," she said.

"It's a very odd conclusion to jump to. What made you think it?"

Florence floundered. "Well ... you say your life is in danger and you've coerced a perfect stranger to take part in a deception. It seems the sort of thing a spy might do."

The man looked amused. "Do you know a lot about spies?"

"Not really," Florence admitted, her cheeks starting to burn.

"If I was, I would hardly admit the fact to a complete stranger, Miss..." He tilted his head to one side and gave her an easy smile. "I don't actually know your name, do I."

Florence hesitated. He did not need to know it as they would be parting before long. Which meant there was no reason he should not know.

"Miss Wakechild."

He swept his hat off his head. "I'm pleased to make your acquaintance, Miss Wakechild. Ned Blake at your service."

"It's nice to meet you, Mr Blake. At least, I think it is. If you aren't a spy, why is your life in danger?" Florence asked. "You aren't a detective, are you? Or an agitator for revolutionaries?"

He laughed. "I assume you know as much about detectives or revolutionaries as you do about spies, Miss Wakechild."

She grinned, rather enjoying a frivolous conversation. It wasn't very often that anyone actually talked with her about anything that she considered meaningful. "Only what I've read in Mr Conan Doyle's stories. He writes about a detective who has rather glorious adventures. My sister sends me The Strand Magazine whenever she sends parcels over to us."

"Yes, I've read a couple of them," Blake said, replacing his hat. "Rather far-fetched I think, with all the secret identities and so on. Sadly, I'm nothing so interesting."

"Why do you need me in that case?" Florence asked, feeling slightly deflated.

Blake smiled. "I may have exaggerated the danger a little. I doubt they'd go as far as killing me, though I'd definitely get a beating. My pursuers are looking for a single man not a couple. Together, we can walk right past them and they wouldn't look twice."

"But who are *they*?" Florence unwound her arm from his. "I'm not taking another step until you tell me who is chasing you and why. I don't believe you're a spy, before you ask."

"Would you believe I'm a worthless drunkard and unrepentant gambler trying to escape my creditors?" he asked.

"I'd be more inclined to believe that," Florence retorted frankly. "Though you don't smell like a drunkard at the moment."

Blake's eyebrow rose. "How wonderfully insulting of you. Are all American women as frank as you?"

She was about to reply that no, her frankness was a particular curse to her alone – according to her father – but he didn't wait for an answer. He took her arm again and resumed walking. At the end of the road, they emerged onto Duke Street.

"If you must know, I won more than I was anticipated to at cards. Or rather, I won something I wasn't supposed to. The organisers of the game grew suspicious at my methods. They would gladly carve their pound of flesh, which would inconvenience both myself and the recipient of my message."

Florence hid her surprise. She hadn't expected a working man would be able to reference Shakespeare. The English education system was better than she imagined. The cryptic reference to "something" was intriguing.

"Am I in danger?" Florence asked, glancing back over her shoulder.

Blake smiled reassuringly. He patted Florence's hand, drawing a little closer to her side in the process. "If I thought you were at any risk, I wouldn't have asked you to accompany me," Blake said.

Oddly enough, this did serve to make her feel safe. Perhaps it was his size and the way he appeared to be alert for any risk that was comforting. She looked into his eyes. They seemed honest, but then how could she know? He could be a very adept confidence trickster.

"What did you win?"

Mr Blake grinned. "That's not your business."

"Were you cheating?"

"Absolutely not!" His brows rose skywards but she couldn't tell if his outrage was real or pretend, so was none the wiser about whether he was telling the truth.

"I've been playing for years. After a while you develop

an instinct for when others are, though," he said with a wicked glint in his eye.

Being back on a busy street also helped because if she needed to, she could scream for help.

She nodded. "Very well, but I hope you will take this opportunity to reform. No more drinking and gambling. It only leads to trouble."

"I think I am well beyond any reformation." Blake grimaced. "And I didn't take you for a mealy-mouthed Temperance Leaguer."

"Why not?" Florence asked sharply.

He looked her up and down. She felt his eyes raking over her and it made her shudder with indignation. Definitely indignation.

"No wire-rimmed spectacles or severe bun, and your clothing is far too bright."

Florence eyed him coldly. Her skirt was a vibrant cobalt blue, matched with a short jacket of yellow, embroidered with cobalt blue flowers. The advantage of being the daughter of a dye manufacturer was having access to whatever colours she wished. That didn't mean she was too frivolous for opinions on the state of the world. As a matter of fact, she did wear spectacles, but only for reading. Anticipating a dull afternoon with Cordelia and Violet in Lewis' tea rooms, she had concealed them at the bottom of her bag along with a copy of *Little Lord Fauntleroy*.

"Do you assume any woman who has the inclination to improve mans' lot in life must be a starched-bloused harridan in grey? I have a good mind to leave you to your fate! Your opinions need challenging."

"Indeed they do." Blake grinned again. "When we get to safety, you can lecture me over the evils of drink and vice another time."

They passed a clockmaker, a watchmaker and a police station. Somewhere in the vicinity was a school because she could hear children shouting. It was exciting to be amid the bustle. No matter where you went in Liverpool, it seemed like everyone belonged, from the dock workers who carried heavy boxes from one side of town to the other, to the shopkeepers who served their customers with a friendly smile and warm welcome. Though the assumption of a warm welcome was perhaps naïve, given their current escapade.

Blake glanced behind him occasionally. On the third turn, he stopped abruptly. Presumably he saw his pursuers because he smoothly wheeled round, directing Florence's attention to a nearby store window. He bent his head to hers and waved his free hand, as if pointing out something for Florence's attention. His breath was cool on her neck and Florence's cheeks began to grow warm as the fine hairs at her nape lifted slightly, tickling her.

"What are we doing?" she whispered, sliding her eyes to look at him.

His eyes twinkled and he looked as though he was enjoying himself despite the jeopardy facing them.

"We are discussing furnishing our home as newlyweds.

You're telling me those lamps would look well in our parlour."

"Nonsense," Florence retorted, indicating the pair he had chosen; two plump cherubs sitting atop the oil reservoir, supporting the glass shades of a bilious yellow. "They're far too unstable. They'd topple in a breeze. I wouldn't gift them to my least favourite aunt!"

She caught his gleeful grin in the reflection of the window. His eyes creased again, the smile lines appearing at the edges. She had initially thought him too thin-faced to be attractive, but his zeal lit his face up.

"Excellent taste! I knew I had picked the right wife."

"Except I'm not going to marry you," Florence pointed out.

She looked at the window again, this time behind them to the other people in the street. Most appeared to be innocently going about their business, but one man dressed in a squashed-looking hat and sporting large whiskers was walking very slowly on the opposite pavement, looking around him. Florence tensed and looked at Blake's reflection. He was also looking behind him.

"How long must we keep up this charade?" she whispered.

His reflected eyes met hers and he smiled reassuringly.

"Only a little further to go. Tell me, Miss Wakechild, which of these lamps would you choose since you have rejected the cherubs?"

"That one, with the square base and the purple acanthus

flowers on the shade. I'd buy the pair of matching floor standing lamps too."

"Your parlour must be bigger than mine," Mr Blake commented.

Florence felt a blush rising. It was undoubtedly true and she wondered what he would say if she told him the house back in Philadelphia had two parlours interlinked by folding doors as well as a morning and sitting room. Her father had earned his wealth honestly, but it didn't seem tactful to mention it.

"We're talking pretend, aren't we, so it can be as big as we like."

She took Blake's arm again and they strolled towards the Mersey.

"I do enjoy the thrill of the chase," Blake said breezily.

"We're the quarry not the hunters," Florence pointed out.

"Even more thrilling!" Blake grinned, reminding Florence of the Cheshire Cat. Goblin, the enormous grey mouser that prowled around her father's Frankford Creek factory back in Philadelphia, also sprang to mind, and once the image was there, she could not shake it. All the same, she had to agree with his assessment. Racing through the streets had been an exciting way to spend half an hour but now it would soon be over because as they rounded another corner, a forest of masts and brick storehouses that lined the landing stages came into view. They were almost at the docks, not too far from the building where Florence's father had taken an office for the duration of his visit.

Blake's smile vanished abruptly and he tensed. His eyes darted toward the river. He muttered something beneath his breath that Florence only half heard, but she believed it was a very rude word indeed.

"Excuse me for that, but we're not safe yet."

Whiskers was standing on the corner of Strand Street, looking around. Florence had just about enough time to feel smug in the knowledge that she had picked out the right man before Blake seized her hand and pulled her after him down an alley. They barged through a door and Florence found herself in a crowded pub.

More astonishing than that, she found herself in Blake's arms, backed into a corner and pressed tightly against his chest. He was close enough to kiss her and for a couple of rapid heartbeats, she thought that might be exactly what was about to happen.

"Mr Blake!" she gasped, not knowing whether to be terrified or excited, to fight against him or submit wholeheartedly. He wasn't looking at Florence, however, but behind her and his face had changed.

"Shhh!" Blake commanded. He pressed his lips tightly together and Florence realised a kiss was not on the cards after all.

Florence swallowed her protestations – and slight disappointment – and took a deep breath. Beneath the overpowering smell of cigarette smoke and beer that filled her nose, she caught a trace of something sweet and feminine. Cheap perfume. And it was coming from Blake's clothing. She wasn't the first woman he'd spent time with today, and the previous one had been much closer. She pushed him away.

"Really this is enough! I'm not going any further."

"You don't have to," Blake said, looking at her and smiling easily, as if nothing untoward had happened. Unlike Florence's, his heart was presumably not thumping a hundred beats per minute because she'd been in his arms.

"I don't think he spotted us. I can wait it out here if need be. The landlord knows me and will deny I ever came through the door. I'll even find you a boy to escort you safely back to your friends."

"Oh. Well … in that case…" Florence looked around, curious at what the inside of a British pub looked like, her indignation at being surplus to requirements momentarily forgotten. Small tables were set higgledy-piggledy and a long bar ran the length of one wall with men standing at it.

"So this is a pub. I thought there would be a piano for some reason."

Blake barked a laugh, sounding a little like a performing sea lion.

"Have you never been in a pub before?" he asked.

Florence shook her head. "This is only my second time out of America. The first time was for my sister's wedding and we went straight to her husband's estate in Cheshire. It's fascinating here. But look at them," she said, gesturing around to the tables. "Is everybody completely drunk in the middle of the day?"

"Drinking but not necessarily drunk," Blake said.

"Don't they have better things to do? A city as big as

Liverpool must be screaming out for men and women to work."

"Oh yes, it is. If you don't mind slave wages and harsh conditions." Blake's voice was bitter and his lips, which Florence was suddenly conscious were distractingly well shaped, curled scornfully. "I suppose in the glorious post-war utopia of America everybody is paid five dollars an hour and eats roast beef for every meal."

"Of course not! You're deliberately talking poppycock," Florence snapped.

There was a slight flicker of his eyelids. Surprise that she answered back, no doubt. She'd been told repeatedly how meek and well-behaved English young ladies were and had intended to follow suit. It was a shame she had barely lasted a week into the trip before getting into an argument. She took a breath and counted to five before speaking again.

"No, there are plenty of poor workers in America too but that doesn't make it right and it doesn't mean that they shouldn't be properly paid."

"I'm glad to hear you think so." Blake's lips lost their angry curl. They really were very nice lips. Not too plump but not too firm. Very kissable.

"You need to go now," he said. "You'll be perfectly safe. They won't connect us, and besides, their beef is with me."

"What exactly is that beef?" she asked. "I really am aching to know what you won."

"I'm afraid that is going to have to remain one of life's mysteries," Blake said. He tapped the side of his nose. "State secrets. Here, Alfie!"

He whistled, and a small Black boy sauntered over from a table.

"Take this lady back to Lewis' department store. See she gets safely to the window with the hat display and there'll be a cup of mother's ruin for you."

Florence was certain she must have misheard the promise. The boy could be no more than seven.

"Gin! You can't give a child gin!" Florence exclaimed.

"He can if he wants me to take you," Alfie retorted with a cheeky grin.

"The gin is cleaner and safer than the water," Blake answered. He held out a hand to Florence. "Thank you, Miss Wakechild. I'm indebted to you. If I can ever return the favour…"

He left the sentence unfinished, leaving Florence to wonder exactly how he would repay the favour or what favour she might require of someone like him. She shook his hand briefly.

"Come on, miss." Alfie tugged at her skirt. "Let him get on with what he needs to do. Don't let them crack your head, Ned."

They left through the door they had entered through. Turning back, Florence saw Blake weaving his way through the tables towards a staircase. As they left, she risked a glimpse to the corner where Whiskers had stood but he had gone.

Alfie trudged along beside her kicking at bits of rubbish and stones as they walked. His shoes were scuffed and the laces mismatched.

"Will he really buy you gin?" Florence asked, still not able to quite believe it.

Alfie must have misinterpreted her question because he nodded eagerly. "Course he will. He keeps his word, Ned does. He's a good one that one. Looked after me when me dad got so drunk he didn't know which of me to thump."

Florence gaped and Alfie shrugged.

"It's how it goes. Come on, miss. Looking for hats, are you? American, aren't you? My mam was from America. Her mam had been a slave, she had, but my mam was born free and you don't do that no more. I'd like to go there one day. Save up my passage and start a whole new life in the new world. I'll be a millionaire by the time I'm twenty."

Florence looked at the lad. He was thin and his skin had an unhealthy hue. Florence wouldn't put money on him making it to twenty, never mind making his fortune. She bade him goodbye with a shilling as a tip which he seemed happy with and he skipped off whistling.

She walked into Lewis' and discovered the two Lady Griggs still deep in discussion with a milliner's assistant. Her absence had not been noticed and it appeared her reputation was still intact.

Chapter Two

After two hours taking a nap in the room above the pub, followed by a bowl of scouse, Ned felt sufficiently refreshed and was convinced the coast would be clear. He borrowed a razor from the landlord, shaved himself, and had a cursory wash. He left a couple of shillings at the bar for Alfie's gin and cautiously left the pub.

He saw no one he recognised as he took the short walk along the waterfront. The pavements in front of the buildings that lined each dock were full of men – and the occasional woman – hoping for work. They clamoured at the gates of warehouses and shipping offices, calling for the opportunity for work the following morning. So many people desperate to make enough to buy bread. Most of them would be disappointed. Despite Ned's earlier assessment of slave wages, there were many who had no choice but to take the pittance offered.

He wove his way through the crowds, glad that he did not have to join them. He was by no means a rich man, but he wasn't poor. He didn't want to contemplate a future where he might be. He dropped his head in case either of the men he was avoiding were in the crowds. The interesting Miss Wakechild thought she had spotted one but the bewhiskered man that she had fixed her attention on had been completely innocent as far as Ned was aware, and she had missed the real pursuers. Still, she would never know that she had been wrong. Letting her feel clever hadn't done any harm unless she encountered the man at some point and accused him of something.

The director of the White Line Lumber Transportation Company would not normally see a visitor who turned up without an appointment to the office in the Huskisson Building, especially when it was nearing four o'clock.

"I'm afraid it will be completely impossible for you to see Mr Van Hoon," the overly pomaded clerk at the desk told him.

"This says you're wrong," Ned said as he held out a card bearing his initials. "Please take it up."

He felt a great deal of satisfaction when the clerk returned bearing Ned's card and sporting an awed expression less than ten minutes later.

"Mr Van Hoon will see you shortly. Please come with me."

Ned knew the way to the office; however, to spare the young man any further loss of dignity, he immediately fell in behind and allowed himself to be led to the spacious and elegantly decorated office on the fourth floor of the building.

"Thank you, Robbins, I'll take it from here," announced Marius Van Hoon himself. Robbins backed out of the room, giving Ned another awed look.

Van Hoon leapt from the chair behind his cluttered desk as soon as the door was shut.

"Good afternoon, Blake. Did you get it?"

No niceties. Barely even a civilised greeting. Ned put his temper in check. It was a measure of how anxious the older man was to hear Ned's news that his usually faultless manners had been forgotten.

Ned nodded. "I've got it."

He reached into the inside pocket of his coat and once inside the inside pocket, his hand dipped into another pocket, cleverly concealed within a double lining. From this, he retrieved a small package wrapped in a handkerchief, the sort that the pretty Miss Wakechild might to use to dab her eyes when reading a sentimental novel.

On second thought, he couldn't imagine the forthright young woman he had encountered earlier in the afternoon reading sentimental novels. She would no doubt view them as frivolous. She would possibly devour some improving tracts, or of course the works of Conan Doyle. His thoughts strayed idly back to their adventure through the streets and he smiled at the memory of her determined expression. Right now, she would probably be back with her companions, unable to mask her boredom while they sighed at hats. A pity. He'd have liked to have spent more time in her company.

Van Hoon gave a discreet but deliberate cough and Ned returned to the present matter. He tossed the handkerchief and its contents towards Van Hoon, who snatched it out of the air, reminding Ned of the way his mother's footstool-shaped chihuahua used to devour a treat tossed from a hand. Van Hoon unfolded the handkerchief and held up the ring it contained.

"Lord be praised," he said, turning it over from hand to hand. His shoulders dropped a full six inches. "I thank you, my boy. I don't know what I would have done without you."

"Oh I'm sure you would have worked something out," Ned said modestly. "I think this way was probably the most discreet and efficient, however. Fortunately, the fools who I was playing against didn't realise the value of what they had beyond the monetary."

They both gazed at the ring in Van Hoon's palm: two pearls set diagonally from each other in a twisted band of gold. The same ring was conspicuous on Van Hoon's finger in the large portrait done in oils that hung over the mantelpiece.

Van Hoon's son had staked it in a game of Brag and lost it. The boy was twenty-six; a couple of years younger than Ned himself. Despite an education at an excellent school where he had mingled with the sons of the aristocracy and businessmen alike, he had failed to pick up any sense of refinement or class. Even if he couldn't confine his whoring to discreet establishments, he really should have learned by that age not to frequent cheap brothels wearing very expensive and very distinctive heirlooms. The scandal, if it had become known, would have been extremely damaging. It was only Ned's skill at gambling, combined with a little sleight of hand, that meant he had been able to win it back from the pimp in the brothel.

Van Hoon unlocked the drawer of his desk and put the ring in a small box, then locked it again. He smiled up at Ned.

"Now, how about a whisky?"

"Gladly. Only the good stuff, mind," Ned said. "I had to drink enough gut rot to get those scoundrels drunk enough that they didn't notice I played a ten of spades twice."

"Old Midleton from County Cork. I never drink anything but the good stuff," Van Hoon announced. He paused in the process of taking the stopper out of a decanter. "I hope you weren't caused too much trouble?"

"Nothing I couldn't deal with efficiently." Ned accepted the tumbler of neat whisky and swirled it round. The aroma wafted to his nostrils. Rich and peaty. The good stuff indeed. Mind you, Van Hoon could well afford it and Ned had probably just saved him somewhere in the region of five or six hundred pounds, not counting the peace of mind that was beyond monetary value.

"Your good health," he said, raising the glass to Van Hoon.

They sipped the whisky. It was very good.

"No, I had no trouble," Ned repeated. It was a lie. He'd

got out of the gambling den in the cellar of the Pembroke Place brothel by the skin of his teeth, and only after thumping a couple of pimps. Once again, he thought of Miss Wakechild and her pluckiness in accompanying him. Thank goodness he hadn't needed to fight or run. The size of the men who had been chasing him was enough to make any sane man quake.

"I came across a most delightful young woman in the process," he commented. "An American. Gorgeous auburn hair and a lovely figure that Rubens would have delighted over."

"A redhead." Van Hoon raised an eyebrow. "Surely you aren't referring to the Wakechild girl?"

Ned prided himself on not often being caught unawares but now he blinked in surprise at hearing the name. He almost confirmed Van Hoon's guess but caught himself.

"It's possible. Who is she?"

"Her father is one of these upstarts whose family made their money in the past twenty years manufacturing and selling chemical dyes. He's come over here to try buy a titled husband for the girl. Done it once already with the older sister. Got her a baron from Cheshire. I've met the father but I've not had the privilege of speaking to the baroness or her sister."

There was clear contempt in Van Hoon's voice, accompanied by a curl of the lip. Ned finished his whisky but there was suddenly a bitter taste in his mouth. Miss Wakechild had mentioned in passing something about her sister's husband's estate in Cheshire, but it hadn't leapt out as significant at the time. It made it even more remarkable that she hadn't been diligently guarded by an aged aunt chaperone or, at bare minimum, a maid.

"So she's here to find a husband?" he mused.

"Not just any husband before you get your hopes up. She's got her eye on an aristocrat. Those of us without a title may look on in vain." He huffed and curled his lip at Ned. "Simply having money isn't good enough for their sort. These women are scrabbling around, whoring themselves out for the chance to wear a tiara and a scrap of ermine. Detestable things. It's becoming quite a thing from what I understand."

Ned bit his tongue, aghast at Van Hoon's audacity at condemning the family. Considering the service Ned had just undertaken for him, the man had a bare nerve criticising anyone else's offspring. All the same, a little of the admiration he had felt for Miss Wakechild faded away. She had seemed quite unlike other women he had known. The look of all-embracing boredom on her face as she had stood alone in the crowd of fluttering ladies cooing over hats had been remarkable. She'd been like a swan in a hen house. She'd been forthright, adventurous, and intelligent. And yet apparently, she was just one of the many women for whom a title was the ultimate trophy.

"It could have been her, I suppose," Ned said, pretending to think hard. "Though the woman I met didn't seem like a spoiled heiress. She sounded quite passionate about reforming the poor, misbegotten working man." He thought for a moment then in the spirit of fairness, added, "And improving his life."

Van Hoon tutted. "I wonder if she airs such ideals to her father. He's rich, though not in the league of the Vanderbilts or the Astors, and I cannot imagine him throwing away profits on building garden plots for his employees."

He refilled his glass and offered the decanter to Ned. Ned declined. He was rapidly finding himself wishing to be out of the man's company. Van Hoon put the stopper back in and took it back to the tray.

"I have heard the family will be attending the Earl of Merseyside's post-race reception at the Wellington Rooms tomorrow evening. I am honoured to be attending so I will do my best to have a good look at the girl. It's a shame he chose to hold it there rather than at Castle Ainsdale, but there we go. Perhaps she might be induced to marry someone without a title but with a full bankbook, prestige, and a good business to invest in, if the offer was attractive enough."

Ned was sufficiently adept at commanding his features so he managed not to raise his brows in surprise. Not at the information that Miss Wakechild would be attending the event, but at Van Hoon's ambition after he had made it clear the woman wanted a baronet at the bare minimum.

"Really? You think she might consider marriage with Willem?"

Ned pictured the Van Hoon heir. A reckless wastrel who had been loathsome as a youth and seemed no better as an adult. He was hardly an ideal match for any woman. Ned found himself growing quite protective over Miss Wakechild's person. No one, least of all a woman who seemed shocked at the idea of consuming alcohol in the afternoon, should be forced to marry a man who was inebriated by noon, frequented downmarket houses of ill repute, and gambled uncontrollably.

Van Hoon patted his thinning hair, preening like a peacock. "Possibly for Willem. Possibly for myself. I've been a widower for three years now. It's time to throw off the mourning."

The struggle not to show his distaste was growing harder for Ned. The old man was in his sixties and was seriously considering taking a bride who must be forty years his junior.

"Now that's interesting," he managed. "I might be in a position to attend the event myself, though not in any capacity where my path will cross with Miss Wakechild or yourself, I'm sure."

"What is your business there?" Van Hoon asked, eyes lighting up.

Ned smiled tightly. "You don't really expect me to answer that. Discretion is paramount, as I'm sure you will appreciate."

"Of course," Van Hoon said quickly. He looked pointedly at the desk. "Yes, of course you know I'm indebted to you and your discretion. What did we say, thirty pounds to sort the matter? A banker's draft?"

"Cash would be preferable," Ned said. He smiled. "Yes,

thirty was the sum, plus reimbursement of my original stake in the game. That was ten pounds."

Van Hoon unlocked his cashbox and counted out a mixture of one-, five-, and ten-pound notes. Ned slipped them into the secret pocket of his coat, except for three of the ones and a five, which he put into his wallet. It was not wise for anyone to carry that much money openly, but a man should never have an empty wallet.

"A pleasure doing business for you. Any time you need my services, please don't hesitate," he said. He raised a brow. "Though perhaps have a word with your son about the women he takes drinking, and the advisability of not wearing easily identifiable jewellery. There are discreet houses in almost every town where a young man can find carnal relief without having to resort to that sort of area."

"Oh yes, I shall certainly be having words with my young boy," Van Hoon said.

Ned smiled and inclined his head, determined not to shake hands. Just as he reached the door, Van Hoon called out his name.

His full name.

Ned stopped. These days, few people knew him well enough to know how he'd been christened. There were fewer still whom he permitted to use it. Van Hoon was in the first category but not the second. He turned back but did not leave the doorway.

"Yes?"

Van Hoon drummed his fingers together. "I heard

interesting news from Yorkshire when I was at my club down in London last week."

Ned tensed. Every part of his being was preparing to storm out of the room. Members of Van Hoon's club would be businessmen and traders, grown wealthy in the past twenty or thirty years, but not gentry. Doubtless they enjoyed gossiping just as anyone might.

"I can't imagine how interesting any news from Yorkshire might be to me," Ned said.

He turned and walked away, letting the door swing closed behind him. His mood, which had until that point been quite good, darkened. He made his way down the back stairs to the ground floor. The increasingly angry and desperate workers were still there, which was fortunate. It would give him the cover he needed to slip away just in case the brothel muscle had found him. Not that it mattered now. The ring was safely back with its intolerable owner. Ned had been well paid for his work and had not thought it necessary to mention that as well as the ring, he had won a further nine pounds and eight shillings. One of the advantages of his commissions which involved gambling was making extra cash on the side.

Nevertheless, he did feel tainted by the whole matter. Providing a discreet service for the wealthy finding solutions and resolutions to matters was a way to make a living, but it was no life. It made him feel...

He sought for the word to best describe his distaste.

Squalid.

But it was something he was good at; he was using all

his talents, and at least he was working and making a living.

He walked out into the warm early evening sunshine, digesting the information he'd learned. So, the intriguingly outspoken and impetuous Miss Wakechild would be attending the reception given by the Earl of Merseyside. Ned couldn't help but grin, wondering what the hallowed ranks of the nobility would make of her, and which earl or viscount she would have her eye on. The race meeting that preceded the evening was a minor one in the calendar; not grand enough to draw the gentry from all over the country, but there would be a few men of title attending. Obviously, there were enough impoverished landowners who were happy to take American wives with all that wonderful American wealth. Some of them might even use the money to improve their estates beyond their own houses.

He strolled over the road and found a wall to lean against while he let the sun warm his face. He inhaled deeply, thinking about the task he had been approached to undertake that would have taken him to the earl's reception. He had initially declined because there was always a risk of seeing familiar faces at large gatherings and he wanted to keep a low profile while he was able, but now he reconsidered. The commission would be simple compared to retrieving the ring and he decided he would quite like to see Miss Wakechild in action.

He walked back to his two-room lodgings and changed into a more respectable outfit. He put his fee from Van Hoon in the secure box that he had padlocked to the iron frame of his bed. His funds had been running low and the job had come at a useful time. It was quite staggering to think how much he had earned from a night of drinking and cards, but it was a measure of how desperate Van Hoon had been to retrieve the ring.

The money would keep Ned in what his landlady described as an "elegantly furnished" pair of rooms, a bathroom and toilet between four occupants, and breakfast every day, plus supper on Sundays. It wasn't home though. He was making enough to survive on, but not much more. Some jobs earned him a bonus and he knew that compared to a dock worker or a clerk, he had no complaints, but for how long would he be able to continue doing what he did? In a bank in Leeds, there was a deposit box containing a few pieces of jewellery which were of real value. The problem was that they were also of sentimental value, having been inherited from his dead mother. He would have to be in severe straits to consider pawning or selling them.

The thought of Yorkshire nagged at him like a bad tooth. His past was catching up with him. People knew where he was. In less than two months, he could be trapped in a life that he had rejected, or been ejected from. Of course if the coin fell the other way – landing on tails, he thought with a grim irony – then the life he had now would be all he could ever expect. He needed to make plans.

He'd had two undertakings relatively close to each other in Liverpool, which meant that he should probably leave the city soon before his whereabouts became known too widely. Bloody Van Hoon wasn't known for keeping his counsel.

He flipped open an old copy of The Strand and found a chapter of *The Adventure of the Copper Beeches*. He smiled grimly to himself at the latest escapades of Holmes. A consulting detective with rooms of his own in London. A man able to command vast sums for his expertise. What Ned wouldn't give to be in that position. A consulting dilemma-solver. Obviously he would have to think of a better term for it.

He paid a visit to Mr Halliwell's home in Allerton to hear what the commission would entail. As he listened to Mr Halliwell explain what he needed of Ned, he daydreamed of a set of rooms where clients came to him rather than him having to traipse around to their abodes. It was a pleasant fantasy but that's all it was.

He agreed to take the commission, though it sounded dull. The opportunity to attend the event that Miss Wakechild would be at had fallen into his lap and he wasn't going to ignore it.

His father had believed coincidences were a sign from fate and should be acted upon. Ned thought they were just happenchance, but he was not going to let this one pass him by.

Chapter Three

"Would you look at this rabble!"

Florence's father was standing at the window of the office he had taken in the Huskisson Building. Beside him stood Arthur Seachie, proprietor of Seachie's Distillery. It was he who had spoken. Florence had met him before and taken a dislike to him that she had thought was unfair. Hearing the contempt in his voice now, though, she decided it was well founded. He was referring to the throng of men who stood in groups around the doors to office buildings all the way along the waterfront. They were dressed in cheap working clothes that had seen better days, but appeared perfectly civil.

"Cordelia and I passed them coming here. She was quite reluctant to let me walk across the street alone. What are they angry about?" Florence asked as she joined her father and Mr Seachie at the window.

"Wages. It seems the cost of rent is increasing and they

want more for nothing," Mr Seachie said. He clenched his fist and rested it against the window as if he'd like to smash it through. "The grain shipping company charges me more and the porters and lumpers at the docks here grumble all day long. My factory labourers are just as bad. I imagine it's the same on your side of the Atlantic?"

"Well, yes," Clayton Wakechild replied, his eyes still on the men and women gathered outside. "It's a difficult matter trying to do the best for everyone. I have a household to run and dependents to provide for. The shareholders have come to expect certain dividends, but of course the men and women in the factories expect and need their own increase in wages."

"And why shouldn't they?" Florence asked crisply. The conversation with the intriguing Mr Blake was fresh in her mind, and his comments about slave wages still rankled. "Our lives have improved as a result of their labours. Why shouldn't theirs?"

"If they want to improve their lives then they should improve themselves," Mr Seachie said, giving her a slightly condescending look.

Florence ignored it and beamed at him.

"I absolutely agree. In fact, one of the things I want to do while I'm in England is pay a visit to the garden villages established by some factory owners and a few of the more enlightened landowners. I want to see what improvements we can take back to Philadelphia with us. Have you ever considered establishing one, Mr Seachie?"

Mr Seachie looked unimpressed at her suggestion. "I

don't think that's quite what I meant. I was thinking that if they wanted to improve their lives then they should work harder for promotion and thereby put themselves in the position to earn a higher wage."

"Well, yes of course," Florence said patiently. "Isn't it our duty as their betters to help them achieve that?"

Mr Seachie bestowed upon her another patronising smile. "Great Scott, no! If a man achieves anything, he must do it with the sweat of his own brow, not anyone else's."

Florence smiled. Out of the corner of her eye, she saw her father's brows shoot down and curbed her first response.

"Of course," she said demurely. "I have ordered some tea to be brought up. While we drink it, you must tell me about your journey to becoming owner of Seachie's Distillery. I believe the mill was your father's originally. Or was it your grandfather's?"

"My grandfather built it," Mr Seachie said slowly. He looked a little puzzled, as if he suspected Florence was taking a jibe at him but her tone had been deferential and there was nothing critical in her words themselves. "I'd be delighted to tell you more about our history on another occasion, but now if you will excuse me, I have a meeting to attend to."

He left the room, with smiles and polite murmurings on every side.

"What was the purpose of that little display?" Clayton Wakechild demanded as soon as Mr Seachie had left and the tea had been brought.

Florence poured the tea and passed the cup to her father. "By that 'little display' you mean questioning that awful man's opinion of the workforce? I believe it was necessary. Didn't you hear the contempt in his voice?"

She took her cup and saucer back to the window and looked out at the group below once more. How many were there? Forty or fifty, all wanting work. No wonder there was no incentive for their employers to raise their wages when they had so many ready to fill the positions.

"Yes of course I did," Clayton replied. "But you need to learn to be more cautious. Especially in Great Britain. They really aren't as used to young women speaking their minds as we are at home. And if you are to find yourself a husband among the aristocracy, then we will need to…"

"Let me stop you there, Daddy," Florence said firmly, turning away from the window to give him her full attention. She knew what he was going to say. It had been the main reason for their coming to England and she was determined not to have the argument again. Her stomach grew painfully twisted whenever they discussed it and made her wish she could run from the room.

"I have no intention of being sold off to some titled nightmare just to raise your status back home."

"I'm not going to sell you!" Clayton said. "That's a horrible way of putting it."

Florence wrapped her arms tightly around herself and stroked her thumbs across her upper arms, as if she could ward off the feeling of misery through such self-consolation. "Traded or bartered, if you prefer. The husband gets a large dowry and you get to drop his title into conversation. It's all rather lovely for both of you but I have to admit I fail to see what I gain from it."

"You get a husband to care for you and give you children," Clayton said, ticking his finger at her. "You get a house of your own to run as you like and won't be beholden to anyone when I'm no longer with you. I'm not going to see you become an old maid like your Aunt Patricia having a couple of rooms in our home. Would you really like to be fifty and living with your brother, Ashley, and whomever he settles on when I pass away? Your mother wouldn't have wanted that and I don't believe you do either when you bother to give it some rational thought."

Clayton averted his eyes as he spoke of Lavinia. They had really loved each other and at times his grief was still an open wound for the world to see. Regretting her tone, Florence left her seat in the window and moved to the settee. She took her father's hand, feeling the smooth gold wedding ring that he still wore.

"Mama wouldn't have wanted me married off to just anyone for the sake of a roof over my head. She didn't want that for herself. She wanted to marry you."

"The husband I want for you won't be 'just anyone'. He will be an aristocrat. I'm determined of it," Clayton said. "He'll have a mark of refinement that comes with decades—no, centuries—of titled ancestors. That's not something that money can buy. You'll be able to walk into any establishment in America or England with your head held high, knowing that your husband's ancestors were aristocrats before our country was even freed from the British yoke."

"Not necessarily!" Florence recognised the light that filled her father's eyes; at once dreamy and enthusiastic. Once he had that mood on him, he was prone to all sorts of wild ideas. She sat on his lap and wrapped her arms around him, planting a kiss on his forehead.

"You've already tried it once when you married Cordelia to Twemlow. He's got a title and a house that's practically a castle, but even then you barely scraped a seat in the upper circle at the New York Opera last August. What makes you think it will be any different if you marry me to another baronet?"

"You know it goes without saying that I have the utmost respect for Lord Griggs and I don't believe there is a worthier baronet in all the British Isles, but I'm aiming higher than a baronet for you." Clayton sucked his teeth and put his finger to his lips before continuing.

"Taking you into my complete confidence and knowing you will keep it, I must admit that your sister's husband was the highest rank that I could manage to take an interest, considering I am not in the league of families such as the Vanderbilts or Jeromes when it comes to the size of your dowries."

He chucked Florence beneath the chin, smiling warmly. "The fact that Cordelia has the avarice of a magpie and the conversational skills of a trained cockatoo didn't help matters."

Florence giggled. Clayton nudged her off his knee and back onto the sofa. He stood and tugged her back on her feet where he looked at her with the keenly intelligent expression Florence had inherited from him.

"You are different from Cordelia. You are witty, kind, and intelligent. With you at his side, a man could really go places. With the right husband, you will most certainly go far. Could you expect me not to boast that my daughter was a countess or a duchess and beloved by all her husband's tenants and servants, and your children the descendants of centuries of nobility?"

Florence pressed her lips together as emotion filled her. His obvious pride was clear to see, even if she disagreed vehemently with his plans for her. She had always known she was his favourite child. She loved him so much that she didn't even mind that he habitually left "beautiful" off his list of her attributes. Kind friends said she was interesting or attractive, or said there was something about her that was intriguing. Having no plans to marry or to win the eye of a man, she was content with that.

"I could go far by myself if I had the chance," she said. "I could be beloved of your workers. I could run the factory alongside Ashley. Better than he could, if truth be told."

"Do you think perhaps you should tell a little less truth, my dear? It can be unkind at times. Your brother would be hurt to hear you compare yourself to him."

But Cordelia would presumably not be hurt by their father's comparison and judgement on her intelligence, Florence thought darkly. As far as Clayton would see it,

Cordelia was a mere woman and wasn't expected to feel as deeply as a man when it came to pride. Florence veered between affection for her father and exasperation at him. She breathed in slowly and counted to five, reminding herself that he couldn't help his old-fashioned attitudes.

She reached up and planted a kiss on his cheek. He was wearing whiskers and they suited him. She stood back a little and regarded him with an analytical eye. At fifty-three he was still good-looking, with a full head of chestnut hair that was only receding slightly at the temples, and a twinkle in his hazel eyes.

"Do you know, Daddy, perhaps it's not me who should be looking for an aristocratic spouse, but you. You're still closer to fifty than sixty and you're very handsome. I bet there are twenty or thirty titled daughters who would gladly marry you."

Clayton's mouth twisted down. "No, thank you very much! I've always found it distasteful in the least to see a couple walking arm and arm and not know whether I should congratulate a fellow on his wife's or daughter's beauty. I'm perfectly content being an old widower and since your poor mother's death, I have no urge to replace her."

Florence walked to the window and stared out. There was still a handful of men and women lingering by the side of the road. They had not given up hope of finding employment today. One figure in particular caught her eye and she felt a spasm of excitement.

"Mr Blake," she murmured to herself.

"What did you say?" her father enquired.

"Oh nothing."

Blake had been inside the same building she was in; she was sure of it. She wondered what he had been doing there. Possibly looking for work himself. Or was this where he was delivering his mysterious item? She peered down as he walked across the road, swinging his arms jauntily. As he reached the other side of the street, he turned back and looked up at the building. Florence thought for one moment that he knew she was there, but his gaze was levelled at a floor lower down.

"Who else has offices in this building?" she asked.

Her father shrugged. "I don't know them all. Mainly shipping companies, or those who use them frequently, such as Mr Seachie. The harbour master has an office on the ground floor. In fact, there are a couple of men I need to go down and pay a visit to. Van Hoon on the fourth floor and Kettering on the second. Why are you interested?"

Florence looked down again. Mr Blake was still standing where she had spotted him, looking up intently. She felt a blush creep around her throat and across her bosom.

"Just curiosity," she answered.

"Well, my dear," her father said, "as much as I am delighted you came to visit me, I have work to do. Let me accompany you down the elevator to the lobby. I'll hire you a cab to take you back to the hotel."

"Oh there's really no need," Florence replied. "It's only a few blocks. I am sure I can find my way."

Her father put her arm under his. "I have no doubt that

you can find your way, but I would like to see you being safe. With rough men and women standing outside the building, I would be fearful for your well-being. They're all so ragged-looking."

Florence hid her disdain at her father's assessment. The crowds of would-be workers were plainly dressed and some were in clothes that had clearly seen better days – or years – but there was nothing to suggest they were dishonest. The atmosphere in the pub had been quite welcoming in fact.

"Daddy, just because those people are working men and women does not mean they are untrustworthy, but if it makes you happy, I'll let you find me a cab."

"You will indeed. Aside from your safety, we have a reputation to uphold. I won't have it said that Clayton Wakechild's daughter had to walk through the streets."

Florence hid a smile. If only her father knew what she had been getting up to earlier in the day, he would have a fit! It made the adventure seem all the more thrilling.

She waited patiently in the lobby while her father instructed the doorman to summon a cab. Before they parted, her father kissed her cheek.

"Promise me you will be on your best behaviour tomorrow night and you won't make any ill-advised comments regarding working conditions or social improvements. It was very good indeed of Lord Griggs to get us all tickets to the ball and this may very well be the chance that we need to enter you into society." He rubbed his hands together excitedly. "There will be at least seven men with titles attending from what I have managed to discover."

Florence's heart sunk. The ball hosted by the Earl of Merseyside was the sole reason for them staying in Liverpool this week before journeying on to Leamington Spa. She had a beautiful dress that had cost a small fortune, but which made her feel like the centrepiece of a banqueting table. She would rather have traded it for her nightgown, peignoir and a good book, but there was no escaping the event and it meant so much to her father.

"I can't wait to go," she lied. "I'll dance with every old duke I can and listen to all the boring earls talking about racehorses and the stuffed fox heads they have lying around their castles, and make them all fall in love with me."

She tried not to giggle at the shock on her father's face, well aware that he didn't find her flippancy amusing. He gave her one of his few severe looks.

"Florence, you heard the conversation regarding finances not fifteen minutes ago. This trip to England has cost me a small fortune and I expect you to take every opportunity that comes your way to enter the highest society. We will find you a husband among the aristocracy, be sure of it."

"I'll be on my best behaviour and take every opportunity," Florence said. *And I'll make sure your investment pays dividends*, she very much did not add aloud.

She swept out of the building and into the waiting cab. She risked a glance to the side, but Mr Blake had gone.

Back in her private sitting room in the Midland Adelphi

Hotel, she ordered a pot of coffee with cream and a slice of coffee cake. There was over a day before the ball and she was sure that by then she would have walked off the cake well enough to be able to fit into her tightly laced dress. She must have lost weight this afternoon practically running through the streets at Mr Blake's side.

What an adventure the day had been. She'd been in England for under two weeks now and nothing had come close to the excitement of one morning in Liverpool! What a pity she was unlikely to meet him again.

Chapter Four

Ned didn't know what strings Mr Halliwell had needed to pull, or the favours he had called in, but the man for whom he was working that evening had somehow managed to find Ned a position as a waiter at the ball. From the refreshment room where he stationed himself, Ned was in a perfect position to watch the guests entering the octagonal hall of the Wellington Rooms.

Naturally, being conscientious, he was alert for the arrival of Mr Halliwell's wife and her two daughters and kept his eye fixed on the entrance. As such, he was able to observe Miss Wakechild entering in the company of a woman who was alike enough they must be sisters, and the man who was presumably her husband. The couple entered first, then Miss Wakechild followed them, walking on the arm of a man who must be her father.

He was good-looking, trim for his age, and walked with confidence. The sister was smiling widely but Miss

Wakechild's expression was similar to the one she had worn while she had stood in the street not looking at hats, and for a moment Ned was disappointed to think she was one of those women who delighted in finding everything dull. He looked again and noticed there was an added shadow of trepidation in her eyes and her shapely neck had a visible tension to it. The day before, she had looked merely bored stiff. Now she looked as if she wanted to run and hide. Mystifyingly, Ned felt a tug in his chest from heartstrings long grown rusty from unemployment.

The two women went into the ladies' cloak room and the men into the gentlemen's hat room before they all emerged a short while later and reunited. Divested of her cloak, Miss Wakechild was dressed in a gown of pine green, with full sleeves and a commotion of gathered skirts. Trimmings of lavender-coloured tuille tempered some of the vibrancy and the low plunging neckline was discreetly festooned with more tuille, but the effect was still eye-catching. It seemed a rather daring shade for a young, unmarried woman.

Ned assumed the dye manufacturer's daughter was taking the opportunity to advertise her father's merchandise and by extension her ample dowry just as much as she was displaying her ample décolletage. She wore the obligatory long white gloves with a single diamond bracelet on her slender wrist. Her hair was piled high and dressed with small purple and white flowers but Ned noticed a gold comb nestled in the red tresses. It sparkled with too many diamonds to be subtle and was a faux pas that she might not be aware of. One piece of jewellery was sufficient.

In comparison to the English girls wearing pastel shades or white, she stood out like a beacon. He wondered whether she was unaware of the impropriety or simply didn't care. If she wanted to make a statement of wealth and availability, she was succeeding amply.

Ned's weren't the only eyes that fell on her, looked away, then back again for a further, closer look as she joined the receiving line to pay her respects to the Earl and Countess of Merseyside. Ned wondered if any of the party were aware that there were whispers that followed the glances. Her father seemed oblivious at least, gazing around the room with too much obvious interest.

Miss Wakechild reached the head of the line and dropped into a smooth curtsey. The old earl's eyes followed her as she stood, but if she thought that she might find a husband there, she was mistaken. The eldest son was already married and the younger boy had shocked society by announcing an interest in Roman Catholicism and intending to take the cloth. Still, there were introductions aplenty to be made tonight. He had seen a list of the attendees and there were two viscounts and a handful of baronets, as well as members of what passed for high society in Liverpool. Miss Wakechild was bound to find a man she could captivate into marriage.

His attention was drawn to the door as Mrs Halliwell and her two daughters entered and Ned's mind turned to work. It did occur to him that it was odd that Mr Halliwell would engage Ned to spy on his daughter rather than asking his wife for her observations and opinions, or even speaking to the girl herself. If Ned was ever induced to marry someone, he would need to be able to talk to his wife about his worries and plans.

Fortunately for Ned – and Mr Halliwell – Miss Halliwell preferred sitting on one of the sofas in the refreshment room and talking with an array of suitors to dancing, meaning that Ned was able to keep a close watch on her. Miss Wakechild didn't enter the refreshments room but from where Ned stood, he could see across the octagonal atrium into the ballroom. He occasionally caught a glimpse of her over the next hour as she was introduced to various other guests, then dancing in the arms of various men – including, he noted with a slight taste of bitterness in his throat, Marius Van Hoon – and looking slightly more at ease than Ned liked to see.

His stomach jerked when he saw her dancing with Viscount Stretford, or *Stuffy*, as the Honourable Robert Erskyn has been known in his youth because of the reputation he had for snoring when hay asthma was upon him. Ned drew further back into the room.

The pang in his stomach took him by surprise as she spun around in a whirl of green and lavender. Did Ned want to be in that throng, polkaing and waltzing in a dress coat and white cravat? Not really. They were not his people, that was not his life, and he was content with the role of onlooker.

All the same, he'd happily exchange places with

Stretford or the Van Hoons for ten minutes to dance in the arms of Miss Wakechild.

Florence had no idea why she found parties exhausting. They should be enjoyable. They were supposed to be enjoyable, and by all accounts everyone else she knew found them so. They just made her anxious.

Perhaps it was knowing she was on show. Everything, from her clothing to her conduct and conversation to whom she danced with and how well, would be scrutinised. The man in whose arms she was currently being waltzed – quite well to give him credit – was a viscount, so she was painfully aware that her father would be watching from the side of the room, hoping she was captivating him with her feminine graces.

"I do admire redheads," Lord Stretford said as he moved Florence around the dance floor. "There's something so fiery in your nature. Boadicea, who fought the Romans and razed Chester to the ground, was a redhead, you know. Queen Elizabeth another. Their hair must have had something to do with it."

He guffawed at his wit. Florence gritted her teeth and affected amusement. She had never felt less like the stereotype. Sadly, Viscount Stretford fulfilled every stereotype of the brainless heir who would have been nothing without his ancestors.

"Yes, I can well imagine Boadicea finally laid waste to

Colchester after one too many comments about her hair," she said sweetly. She smiled up at him, batting her eyelashes to divert him away from the correction. He looked puzzled, then gave another loud chuckle and beamed at her.

"Americans are so refreshing. You must grant me the pleasure of accompanying me into the refreshment room. Mother will love to meet you."

Florence had at least managed to persuade her father to allow her ten minutes respite after each three numbers she danced, so after the music died away, she declined the offer of meeting Lord Stretford's mother and walked over to her father. Clayton was bowing deeply to a man of roughly his own age. The man walked away towards Florence so Clayton would have been oblivious to the slight smirk he wore, but it felt like a slap across the face to Florence.

"Who were you talking to, Daddy?" she asked.

"I have been conversing with Sir St-John Bransdale. I have discovered him to be a second cousin once removed of your mother. He's a baronet."

"Daddy, you're practically bouncing up and down," she whispered. "Why does that matter? Did he even know who you were?"

The excitement ebbed from Clayton's face, causing Florence a pang of remorse.

"Well, he didn't at first, until I appraised him of the nature of our connection."

A sour taste filled Florence's mouth. Presumably her father had been asking too many questions. That would explain the smirk on the baronet's face. It was heartbreaking to see her father's demonstrable excitement, but there was also a hint of contempt that she couldn't quite quell at how easily impressed Clayton was, and how gauche he must seem.

"I'm sure your mother would have loved to know we had been making connections with her family," Clayton continued, oblivious to her misgivings. "Do you think I should offer him my card and ask him to dine at the hotel with us?"

Florence glanced over to where the baronet was now standing. Her eyes met his and he lifted his head slightly so that he appeared to be looking down his nose at her. He turned away without acknowledging the contact. Florence flushed with anger.

"Absolutely not. I'm sure Mother wouldn't want to think of any of us demeaning ourselves to try to curry favour with relatives who barely acknowledged her. Did Sir whatever-his-name-was even send a card of condolence when she died?"

As the words left her mouth, she realised she'd been too blunt. She reached for her father's hand and pressed it tightly.

"I don't recall," Clayton said softly. "There were some cards from England."

"I know there were, Daddy." Florence hadn't realised at the time, being too young and grief-stricken, but when she had found them a few years earlier, she had discovered that the only cards from her mother's homeland had been from friends not family. It made Clayton's determination to marry his daughters into the aristocracy that had rejected their mother all the more incomprehensible to Florence.

"Well, I'm very pleased that you had such a nice chat with him, Daddy," she said kindly. "I'll bet there are lots of interesting people you could talk to about business so don't worry about seeking him out again."

She kissed his cheek and went straight to the ladies' sitting room where her sister was taking a cup of punch. Cordelia waved.

"How goes it? Have you been proposed to yet?"

"No, but I think I've managed to prevent Daddy from making a huge social faux pas by inviting a baronet to tea."

Cordelia winced.

"Goodness me." Florence sighed, dropping carefully onto a comfortable chair and glancing at the clock on the mantlepiece. "It's only ten. We can't leave for another hour. I don't think I'll be able to hide in here for that long."

"Florence, you really have to get over this aversion to fun," Cordelia said with an eye roll. "You certainly can't hide here all evening either. Papa is counting on you to meet someone at one of these events."

"I'm not averse to having fun. I just don't find crowded places fun. Everything is too loud, for one thing. The music from the quartet competes against the conversations and they all conspire to wage war against my ears and brain." Florence fanned herself rapidly. "Why do people have to talk when they dance? Isn't it enough to enjoy the music and the feelings? Do you remember when I was twelve and Daddy threw a surprise party for me? I cried, and everyone was so kind, but I knew really no one understood why I hated it. I would much rather have gone to a tea room and had cakes with a few friends."

"Yes, I remember," Cordelia said. "You ended up running out and going into the garden to pick flowers. Miss Franklin was going to be cross with you until she saw how neatly you had arranged them all in rows according to size on the veranda. You were a strange child."

"I don't suppose I'd be allowed to go arrange flowers now," Florence said wistfully. She examined her dance card. "Viscount Sheernall is next, which will please Daddy, though he's not for another two dances. Then a Mr W. Van Hoon. I've danced with his father already. He kept looking down as if he were trying to see down the front of my dress."

"He probably was." Cordelia giggled. "Men either like breasts or rears, according to Twemlow. Speaking of whom, I'm going to go find him in the refreshment room. We're allowed to dance together occasionally and I don't want to miss the opportunity. Come with me and see if there is any rose blancmange left. It's quite sublime."

The sisters walked arm in arm between rooms. From the back of the refreshment room, Lord Griggs raised his glass at the women and Cordelia waved her fingers, her smile widening.

"You really like Twemlow, don't you?" Florence commented, seeing her sister's eyes light up at the sight of Lord Griggs weaving his way towards them.

"Yes, I'd go so far as to say I almost love him. I'm very

lucky. I don't think Father would have made me marry him if I'd hated him on sight, but I was very relieved to discover how well we get on." Cordelia turned to her sister. "He won't make you marry a man you detest either. He won't let you be miserable or mistreated. He wants you to be happy."

"He wants me to marry someone he can brag about back home and whose name will open doors," Florence muttered. "The higher up the ranks of the peerage, the better."

"Well, you're prettier than me and cleverer so you should aim higher than a baron," Cordelia whispered as her husband sauntered towards them. "Though not too high or I'll be jealous. You're the prettiest girl in the room by far. Certainly one of the richest. And I'd love for you to find a husband who lives in the North so we aren't too far away."

"That's about the only thing which makes the idea tolerable," Florence replied.

"I'm going to steal my wife for a dance," Lord Griggs said. "Will you be alright here, Florence? It isn't really done for young ladies to be left alone but rules are so often relaxed that barely anyone would comment, and if they do, I'll throw down the glove and shoot them."

Florence laughed. "Of course I will. If anyone looks at me askance, I shall go stand close to a group and pretend I've been momentarily edged out."

Cordelia kissed her cheek and walked off arm in arm with her husband. Florence turned her attention to the table laden with cold cuts and sandwiches. She wasn't hungry but a glass of champagne was tempting so she edged her way through the groups of guests to one of the waiters who stood by the table. He was side-on, so she didn't recognise him. He turned on her approach, as if alerted to her presence, and she found herself face to face once again with Mr Blake.

At first, she didn't believe it was him. He was smartly dressed in the uniform worn by the other staff. His hair looked darker and was slicked back with pomade, and he was clean-shaven. She raised her eyes to meet his and was delighted to see he looked as astonished as she was.

"Mr Blake, you are the last person I would expect to meet! You aren't a waiter. What are you doing here? Are you evading somebody else? Did you dash in here in search of another woman to whisk away to help you on your adventures?"

She was feeling flustered, aware she was talking too much and all of it nonsense. She was growing hot and by now there must be a fully scarlet blush spreading across her entire chest, neck, and face. She stopped talking but gave a nervous giggle that made her want to curl up in embarrassment.

"Miss Wakechild! Good evening. How delightful to meet you again."

Mr Blake plucked a champagne bottle from an ice bucket and poured it with an extravagant flourish. "Would you care for a glass of champagne?"

Florence accepted it gratefully and took a sip before the bubbles had even subsided. It was sharp and cold, the sensation momentarily managing to level her heightened mood.

"As it happens, I am a waiter tonight, and I am here on behalf of another woman," Blake said.

"Oh."

Florence sipped the champagne again. She shouldn't be disappointed. There was no reason at all for his business to be any concern of hers. Nevertheless, she did feel a ripple of disappointment.

He gave her a discreet smile and leaned in. "That is, I am here on behalf of a father who is interested in what his daughter is doing and who she's doing it with. This is what I do, you see. People pay me to sort out their difficulties."

"Oh," Florence repeated. She stepped towards him, immensely intrigued by what he was saying.

"It isn't me, is it?"

He laughed then gave her a measured look. "Should your father be concerned about what you are getting up to?"

"Not at all," she said, ignoring the fact that the day before, she had been racing through the streets of the city with this intriguing man and her father probably should be very concerned. "Though he is determined to find me a husband so I'm sure he'd like to know if I have any preferences yet."

"Do you?" Blake asked. He gave a discreet cough. "Pardon me, that is absolutely none of my business."

"No, it isn't," Florence agreed. She gave a slight sigh.

"Though I don't. Now tell me, what are you doing now concerning this young lady?"

"I am watching who she dances with and how many times she dances with a particular gentleman. Whether she takes his arm to go dine. How many glasses of champagne she has had. Any other pertinent facts that her father should be concerned about."

"So you are a spy," Florence breathed.

He looked slightly taken aback.

"Yes, I suppose tonight I am. Very insightful of you. Would you care for another glass of champagne, Miss Wakechild? Or perhaps some fruit punch or iced water?" He indicated her empty glass. She hadn't even been aware of finishing it.

"More champagne, please. It's so hot in here. My sister told me that England did have some nice weather occasionally, but I didn't believe her. I think I'd have worn a completely different dress if I had."

Mr Blake looked her up and down. He did it discreetly but she felt his gaze roving over her. It was the fanciest piece she owned and most definitely did deserve the description of gown rather than a dress or a frock. She'd chosen the green specially to match her hair and she knew that she looked impressively eye-catching. That was the idea, of course, she reminded herself a little guiltily. To catch the eye of an earl or a duke, not to spend her time gossiping with a waiter and risking rumours. She moved slightly around so that she was standing beside him and not obviously conversing.

"Who is the young lady?" she asked.

Blake dipped his head slightly. "That one with the pale pink dress and an array of rosebuds in her hair."

Florence glanced at the woman he was describing. She looked about eighteen and was very pretty with delicate features and corn-blonde hair. Her dress was a gorgeous affair of lace over satin. There were three young men clearly vying for her attention and she was smiling at each in turn.

"They all appear to have champagne," Florence commented. "Which is the man she is supposed to marry or to avoid?"

"Her father wants to her to marry the stout fellow with the Van Dyke beard. Rumour has it she prefers young Mr Thorntree. What do you think?"

Florence walked around to his other side and selected a small, iced biscuit from the table. She'd been closer to him when she was in his arms but now she was more aware of his presence. She inhaled and caught a scent that was slightly peppery. She looked up at him out of the corner of her eye. His eyes were on her rather than on the young woman he should be evaluating and that gave her a small frisson of delight.

"From here it's hard to say. Would you like my assistance again?"

Blake tilted his head down.

"What do you have in mind?"

She glanced at the glass in her hand. "Without appearing too indelicate, your young quarry has been drinking quite a lot of champagne. At some point I'm sure she'll have to make use of the powder room. I'll go in and make her acquaintance if I can. She's more likely to open up to another woman than to a waiter. After all, you can hardly go up to her and say 'Good evening, Miss Eyelashes, would you have some more champagne? Oh, and while you are here, do you plan to elope with any of the gentleman?' Can you?"

Blake snorted then covered it with a sneeze, causing Florence to giggle.

"That's very true. Miss Eyelashes though?"

"Haven't you noticed how fine they are? And by fine, I mean admirable of course rather than thin. Which they really aren't. I can see them fluttering from over here. Haven't you noticed?"

"Yes, they are good," Blake said. "Dark eyelashes are the envy of every redhead, I assume?"

She acknowledged the truth with a small dip of her head. There was a lull in the other room as the music came to an end. Florence gave a start and glanced down at her card.

"Oh lord, I have to go," she said, handing Blake the empty glass. "I'm supposed to be dancing next. I'll go do your mission for you if I can. If I find anything out, I'll try to speak to you again before the end of the evening."

She hurried through the refreshment room, smiling at the people she passed. She couldn't say whether it was the two glasses of champagne she had drunk in quick succession or the snatched and illicit conversation with Mr Blake that had done it, but her mood had lifted and she was looking forward to dancing. As she crossed the entrance hall, she saw her father talking in an animated fashion. The victim was a younger man in an immaculately cut evening dress that fitted his tall, broad frame perfectly. She waved at her father and passed by. She heard him murmur something to the other man, then he called her name.

"Florence, a word quickly."

She turned to face him, smoothing her skirts down and beaming. His face was surprisingly severe as he walked towards her, and she felt a slight shimmer of unease.

"Daddy, are you having a nice evening still?"

The young man smiled and bowed. Florence curtseyed back, thinking how much nicer he was than the self-important baronet. "Excuse me, Mr Wakechild. I'll leave you to speak with your charming daughter."

"I see you've found someone else to talk to. I'm about to go dance with a viscount," Florence said.

Mr Wakechild continued to look solemn. "Cordelia told me she left you in the refreshment room alone. I looked in to find you and unless my eyesight is starting to fail me, I thought I saw you in conversation with a servant at the back of the room!"

Florence swallowed. Of course she would have been spotted. How stupid of them both to lose sight of where they were.

"We weren't really conversing," she said quickly. "I asked about the provenance of the champagne and he was kind enough to tell me. Do you think we could visit France before we return home? I'd love to see where the grapes grow. Apparently, it can only be called champagne if…"

"Florence, stop gabbling," Mr Wakechild said sternly, holding up a hand to cut her off. "This is not the time or place for a discourse on grapes. You can't keep Viscount Sheernall waiting, and I interrupted a conversation to speak to you. That interesting young man has made a fortune through his business of brass engravings."

"And I bet he did it without a title," Florence muttered.

Clayton glared at her. "We'll talk about your conduct tomorrow, but once you have finished each dance, I expect you to return either to my company or your sister's."

His tone left no room for protest.

"Yes, Daddy," she answered meekly, determining that she would look for Cordelia not him. She walked towards the ballroom in search of her partner.

No, not in search of him, she corrected. She was required to make herself visible and wait for him to approach her. How stupid all the rules were. Her jaw tightened. She took five deep breaths as Miss Vavasour, her last governess, had taught her.

It didn't help. Rather than looking forward to the rest of the evening, the thought of an interview with her father was a dark cloud blotting out the rest of the evening's sparkle.

Chapter Five

The conversation took place the following morning in the sitting room of the Wakechild's suite at the hotel. It was luxurious surroundings for a scolding but that didn't make it any easier. Florence could count on one hand the number of occasions Clayton Wakechild had raised his voice at his children, so as always, the lecture was delivered in a calm and quiet tone that resonated with disappointment rather than fury. That only made it worse to hear, of course, as the disappointment burrowed deep into Florence and nested where it would be able to wake and remind her at any moment.

"Last night you were almost noticed for the wrong reasons. Conversing with lower classes, and a male at that! Do you want to be ruined and stand no chance of marriage?"

"Daddy, we've spoken about this already time and time again," Florence said. "I don't want to be used to further your business like a piece of machinery, and your obsession with the aristocracy is silly. The nicest person there was the brass engraver."

Her father sighed. "It isn't the business; it's our family. We're new money and I'm tired of doors being closed to me. To my children. Ashley needs a wife and he's been rejected twice."

Florence felt a twinge of guilt. Not having an aristocracy in place didn't mean there weren't vigilantly regulated levels of pre-eminence in American society. The older the wealth, the higher up the tiers of the de-facto aristocracy a family was. The Wakechild's fortune came from manufacturing and trade, which in itself was bad enough for the members of society who had made their money in earlier generations. Florence's grandfather had started Wakefield Dye Manufacturers, though it had been Clayton's ambition and business acumen that had seen profits soar and the premises expand. One generation was too short a time to see if the wealth would last. Doors were indeed closed, so it was little wonder Clayton wanted to use his children to advance all their causes. It rankled that she should be used to help her brother's marriage prospects, however, and there was no guarantee it would work in any case.

Lavinia Bishop, Florence's mother, had been the daughter of a baronet, and her family had rejected her for that very reason. It had done no good to the family for Clayton to parade his own aristocratic wife.

"I'll be frank with you, as you are usually blunt with

me," Clayton said. "You are getting older. By your age, your mother had one child and was pregnant with another."

"And what good did that do her given that she's been dead for the past fifteen years!" Florence exclaimed.

Her father drew a sharp breath and turned away, suddenly engrossed in the painting of a pastoral scene on the wall.

Florence clapped her hands over her mouth. "Daddy, I'm sorry!"

Clayton turned around slowly and shook his head sorrowfully.

"I imagine you are, Florence. Nevertheless, your words were hurtful. You have a tendency to speak too forthrightly, even for my considerably broad-minded tastes. An unintentional wound can cut as deeply as a deliberate one."

He left her alone.

With the memory of that difficult conversation repeating itself in acute detail inside her head, Florence had no urge to venture further from her suite of rooms than to the almost identical suite on the floor below, which Cordelia and Twemlow were occupying.

"I've disappointed him," Florence sighed, picking at her scone. "I need to behave with dignity or I'll never find an earl who will take me on, and it matters so much to him."

"Yes, it does seem unfair that we're expected to display every grasp of etiquette while they can behave as they choose," Cordelia said darkly, eyeing Twemlow who was lounging on the settee in the bay window, smoking his pipe.

"We know the rules," he said with a shrug. "We've known them since birth, that's why we get to break 'em."

Cordelia glared at him. He blew her a kiss.

"You'll never catch me addressing a lord as 'Sir' on a first meeting, my beloved."

"That's my point. It's just rules. You even have books listing them," Florence said. "I believe anyone could be taught to show the same manners a baron displays. Why, the waiter I spoke with last night had enough civility that even he could have passed a quarter of an hour in a drawing room without his background being called into question. He was much nicer to talk to than that awful viscount who kept telling me about breeding horses. Swap clothes and you'd never tell the difference between them."

She paused with her teacup halfway to her mouth as her brain fizzled with an idea.

"Oh my!"

"Are you ill, Florrie?" Twemlow asked.

Florence slowly lowered her teacup. "No. I have just had the most marvellous idea of how to prove to Daddy that it is all completely arbitrary." She looked at her sister and brother-in-law. Her mood, which had been skulking in the depths of despondency, soared. She stood, hands by her side as if she were declaiming from a podium.

"I shall find a common man and transform him into a fine lord."

"I think creating new peers is beyond even your considerable talent." Cordelia laughed.

"Of course I don't mean to create a real one," Florence

said. "But that's my point really. These titles were created centuries ago. I propose to create a counterfeit viscount. Then I'll present him to Daddy at a party or something and show him just how silly the determination to marry us to titles is. We shall train him in how to behave, clothe him appropriately, and teach him all the right points of etiquette."

Twemlow gave a barking laugh. "Do you think that's all there is to it, Florrie? Cutlery and clothing? You will never succeed in a hundred years."

"Oh do be quiet, Twem," Cordelia said. She walked over and sat on the chair beside him and flicked the end of her shawl at his face. "I've seen you wipe your nose on your cuff when you think no one is looking, and you told me after we married that your grandfather barely knew how to count past fifty until he was nineteen. If you are our benchmark, I'm sure whatever chimney sweep or stevedore Florence picks will have no problem."

She bent over and kissed his forehead. He grabbed her around the waist and pulled her onto his lap.

"Very true, my dear. Go back far enough and our ancestors were throwing bones to dogs and eating off the tip of a knife."

Watching the affectionate bickering, a warm glow spread over Florence. Their marriage has been one of practicality. A title for Cordelia and a welcome injection of cash into the Griggs estate in Cheshire, where the mill owners and tenants were struggling to pay the increased land rent. Still, it had turned out that the pair were well matched: both even-tempered with a love of gossip and social engagements. It occurred to Florence for the first time that such a match would not be unbearable if she was forced into it. But how lucky would she have to be? It was not something she preferred to leave to fate.

"I don't mean to pick a chimney sweep or a stevedore," she said. "Having to educate somebody to read and write or spell would be too hard. A man of the middle classes or a worker in an office of some sort would be best. I bet it would only take a few months."

"Suddenly a betting woman, are you!" Twemlow swung his feet to the ground and pushed his considerable frame upright, upending his wife in the process. "If you can find a man, then I will place a wager. What do you say to a hundred dollars that you can't create a viscount before you leave England?"

Florence hesitated. A hundred dollars was an awful lot of money, but if she won that amount back from Twemlow, just think what she might do with it. She could bring to mind three or four worthy causes off the top of her head. Of course, the main prize would be the victory of being able to prove that a title did not make the man and that a veneer of respectability was enough to make him attractive to the old money who guarded the doors to society with greater ferocity than Cerberus in Hades.

Twemlow grinned at Cordelia. "And what about you, my pet? Do you think your sister is apt to fail or succeed? Will you stand with or against your husband in this?"

Cordelia kissed him on the cheek. "As much as a wife

should obey and support her husband in all matters, I know how formidable my sister can be. I will remain impartial, but I will help pick the time and place for the hoax to be tested. There must be a ball coming up."

"I wouldn't want to embarrass him publicly," Florence cautioned. What had started out as an idle thought was rapidly becoming reality and she'd need to give it careful consideration.

"Florence, do you have anyone in mind?" Twemlow asked.

"I believe I do," Florence said thoughtfully. Until that moment, she hadn't admitted to herself that it was Mr Blake's general demeanour that had made her think of the reckless scheme, but of course it was him she had in mind. She would have to pay him, of course, but he'd proven he was happy to take on all sorts of commissions and she needed to contact him anyway to tell him what she had discovered about Miss Halliwell.

"The waiter with the champagne from last night. He was charming and he referenced *The Merchant of Venice*, so he obviously has a little education."

The quote had been from their previous encounter, but she didn't consider it wise to admit to that.

"Well, he sounds ideal," Cordelia said. She stopped talking and peered closely at Florence. "My goodness, Florence, your cheeks are perfect roses. Are you sure you aren't ill?"

Florence touched a fingertip to her cheek. Sure enough, they were warm. "I couldn't tell you why," she said.

"No, I am sure you couldn't think of a single reason why talking of a good-looking, partially educated working man who quotes Shakespeare would make you get overheated," Cordelia said wickedly.

"I didn't say he was good-looking," Florence said.

"I saw him, remember?" Cordelia sniggered.

Florence smiled. "There was certainly something striking about him. I just need to find him and ask him if he will partake."

"Well, he sounds perfect," Twemlow said. "To our wager."

Florence walked back to the table and poured three fresh cups of tea. She handed them round and raised hers. Excitement made her stomach bubble as if she were drinking more champagne.

"To our wager."

Three days after the ball, Ned paid a visit to The Admiral Nelson pub and discovered there was an envelope waiting for him. He opened it with some trepidation to discover it contained a calling card informing him that Miss Wakechild was available to greet callers every afternoon between two and four in the Rose Salon at the Midland Adelphi Hotel. It was dated two days previously in pencil on the back, but there was no other message.

Alfie was sitting in his corner and a quick chat confirmed that the note had been delivered by hand by a member of the Postal Service, pre-paid. The hotel was no more than a twenty-minute walk and Miss Wakechild could have probably found the pub again, but delivering it herself was completely out of the question for a woman in her position and sending a runner from the hotel would have opened her up to more possible scandal. Ned was impressed that she was being cautious.

He noticed with some concern that Alfie had a swollen lip and was sitting gingerly. Remembering the sting of the cane or strap on his own tender backside, he felt a rush of anger. After intervening to stop the boy's father from delivering a kicking, Ned had developed a disconcerting feeling of responsibility for Alfie in the month that he had been in Liverpool. Before leaving Liverpool, which he planned to do in the next fortnight, he would seek out the boy's father and have some strong words. A clip around the ear for disobedience or cheek was one thing, but this was brutality.

The time was a quarter to three. Ned had no other plans for the afternoon beyond checking on Alfie. He returned to his lodgings and washed and changed into his best suit of clothing; the one he wore when trying to impress potential clients. It would never buy him entry to the fashionable salon ordinarily, but armed with the calling card, he would be granted permission to enter the hotel and move among the cream of society. He arrived with half an hour to spare before the time for paying calls in the afternoon ended.

He stood in the doorway, hesitating before making his way inside. A memory stirred of a visit to Harrogate with his mother and siblings many years ago. The hotel had been nowhere near as imposing as this one, but for a brief moment, he was transported back to a childhood of luxury and excitement with a family that loved him. He'd spent so long living outside that sort of life that entering it again felt unnerving.

He straightened his shoulders and lifted his head. Ned Blake was a man who walked into gambling dens and brothels without a second thought. He'd be damned if he was going to let a tea room full of women daunt him.

The Rose Salon was a public room on the first floor used by guests to receive visitors. As its name suggested, the walls were painted with shades of pink and red, with heavy pink drapes at the windows. The gas lampshades were shaped like rosebuds and each table bore a vase with the flowers. It was oppressively feminine and made Ned itch to leave.

Having said that, there was a pleasant hum of different conversations, with all the small tables occupied by a mixture of old and young women and their guests. Some were mothers with children, others stately matrons supervising daughters. There were one or two couples discreetly courting so Ned's presence wouldn't be too out of the ordinary. He saw that Miss Wakechild was sitting alone at the far end of the room in the corner where the two windows granted the best of the afternoon sunlight. She was sitting at a table for two with a pot of coffee and a plate of biscuits in front of her and was reading a book. Most charmingly, in Ned's view, she had a pair of spectacles balanced on her neat nose. He wondered if she had sat there every day since leaving the message and how many more she would have been prepared to wait for him. His nerve endings twanged with excitement as he speculated what she might have to tell him.

The salon was attended by a steward whose immaculate appearance made Ned feel positively scruffy. He asked Ned to wait at the entrance while he took the card to Miss Wakechild. Ned took a moment to admire her from a distance. Her hair was topped with a small green hat with a veil and she wore a cream blouse with leg of mutton sleeves and a large bow at the front. Her skirt was olive green with a waterfall of burgundy ruffles at the front. In comparison to many of the other women, she was simply dressed considering she was probably one of the richest there. It was a striking contrast to what she wore to the ball and Ned felt as if he'd been given an insight into the public and private woman.

As the steward spoke to her, she cast her eyes to the door and spotted Ned. She gave him a cautious smile and spoke to the steward, who returned and led Ned towards her table. Miss Wakechild ordered a fresh pot of coffee, put her bookmark in place, and closed the book. Ned couldn't resist glancing at the title, but she turned it over, giving him a measured look. It would be nothing frivolous or amusing, Ned suspected. She seemed the sort of woman who would read improving materials.

She removed her spectacles and put them into the case, then put both case and book in a bag at her feet and asked

Ned to sit down. They made inconsequential chitchat about the weather until the coffee was delivered and poured by a pretty young waitress. Ned gave her a wink, then regretted it when Miss Wakechild caught his eye. Finally guaranteed some privacy, they smiled at each other, she nervously, he trying to appear trustworthy and respectable.

"I wasn't sure if you were going to come," she said.

"My apologies. I only received your card today. I'm afraid I don't frequent that pub every day."

"Don't apologise. A man who doesn't spend his days in public houses is better than one who does. Although if I hadn't been able to leave a message for you there, it would have been a great deal more trouble, I suppose, so I shouldn't really mind."

Ned decided not to point out the obvious answer that just because he didn't spend his days in that particular establishment didn't mean he wasn't in another.

"Yes, what would you have done?" he asked.

Miss Wakechild tilted her head slightly to one side. "I suppose I would've tried to contact Mr Halliwell and ask him how he contacted you."

"Very resourceful." He hid his shock that she might be so bold and leaned slightly forward. "I assume it is to do with Miss Halliwell you wish to speak with me as we did not manage to confer at the ball?"

A slight frown crossed Miss Wakechild's otherwise smooth brow. "Yes, I'm afraid I was unable to get away to speak to you before the end of the evening. My family commanded my attention. However, I did manage to see Miss Halliwell."

"Oh bravo, Miss Wakechild. Did you manage to ascertain which of her suitors she is inclined to favour?"

He'd been watching her face rather than what her hands were doing so was surprised when her coffee cup rattled in the saucer. His eyes glanced down to it and when he looked up again, she had begun to blush.

"I don't think she favours any of the men," she said quietly.

"No? You managed to form quite an acquaintance in a short space of time. I'm impressed."

Miss Wakechild pressed her lips together tightly.

"What aren't you telling me?" Ned asked slowly.

He wasn't sure there was more, but his intuition paid off, because her eyelashes fluttered. Pale and coppery in colour, they were nowhere near as impressive as Miss Halliwell's, but they framed a pair of extremely intelligent eyes that were currently hiding something.

Miss Wakechild gave a sigh. "Can we not just leave it at that? I imagine she will wearily accept whichever man her father decides to foist on her."

"No, I think you know something else and you're not telling me. I don't think her father would be satisfied knowing that."

Her eyes locked on to his. He imagined she could be formidable when she wanted to be.

"I don't care what her father thinks. I have absolutely no knowledge of who he is and besides, this is your commission, not mine. Without my help, you would not have even learned this, and you would never be privy to…"

"Privy to what?" he asked, sitting forward again, genuinely intrigued. "Play fair, Miss Wakechild. Now you've slipped up, you have to tell me."

"Very well." Miss Wakechild glanced around the room, then leaned forward across the table. "She was with another young woman in the powder room, and they were kissing."

Ned was a man of the world. He'd met women for whom the attraction of their own sex was greater than that of men. Determined not to show his surprise, he picked up his cup and sat back in his chair, taking a drink.

"I assume you don't mean a sisterly peck on the cheek?"

Miss Wakechild flashed him a stern look. "I do not, and even if it had been, the placement of their hands would have left the matter in no doubt!"

Ned coughed, the coffee almost making a second appearance. He quickly wiped his lips with his napkin.

"Oh dear, Mr Blake, I hope you aren't going to expire on me." Miss Wakechild was watching him with an amused look on her face. "Are you more shocked about what she was doing or that I told you about it?"

"Probably more that you don't appear shocked yourself," he admitted.

"Do you think schoolgirls don't have mad passions for each other? Besides, I have a godmother back home who has lived for years with her companion. It's an open secret that they are lovers but, as everyone is so polite in society and they are discreet, nothing is ever said."

She took a sip of coffee then placed the cup and saucer back on the table. She reached out again and adjusted the handle of the coffeepot so that it pointed in the same direction as that of her cup. She nodded to herself. Ned wondered if she was even aware she was doing that.

"I would strongly advise you to tell Mr Halliwell nothing of this, but suggest to him that his daughter might benefit from a trip around England with a companion. The ... friendship, shall we call it, might draw to a natural conclusion or they will find a way to reconcile their inevitable parting. Or they may even be fortunate enough to be allowed to keep their happiness."

"Why are you so concerned with Miss Halliwell's happiness?" Ned asked. "Until three days ago, you knew nothing of her existence."

Miss Wakechild pressed her lips together again and her eyes grew tight at the corners. "Because if I can ensure a woman is not manoeuvred into a marriage that will bring her misery, why would I not do what I could to help her?"

Ah. There it was. They had reached a moment of significance. She was in search of a husband and may have different opinions on a suitor to her father. Ned said nothing as he waited for Miss Wakechild to collect her thoughts. He didn't have to wait long but it was interesting to see the way her eyes moved around the room. Was she watching the other groups or looking at something within her mind? He'd love to know. He'd love to know a lot about her, he realised.

Finally, she blinked and folded her hands together.

"There is another matter I wished to speak with you about, Mr Blake. I have a proposition for you myself."

"A proposition for me, how intriguing!" he said softly.

"A business proposition," she replied, giving him another of those long looks that were quite captivating in their sincerity and almost made him feel abashed at flirting.

"Of course. What is your problem? Some jewellery you have lost in a game of dominoes that you'd like me to reclaim. An unwanted suitor you wish me to deter, or a wanted one whose affections you wish to confirm?"

"Nothing so commonplace," she replied.

Her eyes darted around the room, down to the table, up to his face. Her lips twitched, pulling the corner into a slight smile. "Shall we have some more coffee? Or would you prefer to switch to tea? I fancy some crumpets too."

"Whichever you prefer," Ned answered, not surprised at the change of subject. Clients often took a while to admit to what they needed him for. He would have chosen tea but, as it appeared he was about to be employed in her service, she could dictate what they had. Also, she would be paying the bill, or rather, her wealthy father would.

She sighed and lifted her chin, looking irritated.

"Mr Blake, I hate being asked to choose on behalf of others. It means I spend my time worrying I made the wrong decision and second guessing myself. Just tell me which you would like."

"Tea," he answered. "Please."

"Thank you." She smiled, her jaw losing some of its

tightness. She waved a hand discreetly and a waitress glided over almost immediately and took her order.

"Miss Wakechild, if you will excuse my extreme overfamiliarity, you are a most fascinatingly direct woman."

"Yes, I've been told so repeatedly." From her tone, it sounded like those occasions had not been complimentary.

"I like it," he hastened to add. "It's refreshing."

Her eyes narrowed as if she wasn't sure he was telling the truth. He smiled and leaned confidentially towards her, hoping that would convince her.

"Why don't you tell me what you need me to do? Please extend your directness to telling me how I can help you."

"Thank you, Mr Blake. It's quite refreshing to meet a man – anyone in fact – who seems to truly believe that my directness is not an annoyance. If you are lying, you do it very sincerely, which gives me confidence." She gave him a sweet smile and leaned forwards as if about to impart something highly confidential. Ned's pulse sped up a little and he leaned closer.

"I wish you to help me perpetrate a hoax."

Chapter Six

Fortunately, Ned was saved from reacting to the unexpected revelation because at that moment, a large pot of China tea arrived, accompanied by a plate of buttered crumpets. The smell and the sight of the holes dripping with melted butter and honey momentarily transported him back to a happier childhood.

"I haven't eaten crumpets in more years than I care to remember," he murmured.

"I never had them before I came here, but they're delicious," Miss Wakechild said. "Please help yourself."

Ned bit into one and chewed enthusiastically. As much as he wanted to continue with the conversation, he wasn't going to decline the offer.

"A hoax, you say. Who would be the victim and what would it entail?" he asked between mouthfuls.

Miss Wakechild beamed. "I'm so pleased you didn't

immediately refuse. I knew you were the person I would need to help me as soon as I thought of the plan."

"I'm not sure it's a compliment," Ned said, frowning, "that I'm the first person who came to mind when you're contemplating something illegal."

Miss Wakechild's mouth dropped open. "What makes you think it's illegal?"

"Hoaxes usually are. They're a type of fraud after all."

"That's true," she said slowly, as if the idea was only just occurring to her. "But this one isn't. At least, I'm not intending to defraud anyone."

Ned poured the tea. By now it would be starting to stew. "I dance around the edges of legality occasionally. I do try to stay on the proper side, though. I don't fancy getting myself jailed or hanged."

Miss Wakechild nodded, clearly approving of Ned's commitment to ongoing existence. "Well, no, of course you don't. I can completely see why the thought of prison or the noose would concern you. No, I don't think that would be the case at all with what I'm proposing."

"What exactly are you proposing? You still haven't told me," Ned prompted.

"I'm sorry, you're right. I want you to pretend that you are a viscount and let me introduce you to my father."

Ned felt his eyebrows shoot up. He wouldn't be surprised if they were adjoining his hairline. His first instinct was to get up and walk out. A smaller instinct, however, was to hear her out. That was the one he listened to.

"Miss Wakechild, is *this* the hoax? Will I turn round to discover a group of people standing behind me and laughing because I believed you even for a second?"

"Not at all," she replied earnestly. She leaned towards him. "I mean every word. I need a viscount. Not a real one. That is the point of the hoax. I shall train you in the correct manners of speech and behaviour, then at some point we will attend a social gathering and introduce you as a viscount. We'll have to think of a title but that can wait for now. My sister's husband thinks it can't be done and I think it can. We've made a wager and there is money at stake."

Miss Wakechild was growing more animated as she spoke. She clearly believed she could do it. Ned wondered if she was genuinely addled in the head or suffering from some female infirmity that had caused her to come up with such an odd idea. It was very clear she knew nothing about the British aristocracy if she thought that simple manners was all that was needed to appear convincingly noble.

Then again, Ned could think of at least one earl who had regularly called his footman a bastard in private and told him to fuck off if the door squeaked as it opened.

"Ah, money," Ned said. "I wondered when we would come to that. So it's a bet? How much will you earn if you win?"

Miss Wakechild grew solemn for a moment, then looked at him and gave a small smile that was awash with pathos. "The amount is incidental. Naturally I would pay you well for your time and effort."

Ned sat back and folded his arms across his chest,

wondering what sort of fee he could charge for something that went so far beyond any of his previous commissions.

"Miss Wakechild, what you are proposing is most definitely fraudulent and, depending on the circumstances, almost certainly illegal. I'd expect to be well remunerated."

"I'm not asking you to try and gain entry to the House of Lords or to swindle a widow out of her jewellery by offering marriage," she said. "The only victim would be my father. He is the only one we will need to trick."

That was unexpected. Ned scratched a thumb across his jaw. "And the reason for this trickery? Do you dislike your father?"

"Not at all. I love him dearly," she said indignantly. She looked puzzled. "What makes you think that?"

"Because you're prepared to ask a stranger to help you deceive him and potentially humiliate him in public. I'm confused," Ned admitted.

Her eyes widened. "I don't want to humiliate him, and certainly not publicly. I'd tell him in private once I knew he was convinced."

"What do you expect to happen if we manage to pull off our deception?" Ned's head was beginning to ache. His relationship with his own father had been strained but even he hadn't resorted to this sort of jape.

"I want to prove to him that a title does not make a gentleman and that a man's character does not result from simply possessing one. What is a title other than an accident of birth? Being a duke does not in itself make a man kind, principled, or well-mannered."

She paused and frowned slightly, thinking about her judgement.

"It might have for the first in the line because there would have been a reason for the creation of the title, but his descendants are of no greater moral superiority than you or I or the waiter."

"You sound very contemptuous for somebody who has come over here to try to sell herself to a nobleman," Ned remarked.

"I didn't come, I was brought!" she snapped. She made a little strangled noise and looked down at her hands. "It was not my idea."

Her shoulders dropped. Beneath her outwardly confident manner, Ned caught a glimpse of someone altogether less full of bravado.

"My apologies," he murmured.

"I suppose it's common knowledge why we're here." She sighed, looking back up at him. "It's fair to assume that I'm dazzled by the idea of becoming a baroness or countess, but unlike my father, I don't care a damn for titles or tiaras."

"Well, I'm in agreement with you there," Ned said calmly.

His memory trailed back to the comment Van Hoon had made about the Wakechilds being on a quest for a titled husband. He'd initially assumed Miss Wakechild had a naïve and starry-eyed view of the aristocracy and wanted to marry into it. Now it appeared she wanted entirely the opposite.

"I have to admit to being tempted to accept, but before

I agree to your scheme, tell me how exactly you, an American woman, will train me to deceive Englishmen?"

Her eyes lit up. "Well, that's the beauty of this. I don't expect you to fool English men, just the one American. Also I have a book."

"A book?" Ned blinked.

"Yes. I found it at my brother-in-law's house when we were there last time I visited. It's fascinating." She delved into her bag and brought out the book she had been reading when Ned had arrived and presented it to him.

Manners and Rules of Good Society or Solecisms to be Avoided.

Ned flipped it open to discover the author was a nameless "Member of the Aristocracy" and this was the fifteenth edition. He had never seen such a thing in his life and had to make quite an effort not to burst out laughing when he saw the earnest look on her face.

"There are so many different rules and points of etiquette. The order of precedence going into dinner, how to address the younger son of an earl, why my sister's mother-in-law is Lady Violet Griggs, not Lady Griggs. My goodness, it's fascinating. I read it in one night and was late to breakfast the next morning."

Ned threw his head back and laughed. "It's confusing, I'll admit. Manners can be learned and anyone with a memory can remember how to address a person, but I can't pretend to have acres of land and a deer park, or an old hunting lodge."

She shrugged. "We have a grand house already back home. What would I do with those? Take my sister and her husband, for example. He has a rambling old house in a fairly passable area of Cheshire but the whole thing was on the brink of rack and ruin before he married Cordelia. Why, just to have a bath required an hour's preparation and half a dozen poor maids carrying pails of water while she waited and shivered."

"So your criticism against the nobility is that they have cold houses," Ned joked.

She sat up straight and eyed him strictly. "No, my criticism is that despite having decades—centuries in fact—of influence, what does it amount to? Surrounding old houses with great swathes of land which, from what I understand, barely bring in enough revenue to subsist on in terms of agriculture. The only thing these people have over the rest of us is that they have been in possession of the land and the titles for longer. Why does that automatically entitle them to more respect? What makes a baron better? What gives more value to a viscount?"

"What makes a duke desirable?" Ned interjected.

"Yes!" She smiled. "Also that's very funny. So, will you do it?"

Ned sucked his teeth. He had no other obligations and he'd be paid for it. The role itself would be easy enough but there would be implications concerning which event she named. He couldn't appear at a race meeting or a ball, for example, but a house party could be manageable.

"Give me two days to think on it and decide my terms, if I decide to take your commission. I'll send a message to you here."

"I've enjoyed your company. Come in person," Miss Wakechild said. "I'll give you my card. Shall we say two-thirty in my suite two days from now? My sister can be there so there is no concern over being unchaperoned."

She gave him a card from a little silver case and he slipped it into his breast pocket.

"Thank you for a very diverting afternoon," he said, taking her hand.

"Thank you for approving of my scheme," she said.

"I haven't yet," he pointed out.

He left her sitting there. He turned back at the doorway, but she was already deeply engrossed in her book. It was very tempting to turn back and agree on the spot, not least because it would mean spending time in the company of Miss Wakechild.

Once Mr Blake had departed, Cordelia and Twemlow left the table where they had been sitting, partially masked by a large potted fern, and joined Florence.

"Well?" Florence asked. "What do you think? He seemed interested in the idea and I didn't even talk specifics regarding a fee."

"He didn't? Are you sure he isn't a confidence trickster?" Cordelia asked.

My Fair Lord

"Unlikely," Twemlow said. "More likely he jumped at the chance to spend time with a charming young lady and get paid for it. Very sensible."

Florence blushed. "Do you think he could pass as a viscount?"

"He needs a haircut and he'd suit a pair of whiskers, but he's got a good figure and an aristocratic profile," Twemlow said. "I wouldn't be surprised if one of his grandparents or great-grandparents was a marquis' by-blow. What do you know of his family?"

"Nothing," Florence said. "When you say 'by-blow' you mean an illegitimate child, don't you?"

"That's right. There must be hundreds of people out there with a little blue blood thanks to an indelicate dalliance with the lord of the manor. That's how half the nobility got started if you think about it. Royal bastards, you know."

Cordelia coughed meaningfully and gave Twemlow a stern look. "Florence, are you sure you need to go to all this trouble when you could just ask my husband to open his mouth and prove his complete lack of breeding?"

Twemlow winked at Florence. "Your way seems much more fun. He seems a good choice. Once he's dressed appropriately, he will certainly look the part."

"Having seen him, I'm very tempted to come in on your side rather than remaining neutral. His accent is intriguing. Not at all local to this area but I can't place it. Perhaps Twemlow can enlighten us."

Twemlow shrugged. "Northern of some sort. Couldn't say whether it's Cumbrian or Yorkshire."

He helped himself to the last crumpet, much to Florence's annoyance. Cordelia smoothly moved the teapot out of his reach.

"I'm sure you will work wonders on his manners, Florence dearest, though I'm not sure you will need to," she said. "I could tell from your face that he's perfectly captivating. Put him in company with Aunt Patricia and her clutch of hens and they'll practically swoon when he turns those gorgeous eyes on them."

"Honestly, wife of mine!" Twemlow coughed on a crumb of crumpet. "You two are like a pair of schoolgirls. It's quite startling to see what effect a good-looking man can have on women, you silly things."

"Our interest is purely sociological," Cordelia said primly. She winked at Florence. "Of course I'm sure it will be perfectly advantageous when it comes to fooling anyone. They won't be able to see past his looks, though I'm not sure if that holds true for Papa. You could tell Aunt Patricia he's the King of Sweden and she wouldn't doubt it."

"Do you think so?" Florence asked eagerly.

Cordelia gave Florence an infuriating smile.

"I'm sure of it. Why, you were practically eating his words. The two of you were quite rapt in each other; leaning your heads close and giving him that coy little smile. Of course, I couldn't see if he was smiling back from where I was sitting, but I expect he was. It looked quite flirtatious."

"Well, it wasn't!" Florence exclaimed in surprise. She would not call herself a practised flirt, though she'd had the occasional sweetheart and indulged in plenty of idle chat with her elder brother's friends when she had been younger. She had enjoyed their conversation and the slightly teasing nature of it. Mr Blake was extremely charming in a rough and ready sort of way. There was something that drew her to him inexplicably.

"It's the prospect of what I can do with him," she said.

The triumphant gleam in both Twemlow and Cordelia's eyes made her listen more carefully to the declaration she had just made.

"I mean, what I can do with him to sculpt him into the sort of man he needs to be in order to fool Daddy," she said quickly.

"Of course," Cordelia replied. "Have you considered where you're going to carry out your lessons? You can hardly invite him back to the hotel to teach him. You'll get a reputation for yourself."

Florence wrinkled her nose. "I suppose that's true. I'll have to give it some thought. I haven't really planned it all out yet. It's very spur of the moment."

"Why not bring him to Goreswarth Chase with you when you come back in a fortnight?" Twemlow suggested. "We can put him up in one of the guest suites and there are hundreds of pieces of silver for him to learn how to use."

Florence brightened. "That sounds fine. He can hardly come to Leamington with Daddy and me. He can have two weeks—a fortnight, I do love that word—to get his affairs in order then we can send for him."

Twemlow clapped his hands. "That's perfect. You'll have a week to begin his education, then we'll see if he can pass as a gentleman at the county fair. Do that then I'll set a date to introduce him to your father."

"And you're perfectly happy for us to use your house?" Florence asked.

"Yes, of course we are," Cordelia said, taking her hand. "It will give us something to do while the men are off fishing. In fact, Twemlow, you can take him with you one afternoon. He needs to learn how to make tedious small talk after all."

Florence smiled nervously. Suddenly everything was becoming more real. Her resolve wasn't exactly breaking, but it was certainly stretching a little more than she was comfortable with. Mr Blake hadn't even agreed to take part and Cordelia was already choosing a room for him.

Her misgivings might have seen her calling the whole thing off until she dined with her father, Cordelia, and Twemlow. Mr Wakechild had returned from an excursion in high spirits and commanded a table in the centre of the room beneath the brightest of the gasoliers that sparkled above.

"Florence, I'm delighted to tell you that despite your rather inappropriate habit of spending the evening talking with waiters, you did manage to catch some attention on the night of the ball." Clayton Wakechild bestowed an approving smile on Florence. "One man in particular has expressed interest in meeting you again."

"Oh, well, that's very gratifying to know," Florence said as she helped herself to another lamb chop and sprinkled it with mint sauce.

"Aren't you going to ask who it is?" Cordelia prompted.

"Oh yes, I suppose I should. Who was it, Daddy? The brass engraver?" she asked, remembering his polite bow. "Not Sir St-John I hope."

"Viscount Stretford."

Florence wrinkled her brows. "I'm afraid I don't remember him. Did I dance with him or just talk?"

"You danced."

Her father described him, and slowly a portrait painted itself in Florence's mind. She pursed her lips.

"Yes, I remember him now. He commented on my hair and said it reminded him of Queen Elizabeth."

"There you go, what a lovely compliment," Clayton said.

Florence picked up her fork. "I suppose so. He was very dull and quite stupid. He seemed to think that it was being a redhead that inspired the Virgin Queen to greatness, and he thought the Iceni lived in Chester."

"Iceni? I'm not familiar with that family. Were they at the ball?" Clayton waved a hand dismissively. "Whether or not Lord Stretford knows them, he's from a very old family not too far from Manchester. You would be quite close to Cordelia. That would be nice for you both. When you go stay with her, we should arrange a meeting between you and he for a day."

Florence had intended to reprimand her father for his dreadful lack of historical knowledge, but it went completely out of her mind upon hearing the plan. Her expression must have revealed something of her state of mind because Cordelia patted her arm.

"That would be lovely, wouldn't it?" Cordelia asked.

"I believe Manchester is very industrial, isn't it?" Florence replied.

"Naturally the city itself is, though there are some lovely parklands surrounding it. Even so, we'll have him visit us instead of you going there," Twemlow said. "We can go fishing. A picnic by the river would be a pleasurable way to spend an afternoon, and perfect for courting."

Florence's hand tightened around her fork. "I don't want to be courted. I meant, what exactly does he hope to use my dowry for? Does he have a job?"

Her father and sister exchanged a glance full of humour. "Of course he doesn't have a job, he's a viscount."

"Yes, but Twemlow is heavily involved in his tenants' mills and farms," Florence pointed out.

"Probably more than their owners would like, if I'm perfectly honest. I think it's a fine question for Florence to ask," Twemlow said, giving her a smile. "I believe he breeds horses for steeplechase."

Cordelia gave Florence a wicked grin of only the sort a sibling could manage. "There now. A horse breeder *and* a member of the aristocracy. That's a fine combination."

"He seemed perfectly pleasant and he was good-looking enough, if you excuse his slightly reddened complexion. I imagine that's because he spends all his days out of doors with his horses," Twemlow said.

Clayton reached for his wine glass and smiled at Florence over the top. "Do you know, I think we should forego visiting Leamington Spa. I've a couple of men I could do with visiting in Lincolnshire and there is precious little to occupy you there. You should go straight to Goreswarth."

"But we were going to go see the elephants in Leamington," Florence protested in dismay. Her whole family were in conspiracy against her and the room began to feel stifling.

Clayton looked at her over the top of his spectacles, shaking his head slightly.

"The elephants can wait. We need to strike while the iron is hot with Lord Stretford. I think the matter could be quite settled in a few weeks. We could even extend our visit long enough to see you married before autumn and spare us the inconvenience of returning to America and back again."

"No!" The thought of not returning home and seeing her friends, but instead being married off to a stranger, sent shudders of trepidation through her limbs. Her stomach felt both tight and empty at the same time. Her throat began to tighten. In a moment, she knew her eyes would begin to tickle and then she would cry.

"I don't even remember a conversation with him other

than the one I mentioned. I absolutely cannot marry a man I don't even know!" she exclaimed.

"Lower your voice," Clayton commanded in a discreet hiss. He laid his fork down and glared at her. "I absolutely will not stand for your continued obstinacy. If I find the viscount agreeable, then there is no reason you shouldn't."

"Daddy, please, don't make such an important decision for me," Florence begged. She was mindful enough to keep her voice to a low whisper but hoped he would hear the urgency in her tone and realise how important this was to her.

"I will consult you once you have made any sort of effort to become acquainted with the viscount, but I am not going to let this opportunity slip through our fingers," Clayton said. "I think we shall leave Liverpool the day after tomorrow. I'll inform the manager first thing in the morning that tomorrow will be our last night here."

Florence dropped her head. She got her obstinacy and single-mindedness from her father and knew that once he'd made his mind up, he rarely, if ever, changed it. She toyed with her food for the remainder of the meal, her appetite completely gone.

The need to get Mr Blake to agree to her plan had intensified. The trouble was, she could no longer wait for him to return to keep their appointment. She would have to brave the streets of Liverpool and seek him out in person, which would mean returning to the Admiral Nelson pub.

As her maid helped her dress for bed that evening Florence smiled sweetly.

"Dottie, how would you like to come with me tomorrow to see a little more of the city? We'll go buy some cakes while we're out."

Dottie readily agreed. Florence twisted the ends of her hair around her fingers and smiled at her reflection. At least her father couldn't fault her for going unchaperoned.

Chapter Seven

When Ned visited the Admiral Nelson the morning after meeting Miss Wakechild, Alfie was sitting in the corner of the pub as usual. He looked up when Ned approached him and gave a weak wave. Ned stopped short, horror-struck. Alfie's face was a mess of cuts and bruises.

"Who did this to you?"

Alfie shrugged and dropped his head. "Who d'you think?"

Ned grew hot to the bones, filled with incandescent rage. Alfie's father of course. He sat on a stool beside the child and gently lifted Alfie's chin. Alfie's dad was close to fifty and had sired more children on a succession of unfortunate wives than a tomcat. He was a large man who wore brass rings on three of his fingers, which were responsible for the wounds.

"Why?" Ned muttered through gritted teeth. A stupid question. Carver Clarke didn't need a reason. Drink.

Tiredness. Just because the mood took him. Ned was already making up his mind to deal with this once and for all, even before Alfie peered at him through swollen eyes.

"Some bloke came looking for you. Worked at the docks."

"A porter? Someone from the ships? Did he leave his name?" Ned asked.

"No. A fancy bloke. From the offices, not the dockside. Showy clothes and an ugly ring on his finger."

"Was it two pearls?"

Alfie nodded and grinned, even though it must have been painful. "That's right. Do you know why toffs always like things so ugly? Anyway, he wanted to leave you a message. Knew you came here occasionally. He gave me five bob. Can you imagine it? Me with that sort of money. Course my dad took it straight off me. Took him a fight though."

Alfie sat back on the stool and winced, tugging at the cloth around his neck. There were clear finger indentations visible beneath the collar of Alfie's ragged shirt. Ned didn't need to see beneath the shirt to know there would be more bruising and probably cuts all over the stick thin body. His jaw tightened, teeth grinding in fury. Ned knew about thrashings. Knew about vindictiveness too. Five shillings was almost a week's rent. Or more likely a hell of a lot of cheap whisky.

"Aren't you gonna ask what the toff wanted?" Alfie asked.

"What did he want?"

Alfie managed a feeble grin and reached out a hand.

"Will it cost me five bob as well?" Ned asked.

"I'm not stupid, me. Gin for a week and buy me a pie now. I chucked up my bread and scrape after my dad laid about me."

"I'll do better than that." Ned walked over to the bar. Meggie Gallagher, the landlord's daughter, was polishing glasses.

"Is your upstairs room free?" he asked.

Meggie tilted her head on one side and fluttered her lashes. "Yes, it is. My dad will be back from the bookies in ten minutes if you can wait that long, but don't let him know I'm with you. We can talk prices when we're up there, but for a fine gentleman like you, I'm sure I can give good terms."

Ned suppressed a sigh. Of course that was what she would assume he wanted the room for. "I'm flattered but I want it for Alfie. The bed, some hot water to wash himself in, and a pie and half a pint of mild. Also a place to hide out. I'll pay you three shillings for the room and another two not to let his dad know he's up there."

She looked a little disappointed. "Another time maybe. I'll gladly help the kid out."

"I'll take him up myself," Ned said. He turned to go back to Alfie, but the barmaid leaned over and grabbed his sleeve. He looked back, raising an eyebrow.

"Someone needs to sort that bastard out, you know," Meggie muttered. "It's not right. I mean, all kids need a slap for cheeking their mam and dad occasionally. Lord knows I had enough of it in my time, but that's too much."

Ned nodded. "It'll be the last time he does it, I can tell you for nothing."

Soon Alfie was settled in the upstairs room. It was small but neat with a comfy chair by the fireplace and a cheerful patchwork quilt on the bed. The water that Meggie brought was warm. Alfie had clearly never seen anything as luxurious before.

"Stay in this room. Wash yourself and eat your pie. Even have a sleep if you want," Ned told him. "If your dad comes looking for you, Meggie won't let on that you're here."

"Thanks, Mr Blake." Alfie's brow furrowed. "That man said you might not be going by the name Blake here. Do you have another name?"

Ned smiled tightly. Damn Van Hoon. Ned cursed himself afresh for keeping up with old acquaintances. Couldn't a man ever escape his past?

"Not anymore. I'll see you later."

He made his visit to the Van Hoon offices first. The father and son were together. Willem Van Hoon stuck out his hand.

"Ned! So good to see you. Can't thank you enough for what you did for me. We're just about to head out to Murray's Chop House for a spot of lunch. Care to join us? I'll stand you a pint of porter."

Ned shook Willem's hand. "Regretfully, I have other

business to attend to that prevents me from accepting your kind offer. You came looking for me at the Admiral Nelson. What did you want? Have you got yourself into any more trouble? If so, it'll have to be quick because I'm very soon to be otherwise engaged."

Miss Wakechild's proposal was delightfully odd. He'd rather work for her than the Van Hoons again. He intended to leave Liverpool soon in any case, and the prospect of sorting out Willem's mess again made up his mind there and then that he would accept Miss Wakechild's curious offer of employment, regardless of any qualms he might have about the success of her plan. He'd move lodgings and change his name for couple of months until any trail that had followed him as far as Liverpool might go cold. He'd stipulate that wherever they carried out the meeting would be at a private event too.

"There's no trouble," Van Hoon said. "Possibly some benefit to you though. People are looking for you. Those in the know want to know what your intentions are."

"I don't have any intentions that should concern anyone," Ned said, flashing him a hostile look.

"A certain lady is nearing the end of her period of confinement," Van Hoon said.

Ned's guts clenched. He smiled, though it was more baring his teeth in what he hoped Van Hoon would realise was a warning.

"Well, how wonderful for her. However, I said that is nothing of interest to me."

"The child will be born in a matter of weeks," Willem added. "Aren't you eager to find out if it lives?"

Ned sat down on the Chesterfield sofa and gave a heavy sigh.

"As eager as any disinterested party who hopes for a safe arrival for the child and health for the mother."

Of course he did. Only a monster wouldn't. He ran his hands through his hair and across his face.

"Willem, I'm ruing the day when I offered you my assistance. I should have stuck to people who don't know my past. I want nothing to do with events up in Yorkshire and if you're a friend to me at all, you will deny having spoken to me."

He watched the expression of disapproval form on the face of the elder Van Hoon. He didn't care. The Van Hoons had enough potential scandals in their own lives that Ned could make known if he chose to, though he hoped he wouldn't have to resort to blackmail. It was so demeaning.

He didn't have many qualms about masquerading as a viscount, he mused as he left the office. In fact, the thought of playing the role made him want to laugh. He'd spent years becoming whatever he needed to be, but that was a role he'd never played.

It occurred to him that he was wearing the suit that he had worn to meet Miss Wakechild, which might be ideal for visiting the Van Hoons, but not for his next meeting. He returned to the Admiral Nelson, removed his tie, starched collar and waistcoat, and left them with Meggie, along with a shilling and the warning not to sell them before he came back. Having done so, he made his way along the river front in the opposite direction of the Van Hoon's office, almost three miles down to the much less salubrious docks where Alfie's drunken wastrel of a father scraped a living cheating working men at cards.

He spotted Carver Clarke sitting on a stack of crates, winding a length of rope, and laughing with two other men. Carver was wearing a battered top hat jammed onto his straw-blond hair and a garish waistcoat of green and yellow stripes that looked almost new. It wasn't hard to imagine where Alfie's money had gone. The men looked over at Ned as he approached, eyes flicking up and down him. Ned flexed his hands and squared his shoulders then tilted his hat back. He took a deep breath.

"Carver Clarke?"

He stalked over to the group, rolling up his sleeves, the anticipation building inside him until the muscles in his arms began to sing.

Very soon he would have another compelling reason to disappear without a trace.

Ned returned to the Admiral Nelson later that afternoon to collect his clothing and check on Alfie. He walked gingerly into the pub and took a seat in the corner, waving to Meggie's father, Eoghan, who had returned from the bookmaker's. He signalled to the bitter pump and eased himself onto the wooden bench while he waited for his pint to be pulled. His ribs ached and he knew without seeing his reflection in a looking glass that there would soon be a bruise spreading over the left side of his jaw. He'd got a cut beneath his left eye along the cheekbone that he hoped wouldn't scar. Damn Carver Clarke and his bloody rings. He needed a cold cloth or a steak to take the swelling down if he had any hope of the injuries subsiding before he saw Miss Wakechild two days hence.

Eoghan brought a pint mug over and put it on the table before Ned.

"What have you been getting yourself into?" he asked.

"I've had a talk with Alfie Clarke's father," Ned mumbled, discovering that talking was quite painful through a split lip.

"I don't mean that," Eoghan said. "That lady has been waiting for you. Looks important."

He indicated with a thumb to the table beside the door where a woman sat, her face obscured by the heavy veil that fell from her hat, in the company of a young black, maid. Neither had drinks. As Ned and Eoghan looked over at their table, the veiled woman stood and walked over. A sinking feeling filled Ned as he recognised the determined walk. He could already picture the expression he would encounter before Miss Wakechild even lifted her veil. In an ironic recreation of Ned's reaction to seeing Alfie, she stopped as she got close.

"What happened to you?" she gasped.

"Nothing important," Ned said.

"You're lying," Miss Wakechild said severely. She lifted her veil and her eyes were indeed wide with horror. "Don't stand there with a face like an artist's smock and tell me nothing has happened."

Ned reached for his glass. His hands were bare and now he noticed how the knuckles on both hands were red and scraped. He saw Miss Wakechild looking at them, her eyes widening.

"I didn't say nothing. I said nothing important." He glowered at her and took a long drink before turning his attention back to her. "There was a slight differing of opinion, but it was solved very easily."

"With fists?" Miss Wakechild raised her eyebrows. Her lips curled with distaste. "It's blatantly clear that you have been in a fist fight. Mr Blake, I'm very disappointed in you. I thought you were better than that!"

Ned put the glass down on the table slightly harder than he intended, causing it to make a sharp bang. Miss Wakechild jumped.

"What are you doing here?" he asked brusquely. "We aren't supposed to be meeting for another two days."

"I've been forced to bring our meeting forward. Now, seeing you in this sorry state, I wonder if I have taken on more than is wise! Good afternoon to you, Mr Blake. Dottie, we're leaving."

The maid stood. Miss Wakechild turned on her heel, pulling her veil back over her face as she walked towards the door, and with her went Ned's opportunity for a quiet place to lie low. Cursing between his split lips, he downed the rest of his pint and chased after them.

Florence walked out of the Admiral Nelson and heaved a mighty sigh of frustration. Mr Blake had clearly gotten into a fight. Presumably, it was the result of taking on another disreputable job. She adjusted her veil and turned to her maid.

"Come along, Dottie, our business here is done."

"Miss Wakechild, please wait." Mr Blake appeared in the doorway. Florence's belly gave a little flip as if it were happy to see him, which was so far from the truth to be laughable.

She flicked her hand towards him. "Go back inside. Drink your beer and nurse your injuries. We have nothing more to say to each other. I see you are completely the wrong person for my proposal."

She winced and her previously traitorous belly now twisted as she saw all her plans going up in smoke.

"How could you get involved in violence!" she exclaimed.

"Let me explain. It's not what it looks like," Mr Blake said, moving slowly towards her. "I haven't been brawling."

She should hear what he had to say before rejecting him. There was absolutely no way she could find anyone else at such short notice. "Really?"

She put her hands on her hips and stared him down, realising belatedly that Dottie was watching with fascination. She was twenty-two and had been Florence's personal maid for six years, rising from being a general chambermaid to being something closer to a companion and friend. She was perfectly entitled to be nosy, having been summoned on Florence's excursion to the pub, a place she could hardly imagined they would end up in. Thank goodness she knew Dottie would act with complete discretion. She stuck her hand into her bag and gave Dottie a handful of coins.

"I need to have a conversation with Mr Blake. Please go and look in that bookshop. See if you can't find us something new to read while we're in the countryside. Choose whatever you like."

Dottie hurried off eagerly, Florence having given her the ultimate inducement. She was a bright girl who was educated well beyond what was necessary for her station (or as many would unfairly consider, her race) in life. In Florence's opinion, she should be a schoolteacher, not drawing baths and sticking combs into Florence's hair.

"Mr Blake, you have approximately five minutes to explain, before Dottie returns with an armful of new books. She never wastes time browsing."

"Thank you," Mr Blake said. "I had hoped to look less alarming by the time we met. I really didn't want to jeopardise the arrangement. I intend to agree to your proposal, with a couple of minor requests."

He looked and sounded sincere. She would never get an

opportunity like this again. Now that an actual suitor had appeared, she needed his help more than she could let on. She was on the verge of accepting him but hesitated, knowing she often acted too eagerly.

"I'm very tempted to take you on as a project," she said with as much haughtiness as she could manage, "but before I do, I need to know who you have been fighting and what you were carrying the other day when you involved me. It's one thing taking part in a deception such as I am proposing and quite another to bring my family into connection with the law. If we do this, we'll be going to my brother-in-law's estate in Cheshire in order to carry out the lessons somewhere less visible. I need to know if you are involved in anything criminal and if I'm likely to put myself or my family in danger. I absolutely cannot have them connected with scandal or criminality."

Mr Blake's fingers strayed to his jaw and he rubbed at the bruise. It looked very painful and she couldn't help the pang of sympathy that shot through her.

"Cheshire? Well, I could do with leaving Liverpool so that's ideal. Miss Wakechild, I can promise I am not a criminal. The men who were pursuing me the other day, however, were definitely not what we'd call desirable figures."

"That isn't an answer," Florence said.

"You are relentless, aren't you," Blake said, giving her a slight grin.

"So I'm often told." She stared back directly, not smiling.

"Very well. A young man in my acquaintance had

inadvisably got himself entangled with a young woman—note I don't use the term lady—and while in her company had been embroiled in gambling. He went beyond his means and as a pledge, he left a ring that would have identified the family and caused extreme embarrassment to his father. I took on the commission of charming myself into the game and retrieving the ring. When the men realised that they had lost the opportunity to blackmail a particularly prominent person, they decided to try to retrieve the ring."

He inclined his head towards Florence in something approaching a bow. "Thanks to your participation, they didn't find me and I was able to return it to its rightful owner. He and his father were extremely grateful."

He gave her an open smile and she was struck again by how charming he could be. Perhaps a viscount was too low. Should she make him an earl or marquis?

"Is that why you were at the Huskisson building later that afternoon? I saw you from my father's window, though I doubt you saw me. Does the person in question have an office there?" Florence asked. She suddenly connected dots and, forgetting she was angry with him, leaned forward eagerly. "Is it someone I might know?"

Mr Blake rolled his eyes. "You're too sharp for your own good. You almost certainly know them, but on my honour, I'm not going to tell you the name."

"Well, that's a real shame," Florence said. "But I suppose it's good that at least you are a man of your word."

"Absolutely I am. My integrity is everything to me, Miss

Wakechild. I move in some shady circles but I never lower myself to breaking the law." Mr Blake lifted his chin and eyed her solemnly. The effect would have been more convincing if he hadn't been sporting his bruises. "I can be devious but when I give my word, I keep it. Is that a good enough answer for you?"

Florence nodded thoughtfully. "I think it is. But you haven't told me how your injuries came about."

Blake's eyes narrowed, his straight brows almost meeting. He looked furious, though not at Florence's persistence.

"They are unconnected."

He stopped speaking and looked as if he was thinking deeply.

"Will you come with me? I have something to show you that will explain everything. Bring your maid too. I see she is returning and yes, she has three books."

Immensely intrigued, Florence followed him back inside the pub. He led her past the bar and upstairs. Dottie trailed behind, her eyes gleaming with interest. Mr Blake stopped at a door and knocked.

"Are you decent?"

A high voice answered the affirmative. It sounded either young or female. Florence wasn't sure which.

"Is this a house of ill repute?" Dottie asked in a scandalised whisper.

Florence hushed her. She should be shocked, but she was immensely curious as to what she'd see behind the door.

"Do you think I'd take anyone like your mistress somewhere like that?" Mr Blake asked Dottie, his brows raising in amusement.

"I'm not sure I'd put anything past you," Florence said.

Mr Blake grinned and opened the door.

Chapter Eight

They entered a small bedroom, sparsely furnished. A young boy was sitting on a chair. He gave a wide grin on seeing Mr Blake. Three of his front teeth were missing.

"This is Alfie. Do you remember him? He took you back to Lewis' on the day we first met."

"Yes, I remember. Hello, Alfie," Florence said.

She took a closer look at him. He was much cleaner now and wearing a better fitting shirt, but also an adult's yellow and green waistcoat that drowned his small frame. His face was covered in a multitude of little scabs and bruises that were not quite as fresh as Mr Blake's, but still recent and his lip was puffy.

"What happened to his face?"

Mr Blake held a hand up and slid his eyes towards Alfie. Florence nodded, understanding.

"Alfie, nip down and buy yourself a twist of pork

scratchings." Blake flipped him a coin. Alfie caught it in mid-air and skipped out. When he had gone, Florence turned back to Mr Blake.

"Did he get into a fight or did somebody attack him?"

"His dad did it. Alfie came into a bit of money but his dad took it. Alfie fought to get it back but he was never going to win against someone who spends his days heaving about crates and barrels."

"That's dreadful. Something needs to be done." Florence felt her hands curling into fists. "Where can I find this man?"

"You won't find him," Blake said firmly, "and even if you could, I wouldn't let you go off to confront him."

"That choice is not yours to make on my behalf," Florence said indignantly.

Blake folded his arms across his chest. "It isn't a choice I am prepared to let anyone make. What would you do? March up to him and tell him to reform his ways?"

"Well, yes. I suppose so." Florence could feel herself getting flustered. "That is, I would inform him that the police would be getting involved if there was a repeat."

Blake's mouth twitched. She thought he was about to smile but he controlled it.

"He'd snap your neck before you got three words out. People like you don't go after men like Carver Clarke. The police wouldn't touch him either."

A finger of ice traced itself down Florence's spine, causing her to shudder; it was not the words as much as the tone of his voice. She had never heard him sound so serious.

"Well, something needs to be done," she protested.

"It has been," Blake said quietly. Their eyes met and the hardness she saw in his was so alarming it caused her to take a step back. More dots joined. She looked him up and down.

"What did you do?" she asked in a whisper.

"Enough that he won't be so quick to beat anyone again."

There was a quiet determination in Blake's voice. It was like listening to an iron bar speaking. She looked Blake up and down, drinking in the livid bruising on his face and imagining more beneath his shirt. The hair at the back of her neck prickled.

"Have you murdered him?" Dottie, standing by the window, gave a squeak of alarm.

Mr Blake's eyes widened. "Good grief, Miss Wakechild, your maid does seem to have a dreadful opinion of me. Of course I haven't murdered him."

"There, Dottie, don't be so foolish," Florence said, slightly relieved that Dottie had asked the question she had been wondering herself and even more so that the answer was negative. Blake's next words were not so comforting, however.

"You don't murder somebody like Carver Clarke. That's too dignified a word. You put the animal down."

"Oh!"

Blake's eyes flickered and for a moment Florence saw pure fury.

"I have done neither, however. Let's just say I

demonstrated how it feels to be on the receiving end of a solid beating and Mr Clarke will think twice before laying his hand on the boy again."

He lifted his chin, displaying the profile that Twemlow had praised.

"Oh thank goodness," Florence breathed. "I mean, thank goodness you didn't kill him. Also thank goodness he won't hurt Alfie anymore and got what he had coming to him."

Alfie wandered back into the room holding a brown paper bag and crunching on something enthusiastically. The smell of fat and salt rose enticingly from the bag. He was tucking into his treat as if there was no tomorrow. For him, with a brute of a father, perhaps there was no guarantee of a tomorrow. Florence's stomach tightened.

"What will happen to him now?" She asked Ned quietly so that Alfie didn't hear, but he looked towards her from his spot by the window.

"He's a bright lad," Blake said. "Quick on his feet. Sharp too. The sort of boy that could be made something of if he had the opportunity." He gave a gentle cough. "Miss Wakechild, something extremely untoward has just occurred to me."

"Yes," Florence said, giving him a big smile. "Yes, Alfie can come with us."

He looked astonished. "How did you know that is what I was going to ask?"

She tilted her head on one side to look at him, wondering how he could be so unaware. "Because you brought him here. You are taking the time to care for him and now you want to ask something of me. What else could you be asking me?"

Blake smiled, his eyes crinkling at the corners. "I'm not suggesting we turn him into a viscount, but with a bit of education, some manners, and enough food to fill his belly, he could make a passable servant. Not at the house, of course, but downstairs. Will you do it?"

"How can you even doubt it? We can't possibly leave him at the mercy of someone who would do that to him."

"Thank you." Mr Blake took her hand. She looked at her hand contained in his. His fingers were slightly calloused. Not the hands of a nobleman. She'd have to invest in some lanolin ointment to help soften them. She curled her fingers slightly around his, and he made a soft noise in the back of his throat, something between a sigh and a grunt. Florence slipped her hand free, wondering if she had upset him, and went to Alfie.

"Alfie, would you like to come with me to Cheshire? My brother-in-law owns a house and he could always find work for a clever boy."

Alfie looked interested. "Does he have horses, miss? I like horses."

"Why yes, he does. He has two that pull his carriage. I'm sure he could find you work with them." She thought for a moment, then added, "There is someone I'm going to meet who breeds racehorses. If my brother-in-law can't find you work, perhaps he will."

Alfie beamed. Florence looked at him speculatively, then

at her maid. Dottie's skin was darker than Alfie's but that wasn't necessarily a problem.

"Dottie, you have a little brother, Davey, don't you? I think for one night Alfie can sleep in your room and if anyone asks, you can say he's Davey come to visit you. Will you run ahead to the hotel and ask the porter to find a pallet bed?"

Dottie bobbed a curtsey and left. Alfie barely had any possessions, so Florence, Blake, and the boy were not far behind. As they left the pub, Florence looked up at Blake.

"The man in question whose ring you were returning wouldn't happen to be a Mr Van Hoon, would it?"

Blake's eyes shot wide open and Florence knew she had guessed correctly. "What makes you say that?"

"When I saw you at the Huskisson Building, you were looking up at the windows to a lower floor than mine. Thinking of who owns offices on the third and fourth floor, I think Van Hoon is the most likely candidate to be concerned about things. I also know he has a son only a year or two older than me because I danced with them both at the ball."

Blake's lips twitched. "Very clever, Miss Wakechild. Are you sure you wouldn't like to join me in my line of work?"

She felt her cheeks go red. "Mr Van Hoon senior suggested I might like to meet him with a view to matrimony. I don't like the father, so I certainly don't want to marry the son."

"Why don't you like him?"

She sucked her lip and shook her head. "He just gives

me a feeling. He looks at me as if he is imagining me in my underwear. Or out of it."

Alfie sniggered, stopping abruptly when Blake gave him a stern look.

"I don't imagine he's alone in that, Miss Wakechild," Blake said with a grin that contradicted his admonishment of the child. "You're very eye-catching. Any man with eyes and a pulse would do the same."

"Mr Blake!" Florence's cheeks began to smart. The heat travelled down her neck and she was thankful for the high collar of her dress that would obscure the worst of the redness. "That is a scandalous thing to say! It's certainly not what I would imagine hearing from a member of the aristocracy, so you had better curb your language."

Blake gave a barking laugh then grew serious. "Miss Wakechild, if you know anything about the British aristocracy, you will know it is precisely the sort of thing they would say. The aristocracy love nothing more than rutting with housemaids, seducing their brothers' wives, or imagining their associates' daughters in stages of undress. Their licentiousness knows no bounds. In fact, my unwillingness to grope the village girls is precisely why I would never cut it in some of the finest houses in England."

Florence looked at him. He must be joking. Surely that sort of behaviour wasn't common. He looked contemptuous though, and Twemlow's assessment of him sprang to mind. She had her own reasons for disliking the institution, but Blake seemed genuinely angry.

"Are you a nobleman's by-blow?" she asked.

Alfie gave a barking laugh and Blake coughed. "That's not a term I'd expect a young American lady to use."

"My brother-in-law told me it," Florence explained. "Are you? There's no shame in it. Your father would be at fault, not you."

He folded his arms across his chest then laughed. "You are astonishingly straight to the point. No, I'm not. My father was many things, but as far as I know, he didn't father bastards left, right, and centre. Only legitimate children for him."

He offered her an arm. "Shall we go?"

She took it. As they crossed the street, a man began running towards them. He had a look of fury on his face, though as he charged, he lowered his head.

"Blake, you piece of shite. I haven't finished with you!" he shouted.

Blake swore under his breath.

"Who else have you been fighting?" Florence demanded.

"That's Alfie's dad. You should go."

"That's Alfie's father? But he's..."

"White?"

Florence tailed off in the face of Blake's grim amusement at her assumption that both Alfie's parents were the same race. Now that he drew closer, she saw that even though this man's skin was ruddy and his hair was blond, there was a strong resemblance to the shape of the boy's jaw and nose.

His face looked equally bruised, Florence noted with

some satisfaction. She had thought Blake's injuries were bad, but they were nothing compared to the mess of this ogre's face. He stopped in front of them and flung out a hand towards Alfie, who drew close to Blake.

"That's my brat! What are you doing with him?" He flexed his hands. His knuckles glittered with heavy rings. "Come here you little turd or I'll tan yer hide."

Florence gasped. She had grown up in a home full of affection. Even when her newly widowed father had grown tired of the children's bickering, he barely ever raised his voice. The thought that a parent might speak to a child in such a way was unthinkable. Though she still deplored Blake's use of violence to solve the problem, it was hard not to internally cheer.

"Sir," she said loudly, drawing herself up tall and stepping towards him. "Guard your language."

"Miss, don't," Alfie muttered.

"Who in the Devil's name are you?" Clarke spat.

"I am the woman who is taking your son to a place of safety where he will be treated with dignity," Florence said firmly.

"Is this your doing?" Alfie's father rounded on Blake. "Got some interfering lady philanthropist involved in my affairs? I'll beat you to a pulp and piss on what's left."

Blake stood taller, his frame somehow becoming larger in readiness. If Florence didn't intervene, she was certain there would be a public fight.

"You will do no such thing!" she exclaimed.

Both men looked at her, their faces bearing almost identical expressions of incredulity that she had spoken.

She took a step closer to Clarke, a small part of her wondering what on earth she was doing. "What I mean is Mr Blake has bested you once and he could easily do it again. If I had my horsewhip, I'd thrash you myself for mistreating your child!"

"Miss Wakechild, I think you should leave now," Blake said. He put one hand on her upper arm, the other around her back in a gesture of protection. Usually, she would baulk at such unwanted intimacy but it was so tender that she forgave him.

"We are all leaving," she answered. She took Alfie by the hand then turned to his father.

"You don't deserve a child. Alfie does not deserve a father like you. I'm taking him somewhere safe and you will not stop me."

Mr Clarke didn't move. "I want paying for him. I've raised him since his mam ran off."

Florence whipped out her purse and flung a sovereign onto the pavement, which Clarke immediately dived for.

"Be thankful I'm not informing the police. Come along, Alfie. Mr Blake, if you will…"

She held her arm out. Blake looped his through. The three of them walked away. By the time they turned the street, Florence's legs were shaking and she was glad of Blake's arm to lean on. He didn't say a word as they walked, but his thumb moved over her arm in comforting circles. Alfie, on the other hand, looked jubilant and kept giving her admiring glances.

Dottie was waiting at the door, flirting with the porter.

"Take your brother upstairs," Florence instructed, passing Alfie's hand to Dottie's. Only when they had disappeared inside did she feel her knees beginning to tremble.

Blake turned to face her. "Miss Wakechild, do you need me to take you inside? You are pale."

She shook her head and smiled at him. He didn't return it.

"What you did and said back there was either incredibly brave or incredibly stupid. I can't decide which, so I'm inclined to say both equally. Are you always so reckless?" He glared at her, clearly angry. She felt affronted but recalled the way he had stepped to her side protectively and put his arm around her, and her indignation ebbed.

"It was my recklessness which made me agree to help you. Twice, in fact. It was recklessness which made me offer you my proposition. If you find that is too reckless, then we can end our association now." She gave him a little smile. "Though I would much rather not."

He blew out a long breath and stared into the distance before looking back at her with a smile.

"I had better continue it, if only to protect you from your own actions!"

She smiled back. "Good. In that case, be ready to leave for Cheshire and prepare to work hard. From what I know of you, we have a lot of work to do!"

It was with higher spirits than she initially imagined possible, that Florence bade farewell to her father as they parted on the steps of the hotel.

"We will see you again in a few weeks," she said, kissing his cheek affectionately. "Go have fun making new business connections while we while the days away in the countryside."

"You really don't mind too much?" Clayton asked. "I know you wanted to see some more of the country before we returned to the North. It's good of you to submit to such disappointment so easily."

"Oh I'm sure I'll find plenty to occupy myself," Florence said, hiding her smile as she hugged him.

A day later, she was settled in the newest wing of Goreswarth Chase in a small and comfortable bedroom, though even that was old enough that the room had genuine oak beams crossing the ceiling and floorboards that squeaked when she clambered into bed.

The house was old—positively ancient in places—and had a timeless quality which was the result of so many additions to the original building. The furnishings were dark with the weight of centuries upon them and worn in places from use. The end of Florence's bed had initials carved into the footboard from a previous occupant that Twemlow thought might have been his great-great uncle who had become a bishop.

History and family: after a day wandering the corridors

and observing the way the dimensions of windows and doors changed as she moved from the newest to the oldest parts, Florence began to gain an understanding of why such unending solidity was appealing. Everything in her house back in Philadelphia was new, or no older than two decades at most. Lord Griggs' home was evidence of a lineage which stretched back centuries. It was breathtaking to consider, and Florence found herself envying Cordelia more than she ever expected to. And, to her consternation, found herself more than once pondering if Lord Stretford's family seat was equally ancient and imposing.

The days passed quickly and on the appointed day of Mr Blake's arrival, she and Cordelia sat sketching by the lake where bunches of reeds and water flowers were growing lush in the heat. Neither of them was being particularly successful. Cordelia daubed a couple of splodges of moss green on her canvas then stood back to admire her handiwork. She dropped her brush into the glass jar filled with water and tutted.

"Now I've ruined it with too much working on the reeds. I'm bored of painting in any case. Aren't you? Let's go for a walk into the village. We can take some hothouse fruits to a few of the deserving widows. We have such a glut at the moment."

Florence regarded her own attempt at capturing the scene. It wasn't much better than her sister's. The lake looked like it was floating above the grass and the sheep she had painted on the distant hills looked more like unfortunate clouds that had tumbled from the heavens. She'd gladly work away at it all day – though she knew that would most likely ruin it further – but she had other reasons for not wanting to leave the grounds.

"I'd rather stay here, if it's all the same to you," she said hesitantly. "Today is the day that Mr Blake should be arriving and I thought I might go with Jeavons when he takes the pony trap to meet him from Congleton. I don't want to be too tired by this afternoon."

"*Should* be arriving?" Cordelia gave her a narrow-eyed look that penetrated Florence's belly and made her squirm. "Do you think he won't come?"

"Of course he will come!" Florence exclaimed. She dabbed an errant spot of Van Dyke brown from her brush. "He will be here. If I know anything of Mr Blake, then I know he likes a challenge and won't give up on an undertaking."

She hoped she was right. Before she left Liverpool, she had given him twenty pounds in order to outfit himself as a gentleman and buy whatever sundries he would need. She hoped he was not a confidence trickster who intended to swindle her out of it. It was a considerable sum to have given him and she didn't want to lose it. More than that, she worried that if he vanished never to be seen again it would reflect badly on her judgement. She bit her lip and looked sidelong at Cordelia.

"What if he doesn't?" she whispered.

Cordelia shrugged. "We'll have to persuade the second footman to play the role instead. He has very good legs and would look fine in evening wear."

Florence was still pondering how her sister had come to notice such an intriguing detail when the first footman arrived at their side. He bowed to Cordelia, then to Florence.

"My lady, a gentleman has arrived. He says you are expecting him."

Florence felt a thrill run through her. "Did he give his name?"

The footman looked a little taken aback that Florence had interrupted. His nostrils flared then tightened. "A Mr Blake, I believe, Miss Wakechild." He turned to address Cordelia once more. "Mr Wilikins has taken him to the Summer Room to wait for you."

"Thank you, Johnson. Please inform Mr Wilikins that we'll be along shortly," Cordelia said.

"He's early," Florence murmured as she gathered her easel and paints.

"Leave those. I'll send Johnson back to collect them," Cordelia instructed her. She grinned nastily. "He's such an objectional piece of work. If his father and grandfather hadn't held positions, I'm sure Twemlow would have seen him off years ago."

"Not good legs?" Florence whispered as they strolled back to the house.

"Not at all!" Cordelia said firmly. "I wonder what your Mr Blake's legs are like?"

Florence halted. "I have no idea! I haven't ever looked. And he's not 'my' Mr Blake, thank you very much!"

Frustratingly, once they arrived in the Summer Room – so called because the thick stone walls and narrow windows of the original building made it unbearably cold at any other time of year – Florence was unable to stop speculating about the suitability of Mr Blake's legs.

The man in question was standing with his back to the door, hands loosely clasped behind his back and sporting a pair of lemon-yellow gloves. He was dressed in a frock coat of deep grey and wore a derby hat. He was admiring an old, faded tapestry portraying a pastoral scene of ancient Greece with shepherds and nymphs who would have frozen blue if they had really been in the room, given their lack of clothing. Mr Wilikins was standing in the corner of the room, clearly standing guard in case the visitor decided to abscond with the candlesticks.

"Mr Blake," Cordelia said as she swept into the room.

He turned. His eyes darted to Florence then centred on the baroness.

"Lady Griggs, good morning."

He swept the derby from his head and gave a deep bow to Cordelia then turned to address Florence.

"Miss Wakechild."

His eyes twinkled as he smiled at her, and Florence felt her heart skip a beat. She could not help but blush as she curtsied politely and returned his greeting. He had a debonair air about him and beneath the open coat, she could see he was dressed impeccably in a tailored suit. He wore polished boots that had somehow picked up a little dust. His coat reached to mid-thigh so she had no opportunity to assess his legs.

"Wilikins, please have coffee sent to us."

The butler shuffled obediently out.

"Mr Blake, you are much earlier than expected," Cordelia said.

"Please accept my apologies, my lady. Just as I arrived at the railway station, I happened to see a mail coach coming in this direction and jumped aboard. From the town crossing where it dropped me, I then happened upon a farmer who was kind enough to let me ride with him in this direction. Once we parted, it was a simple matter of walking a couple of miles down a country lane, which was no trouble at all. Quite a pleasant way to spend the late morning, in fact."

"I was going to come in the trap to meet you from the village," Florence said. There was no reason for him to have known that, but she felt put out all the same that her plans had been changed.

"I'm sorry I deprived you of your excursion," he said, giving her a smile that melted away her frustration. "My travelling trunk is stored in the post office in the town. Perhaps tomorrow we can take the trap out together and collect it. I'm quite an able driver."

He addressed Cordelia once again. "My lady, I assume the farmer must be a tenant of yours, given that his holding borders this estate. A Mr Fent?"

Cordelia nodded. "Yes, he's one of our tenants."

"In that case, please would you allow me the liberty of passing on my regards to your husband on the manners and kindness of his tenants. He was a most gentlemanly fellow."

Cordelia gave him a warm smile. "I wholeheartedly agree with your assessment of him; however, Lord Griggs can make no claim to be responsible for his existence. The Fent family have farmed this land almost as long as my husband's family have held it. I believe there were Fents fighting alongside Griggses back in the English Civil War."

"How strange," Florence murmured. "Just imagine! Didn't you say that the title was granted after a Griggs saved the life of one king's illegitimate sons? Just imagine if one of Mr Fent's ancestors had been there instead. Goreswarth Chase might now be owned by Baron Fent and you would be married to plain Mr Griggs, the farmer."

Cordelia gave her a slightly sour look. "I hardly imagine I would be married to a farmer, though I admit it's possible I may have become Lady Fent instead of Lady Griggs."

Florence had obviously touched on a sensitive nerve. She smiled. "Well, in any case it makes my point, doesn't it? An accident of birth or the actions of one's ancestors are enough to change your family fortunes and convey a different path in life upon one's descendants."

She turned to Mr Blake, who had been standing silently during the conversation.

"When we create your family's history, I think your title shall have been given because your ancestor rescued the favourite pet dog of Queen Anne from being trampled by a carriage."

He gave a delighted laugh. "I can think of no finer service to perform for a queen."

"You are both very foolish," Cordelia said with a humorous sigh. She drummed her fingers on the table. "I don't know where Wilikins has got to with the coffee. Mr Blake, let me summon a maid who can take you to your room. I imagine you will wish to bathe and change after walking for two miles."

"Thank you, my lady, that would be welcome," Mr Blake replied.

Once he had left the room, Cordelia turned to Florence with a wicked look on her face that made her look like the young girl she had once been.

"Very good legs indeed," she whispered, a giggle edging her voice.

"I'm sure I couldn't say." Florence giggled. She grew warm inside. It was rare to find somebody who tolerated her sometimes eccentric train of thought. Good legs or not, she decided that she would very much enjoy teaching Mr Blake and was keen to begin as soon as possible.

Chapter Nine

"May I introduce you to Julia, the Dowager Countess of Swan, and Lady Augusta Sugar, Marchioness of Fish. Now, of these two women, which one do you greet first and how?"

Miss Wakechild waved her hand towards the two cut-out paper dolls propped against the mirror. Hiding his amusement, Ned gave a smooth bow, first to the dowager countess and then to the marchioness. Miss Wakechild and Lady Griggs exchanged a smile of amusement at seeing a grown man greeting the dolls with such solemnity. Ned permitted himself to join in.

"Very good. You really are a quick learner." Miss Wakechild consulted her book, pushing her spectacles up her nose as they slid forward. Ned's fingers itched to take them from her face and adjust the temples so they fitted over her ears better.

It was true: they had spent only a week at Goreswarth

Chase and already Ned was able to recite the correct introductions and draw up a list of who should go into dinner first and explain why. It was extremely tedious, but he'd spent enough time in polite society to be able to recall the etiquette. He was content to dance to Miss Wakechild's tune because, despite the building itself being a ramshackle evolution of architecture from the time of Good Queen Bess to fifty years ago, Ned's room in Goreswarth Chase was very comfortably furnished and Lord and Lady Griggs had an excellent chef.

Miss Wakechild selected three new paper dolls and held them out. Ned rubbed his eyes. There were harder ways of earning a living than tipping his hat at fashion cut-outs, but there were limits to his tolerance, and being tested by Miss Wakechild made him feel like a schoolboy being examined on his Latin. He decided this would be the last example for the afternoon.

"Now, we have the daughter of a viscount, the wife of a baronet, and the wife of a knight, who is also the daughter of an earl. Who should you greet first and why?"

"The daughter clearly," Ned said with a grin. "Because she's not yet married and therefore the other two women are of no interest to me, unless of course their husbands are old and gouty and the wives are young and pretty and bored."

"Mr Blake, please be sensible!" Miss Wakechild exclaimed, waving her hands and making the paper dolls flutter. Her brows shot together. "We have to get this right!"

"How can I be sensible when making bows to fish and

swans?" Ned asked, flicking his eyes to her hands. He believed he had made a fair point about her choice of names. They were always drawn from either the paintings that adorned the long gallery where they held their lessons, or items on the tea tray.

From her seat in the window, Lady Griggs gave a hooting laugh. Miss Wakechild tossed the paper dolls onto the table with a flourish. They landed in a pile, gravity caring not a whit for the order of precedence in which they fell.

"There!" She put her hands on her hips and glared first at her sister, then at Ned severely. It made her look quite charming. "Now will you please take this seriously."

Miss Wakechild's cheeks were growing blotchy with anger. Not for a redhead the delicate blush of pink blossom, but the bright and angry red of strawberries. Lady Griggs laughed again but a little warning bell rang in Ned's ear. He had perhaps gone too far in his mockery. It was clear that she really wanted to win the wager and he wasn't really taking it seriously. Having her sister laughing at her would not help matters either.

"I am being serious," he said quietly. "However, I will not be in a position to dictate the order in which I am introduced to these ladies as my host will decide that."

He bent down to pick up a stray baronet who had fallen to the carpet and set him besides his wife.

"Also, it strikes me that as I will be fraudulently masquerading as one of their number, it would be a wise idea to stay very clear of any genuine members of the nobility and confine myself to meeting your father and his immediate circle, don't you agree?"

"It's a good point," Lady Griggs interjected from the bay window where she was sitting with a large embroidery frame, working on a scene of the gardens beyond. "Dear Twemlow is barely capable of recognising his own cousins in a crowded ballroom without me or his mother pointing them out, but you don't want to encounter anyone who will be able to disprove your lies."

Miss Wakechild turned her back on Ned and walked over to look at her sister's progress. Ned joined them, catching sight of himself in the mirror. He clasped his hands behind his back and stared at himself as if looking at a stranger. He was smooth-shaven now but growing a neat pair of sideburns that he was privately quite pleased with. The bruising on his face had all but disappeared and he looked dignified. Once again, he reminded himself that tolerating Miss Wakechild's eccentricities was a small price to pay for a peaceful month when he'd otherwise be dwelling on the future.

"What are you thinking?" Miss Wakechild asked.

He turned his head and bestowed a smile on the sisters.

"I'm thinking it's a beautiful day."

It was true: sunlight streamed through the elm trees, casting black shadows over the gravelled pathways and boxy hedges. At the end of the rose garden was an ornamental fountain and beyond that a small gazebo in the shape of a Roman temple. A gentle breeze made the branches of the trees sway and Ned was hit with the longing to feel it on his skin. It was considerably more inviting than staying indoors.

"Why don't we go outside and practise promenading around the ornamental lake? We don't need to do this inside."

Miss Wakechild walked over to stand at his side. "I agree. Let's go outside and talk as we walk."

Ned met her eyes and smiled. "I knew you wouldn't take much persuasion once you saw how fine it is. Go find your bonnets and whatever else you need and I'll meet you both out in the gardens in a few minutes."

Miss Wakechild tidied the dolls away, but Lady Griggs continued sorting through her box of embroidery silks, then began threading a new needle with sage green thread.

"Aren't you going to come with us?" Miss Wakechild asked.

"No. I'm comfortable here and the light is very good at the moment. Besides, it is likely to rain within the next half hour."

Miss Wakechild glanced back at the sky. "There isn't a cloud to be seen."

"There never is until the moment when there are hundreds of them and the heavens open. The weather changes very quickly here. I'd take galoshes if I were you."

Miss Wakechild wrinkled her nose. "A parasol and shawl will suffice. I suppose I should go summon Dottie to chaperone us. How irritating. I wanted her to stitch the rip in my nightgown but she'll have to trail around after us."

Lady Griggs looked out of the window again. "I can see

you perfectly well from here if you need a chaperone. Lady Violet will be arriving at the end of the month and I want to be able to show her how far I've got with my embroidery. I'm sure Mr Blake is perfectly trustworthy, aren't you, Mr Blake?"

Ned smiled serenely and put his hands together as if he was about to pray, radiating dependability.

"Perfectly so. In fact, it's rather insulting, don't you think, to assume that young people will get up to all sorts of mischief if they're not being watched at every opportunity?"

"Yes, I do," Miss Wakechild answered primly. "This need for chaperones is most tiresome. I believe we could spend hours together and the thought of anything scandalous would not even cross our minds."

"Quite." Ned gave a polite nod to Lady Griggs and left the room. Whatever his faults, he was no debaucher of young women, even ones whose expressive eyes were downright hard to resist. She didn't have to be quite so certain though, did she? A silly idea occurred to him. He went to his room and dressed in his smartest coat and a top hat, added kid gloves to the outfit, and picked up a walking cane.

By the time he arrived in the gardens, he expected Miss Wakechild to be waiting but she was nowhere in sight. Never mind, the air in the garden was fragranced with summer roses. Bushes of red and pink blooms alternated in a chequerboard pattern set among small hedges and Ned spent a few pleasant minutes investigating the contrasting smells attributable to the different hues of petals. It was very pleasing to the senses and a tonic to the soul after the weeks he had spent in Liverpool.

He had walked halfway down the path when he heard the light crunch of a foot on the gravel behind him and turned. Miss Wakechild had arrived. She was wearing a pink straw boater with a large green ribbon and a matching pink and green shawl. In her hand she twirled a green and pink parasol.

Ned stopped walking and let his face take on an expression of astonishment that was not entirely simulated.

"Why Miss Wakechild! How delightful to meet you here."

Ned swept the top hat from his head with a flourish and bowed deeply. Miss Wakechild curtseyed, a little confused by his behaviour if her expression was anything to go by.

"I am so sorry to intrude on your solitude. Had I known you were alone in the gardens, I would never have presumed to visit Goreswarth Chase; however, I was in this area of the county and decided I must see your beautiful grounds. Please accept my apologies," Ned said.

"Oh, I see. You are play-acting!" Miss Wakechild dropped into another curtsey. "No apology necessary, Sir... Sir..."

She stood upright and bit her bottom lip. "I don't actually know what to call you. We haven't given you a title yet, have we?"

"That's very true." Ned rubbed his sideburn with his thumb. "I don't yet have a name. If I am to be a viscount, I must be Viscount Someone or Somewhere. And it's 'Lord' of course."

"Of course. I know that," Miss Wakechild said quickly. "Now let's think. We cannot use a name already in existence."

She looked around.

"Miss Wakechild, do you propose to pick a name out of the air? Am I to be a Fish or a Swan like my cut-out companions?"

"I don't know. I am afraid I don't have much imagination."

"Should I be Viscount Gravel or Leaf perhaps? Why not the Earl of Weathervane?" he asked.

"Oh Mr Blake, you are funny. I didn't see that before, but you are."

Miss Wakechild giggled; a sound which was so utterly unexpected that Ned felt a laugh bubbling up inside him.

They looked at each other, both smiling. A breeze that had been ever present swelled into a gust that was colder than it had any right to be given the sunny day. The fine hairs at the nape of Ned's neck lifted and fluttered, making his skin feel unusually sensitive. He reached a hand up and adjusted his collar.

"I shall accept that as a compliment," he said quietly, replacing his hat and extending an arm. "Shall we walk along the path and see if inspiration comes to us?"

They walked as far as the temple; not really a place of pagan worship but a small folly that stood at the end of the rose garden and looked back at the house.

He glanced at Miss Wakechild. She was staring up at the sky but must have been watching Ned out of the corner of her eye because she turned her head to him, tilting it on one side. Over the top of the house, as the baroness had predicted, there were gathering clouds. Fluffy to begin with, but growing heavier where they met and joined.

"Shall we return?" he asked.

"I think we're safe from rain for the time being. Let's walk as far as the village. We should have time before it rains if it's going to, which I doubt. My brother-in-law says the Cheshire plains rarely get rain to the extent the Peaks do."

One thing Ned appreciated as a commoner was the opportunity to be truly alone with no one caring what he got up to. For the upper classes, it was rare to get a moment alone without a servant of some sort bustling around and inevitably reporting any gossip back to the Servants' Hall. He didn't care himself, but for Miss Wakechild and the family, it wouldn't do to have talk.

"Your sister won't be able to see us," he pointed out, gesturing to the figure of Lady Griggs silhouetted in the window, the visible but distant chaperone.

Miss Wakechild grinned. "Precisely. I'm already the subject of talk because I'm American, according to Dottie, and therefore of as much scientific interest as a kangaroo in the zoo. I'd like to have a few minutes of freedom, if you'll come with me."

Ned looked around. Even though he and Miss Wakechild appeared to have some privacy now, it was illusory. There were two gardeners working away on the ornamental hedges off to the right of the rose garden. Everything in society was designed to ensure people behaved as they should and woe betide anyone veering off course. Women had it worse and it must grow wearisome.

"A short walk, but only to the village green," he agreed.

He held an arm out for her to take and together they strolled across the lawn towards the rear of the estate where an iron gate in the wall led to Goreswarth village. The houses looked picturesque and the village prosperous, with a rectangular green. Three shops, a forge, and a small inn were set on one side while a row of neat cottages edged another.

They walked around the pond in the centre of the green, where five ducks and a moorhen were clustering round a pair of well-dressed gentlemen throwing them sponge cake. At the third side of the pond stood the church of St Paul which, Miss Wakechild informed Ned with wide eyes, had stood for almost four hundred years. It clung to one edge of the grey stone wall as if it were trying to hide from the rest of the village. Slanted sunlight filtered through the sycamore trees, dappling the gravestones which stood amid lovingly tended grass. A more idyllic scene was hard to imagine.

They watched the two gentlemen for a moment, placing bets on which duck would get the most cake, then walked back towards the gate. The sound of a tuneful baritone humming wordlessly came from the open window of the vicarage. Reverend Reed was presumably deciding on the hymns for the Sunday service.

"I should have gone into the church as a young man," Ned commented. "My family expected me to."

"You wanted to join the clergy?" Miss Wakechild's eyes grew wide, as if she could no more imagine Ned in the pulpit than he himself had.

"Not wanted to. The expectation was on my father's side," he corrected. He clamped his lips together. How had he managed to let something so personal slip out? He never talked of his family to anyone. No one ever grew close enough to care to listen to him, but he found himself wanting to continue.

"There are many roles a man can take which require only a half-hearted commitment, but for a life serving the Almighty, I believe it must be fully given. I, poor sinner that I am, lacked the necessary conviction. We quarrelled about it on several occasions until my father finally saw it wasn't something I had enough faith for. I was too impulsive and wayward."

"In that case, you were right to choose otherwise and fortunate your father saw sense," Miss Wakechild said. She wrinkled her brow. "Does your father approve of your current choice of career?"

Ned looked away, only now seeing the snare he had set for himself and unerringly walked into.

"My father died before I was able to embarrass him with the knowledge of what I had become," he said briskly.

"I'm sorry."

Miss Wakechild pressed her hand onto his. It was a small gesture and there was no reason for it to create such a large lump in Ned's throat. He didn't miss the old man. Hadn't for years. His death wasn't the tragedy that a woman from a loving family would assume it was.

"Thank you."

What more was there to say?

Ned held the gate open for Miss Wakechild. As they passed through, he noticed the stables were on the edge of the property, closer to the village than the house. Seeing them reminded Ned of something he had been meaning to do and the lull in the conversation caused by the awkward exchange needed filling.

"Could we go pay a visit to Alfie?" Ned asked. "I haven't seen him and I'd like to know if he is doing well."

"Of course, I should have thought of that myself," Miss Wakechild said. "We can go to the stable yard now. He's sure to be there."

In the stable yard a groom was leading Lord Griggs' carriage horse across the straw-strewn yard. Alfie was sitting on a bale of hay beside a couple of lads a few years older. All three had brooms resting across their laps. Alfie jumped off when he saw Ned approaching, then hesitated as if unsure that he was allowed to do that. When he saw Miss Wakechild, he looked even more uncertain. He pulled the cap from his head. His hair had been shorn close to his head and was now practically nothing more than a black fuzz. It made him look desperately young.

"It's alright Alfie," Miss Wakechild said. "You can come and talk to us."

"Thanks, Miss. I've got a break, but I wasn't sure if I'm allowed to leave the yard."

Miss Wakechild looked surprised, as if such a thing as being constrained never occurred to her before.

"Well, I shall answer for you, if that is the case. Please come and talk to us for a minute. Your bruises are healing nicely, I see. Are they treating you well?"

Alfie raised his brows and twisted his mouth slightly uncertainly. Ned looked around. The stable yard was a hive of activity, but most of it was momentarily paused at the arrival of the American visitor. The two stable boys were openly staring.

"Let's take a walk," Ned suggested in an undertone. "If there is anything Alfie needs to say with regard to his treatment, he would hardly confess it in front of the people responsible."

Not even in private, given how many years of suffering the child had endured at Carver Clarke's hands.

"You're right; I didn't think," Miss Wakechild said. She held her hand out.

"Come on, young Alfie. Come and introduce me to the horses in the paddock. Have you learned their names yet?"

Ned followed behind as the woman and boy picked a relatively clean route through the yard and down to the enclosure where four horses were grazing. The two of them chatted as they walked and Ned felt confident that if anything was amiss, it would be revealed by the time they reached the horses. Something in Miss Wakechild seemed to invite people to share confidences. Ned had surprised himself on that account more than once.

As they watched the horses make their slow way from hay bale to thistle, Alfie told them of his experience.

"There's always bread and scrape for supper, but they only give me milk or water to drink. I miss gin. The lads are ok. Bit of teasing but I've had worse."

"Teasing? How do you mean?" Miss Wakechild asked.

"Say they're gonna use the saddle soap to clean me face white."

"That's dreadful! Do you want to leave?" Miss Wakechild asked.

"No. I don't want to go back to me dad," Alfie said, far too quickly for Ned's comfort.

Miss Wakechild patted his hand. "No, of course not. But perhaps the kitchens or gardens might be better for you than here if the boys aren't kind."

Ned grimaced. Liverpool was a port city filled with people from all over the world, of every race and colour. Goreswarth was not, and Alfie was the only person in the household whose skin was dark. It was bound to be commented on wherever he was sent.

Alfie shook his head and wiped his nose on his sleeve. "I like it here. I'll make them eat the bar if they try that thing with the soap, don't you worry. I haven't got to touch the horses yet, only shovel their shit, but one day I'm going to ride one."

Miss Wakechild coughed delicately and bent her head.

Ned thought she might be hiding a smile rather than shock but even so, he shot Alfie a look over her head. It was hard to chastise the boy for his language when he had such determination in his voice that Ned could well believe he would ride his horse one day. After all, some dreams must come true, for some people.

Chapter Ten

Florence and Ned returned Alfie to the stable yard and made their way back toward the house through the rose garden.

"I do hope we've done the right thing bringing Alfie here," Miss Wakechild said.

Ned nodded thoughtfully. "I think we have. He's looking healthier and he seems happy. He's away from his dad and not getting beaten. He's a quick lad. If your brother-in-law is happy to keep him, I don't see why it won't work out well."

They passed through the beds of pink roses where the scent was strongest. They both inhaled deeply at the same time, caught themselves, and looked at each other. They both laughed.

"They're the nicest scented," Miss Wakechild said.

Impulsively, Mr Blake twisted off a flower from the

nearest bush and held it out to her. "Here, now you'll have the scent with you as we walk. I'm sure Lord Griggs won't begrudge you one."

Miss Wakechild broke into a smile. "Why, Mr Blake, how gallant of you. Will you fix it into my hatband?"

Ned leaned close and fixed the stem into the wide ribbon of her hat so that the bloom faced forward, slightly in front of her ear. Miss Wakechild titled her head to one side, then straight again. She raised her eyes to his, her pale lashes framing the hazel subtly.

"There, very pretty," he said. He wondered if he should clarify he meant the flower but decided against it, realising that would imply Miss Wakechild wasn't herself pretty. With the sunlight accentuating the deep golden tones in her red hair and the sweet expression in her eyes, she was very pretty indeed.

Ned still had his hands raised and it would be a matter of a moment's work to place them onto her cheeks, draw her closer, and kiss her. His heart thumped as he considered doing it. Miss Wakechild's lips parted slightly and she pulled slightly at the lower lip with her teeth. Was she considering the same thing? So much for high and mighty talk of not getting up to anything when they were unchaperoned! As much as he was tempted, sense overtook Ned. She was employing him to act as a viscount, not romance her. He stepped back and straightened his cuffs.

"You should have one too. But not a pink one." Miss Wakechild walked to the next set of bushes and twisted a crimson flower off. "May I?"

Ned nodded and she slipped it into his buttonhole. "There, very handsome. We'll make a viscount of you yet."

"Viscount Rose," Ned said.

They smiled at each other.

"Perhaps not."

A gentle but unwelcome smattering of rain fell then immediately ceased. They both looked upwards. The clouds had finally won their conquest of the sky, gathering closely, and the next assault would be harder.

"I think our luck has finally run out and the rain is starting. We had better turn back," Miss Wakechild said.

"Yes, you're right. If we make haste, we shouldn't get more than slightly damp." Ned put his hands into his pockets and turned towards the house.

"Mr Blake?" Miss Wakechild twirled her parasol, looking at him. "I think now would be an appropriate time for you to offer me your arm, don't you think?"

"Oh yes, of course." He held out his arm and she looped hers through the crook of his elbow.

"There's something I need to discuss with you, but we'll have to do it as we walk," Miss Wakechild said. "The day after tomorrow is the Charter Fair in the village. From what my sister tells me it's great fun. I was hoping we could go together. I won't introduce you as a viscount yet, but I think you will be able to pass as a gentleman and it would be good to take you out in a social setting."

"That sounds lovely," Ned agreed. "I would be honoured to accompany you for the day."

"Oh I'm afraid it won't be the whole day. The fair lasts

all day but I can only attend in the morning." She frowned. "I have to say I'm looking forward to that much more than the evening."

"Why, what's happening in the evening?" Ned asked, slowing down.

Miss Wakechild's answer was frustratingly interrupted as a more violent spattering of large raindrops fell. On unspoken agreement they both quickened their pace and headed for the refuge of the covered pergola.

"Why will the day be better than the evening?" Ned asked again once they reached shelter.

"My father has begun to rumble about brokering a marriage for me. That's part of the reason that we came here sooner than expected. The man in question has an estate somewhere near Manchester. My poor long-suffering brother-in-law is being asked to host him so we can meet."

She grimaced more openly.

"He's coming in the late afternoon and staying overnight. Then the following day we're going to go on a picnic so the men can go fishing. His sister will be accompanying him. You'll join us for everything, won't you? It will be the perfect opportunity to practise dining formally in the evening and will make the numbers right."

"Your suitor won't be coming to the fair?" Ned asked.

She shook her head vigorously. "No, I have asked Lord Griggs not to invite them to arrive too early. I intend to enjoy myself there."

"Don't you think you'll enjoy yourself if he's there?"

Ned asked curiously. Finding a suitor was the whole purpose behind her visit after all.

"I have no idea, but I don't want to risk it. He's not somebody I particularly care about knowing, and inviting him was not my idea. I'll do it under sufferance because that's what my father expects me to do." She turned to Ned and took him by the hand.

"Will you join us for everything? I need a friendly face."

She really did look apprehensive, so he ignored the faux pas. Besides, her fingers intertwining with his, coupled with the entreaty in her eyes, made him feel rather giddy.

"Of course. I will be delighted to. Does this suitor have a name?" he asked.

"Oh yes. He's called Viscount Stretford. Robert Erskyn I believe is his name. His sister is the Honourable Minerva Erskyn."

Ned's chest tightened as the planned visit became altogether more complicated. He took a deep breath, consciously trying to relieve the pressure. He knew Stuffy and Minerva Erskyn. More crucially, they knew him.

Extricating Stuffy from an embarrassing entanglement with a music hall performer had been one of Ned's first successes years ago when he had first started out in this role. They were pleasant enough individuals, though neither was particularly overburdened with brains in any way. Despite that, even with a smart new suit of clothes and a fashionable Devil-may-care haircut, there was no way Ned could spend even ten minutes in their company without them claiming recognition. The entire deception would be revealed, but more crucially, they knew Ned by his real name and what he was running from.

He had two days to think of how to get out of it without revealing anything to anyone. It was going to take quite some thinking.

Miss Wakechild was still staring at him with an expectant look on her face.

"That all sounds perfectly wonderful," Ned managed to say, even sounding like he meant it.

"I'm so pleased you feel that way," Miss Wakechild said, and Ned immediately curled up inside at the thought of disappointing her. He escorted her as far as the entrance hall then bade her farewell.

He was still feeling restless after dinner and it wasn't raining hard enough to put him off walking out again. He'd grown up in Yorkshire after all, where the rain lashed the cliffs and hardy men went about their business. He let himself out into the grounds and paced back and forth.

The night was quiet except for the occasional voice from the village. He walked to the pub and bought a pint which he nursed in the corner while he mused.

He had two days to think of a way of avoiding the visitors. Perhaps an urgent summons back to Liverpool or elsewhere that would see him called away, while expressing his regret at missing such a delightful opportunity to showcase his newfound gentility. No, that would never do. No one knew he was here. A sudden illness, perhaps?

He wasn't overly concerned. Something would occur to him. Something usually did.

Florence looked at her list and after some consideration struck a light line through *Introductions*.

The aborted afternoon lesson and Mr Blake's gentle mockery still played on her mind and would do so every time she thought about repeating the activity. He'd made a valid point anyway, that as long as he knew how to respond using the correct forms, he did not have to make the choice of when and to whom he would be introduced. Her father was the only one whose opinion mattered.

All in all, it had been a productive afternoon and Mr Blake looked eager to join her at the fair and help entertain Viscount Stretford. She bit her lip. She drummed her fingers on the edge of the writing desk. He had seemed less eager to do the latter, and thinking about it, the reason was obvious to her. His confidence was lacking. She would have to find a way of convincing him that he was well on the way to proving he could pass in society. Why, their walk through the gardens and into the village had been most pleasurable and she doubted the time spent with Lord Stretford would be any more so.

Tomorrow's lesson would be on topics that must never be discussed in polite company and useful ones to start conversations after a lull. Being armed with ideas of how to converse would ease his mind. She decided to retire to bed with the book on etiquette. *Manners and Rules* had become her curriculum and Bible in all things concerning the wager. She should probably offer it to Mr Blake so he could study it himself, though she enjoyed being the one to instruct and impart knowledge.

She had let Dottie retire to her own room once she had helped Florence out of her stays and into her nightgown so all she had to do was go to the window to draw the drapes herself. It was still light outside even though it was now after half-past nine at night. It seemed a shame to cut out the remaining light but once she got into bed with her book, she would read until she fell asleep. Going to sleep in the light was very different from being woken at six.

Her room looked out over the gardens. She smiled to herself. The walk with Blake had been very pleasant and she imagined she could still smell the scent of the rose he had picked for her though it now lay on the dressing table at the other end of the room. Perhaps she would press it like she had done when she was a child. Cordelia was bound to have a press somewhere.

She looked down and spotted a figure walking purposefully through the gardens. At first, her nerves flickered at the thought that it was an intruder, but then she recognised Mr Blake. How odd to be going out at that time. She drew back behind the heavy drapes so that if he happened to look up, he would not see her and think she was spying on him. He walked the path that they had taken earlier in the day. Perhaps he was going to see Alfie again as the stable boys were quartered in rooms above the stables, but he turned towards the gate that led to the village. Florence narrowed her eyes. What could he be doing out there at this time of night?

The realisation struck her that she did not know much about him and had no real idea whether or not he was trustworthy other than his word, which could easily be false. Possibly he intended to try to find work in the village. Her frown deepened. She was paying him well for his time as well as his board and lodgings, plus if they won the bet, she had promised him twenty pounds from her winnings. He had no need to be finding extra ways to make money.

She drew the drapes together sharply and retired to bed. She should try find out more about him.

The following day, she examined him for signs to indicate he might have stayed out late drinking or gotten into a fight – the confrontation with Alfie's dad returning to her mind – but his face appeared clean and he didn't even look tired. She couldn't ask him without revealing that she has been looking at him, so she had no choice but to leave the matter.

As is often the case when one anticipates an event, the interim days feel like a trial. Florence's brain was occupied by mundane matters for the entire day before the fair and she could not find adequate leisure time to muse over the mystery of the night-time walk. She had to decide on an outfit for the fair, another to wear for the formal dinner with Lord Stretford, and yet another for the picnic. The rain came down all morning, which was disappointing because Florence had hoped to go watch some of the side shows being erected. She had visited the state fair back home every year since she could remember, but Cordelia assured her that this was quite different.

"Perhaps I should just wear a tag around my neck like a prize ewe as I'm being offered as livestock," she raged to Cordelia.

The weather had cleared by the afternoon and they had taken their easels down to the lake once again in an attempt to capture the scene they had failed to before.

"You are," Cordelia said, flashing Florence a wicked smile. "I don't know why you're so intent on railing against it. Do you really think Daddy will suddenly decide you can marry a market gardener if he falls for your trick? Do you think he'll even fall for it?"

Florence sat back with a sigh of irritation. "I don't know. Hopefully dinner tomorrow night will give me an idea whether Mr Blake can even pass for a gentleman. He looks the part and I'm sure he'll be able to remember the order of precedence and suchlike."

"You've made great progress with Mr Blake, I must say. He's quite the gentleman now and can converse on the most boring subjects just like Twemlow can. Yesterday I overheard them discussing whether there is a future in alum production now that artificial dyes are becoming more popular. It's a shame Papa can't get to know him as he actually is. I'm sure he'd have some opinions about that."

"I feel that you and Twemlow have not made the most of your fortune," Florence mused.

"We have made every advantage," Cordelia replied,

sounding confused. "I have installed a water closet and we are planning a system of heating for the upper rooms which will save the scullery maids carrying endless buckets of coal up and down the stairs. Not forgetting the new carpets and drapes in the billiards and music rooms."

"I don't doubt that you've made improvements throughout the house," Florence said, choosing her words carefully, "but I thought Twemlow had plans for the estates. When we first met him, he spoke of developments in farm machinery to increase the productivity of the tenant farmers by almost a quarter, and a system of drainage to divert the water flow from the river to the lake."

"We'll get round to that," Cordelia said, waving her paintbrush in the air, sightly impatiently to Florence's mind. She suspected she had prodded a nerve.

"Of course those matters are important to us and we are just waiting for one or two of our investments to mature. Also, we have invested in the planning of a park. The federation of mill owners have purchased land for the purpose on the outskirts of the nearest town. They want a lake with small rowing boats in the nearby town so Twemlow and I have made a sizeable donation. It will be known as The Griggs Lake."

"Well, that's good, I suppose," Florence said, keen to avoid her sister dropping into a sulk. "It is important for the working man to have some leisure at his disposal."

She thought of Alfie, whose only comment when he had been deposited in the care of the housekeeper had been that there was so much grass.

"It's good for mothers to have somewhere to take their children too," she added.

Cordelia beamed. "Exactly! It must be at least as much benefit as new ploughs. And you must remember that not all of Twemlow's tenants live in farms. A good deal of the rent comes from mills and other factories. Urbanisation is encroaching on us. Soon the villages will become towns and the towns may well become cities."

"Well, that's good, isn't it?" Florence asked. "More jobs for people and new facilities."

"I suppose so, but it will be a great shame if half the estate gets given over to building houses and hospitals and schools," Cordelia said, giving a yawn.

"Not for the people using them," Florence said quietly.

Cordelia gave her a sidelong look. "When you speak in that tone, I find myself hoping you won't marry a landowner—for his sake, not yours. When you get your hands on his estate, you'll have turned it all into public baths before your first anniversary."

"In which case, it would be a year well spent," Florence said firmly. She grinned. "Perhaps I don't need to prove Daddy wrong. Maybe I should just begin every meeting with an earl by asking how he intends to develop his land until they all run screaming with the fear that I'll sell their family jewels."

"Or one of them will completely charm you with his intentions to build schools for girls and gardens outside every house. Then I believe you could be persuaded to marry a viscount after all," Cordelia said with a smug look on her face.

"Nonsense," Florence said briskly. Such a man wouldn't exist, but if he did, what an enticing prospect that would be. Honesty compelled her to amend her declaration. "At least, perhaps if I picked him I might, and if I did, I can absolutely assure you it would be for some reason other than his title."

Chapter Eleven

"Mr Blake, you are a common man. Do you believe that parks are of as much benefit to the working class as developments in machinery?" Florence asked as they sat together in the dining room later.

Florence wasn't really concerned that Mr Blake would fail to pass as a country gentleman. He dutifully worked his way through the rehearsal meal of empty plates using all of the cutlery accurately from fish knife to grape scissors. If the servants who moved silently around the room thought their behaviour odd, they made no sign of it. Presumably they would save their gossip about Lady Griggs' odd sister for the Servants Hall. She considered asking Dottie but on balance preferred not to know.

"You have a delightfully flattering turn of phrase, Miss Wakechild," Mr Blake answered, laying down his dessert fork. "If a landlord already treats his tenants fairly and has provided for their basic needs, as I believe Lord Griggs does, then, yes, I firmly believe that the soul needs to be nourished. I consider the opportunities for leisure more important for those who must labour for their bread than those whose lives are generally comfortable."

"That's a very radical opinion!" Florence said, startled by the depth of feeling that was apparent in his voice.

"It's shameful that it is viewed as so radical," he said. He picked up the fork again and twisted it between his fingers, back and forth from thumb to little finger. It was quite compelling to watch and Florence wondered how long it had taken him to perfect the motion.

"There are too many who see their tenants as a commodity to increase their wealth and don't give a damn if their cottages are tumbling into the sea. We who have the good fortune to be born into riches should never forget upon whose backs we have made our fortunes."

"We?" Florence wrinkled her brow.

Mr Blake stopped the fork twisting. The side of his eyes tightened, then he smiled up at Florence and the tension was gone.

"I am trying to remember the role I will be playing. A viscount such as I am pretending to be would say 'we', wouldn't he."

"Of course." Florence walked to the dining table and straightened the cloche over a serving dish. "Though I'm not sure a viscount would hold such views."

Ned grimaced. "Probably not. No one likes to be confronted with the arbitrariness of their luck, and there are many noblemen who see it as their right, without acknowledging any responsibility. Isn't that the point you are trying to make? I shall do my best to conceal my opinions and stick to talking about the weather and the fashion in cravats."

He smiled but it didn't look as though it was wholehearted.

"Are you nervous about the dinner?" Florence asked, coming to sit beside him. "You shouldn't be. You're doing exceedingly well and I am sure nothing in your manner will let you down. Why, I am quite convinced Lord Stretford will have nothing on you when it comes to manners. You look as dashing as I remember him looking the night of the ball."

Mr Blake cocked an eyebrow. Florence bit her lip, not having meant to be so forward. She remembered Lord Stretford's appearance being good, coupled with the sense of dancing in his arms being quite pleasurable. Now she found herself wondering what it would be like to dance with Mr Blake.

That was something they hadn't really touched upon yet, but it was possible that Twemlow would pick a country house dance or ball of some sort for the location of the deception. He'd promised it wouldn't be a very public arena. It was something she would have to rectify as soon as her mind was able to concentrate on it, which would not be until after the visit was over. For the rest of the day, she would have to practise the piano and singing so that she did not embarrass herself when Lord Stretford inevitably asked her to provide some entertainment. The honourable Minerva had an excellent singing voice by all accounts.

"Mr Blake, the afternoon is your own," she said once they had finished their real lunch. "I'm afraid I shall be secluded away in the music room."

"You sound delighted at the prospect," he remarked, raising a brow.

"I do love playing, but only to entertain myself. I dislike an audience. The kind of pieces I enjoy are not necessarily what I would choose to play in company."

Mr Blake's eyes glittered. "I'm intrigued!"

"Don't be. I made it sound much more interesting than it really is. I just enjoy the gloomier Beethoven to the pretty melodies of Mozart. My father says it isn't very ladylike." She stopped and gave a little cough, aware she had been talking too much.

"Anyway, I shall see you later. You may do as you like. Read, go for walks, explore the village."

Florence was unaware what Mr Blake did with his time but she spent the afternoon in Cordelia's music salon, learning how to play the music for two sonatas by Mozart and two country dances, which, Cordelia assured her before departing to organise the Rose Queen procession, Lord Stretford would enjoy hearing. It was a nicer afternoon than she anticipated, with a gentle breeze blowing through the open window and a pot of tea at her side. Once she was sure she could play all the pieces skilfully enough to accept compliments without growing bashful, she threw caution to the wind and let her fingers find the opening notes Beethoven's fifth concerto. It didn't matter that she didn't have a sheet of music. Once she had a melody in her head, she rarely forgot it. She played it twice then moved on to the slow, ponderous first movement of the Moonlight Sonata, closing her eyes and letting the sound lull her senses. She lost herself so deeply in the music that the sound of the bell for afternoon tea took her by surprise.

As she left the room, a voice muttering to itself caught her attention as she passed by the door to the billiards room. Mr Blake was in the room alone. He appeared to be halfway through a game against himself. He was standing with his back to the door but turned as she peered inside.

"Lord Griggs very graciously said I was free to use the table whenever I liked," he said. "Does he spend his evenings playing in here while his wife serenades him from next door? How charming."

Florence's stomach tightened thinking that she had been overheard indulging herself. "You heard me?"

"The windows are both open and it's impossible to play Beethoven quietly. Nor should you."

"Do you know who Beethoven is?" she asked, walking further into the room. It smelled of Twemlow's tobacco, slightly of port, and now of whatever cologne Mr Blake was wearing. A very masculine, attractive mixture.

He leaned against his billiard cue. "Of course. That is, I am not just a music hall man."

"Oh! I'm afraid I did not imagine you being a musical man of any sort. I'm sorry, I really should not assume anything. You have hidden depths, and every now and then I get a tantalising glimpse inside your head."

He laughed and lined up another shot that looked impossible, but when he struck the ball, it hit another that somehow skirted around a third and into a pocket that Florence had not expected.

"Bravo!" she exclaimed. "Are you a conjurer as well? Is there anything you can't do?" Florence walked closer to him, enjoying the way his eyes flickered as she grew closer.

"There are plenty of things I can't do."

"Do you dance? That is, can you dance?" Florence dropped her eyes. "It's something we haven't practised and when I was thinking of Lord Stretford before, I remembered the ball. Then I thought that my brother-in-law might choose somewhere with dancing as the scene."

"I can dance a little, but I suppose that is something we should consider," Mr Blake said.

"Perhaps when Lord Stretford has left that can be something we could work on," Florence said.

Their eyes met. Mr Blake inclined his head. "I would be delighted."

"Will you really? You say that about meeting Lord Stretford too, but I think you didn't sound certain."

He smiled, though she noticed his eyes glinted and the edges tightened.

"What else is there to know about you, Mr Blake?" she asked, pushing on even though a little voice at the back of her head told her to stop. "I know so little about your past."

Mr Blake turned back to the table and potted a ball

smoothly into the furthest pocket before turning back to her, leaning against the edge of the billiard table.

"How much do you know about any of your employees, Miss Wakechild? What is Dottie's favourite colour, for example? Does that excellent chef have a good singing voice? How many of the workers in your father's factory prefer raspberry jam to gooseberry? I am here because I'm paid to do a job and I'm doing it. You don't need to know everything about me."

"Dottie likes lemon yellow, actually," Florence snapped. Mr Blake took a step toward her but she waved a hand to ward him off. She walked to the pocket he had sent the ball into and retrieved it, giving her an opportunity to collect her thoughts.

"I may not know my employees' favourite flavours of jelly, but I always take a reference or resume. Perhaps I should have done the same for you."

She put the ball back on the baize and walked past Mr Blake to the doorway. "I'll leave you to your game. Good afternoon."

"Don't go," Mr Blake said quietly.

Florence paused and half turned back to look at him.

"I'm sorry. I didn't mean to offend you. I'm quite a private person and not used to my clients taking an interest in me personally. Usually they are only concerned with what service I can provide and how quickly I can complete it. There's really very little to know about me. I am partial to rhubarb jam and I can't hold a note in a bucket."

Florence smiled, feeling it was still a little forced but appreciating his attempt at reconciliation.

"Thank you, I appreciate your apology and your understanding. I will still leave you to your own devices as I was on my way to take tea with Lady Griggs before I stopped in here."

He nodded and Florence turned away, then back again immediately.

"It's hard to think of you as just an employee when we're spending so much time together. I shouldn't let myself forget that. I'll do my best not to from now on."

She'd lost her appetite for sandwiches so made her apologies to Cordelia and went back to her room. Tears of humiliation sprang to her eyes. She blinked them away and pressed her lips together tightly. Mr Blake had been right to chastise her nosiness. It was her fault for not looking more closely into his background but inviting him into her rash scheme without care and attention. Now she had gone too far to go back. He was an employee not a friend. However curious she got, she would refrain from questioning him about anything personal. She was his client. Their relationship was purely business, and she must not forget that.

So why did every moment spent in his company feel like the best part of every day?

The morning of the fair was overcast. By the time Florence and Mr Blake watched the pretty fifteen-year-old daughter of Goreswarth's doctor crowned Rose Queen by Twemlow, the sun was poking through the clouds, though it was still chilly. Florence was glad her muslin dress had a matching peach lace shawl with fringed edges to add a little warmth. To the sound of church bells pealing, Maisie Collins and her Rose Squire, Ollie Beadsley, walked onto the ivy- and rose-festooned pontoon in the centre of the village pond followed by a progression of sweet young children. The servants of Goreswarth Chase had been given the day as a holiday to attend the fair, so, to loud cheers, Twemlow and Cordelia as Baron and Baroness Goreswarth took their places in the tableau. The pontoon had been securely tied to submerged stakes at each corner and there was little to no chance of that capsizing, but all the same, Florence had to giggle at the nervous expression on her sister's face.

"She doesn't like being on water," she explained to Mr Blake as they joined the fairgoers in throwing rose petals and stems onto the pond, trying to land them on the platform. "When we first left New York, she didn't leave her cabin for the entire journey and she declared that she would marry whoever father picked for her, if only she did not have to venture back on board for at least a year."

"Do you feel the same?" Mr Blake asked.

"Absolutely not," Florence declared. She paused, thinking. "Do you mean about sailing or husbands? If I have to marry, I won't be choosing a husband on the basis of avoiding a steamship. If you mean being on water, I love sailing. I do believe if I ever have to live away from America, I shall be back and forth every four or five months just for the fun of crossing the ocean."

"You sound so enthusiastic you are making me tempted to make the journey myself one day."

"To America?"

Blake shrugged. "Perhaps to America. There's a fortune to be made out there, as your father knows. A man can start afresh."

He sounded wistful. No, not wistful exactly. Contemplative.

"What are you starting afresh from?" Florence asked. She held a hand up, reminding herself of her promise. "No, I'm sorry. I'm doing it again, aren't I? Don't tell me anything you don't want to. Oh look! A swingboat! I've never been on one. Will you ride with me?"

Without waiting for his answer, she walked to the brightly-coloured frame of wooden boats and paid the twopenny fare to the boy holding the ropes of a spare boat. She and Blake climbed aboard, laughing as they sat opposite each other and bumped feet as they reached for the ropes.

"Not quite the sea, I'm afraid," Mr Blake said as they swung wildly back and forth tugging on the ropes to propel them higher.

"It's about as choppy," Florence pointed out, clutching the end of her shawl with one hand lest it fly away. She felt quite light-headed as she got off and had to lean on Mr Blake to steady herself. He took her by the arm, gallantly letting himself bear her weight. She smiled up at him. They were friends again, as much as their relationship allowed.

It was altogether the most marvellous morning. They failed to win a coconut by knocking down balls, though they saw Alfie win three in succession before the vendor stopped him playing for a fourth time – a childhood most likely spent throwing stones at stray dogs and harbour rats, which accounted for his deadly accuracy, according to Mr Blake. They listened to the display of music from a steam-powered organ with moving animals, drank ginger beer, and had great fun on the busiest attraction of the event: a wondrous mechanised roundabout of wooden horses, each of which moved up and down as if they were truly galloping. As Florence accepted Mr Blake's hands to help her slide off the painted saddle, a raucous booing and cheering fill the air.

"What's that?" she asked in alarm.

Mr Blake peered over the crowds. "The prize fighter. Let's go look."

They walked towards the sounds. A square of grass in front of the inn had been roped off, and three sides were surrounded by people watching. A painted sign proclaimed that anyone who lasted in the ring with Maximillian Rafferty until the bell rang would receive their money back, plus five guineas. A burly, bald man who was naked to the waist and the butcher from the next village over were preparing to spar. The bell rang and to loud cheers, the butcher darted forward, one fist raised to shield his face, the other aiming for the fighter's belly. Maximillian Rafferty –

assuming this was he – stood his ground, a wide grin showing far too few teeth.

"That's absolutely barbaric!" Florence exclaimed.

"Oh I don't know." Mr Blake narrowed his eyes and looked at the muscular fighter. "The rounds last only three minutes and it isn't in his interest to do anyone a lasting injury. So long as you're quick on your feet and keep out of reach, I don't see why it wouldn't be an easy way of making money."

"Don't you dare even think about that!" Florence exclaimed, rounding on him with her arms folded.

"I wasn't." His face took on an expression of injured innocence.

"You're lying!" Florence replied sharply.

Blake confirmed it with a grin. "Don't worry, I'm more than capable of dodging a fist if I did decide to take my turn in the ring. Though your concern for my welfare is touching."

The butcher clearly wasn't capable of dodging because at that moment, a loud grunt shot from his throat as he took an elbow between the shoulder blades and dropped to his knees. Florence winced and looked away as he struggled to rise to his feet.

"I'm not concerned for your welfare. I'm concerned that I won't be able to produce a viscount for my father if you're laid up in your bed with a broken arm or cracked skull!"

"Oh I don't suppose I'd get that badly injured," Blake mused, rubbing his forefinger against his temple, as if probing for an injury already. "Besides, we have another few weeks and you can always tell him I fell from my horse as we hunted on my estate. That would be a respectable way of doing myself an injury."

Before Florence could demonstrate her appalled response, Cordelia swept through the crowd and took her by the arm.

"Florence, there you are. I've been looking everywhere for you! Good afternoon, Mr Blake. How do you do?"

Mr Blake bowed, greeting Lady Griggs with perfect manners. Florence would have approved if she hadn't been so concerned that he was about to step into the ring and do himself an injury. The butcher had surrendered to his inevitable defeat and was staggering from the ring to sympathetic catcalls.

"Florence, why are you still here and not preparing for Lord Stretford's arrival? It's almost two. We need to go back and dress for the afternoon," Cordelia said.

Florence looked at the clock on the church tower and her stomach dropped. Where had the time gone?

"I'll come now, Cordelia," she said. She fixed Mr Blake with a stern look. "What you do is up to you, but I would really prefer that while you are in my employ, you do not damage yourself or put my wager in jeopardy."

"Florence, you do worry unnecessarily," Cordelia said as they walked away. "Men, especially young virile ones such as Mr Blake, are like puppies and need to get rid of their excess humours. They show off to their friends and strut around like gamecocks. Look, my husband's valet is about to try his luck. I'd stay and watch if I had time."

"Twemlow won't mind if he gets a beating?" Florence asked, now more aghast than ever.

Cordelia patted her arm. "It will only be a mild one. Mr Rafferty understands exactly what to do and where to hit them so they feel brave for trying. Twemlow wouldn't let him come every year if there was any real danger. You don't really understand men, do you?"

Florence shook her head, unable to argue with that. There was logic in Cordelia's words, even though the whole thing seemed ridiculous. She looked back over her shoulder. Mr Blake was no longer standing where she could see him. She hoped he had gone off to find other amusements and would have the sense not to risk it. As she walked, she couldn't help but feel that something was changing inside her that made it hard for her to leave the company of Mr Blake behind. For now, she had more pressing demands upon her time: the visit from the potential husband.

On reflection, she would rather square up to Maximillian Rafferty herself.

Chapter Twelve

Ned walked around the entire fair once until he was sure that Miss Wakechild had definitely gone back with her sister to Goreswarth Chase. He spotted Alfie running after a football with the other stable boys and a handful of other children from the estate. He was laughing and jostling and looked to be having the time of his life. He seemed to have grown, too, though perhaps it was not walking with a nervous stoop that did it.

Ned smiled to himself. Even if Alfie had to return to life in Liverpool with his father, he would return with a month or more's worth of better food in his belly and greater confidence. It was Ned's great wish that he might not have to return at all. It might be possible to persuade Lord Griggs to employ the boy permanently. He was quick and bright, and Ned saw no reason why he might not do very well for himself. Not everyone was given that kind of chance and he hoped Alfie would be sensible enough to take it if it was offered.

Deep in thought, he walked back to the ring to find Maximillian Rafferty. He hesitated by the sign and took a deep breath, not at all sure that this was the right thing to do. There were probably other ways in which he could suggest to Miss Wakechild that he had already encountered Lord Stretford and therefore the ruse wouldn't work, but a black eye would be a convincing reason to avoid company.

It was a dirty trick to play on Miss Wakechild, but it was the only way Ned could think of to get out of meeting Stretford. If he could have thought of a different way, he would have done, but nothing had presented itself.

He knew he was telling himself a lie. He wanted to fight. He didn't relish the thought of getting beaten because of the pain that would result, but he wanted that feeling of his muscles burning and relying on his wits, speed, and strength to keep him sharp.

He took one more look about him. There was definitely no sign of Miss Wakechild. He paid his three shillings to the hawker who stood beneath the sign and nodded to Maximillian Rafferty in greeting. Rafferty nodded back amiably.

"How many have beaten you today?" Ned asked.

"No one."

"That's good." Ned removed his hat, coat, waistcoat, and tie and folded them neatly on a stool. "I'd hate for you to lose more than five guineas."

Rafferty laughed good-humouredly. "Won't happen now either."

The crowd was thinning out. No one had taken Rafferty on since the valet had left clutching his belly and groaning. Now a few more spectators drew close.

"Don't hit my beautiful face," he said, stroking his sideburns.

Rafferty laughed and beckoned Ned to step inside the roped area. "Can't promise."

Ned rolled up his sleeves then stepped over the low rope and raised his fists. The hawker rang the bell and Ned darted forward. He got the first punch in, straight at Rafferty's abdomen. It felt like hitting a bag of bricks. Rafferty was well used to the game. He let Ned get a couple more glancing blows in, just enough to give him unwarranted confidence.

Ned knew the game too, though. He ducked and danced around lightly on his feet, making a show of avoiding Rafferty when the colossus began to swing. He knew how to fight respectably and how to brawl crudely. Most importantly, he knew how to dodge a fist when it came to it so the impact was lessened. It struck him that he could actually last the round without injury and win himself five guineas. It was very tempting.

All his assumptions that he could win vanished when Rafferty swung his left fist and caught Ned on the right shoulder. Ned staggered backwards, grunting as waves of pain shot down his right arm. He swung out wildly with both fists, losing all sense of how long he'd been there for.

He felt his fists strike some part of Rafferty, who gave a deep laugh and pushed him away.

Ned sucked in a breath as he stumbled back, breathing heavily and staring at Rafferty, pondering his best move. It was no good getting a bruised belly or ribs with nothing to show for his exertions. He needed something visible. At some point he would have to grit his teeth and let Rafferty get a punch to the face. Only a slight one, though. Ned didn't want to actually be injured, but he had to look gruesome enough that Miss Wakechild would not have him anywhere near her party for the next few days at least.

He danced round Rafferty, ducking back and forth while letting the large man spin on his heels. He felt like a toy poodle baiting a mastiff. Somewhere he heard voices begin to count down from twenty. It was now or never.

He licked his lips, sent a prayer up to anyone watching who might not have abandoned him as a lost cause, and stepped face first into Rafferty's oncoming fist, tilting his head at the final moment so that the blow took him on the side of the face and not straight on the nose. He tasted blood, roared, and threw himself into Rafferty. The prize fighter had not been expecting a return onslaught and landed another punch to Ned's eye. Lights exploded inside Ned's head and he staggered but did not fall. It didn't hurt as much as he expected, but it would leave a hell of a bruise.

Dimly he heard a bell ringing. The crowd erupted into cheers and applause. Ned dropped to his knees and gave a sigh of relief.

"I think I won," he mumbled, letting himself fall fully to the ground, lying back and staring at the sky.

"Yes." Rafferty stood over him, eyes narrowed. He held a hand out and helped Ned up. He leaned in close and whispered to Ned.

"You could have avoided those last two punches, but I think you've done this before. You're an absolute fool. If I lose my pitch here because Lord Griggs thinks I'm beating people up, I'll come after you and finish you off."

"You won't. It was my fault. I'll answer for anything that has to be answered for."

The two men shook hands. Ned reclaimed his clothing and accepted the five guineas, promising himself that some of his winnings would go to a pint of something good to take the sting away. He wiped his mouth and spat blood. He walked away, wincing and rolling his shoulder back. All in all, he was satisfied with how the encounter had gone.

His elation was short-lived as he turned to see Miss Wakechild standing and watching. Her arms were rigid by her side and her face as pale as fine porcelain. She was wearing the same outfit as before, so she clearly hadn't returned to change. He stepped towards her quickly, though each limb felt unaccountably heavy, but she shook her head.

"Don't speak to me!" she hissed.

"I thought you had gone," Ned began lamely. His stomach heaved and he was flooded with shame. Getting bruises was one thing but he hadn't intended for her to see it happen.

"I had. I came back because I just knew you were going to do that!"

Her eyes were bright and she looked on the verge of tears. The sight was like a fist driving into his ribs. It was causing more discomfort than anything Rafferty had managed to inflict.

"How do you think I felt watching you in the ring?" She screwed up her eyes then opened them and glared at him. "Why are you so greedy? You don't need the money. I'm paying you well, though I've a good mind not to after that display."

"That would be fair," Ned said quietly, dropping his head. Let her think it was self-recrimination that made him avert his gaze. In truth, he couldn't bear the expression of misery on her face. "It won't happen again, I can assure you."

Miss Wakechild made an anguished noise in the back of her throat. "I don't want to hear your assurances. I don't want to see you again today. Or tomorrow. Not until Lord Stretford has gone. Perhaps not even then!"

She turned and swept away. Ned's shoulders sagged. He made his way back to Goreswarth Chase and to his room, taking care to avoid the route Miss Wakechild had taken. He sent for water and dabbed at his bruises. When he heard the clattering of wheels signalling the arrival of Stretford's carriage, he forced himself to resist looking out of the window. He didn't want to know how the visit would go. He'd achieved what he needed to do, but the price was far higher than it should have been.

For the duration of Lord Stretford's visit, Ned remained in his room. No one told him he could not leave but he did not feel inclined to do so. There was a knock on the door half an hour before the party set out on their picnic and fishing excursion. He answered it cautiously to find Dottie bearing a book.

"Miss Wakechild said you might want to read this," she said, bobbing a curtsey and holding it out.

Ned relieved her of it with thanks and flopped onto the reading couch. It was the book on etiquette she had shown him back when she'd proposed the scheme. He flicked through it, happening upon a folded corner of a page which turned out to be the chapter on picnics and water parties. He scowled, wondering if she had sent it to him to taunt him, or if she had been perusing that chapter herself.

He cast a look out the window. The day was fresh, with partial clouds providing some welcome shade. Walking through the countryside to indulge in a hamper full of pies and pastries would have been a good way to spend the day. He wondered what Miss Wakechild was doing, whether she was enjoying Stretford's company, and if she was any closer to bagging herself a titled husband. That possibility sent his mood spiralling further into gloom. Miss Wakechild was far too superior a wife for an ass like Stuffy Stretford.

He'd let her down badly, though he could never explain why and that tortured him.

Lord Stretford departed after a late luncheon the

following afternoon. Within an hour, a footman brought a note to Ned's room asking him to attend Miss Wakechild in the Summer Room. Ned freshened up, grimacing as he examined his reflection in the looking glass. He'd suffered a black eye and a cut to the lip, as well as livid bruising across his cheek. He didn't want to appear bearing the evidence of his shame, but he had no alternative.

The Summer Room was the first room he had entered when he had arrived. It was in the oldest part of the house, with a richly carved oak chimney piece and wood panelling that made him think of medieval times where it would have been the focus of the house. Lady Griggs had done her best to bring it up to date with coral and blue drapes that clashed with the worn tapestries on the walls, and a large mirror facing the narrow windows to maximise the light.

Miss Wakechild was sitting in a comfortable wingback chair upholstered in the same colours. Ned wondered if she would leave him standing, but she gestured to a smaller, less comfortable-looking chair that had been placed at a right angle to hers. He sat down. A pot of coffee and a plate of scones stood temptingly on a small table at her side, but there was only one cup and side plate, making it clear it was for her alone. Ned gave her a mental round of applause for the opening strike.

For a moment she was silent, then she pressed her fingertips together and looked at him.

"Mr Blake, I cannot tell you how disappointed I am with your behaviour. I specifically asked you not to fight and you did it the minute my back was turned. I am paying you handsomely and yet you are treating me with contempt. I cannot begin to understand why you did it."

She didn't raise her voice at all. Ned would have preferred it if she had. Her quiet recriminations bored into his conscience, eviscerating him. They were far more effective than any shouting, cutting through to the core of his being and leaving him feeling exposed and vulnerable.

"I apologise," he said, meaning it most sincerely. "I have no excuse, nor will I attempt to make any."

"You ruined my plans to introduce you to Lord Stretford and his sister. It made the party unbalanced and awkward."

She held his gaze, then her face creased into a blend of anger and distress. "Why did you do it? Why can you not take this wager seriously? Don't you realise how important it is to me?"

"Is it so important?" Ned asked quietly.

She leapt to her feet and swept past him to the window. "Of course it is! You know how much effort I have put into training you. Why I spend hours on it. Don't pretend you don't understand." Her voice was high.

"I'm starting to wonder if I do understand at all," Ned said. "Why do you care so much about winning? Yes, I understand your pride will be injured, but you don't need the money you stand to win, you said that yourself. You'll most likely barely break even after paying me, clothing me, and feeding me. Even if it does have some kind of stakes attached to it, it should still be treated as more of an amusement than anything else."

"It isn't just about the money." She folded her arms, mouth becoming an angry line.

"What, then? I understand you don't want to let your sister and brother-in-law win. I do understand the rivalry between siblings, but really, getting angry to this extent is…"

"Oh stop!" Miss Wakechild turned around and stalked towards the dark oak fireplace and stared into the depths. "It isn't just about proving I'm right. There's a lot more at stake."

Her eyelids flickered rapidly as she looked down to her side. The fury seemed to have gone out of her. He nodded slowly as if he understood what was going on inside of her, though in reality he was floundering.

"What?" Ned asked gently. "What haven't you told me?"

"I told you it was purely a sociological experiment. I lied."

Ned blinked. "About what?"

Miss Wakechild clapped her hands together, fingertips pressing against each other. She looked at him sheepishly then walked to the table and poured herself a cup of coffee before turning to him.

"We're recently wealthy and the old families look down on us for it. Daddy finds it unbearable. I told you that my father considers the British aristocracy the height of breeding. Unsurpassable and without imitation thanks to the long line of ancestors stretching out behind them. He believes that marrying into it will elevate his standing back home." She sipped the coffee. "If I can prove to Daddy that all of what he thinks makes a nobleman superior can be learned from a book and none of it is innate superiority, perhaps he will stop demanding I marry someone with a title."

"Ah." The clouds parted on Ned's understanding. There was a certain logic to what she said. It made sense now in a way that it hadn't before and explained her urgency. "So you can marry whom you choose? Is there someone waiting back home in America?"

Miss Wakechild glanced down at her hands. Ned looked at her curiously, then daringly asked, "Or a particular friend such as Miss Halliwell has?"

She shook her head. The insinuation didn't appear to offend her. He'd suspected it wouldn't. She just took another sip of coffee before answering. "So I don't have to marry at all."

"Now you're jesting," Ned replied.

"Isn't it typical that men always think it must be about a man? Why can't I dislike the idea for myself?" Miss Wakechild put her cup down and crossed her arms irritably. "Why would I want to spend my life as someone's wife when I could be my own mistress? I've never met anyone I'm prepared to give up my independence for. My mother hoped I would be my own woman. I remember her as a fiercely intelligent woman. She read everything she could lay her hands on, devoured the writings of Susan B. Anthony. She was firmly in favour of female suffrage. As I am."

"Being a wife doesn't mean you can't be in favour of that, or that you can't read improving books," Ned pointed out.

"I don't want to just read them; I want to put the ideas into practice. I want to make a difference and I can't do that if I'm a wife." She'd begun to wave her arms as she spoke. Now she took a breath and dropped them to her side, the combination of which had the effect of lifting her bosom high in a truly magnificent manner. She took a slightly smaller breath and then fixed a smile on her face that looked well practised.

"I know I'm probably fighting against a tide I can't turn back."

"It depends on whose wife you become, doesn't it?" Ned asked. "The mistress of an estate will have influence over the lives of hundreds of people if it's big enough. Take this place, for instance; your sister could do such good as Lady Griggs. Think of the improvements she has made to this old house and imagine that extended to the lives of the tenants. Her involvement in the plans for the park is commendable, but she could be even more ambitious."

"That's what I tell her!" Miss Wakechild's eyes gleamed and she walked to Ned's side. "I know Lord Griggs would let her undertake any project she chooses. He cares about his servants and tenants and is very forward-thinking."

"Well, there you go," Ned said. "I can see you doing great works in the right place. You're formidable. There are plenty of aristocrats who would be lucky to have you as chatelaine."

"I'll take that as a compliment." She gave a slight smile. "My sister has the sort of marriage that I could only wish for, but most women don't find husbands so liberal. I have friends who are miserable with their husbands and have to ask for more than the most meagre pin money. Why would I risk that?"

Ned didn't have an answer. She was right. Far too many women had been stymied by uncaring or small-minded husbands. His own mother had been. His throat filled with a lump, remembering her. If she had been able to choose freely – or choose not to choose at all – he had no doubt she would have been a happier woman.

It appeared his chastisement was over. Ned eyed the coffee pot and the scones.

"Miss Wakechild, shall I ring for a fresh pot of coffee for you?"

"Yes please." Her eyes followed his, then flickered up and she gave a small smile. "And you may ask the maid to bring a cup for yourself as I have forgiven you."

Ned rang the bell, gave his instructions, and walked to the window. He ran a finger along his jawline, probing the swelling that had started to reduce.

"I wish you had been honest with me from the start, Miss Wakechild."

"Would it have made you take it any more seriously?" she asked.

"Of course it would. If I had known how important it was to you on a personal level…"

She walked to his side and tilted her head slightly back

to stare into his eyes. She lifted a hand and he thought she was about to touch his face. His heart began to race in anticipation of her fingers touching him, but to his disappointment, she lowered it.

"Does your face hurt a great deal?"

"Not as much as my conscience," he answered.

"I'm sure they will both heal in time," Miss Wakechild said.

Her eyes crinkled. Despite her pale lashes, her eyes were remarkably striking. Ned smiled back. His heart sped up and he held his breath, not wanting to spoil the moment.

The maid spoiled it for him by arriving with a tray of coffee. She went to put it down on the table, realised there wasn't space beside the one already there, and began to dither.

"Let me help you," Ned said. He lifted the superfluous tray while she put the first one down, then handed it to her. She bobbed a curtsey and blushed. She was still bobbing as she backed out of the room.

"I don't think a viscount would have done that," Miss Wakechild remarked with amusement.

Ned raised a brow. "Maybe if more of them did, they would be less insufferable."

"What would you do if you did have an estate to manage?" Miss Wakechild asked. "If you woke up tomorrow and found you had become a viscount."

"What a dreadful thought." Ned looked down at the coffee pot then up at Miss Wakechild. She looked a little taken aback at his answer. "I'd build a park full of statues of myself and create a huge fishing lake in the middle," he replied, giving her a wide smile.

"Be serious," she scolded gently.

"I'd invest in the businesses my tenants run. Research new methods of production. Possibly see if a railway branch line could be added. I believe transportation is going to be crucial to financial success." He stopped, slightly taken aback at how easily his answers had come. "Of course, I wouldn't know the first thing about managing one. I'd have to employ an excellent estate manager before I did anything else."

He poured the coffee and handed Miss Wakechild her cup and took his own back to the chair. "That's the thing, you see, Miss Wakechild. An heir to an estate is trained practically from birth in what it entails. Anyone thrust into the role without notice would find it a daunting prospect. I'd pity him."

"So would I," Miss Wakechild said solemnly. "Lord Stretford and my brother-in-law were discussing the trials of finding good managers. My father had the same experience when he opened a second factory."

Ned's curiosity refused to be contained any longer. "Will you tell me how your visit with Lord Stretford went?"

Miss Wakechild lifted the coffee cup then put it back in the saucer, untouched. She pursed her lips before answering. That she had not immediately launched into fulsome praise of the viscount was good in Ned's opinion, though he couldn't work out why it mattered so much.

"It went well, I think. Lord Stretford seemed happy with

his visit. His sister was pleasant. She got on with my sister terrifically, in fact. I think they are hoping to maintain an acquaintance whatever the outcome regarding the two of us."

Miss Wakechild tailed off. She slumped back in her chair, looking weary and dropped her head. Ned sat on his chair, dragging it a little closer. He peered up at Miss Wakechild's face.

"Miss Wakechild? Are you alright?" Ned asked in a gentle voice.

"Yes, I'm fine, thank you for asking. No one else has."

"How did *you* find the visit? Did it make you happy?"

"I find company exhausting at times. Not physically. I'm not one of those women who swoons if I have to walk more than ten paces from the sofa but being entertaining does not come to me naturally."

Her lips twitched into a brief smile that was gone almost before it started. Ned remembered the vibrant figure he had watched dancing with a series of partners in Liverpool.

"Don't you enjoy going to parties and balls? You looked like you were thoroughly enjoying yourself when I saw you dancing at the Assembly Rooms."

She twisted her fingers around the bow at the neck of her blouse. "You look like a viscount. Appearances can be deceptive."

Ned nodded sympathetically as he listened to Miss Wakechild speak, wishing it was within his power to help her out of having to endure such encounters.

"If you have to force yourself to smile then it isn't the right place," Ned agreed. "What would you like to do?"

Miss Wakechild smiled again, cautiously but slightly more warmly. "I think most of all I would like to go to the Carnival in Venice. Then I could wear a mask and nobody would be able to see what I was really feeling."

"Wouldn't it be nice not to have to wear a mask and to be able to show what you're feeling?" Ned asked.

"Yes, I suppose it would." She sat a little straighter. "The problem is that what I am feeling or thinking is probably very boring to most men. I'm not very good at talking with people."

Ned was growing quite astonished at her admissions. He had always believed her so confident and full of certainty. Seeing these doubts and her vulnerability was a revelation. He half wanted to wrap her in a blanket and hold her tight to protect her from a cruel world that did not appreciate her.

"Aren't we talking now?" he asked.

"Yes, I suppose we are, but this is different. We are having a conversation. This is comfortable and I'm not expected to impress you. We are talking about a topic. But most men don't want women to talk about topics. Just to make chat about the weather or food. Well, that's my problem, you see, once I've run out of weather and food, my mind empties and all I can think of are topics. No man wants to be discussing the idea of universal suffrage while trying to waltz."

She looked so downcast. She was right, of course, most

men did not want a woman to be sharing – or even admitting to having – opinions. Truth be told, if Ned was dancing with Miss Wakechild, he would not want to be discussing anything. He'd be content simply gazing at her face and longing to see signs of enjoyment at being in his company.

It was then he decided that although he was her project, she was going to be his. He would teach her to flirt and laugh and dazzle. While she was transforming him, he would turn her into a belle capable of snaring any man alive. While he was at it, he could teach her a thing or two that might make marriage seem a more attractive prospect. He wondered if she had ever been kissed.

He cleared his throat. That line of speculation was a path he should most definitely avoid setting foot on.

"Miss Wakechild, I would like very much to help you prove your father wrong and help you win your bet. I offer my services with complete dedication to your cause and will not disappoint you again. Will you still have me?"

Her eyes narrowed then she sat up straight and gave him a dazzling smile that looked completely genuine and unforced.

"Mr Blake, I'll have you." She thrust out her hand. Ned took it and they shook. "We'll begin again tomorrow."

Chapter Thirteen

Mr Blake appeared as good as his word and arrived promptly for the lesson the following morning. Florence met him in the music room. She had dressed in a gown that was more suitable for an evening than a morning and Mr Blake stopped in his tracks when he entered the room.

"Did I forget an instruction?" he asked, gesturing down at himself. He was wearing his morning suit. It fitted his figure perfectly, drawing attention to his slim build and long legs. "I'm afraid I don't have anything suitable for a ball."

"That doesn't matter," Florence said, walking to greet him and reminding herself to discuss acquiring one for him with Twemlow. That might give her a hint to the proposed location of the meeting with her father, as Twemlow had refused to be drawn on where he was planning to have the bet taking place.

'If you have taught your pupil well the location should make not a whit of difference,' he had said at least twice, much to Florence's vexation.

"I thought we should begin dancing lessons today," she declared. "Cordelia has kindly agreed to accompany us on the piano."

Cordelia had not so much agreed as wearily consented after Florence's repeated entreaties the previous evening. She had told Florence that she had sworn when she married that she would no longer be required to make an exhibit of herself and she would play for her own enjoyment alone. It had taken the promise of afternoon tea in the upstairs room of the Crown and Feathers to secure her cooperation.

"What shall we begin with, Miss Wakechild?" Mr Blake asked. He took her hand and raised it to his lips. She was wearing long gloves but could swear she felt the heat of his breath on each little hair on her arm. She suppressed a shiver of anticipation. Nothing that would require too much closeness, she decided.

"A polka? Or perhaps a Detroit, which is similar. Do you know that?"

"I'm afraid I don't, but I'm your willing pupil," he said, walking into the centre of the room. "I am in your capable hands for as long as is required."

Cordelia shuffled her music sheets and gave a little cough. She caught Florence's eye and winked. "I think I can manage something for the Detroit. You walk Mr Blake through the steps while I look."

Florence faced him. His eyes rested on hers in a manner that made her feel quite disquiet.

"It's a bit like a waltz in places, but slower and we parade around the perimeter of the room in a procession," she explained. "We start by standing in the military position. You are on my left with your hand on my waist and mine on your shoulder."

She paused as a little worm wiggled in her belly.

"Left foot forward, sway backward, foot back, sway forward. Three steps running forward, face your partner, *pas de basque*, side close, side close…" She held her hands out to an imaginary partner and demonstrated the steps to the end of the room, executed a turn, and came back to his side.

"Now you try. But as in a mirror."

Blake had a very good stance. Back straight, shoulders relaxed, and light on his feet. He followed her instructions until he reached the end of the room. He gave a flourishing bow and all three of them laughed. Florence walked to him.

"Very good. Now I can teach you to put a turn in and then we can go back the other way together."

He held his hand out. She slipped hers into it, palm facing downwards on his upturned one. Together they stepped through the dance and promenaded back up the room. They ended the dance facing each other, their bodies less than a foot apart. She curtseyed and he bowed.

"You're a quick learner," she murmured.

He inclined his head. "You're a good teacher."

"I found some music," Cordelia called. "Shall I play for you?"

"What?" Florence dragged her attention from Mr Blake to her sister. For some reason, Cordelia was looking at Florence with a strange expression, eyes narrowed and an odd smile.

"Yes, thank you," Florence said.

She and Mr Blake took up the starting position, danced the length of the room and back again twice, then stopped.

"I think that's a very good start," Florence said once she had caught her breath. "Shall we try another dance or are you too tired?"

"I'm far from tired; I feel invigorated," Mr Blake said. "Lady Griggs, would you happen to have a Viennese waltz to hand?"

"A waltz?" It was a bit old-fashioned but a dance that Florence loved. One where she could glide across the floor feeling like she was floating without having to concentrate on what her feet were doing. It was very intimate though. There wasn't as much space between their bodies as in the Boston. She glanced at Cordelia for guidance.

"It's a perfectly respectable dance," Cordelia said. "Even father has been known to dance it."

"Every gentleman is expected to know how to waltz," Mr Blake said. "I saw you dancing it with the elder Mr Van Hoon, don't forget, so I know you can."

That was true, but dancing with an old man was very different from dancing with Mr Blake who was young and handsome and very charming and who made her grow hot inside when he took her hand. Once she had some time to herself, she would have to examine why she was reluctant to dance with him when she was so very keen at the same time.

"One waltz and then I've promised Cordelia afternoon tea as payment for accompanying us."

Cordelia opened a new piece of music and played through it rapidly. Florence recognised the tune immediately. It was one the girls had learned to play as children.

Mr Blake held his arms out. "Shall we dance, Miss Wakechild?"

She stepped into his arms. "I'd be delighted."

As soon as they began, she knew this would be an experience unlike dancing with Mr Van Hoon or any other partners she'd had before. He guided her around the room, his arms reassuringly firm and his steps confident.

"Mr Blake, you continue to surprise me. You are a very good dancer. You've obviously done this before," she said.

Mr Blake grinned. "Of course I have. I don't know why you think I might not know how to dance. I've been in ballrooms and assembly rooms many times, even if only as an observer, but I've had occasion to dance."

"Tell me some of the times you've danced," Florence asked. "Do you dance for your own pleasure or because you needed to?"

He laughed; a rich, deep baritone. "One time I was asked to get close enough to the wife of a distinguished owner of a department store to discover if she was wearing the perfume given to her by her husband or by someone else entirely."

"Do you mean she might have been wearing something given to her by a lover?" Florence asked. "What did you discover? How did you know which scent she should have been wearing?"

Her mind wriggled with ideas and she began letting her feet move instinctively, content to be guided as she speculated. "I suppose the husband must have…"

"Miss Wakechild, pardon my rudeness, but please allow me to stop you there." Mr Blake gave her hand a gentle squeeze. She returned from her thoughts and looked back into his eyes. He had a playful grin on his face.

"As charming as it is to see your mind at work, this is one of the occasions when conversation should only be on frivolous subjects. Dancing is the perfect opportunity to get to know your partner a little more intimately. I believe that is the purpose of it. Two people, in relative privacy despite being surrounded on all sides." He lowered his head, bringing his lips close to her ear.

"For example, may I dare to compliment you on your appearance this morning. You are breathtaking, Miss Wakechild. If we were at a ball, I would be the envy of every man attending."

"Oh!" Infinitesimal flickers filled Florence's belly, rising up and down inside her. She licked her lips. Should she return a compliment, rebuke him for being forward, or accept it? "I'm not sure that is appropriate at all, but thank you. That's very kind of you to say, though I doubt it is the case."

He sighed audibly and spun her around. "I get the feeling you don't feel too comfortable at getting complimented. I'll make it my business to think of a new one every day until you are able to brush them off with ease."

Her cheeks began to grow hot; the warmth spreading across her face and down her neck. She would be blushing scarlet and he would know how much his words were affecting her.

"I think we know this dance well enough. We don't need to practise any more. Cordelia, you can stop now."

She stepped back out of his arms. Cordelia paused her playing and turned around on her stool.

"Are you sure?"

Mr Blake lowered his arms to his side. He glanced at Florence briefly, then gave a rueful smile. "If Miss Wakechild has decided, we are done. Thank you for your time, Lady Griggs."

Cordelia shrugged and left the room. Mr Blake walked to the piano and began gathering the sheet music and placing it in the space beneath the stool.

"Miss Wakechild, I made you feel awkward. I apologise."

"It doesn't matter." Florence sighed. "I am awkward at times, and as you say, I'm not used to compliments."

"That is one of the greatest injustices of our age." Mr Blake turned to her. "I meant every word I said."

She tugged at her glove, pulling it over her elbow. It felt uncomfortably tight and she suddenly felt very foolish, wearing an evening dress in the middle of the morning. She was seized by the overwhelming urge to be out of it and dressed in a modest, comfortable skirt and blouse more suited to the morning.

"Goodbye, Mr Blake," she muttered. She turned and fled before he had time to answer. She didn't slow her pace until she reached her bedroom and caught sight of herself in the full-length looking glass. She did look attractive in the pale blue gown she had chosen, but hadn't expected Mr Blake to notice. She summoned Dottie and while she waited for the maid to bring fresh clothes, she couldn't help dancing around the room, waltzing with an imaginary partner. If Mr Blake hadn't spoiled everything by trying to be nice, she could have danced with him all day long.

Three days later and with two more dance lessons completed, Florence gave Mr Blake a morning to himself while she caught up on writing her shamefully neglected journal and the sketch she was doing of the gardens. She was sitting in her bedroom, occupied with these tasks when Cordelia walked in.

"I have a letter from Father," Cordelia said.

Florence joined her on the sofa. "He should be arriving in two days. You wouldn't tell me if it was just making arrangements for his room or the menu. What's wrong?"

"I think you better read yourself." Cordelia held out the envelope. Florence had to control herself not to snatch it from her hand. She pulled out the folded sheet and held it up.

My dearest girls, business compels me to return immediately to Philadelphia. I will not trouble you with the intricacies.

Florence gasped. "Do you think there is something wrong? Are we ruined?"

"I don't know. Read on," Cordelia urged.

Suffice to say that I am deeply apologetic that I will not be able to visit you in Cheshire, Cordelia. Florence, my dear, I think it would be wise if you also curtail your visit and return home. I am aware of how unpleasant this news will be for you as you wish to tour more of the country. I can assure you that in the future I hope to bring you back here. I have not given up my hopes regarding your marriage and in fact my correspondence with Lord Stretford has been most favourable.

I am booked to depart from Southampton in three days from my time of writing so will have departed by the time you receive this. Cordelia, I have written separately to your husband entreating him to arrange passage for Florence and also for yourselves. She cannot return unaccompanied except for her maid. I know you have expressed a wish to return home on occasion and it is time your husband was granted the opportunity to see the country of his wife's origin.

I remain your fondest father et cetera, et cetera.

"Cordelia, what do you think is wrong? Is it Ashley? If there are troubles at the factory, Father could just as easily leave it to him, so it must be Ashley." She stood and began pacing to and fro. "This is too worrying. What if father is ill? What if Ashley is? We need to pack at once!"

She pictured her bedroom, neatly organised with books, sketchbooks and ornaments. It wouldn't take more than an hour or two at most for Dottie to pack.

"Florence, you need to calm yourself." Cordelia took her by the arms and shook her gently. "Let me speak with Twemlow and see if Papa has sent him any information that he didn't want to trouble us with. I'll let you know as soon as I hear anything from him, but we certainly won't be leaving tomorrow. It will take at least a week to arrange passage, maybe longer depending on how many staterooms are available."

Florence nodded, seeing the sense in her sister's words.

Cordelia patted her cheek. "Florence dearest, I'm sure there is nothing too bad happening. Father sounds very pleased with you, and Lord Stretford is still a possibility for a husband. You won't have seen the last of him."

"I would happily have done so." Florence drew a sharp breath. "Oh goodness! Oh this is too bad. We've worked so hard and now Daddy is not going to get to see our hard work with Mr Blake."

She screwed her fist up, crushing the letter within. "I'm sure we would've won the wager too. I'll have to speak to Twemlow and have it declared null and void. And what of Mr Blake? I'll have to tell him and say goodbye."

Her lips began to quiver with dismay. They had been making real progress since she had told Mr Blake the real reason and Florence had enjoyed the last three days more than almost all the previous ones she had spent in England. She wasn't sure where Mr Blake was but there was no time like the present. She would not relish telling him they must part, but a painful thing would not grow less painful by leaving it.

Upon enquiry, it turned out both men had gone out together to practise archery on the butts behind the vegetable gardens. The vegetable garden was behind a high wall that had pear and apple trees espaliered all around the inside. A stray arrow flying over could hit a gardener and there would be all sorts of trouble.

Twemlow had just fired and hit the blue circle. Facing the targets, he and Mr Blake did not notice the women approaching across the lawn, so Florence and Cordelia were able to watch Mr Blake take aim and release his arrow. It landed directly in the middle of the bull's-eye.

"Oh, well done!" Florence cried, beginning to applaud. The men turned, saw the women, and both smiled.

"Mr Blake, you are a regular Earl of Loxley aren't you?" Florence said with a laugh.

He froze, his eyes suddenly wary.

"I mean Robin Hood," Florence clarified. "He was the Earl of Loxley, wasn't he?"

"Of course," Ned said. "I wasn't quite sure what you meant for a moment. Yes, he was. It's quite rare to hear him being referred to by his title."

"Now there's a nobleman whom one could admire," Cordelia said. "Giving to the poor, fighting against injustice and so on, all while being very dashing and romantic. Twemlow, you could learn something from him."

"Robin Hood was a fiction," Twemlow said.

"And he only did those deeds after he had lost his title," Mr Blake pointed out. "Until then who knows what kind of earl he might have been had he not been dispossessed."

"Very true," Florence said, warming to the theme. "It's the same conundrum. Was he good because of, or in spite of, his birth?"

Mr Blake gave her a smile. "Perhaps your father should seek to marry you to an outlaw."

"Gosh, now I'm vexed again," Florence said. "That's why we've come out here. I had almost forgotten."

"You're getting married?" Mr Blake asked. His eyes widened and he took a step towards her. Was it Florence's imagination or did he look disappointed?

"I am not," Florence said.

"My dear, did you receive a letter from my father?" Cordelia asked Twemlow.

"Yes, I did." Twemlow notched another arrow, closed one eye, and aimed. This time his arrow struck the centre of the target, close to Mr Blake's. "I shall get straight onto the matter after lunch."

He strolled over to the target to retrieve the arrows. Cordelia followed him. Florence was left alone with Mr Blake.

"Mr Blake, I have the most dreadful news," Florence said. "My father is returning to America and he has told me I have to return too, as soon as possible. Lord and Lady Griggs will be accompanying me."

"You will be leaving?" Mr Blake frowned.

"Yes, it's too bad, isn't it? Our wager must come to an end. I'm sure my brother will not expect you to leave the house until you have found other lodgings and naturally I will pay you the full amount we agreed upon."

"I wasn't thinking of that," Mr Blake said quickly. He coughed. "I mean to say, that is very generous of you, Miss Wakechild, but really there's no need. I'm just sorry that I'm not able to help you win your wager."

"I mind enormously. Not only about the wager but I'm afraid I shall be leaving you unemployed," Florence said.

Mr Blake patted her shoulder. "I am sure I shall find another occupation soon enough. Perhaps I should become a prize fighter."

"That's not funny," Florence said sternly, eyeing his split lip. It had healed well but there was a slight scab that threatened to become a scar. In time it would probably fade completely but it might not. He should probably grow a moustache.

"Also, you're clearly not a very good fighter."

Twemlow and Cordelia walked back.

Florence turned to her brother-in-law. "Do you think I would have won the wager if we had a little longer?"

They both stared at Mr Blake.

"I think it would be very close, even if you didn't," Twemlow said. He stuck the arrows into the grass. "If you will excuse me, I shall leave you. I have a meeting with my estate manager. I will probably take luncheon in my office."

Cordelia accompanied her husband back to the house, leaving Florence and Mr Blake alone once again. She didn't know what to say. No chit-chat came to her head and she couldn't think of a single subject.

"I shall be sorry to part from you. I feel almost as if we have become friends," she said eventually.

"I am deeply honoured to hear you say that," Mr Blake said, his voice low. "So do I."

Impulsively, she touched his arm. "Mr Blake, if you like, you may call me Florence."

His eyes widened, the pupils dilating. He inclined his head. "I will be more than privileged to do so. And in return, might I dare to ask if you would call me Ned?"

"Ned." She smiled. "Edward, I suppose."

He dipped his head, then tilted it one side and she was close enough to believe for one wild moment that he might kiss her. Her heart pulsed as she wondered what she would do if he did, but he straightened up again. She glanced down and noticed he was still holding his bow.

"May I?"

She took it from his hand and tugged an arrow out of

the ground where Twemlow had stuck them earlier and fitted the groove into the string, then pulled it back and took aim at the target. She didn't expect to hit the centre straight off, but she didn't expect the arrow to fall, nor the string to twang back and whip against the inside of her lower arm.

The impact was like the crack of a whip: white hot, instantly numbing, instantly followed by searing pain from wrist to the crook of her elbow. Tears filled her eyes and she yelped at the sharp intensity, dropped the bow, and grasped her arm tightly. Her head began to swim, she turned towards the house, stumbled, and fell.

She was caught before she landed, jerked to safety before impact. She looked up into Mr Blake's eyes, in whose strong arms she was held.

Chapter Fourteen

"Let me see the wound."

Mr Blake firmly prised her hand back from her arm. Her sleeve was fastened with five small mother-of-pearl buttons. Mr Blake unfastened them and pushed the thin lace up to her elbow. Florence peered at her arm, expecting to see blood. To her relief, the skin hadn't broken and there was only a raised line, though it was bright red and swollen.

"You made it look so easy," Florence gasped.

Mr Blake looked shocked. "Was that the first time you have ever tried? I would never have let you if I had realised. You need a wrist guard."

He held her arm gently and ran his forefinger over the length of the welt.

"It won't scar but you should go back to the house and wrap a damp cloth around it. Come on, I'll take you back."

"That was so stupid of me," Florence said as they walked. "Daddy always told me I was far too impulsive."

"It's an easy mistake," he replied. He brushed his finger over the wound again. Caused no doubt by the pain and shock, Florence felt as if her arm had doubled the number of nerves, and each one was dancing.

"I did it the first time I ever picked up a bow. My instructor let all of us do the same thing so we learned to be more careful and respect the weapon."

Intrigued by the curious insight, Florence asked, "Where did you grow up Mr Blake? I mean, Ned?"

He hesitated before answering. "In Yorkshire. I think officially we're still allowed to shoot Scotsmen on sight."

"I wanted to see Yorkshire, and Scotland," Florence murmured. "My mother's grandmother was Scottish. Only just. Her family came from somewhere on the borderlands, in a bit that was sometimes English and sometimes not."

Mr Blake began to lead her across the lawn. "Being Scottish would explain your hair colour of course."

"You won't shoot me though, will you? Even if you're allowed to."

"No, I won't shoot you," he said patiently.

She beamed at him. The pain or shock, or being held so close, was making her feel light-headed.

"My mother used to tell me tales of our ancestors. Not the recent ones who disowned her. Apparently, they were border lords in the olden days and some of them might even have been criminals. My father didn't like her telling me those stories."

She giggled then slapped her free hand over her mouth. Mr Blake was gentlemanly enough not to pass comment.

"How do you feel about returning home?" he asked.

"I really enjoyed my time here even though it is not exactly how I expected to be spending it. It's been better. I've enjoyed our lessons." She wrinkled her brow. "What will you do now? If this were my house, I would say you are welcome to stay until you found another commission, but I can't make that offer on my brother-in-law's behalf."

"I will find something. I'm very resourceful," he said, shrugging.

"Maybe you should go to America," Florence said.

"Perhaps I should."

They stopped walking at the same time. A light buzzing started in Florence's ears. She raised her eyes and met Ned's, seeing the same sense of excitement that was erupting within her.

"Maybe you should *come* to America," she said, emphasising the verb so he didn't miss her meaning.

Ned broke into a wide grin. "Maybe I should."

"The wager doesn't have to be over. It would be even better if you came to Philadelphia and met my father there. He will be surrounded by people who know less about the British nobility." Florence couldn't stop from smiling. "Oh this is wonderful! We'll be home in time to go to the opera and the August salons. Let me go speak with Twemlow immediately. He needs to arrange passage for you too."

"Miss Wakechild. Florence, stop, please! Your wrist. You need put something cool on your arm."

Florence rubbed absentmindedly at the red stripe.

"It barely hurts at all now." It was a little lie. The initial sting had lessened but it was beginning to throb.

Ned gave her a stern look. "It will hurt more later and you don't want to end up with a scar. I insist you get it treated. In fact, I'm going to take you myself." He took her gently by the elbow again and escorted her to her bedroom. Dottie was sitting in the comfy chair darning something lacy that Florence recognised as her slip. Dottie gave a slight squeak when she saw Ned entering beside Florence.

"Oh Miss! Sir! I wasn't expecting you." She looked down at the garment in her hands and shoved it deep into the basket. If Mr Blake had spotted the item, he gave no indication that he recognised it for anything intimate.

"Dottie, your mistress has had a shock and has received an injury. Go and bring a bowl of cool water and some linen to dress her wounds. Perhaps a small glass of brandy as well."

"Umm, Miss, should I do what he says?" Dottie stood and looked from Ned to Florence. Her eyes slid to the half-tester bed with its pretty rose- and grey-patterned eiderdown. Her sense of propriety and inclination to follow orders were clearly at war.

Ned saved her from further anguish.

"Don't worry, Dottie. You stay with your mistress and I will go find the necessary items. Miss Wakechild, let me help you sit."

He escorted Florence to the window and helped her to

sit, fussing around, finding her a footstool, and ensuring her arm was raised on the arm of the sofa.

"Oh Miss, what on earth have you been doing?" Dottie asked after he had left. She looked at Florence's arm and gasped. "That must hurt so!"

"Playing bows and arrows," Florence said ruefully.

"Did you swoon?" Dottie asked. "Did you faint? Did Mr Blake have to carry you?"

"I think you read far too many romances," Florence said, mustering the energy for a smile. "Of course I didn't do any of those things. You know me well enough to know I'm not the swooning kind. And nor did Mr Blake have to carry me."

"Well, that's a waste of an opportunity," Dottie said, grinning. "If I had a gentleman as nice as Mr Blake, I'd have made sure to faint."

"Dottie!" Florence gave a shocked laugh. "Really, you're quite scandalous!"

Ned had shown such tenderness, though, and she would not forget for a long time the way his fingers had travelled over her delicate skin. To think he had been about to suggest staying alone with her in her bedroom! Why, the thought of that made her feel more light-headed than the pain in her arm.

When Ned returned, Florence allowed him and Dottie to fuss around her, wrap her arm in damp bandages – which she had to admit did ease the pulsating pain – and supply her with brandy. Maybe she should have swooned a little bit, she mused as he rearranged a blanket over her lap. She ushered them both out and lay back, eyes closed. Of course Ned would accompany her to America. It was so obvious, so perfect that she did not know why she hadn't thought of it in the first place. They'd had some hiccups on the way, but now nothing could possibly go wrong.

It always astonished Ned to discover how quickly matters could move when people put their minds to it. He'd been used to a leisurely existence, pleasing himself and accountable to no one, but now that he had fallen into the whirlpool that was Florence Wakechild, he was incapable of pulling free of her tug. He understood from casual chats with the domestic servants that it had taken Miss Wakechild almost a full day to persuade Lord and Lady Griggs to agree to Ned accompanying them on the ship to New York and only the threat that she might refuse to return herself or would insist on paying his fare herself swayed them.

So now it appeared he was going to America. It had been a ridiculous impulse but on more considered reflection, it made sense. He was getting handsomely paid and enjoyed spending time with Florence. Most importantly – and something he would never reveal to her – with the estimated date of a "happy event" almost upon him, it would give him the perfect reason to leave England for months if not forever. Let him disappear across the Atlantic Ocean, and let his worries stay behind.

The night before they were due to return to Liverpool,

Ned followed the sound of the piano to discover Florence in the music room, playing the Viennese waltz they had danced to. She was alone so he knocked on the partially open door and walked in. She glanced up, then back at the music and continued playing. When she came to the end, she finally gave Ned her complete attention.

"I'm sorry, I hate to break off halfway through."

"That's reasonable. I don't like leaving matters unfinished either."

The piano stool was as long as the instrument, to allow a pair to duet. Florence moved over and patted the space beside her. Ned sat.

"I don't play, you realise."

"Men rarely have to learn. You aren't expected to woo us by performing. I don't have time to teach you now but once we've won the wager, I could always see if I could pass you off as a music hall artiste."

Ned chuckled then his mood grew sober. Thoughts of what would happen when the wager was over had flashed into his mind on the occasions that it appeared in jeopardy: when he had almost doomed it by fighting and when Florence had been called home. Now he was struck by the realisation that in a matter of weeks, it would be. He would have no reason, or excuse, to remain in her company. It saddened him.

"I imagine you'd lose that wager before you even started," he said.

Florence ran her hands along the keys, her fingers skipping daintily over them in rippling scales. She stopped when it would have meant leaning past him and placed her hands in her lap. Her sleeves were gathered tightly almost to the elbow before billowing out in stiff puffballs over her upper arms. He wondered whether the bowstring had left any trace.

"Ned, you know why I want to win and I know you want to help me, but you were happy to do that before you discovered my real motive. Is it just because I'm paying you? We have never discussed why you are so eager to prove my theory right. What do you have against the nobility?"

Ned sucked in his breath. He couldn't explain that it wasn't the whole of the aristocracy he loathed, merely particular examples. With the prospect of leaving England behind him, he felt safe enough to share more than he might otherwise have. He reached out and ran his fingers over the keys, wondering where to begin and what to omit.

"I grew up on an estate in Yorkshire. When I was a boy of ten, I was discovered picking apples from the trees on the earl's property. I don't know what you call it, but we call it scrumping. The earl apparent whipped me with a riding crop until the blood ran down my spine. Personally. Then, when flecks of my blood spattered his shoes, he gave me a kicking in retaliation."

He slammed his fingers down on the piano keys, creating a discordant blare as the memory of helplessness and agony bore down upon him. Florence jumped. Ned withdrew his hands. He closed his eyes briefly. When he opened them, she was staring at him with a mixture of horror and pity. And something else. It took him a minute to remember the emotion he saw and name it as concern.

"That's barbaric."

He shrugged. "I should no doubt have been honoured that he did not consider the punishment beneath his notice and delegate it to an underling. All it did was make me hate him. I still bear the scars."

Florence drew closer to him, twisting in her seat. Her face was creased with rage. He caught the scent of something floral. Violets.

"That's brutal! Could you not seek justice?"

"From whom?"

Ned played another not-quite-chord, fingers rigid, bitterness rising and ebbing. He had walked away, though, into a life of uncertainty and freedom. The boy who had wept through the night back then no longer cried now.

"It's how things are. A man has power or not through the accident of his birth. In the earl apparent's defence, I had been caught up a tree with an apple in my hand. In other circumstances, I might have been imprisoned as a thief, so I bit my tongue, mopped my blood, and endured the further reprimand my father gave me when he discovered what had happened."

"Ned, I'm sorry," Florence whispered. "What did your mother say?"

Ned's heart cracked. The eruption sent waves of grief bounding through every vein and artery. Many people knew the tale, but he had little to do with them. Soon England, with all its memories, would be left behind. He'd warned Florence not to ask about his past, but now, sitting beside her in solitude, he found the words coming easily.

"My mother had died by then. I mentioned it when we first met, if you recall. Her life had been hard and miserable, so I expect she was relieved to be leaving it. My father lived until I was twenty. At that point, I was thrown out of my home with barely a penny to my name, only the clothes on my back and a few personal possessions. That I am not in the poor house or dead is due entirely to my own wherewithal."

He closed the piano lid softly.

"I don't ask for much in life. A home I can call my own that is more than two rooms. Warm clothes in winter and good food. I was forced to make my way in the world, and I thank Providence every day that I have the brains and the cunning, not to mention a good deal of doggedness, to put myself to good use."

"So what would you do with your time if you were rich?" Florence asked. "I don't mean merely rich enough so you could rent an office and take on these sort of commissions as you chose. What if you were really wealthy? If you had, say, nine thousand dollars a year?"

"An interesting figure," Ned said, wondering if that was what Florence had, or would have when she married. It was a tempting sum.

"I suppose so. A nice round figure, at any rate. What would you do?"

He walked to the window seat and sat down. The sun was going down over the trees in the distance. The landscape was flat and dull. He had an overpowering urge to be back in the place he had once called home where vertical cliffs and rolling moors met.

"I'd buy a house by the sea. I would look for men such as myself who have ambition and drive who are starting out in businesses and I'd offer them capital in return for investment."

"That's what you do with your money," Florence said, joining him on the seat. "What would you do with your days?"

"I don't know," Ned replied. "I can't really conceive of being a man of leisure. Perhaps create photography. Maybe I would learn to paint. Perhaps I would spend it watching the sea change as the seasons turned, with a wife at my side for company."

"The wife you would employ a servant for, so she could have leisure too," Florence said, with a slight question in her voice and a glint in her eye.

"Of course. We could both learn to paint," he assured her.

"Oh I'm dreadful," Florence answered with a light laugh. "No number of lessons could improve my misshapen daubs."

He looked at her, slightly confused. "When I say we…"

"Oh! Yes! No. Of course. I see what you mean. You weren't referring to the two of us when you said 'we' were you. You meant yourself and your future wife. Whoever she will be. How silly of me."

The tips of her ears had started to turn pink. Was that

what he had meant or had he been thinking of Florence in some way, even unconsciously?

"I suppose so," he said. Of course she would never be his wife. She was destined for great things whether or not she married an aristocrat. If it wasn't a viscount, it would be a railroad magnate or one of the great families of American high society. Ned's stomach twinged again. It was happening with such frequency he wondered if he had eaten something that disagreed with him.

She was still looking flustered. "Excuse me. I think I should go and check on Dottie and make sure she has packed everything. It was nice talking to you. I'll see you in the morning for breakfast. Such an early start!"

He stood and held out a hand to help her rise.

"Very gentlemanly," she murmured, her hand still in his.

He grinned and raised it to his lips, resisting the urge to linger. "You see, you will make a gentleman of me after all."

The following day, after having bade farewell to Alfie, Ned was back in Liverpool. With the *RMS City of Bruges* due to set sail at four, he had an hour to idle around while Florence and her sister completed some last-minute shopping. Ned had nothing to buy so ambled along the waterfront and ran straight into Marius Van Hoon.

"Blake! I didn't expect to see you back in our city so soon. Rumour had it you had gone to Oxford, of all places, in connection with a divorce case. Yet here you are again."

Rumours started by Meggie Gallagher, the barmaid at the Admiral Nelson, at Ned's request. He concealed a smile.

"Good to see you in any case," Van Hoon continued. "I could do with your help regarding Willem. He has developed an unsavoury new friendship. Are you able to help?"

Ned concealed a sigh. He'd rather hoped Willem would have learned a lesson. "Sadly not. I have a commission that takes me elsewhere."

"That's a shame." Mr Van Hoon scowled then twirled his cane. "But how interesting. Any gossip to liven an old man's life, may I ask?"

"You may ask," Ned said pleasantly, "however, you won't receive an answer. You know that. Discretion is my byword."

The old man did not take offence, knowing he had benefitted from this too. It didn't stop him trying again, though.

"I see you are dressed like a gentleman. Is there anything the world is unaware of?"

Ned bared his teeth in a false smile. "Oh I'm sure there are plenty of things the world is unaware of. Many that I am too and I'm happy to remain so. I must bid you farewell. I have places to be."

He would have got away with that enigmatic and unrevealing response had Florence not swept up to him briskly. She was wearing a travelling suit with a closely tailored jacket, a rakishly angled hat and half-veil, cream kid gloves and carried a small bag. She looked attractive and excited. She looked, in fact, exactly like the wealthy woman she was.

"Mr Blake, there you are. We need to go. Time and tide wait for no man and certainly not for a woman! Why, it's Mr Van Hoon, isn't it? How nice to see you again. I cannot tell you how much I enjoyed dancing with you at the ball. Mr Blake, I shall see you on board."

She curtseyed to them both and walked away again. Van Hoon's eyes were gleaming as they followed her departing figure.

"Interesting commission. So America is the place, is it? When do you return to our fair shores?"

"I have no idea."

"Is the heiress paying? I never took you for a kept man. Are you getting your ducks lined up in anticipation?"

"Miss Wakechild is paying me for the work I'm doing, and I warn you to keep a civil tongue in your mouth." Ned dropped his voice, tensing his frame, and stepped close to Van Hoon. "In fact, I want you to keep your tongue entirely motionless in your mouth when it comes to Miss Wakechild. And to my affairs, for that matter."

"Of course. I would not dream of interfering." Van Hoon stepped back, a sickly smile on his face. "Naturally as a father I would have some concern for Miss Wakechild. I wonder how much she knows about your past and how much she might like to know about your future. Or perhaps she knows already."

Ned stepped even closer. "I am warning you. There is plenty I could tell the world about your son and his habit for cheap whores and losing heirlooms. I suggest it will be mutually advantageous for us both to keep our counsel."

Van Hoon nodded and stepped back. Ned raised his hat and walked away. He had only taken three paces when Van Hoon called after him.

"You can't run from your past forever. You can't sail away from it either. Enjoy your voyage on the *City of Bruges*. I assume you'll be sailing on her if you're leaving tonight."

Ned's shoulders knotted and it took a great deal of control not to bellow aloud in frustration. What impetuosity had driven him to come somewhere he might be recognised? He should have gone straight to the ship and shut himself in his cabin. He was so close to leaving the country without anybody noticing but now Van Hoon knew not only his destination but his method of travel. His frustration at his incaution did not ease until he was on board and safely in the small second-class cabin. It was only when the ship had left the dock and was on the way down the Mersey that he felt the bonds of anxiety loosening.

So what if Van Hoon knew which ship he'd sailed on. So what if he told anyone who came looking. Anyone would be a day behind, and New York was large enough for Ned to keep hidden. He was booked into a hotel under a different name so even if he was tracked to the city, the trail would go cold. For the next month at least, he did not need to give any regard to what might be happening in England, nor the effect it could have on his future.

Chapter Fifteen

Unfortunately, and contrary to expectation, Ned discovered that his experience of sea travel was closer to Lady Griggs' than Florence's. Much to his embarrassment and discomfort, as soon as the *City of Bruges* reached the open water of the Atlantic, he was hit by unquenchable nausea. For the first twenty-four hours, he could do little more than lie on his bed, groaning and praying that he would not actually vomit into the large porcelain bowl that the steward – with a neutral expression that suggested he had seen many such afflicted passengers – had placed on the nightstand within easy reach.

By lunchtime on the second day at sea, he finally began to feel a little more like himself, and by five in the evening, he decided that, though he was unable to face the dining room, he could stomach some vegetable broth and water biscuits.

He was extremely surprised, when they were delivered,

to find Florence walking into his room just as the steward left.

"Dottie, please wait outside," Florence instructed. "I'll leave the door open as the room needs airing so it will be perfectly proper for you to stand out there. Mr Blake, I thought I had better see whether you were still alive," she said breezily.

She was dressed in a purple twill skirt and jacket with a cream blouse and a small straw hat tipped back on her head. She looked the very image of health and vibrancy and it was all Ned could do not to glower at her in envy.

"Miss Wakechild, I wasn't expecting a visitor! Are you allowed in the second-class areas?" he asked. Fortunately he had washed and dressed so wasn't supine in his nightshirt.

"Undoubtedly not, but at this time of day everyone else is resting or playing games on deck and I won't be missed. Mr Blake, do you object to me opening the window? You need air."

Ned didn't object and Florence opened the catch on the small bullseye porthole. A brisk but refreshing blast of air wafted through the room, smelling of salt and freshness. Ned wished he had done it on first boarding. He lifted the silver cloche to discover a small, lidded tureen and a plate with crackers. A small dish of butter and a dressed orange completed the meal. Cautiously, he lifted the lid from the tureen, praying that he would not vomit at the sight and smell. Instead, he found his mouth watering in anticipation.

"Please don't stand on ceremony for me. Eat," Florence instructed.

Ned obeyed at once. The vegetable soup was smooth and velvety. Both comforting and bland enough that it made him feel instantly better. He buttered a cracker and nibbled it. When it appeared happy to stay consumed, he finished the soup.

"We had lobster bisque and roast pork at lunch. I don't suppose you would like any of that sending down?" Florence asked.

The only reply Ned managed was a shake of his head as he reached for another cracker. Florence laughed kindly.

"Perhaps tomorrow. I imagine the chefs must get used to catering for the seasick. If it's any consolation, my sister has been lying on her sofa all morning with a wet flannel over her face and a peppermint tisane at her side."

Lord and Lady Griggs had taken full advantage of their wealth and status to secure staterooms on the top floor of the ship. Ned could only imagine what their rooms were like if they were large enough to accommodate a sofa. He looked round him. His cabin was small, with a bed with storage beneath it, a washstand, and the dressing table and chair, but little else. Florence looked around too.

"This is very small, isn't it? I'm so sorry Lord Griggs refused to buy you a first-class cabin. It's quite embarrassing."

"It doesn't matter," Ned assured her truthfully. At least he was not in steerage down in the depths of the ship where bunks were separated merely by curtains to offer only a little privacy. "I'm extremely grateful to him for paying for my passage at all. He was under no obligation to do so."

"Yes, but it is rather annoying," Florence said. "I was hoping to be able to continue our lessons as we have a week at sea. With you on this deck and me above, it will make everything so much more problematic. We could meet on the promenade deck to talk and I'm sure I can pay the stewards to look the other way so you can come visiting me."

Ned's plans for the voyage so far had involved not dying of misery or sickness. If he had thought about the remainder of the journey, he might have mentioned feeling well enough to eat, and perhaps recuperating enough to promenade on deck after dark. He made non-committal noises.

Florence pursed her lips. "We'll have to pretend you are someone important travelling in disguise. I shall start a rumour that you are a marquis or earl, or a Member of Parliament."

"I don't think that's such a good idea," Ned said cautiously. The last thing he wanted was anyone beginning to speculate on his identity. He reached for his orange.

"Well, I think it's an excellent idea. That way, when we arrive in New York, everyone will be keen to discover who you are. You will have some history behind you, even if it is only a week old. Father won't even think to question if you are real or not because if he mentions your name, someone will be able to say, 'Ah, yes. That's the fellow who travelled here incognito, jolly good chap' and he'll be convinced."

She had a point. He had boarded the ship under the name Ned Blake. Anyone looking on the passenger lists for

Viscount Telford, the name they had eventually decided upon, would not find anyone of that name.

"Mmm," Ned mumbled. "It's certainly something to ponder. If you will pardon me, however, I think I might need a short nap to allow the broth to do its good work."

"Yes, how insensitive of me." Florence straightened his pillowslip, ridding it of the indentation of Ned's head. Her hand rested in the spot. It was an oddly intimate gesture that made Ned's stomach flutter. She reached out and patted his hand.

"You'll start to feel better soon, I'm sure, and then we can have such fun while we sail. I'm sure you'll love it once you find your sea legs."

She left. Once the steward had removed the tray, Ned climbed back onto his bed. He didn't feel like sleeping but lay with his head on the pillow, reforming the dent Florence had erased and imagining he could still smell the trace of her perfume.

Life on board the *City of Bruges* was wonderfully interesting. Florence had the utmost pity for Cordelia who had not yet left her cabin. Fortunately, Twemlow's constitution was robust so he was able to escort Florence to eat in the magnificent dining room with stained glass lamps, a wide, domed skylight, and chairs which were affixed to the floor but which swivelled to allow the sitter to turn and stand. Florence and Twemlow both agreed that it was an innovation that should be introduced to houses.

Her only disappointment was that Ned and Cordelia were suffering so much, but at least a steward had brought a note from him, thanking Florence for her kind attention and suggesting they meet after lunch for a walk along the promenade deck.

She practically skipped into Cordelia's stateroom. Cordelia was in her customary position on her sofa, a blanket tucked around her to the neck.

"Mr Blake is feeling better. I'm going to suggest a game of quoits this afternoon. Do you think you might revive enough to make a four with Twemlow?"

"I'm not leaving this room until we're safely in New York," Cordelia moaned weakly. She patted the sofa. Florence shuffled onto the end, just about finding space beside Cordelia's stockinged feet.

"You poor thing, you look so grey. Is there anything I can have brought to you? I know Mr Blake revived almost before my eyes when he was eating soup yesterday afternoon."

"I'm content with peppermint tea, milk and rusks, thank you," Cordelia said quickly, her mouth twitching.

"I don't recall you being this ill on the way out," Florence said.

Cordelia winced then to Florence's surprise, she smiled. "I'm not completely sure but I suspect there is an additional reason for my sickness. I might be carrying an extra passenger."

She put her hands to her belly.

"You're with child!" Florence shrieked.

"Shhh! I said I'm not certain. I haven't even told Twemlow, so you must keep it to yourself. In February we thought we were lucky, but it came to nothing."

"Of course I won't speak of it," Florence promised. "How wonderful it would be though. I'll be an aunt and Daddy will be a grandfather."

"He'll be able to brag at being grandfather to an heir apparent. He'll love it," Cordelia said with an eye roll.

Florence took her hand, incensed that Cordelia was probably right. "He'll love it because it will be your baby. So will Twemlow."

"Of course, but it will definitely ease Twemlow's mind if we have a child and he knows his title and estate is in safe hands. These things do matter, however much we pretend they don't. Imagine how awful it would be if everything he has achieved passes to a distant relative."

"I suppose so," Florence said. "At least his ancestors were enlightened enough to allow women to inherit."

She hugged Cordelia. "I won't say anything, but I'll be hoping as hard as I can, and whatever you need, just call for me. Except now I need to go because I'm meeting Mr Blake."

Cordelia waved her off with a wan smile. Florence skipped up to the promenade deck, barely able to contain her excitement.

Ned had a spring in his step too and appeared much more like himself. He was dressed elegantly in a light grey suit with a closely striped, blue waistcoat. He sported a straw boater, a little like the one Florence was wearing.

"Soup must agree with you," she remarked.

He grinned. "I kept the window open and the fresh air has helped me a lot. I must remember that on my return journey."

"Make sure you do. I won't be here to remind you," she answered.

He looked thoughtful. "No. I suppose you will be staying in America if all goes according to plan."

"I suppose I will," Florence agreed. A dash of melancholy took her by surprise. "You could always stay with us in Philadelphia for longer."

Ned gave her look of surprise. "I hardly think your father will want a guest who has been instrumental in deceiving him."

"Oh I'm sure he won't mind," Florence said, waving a hand as if brushing away the concern. "He's bound to see how funny it is once we explain everything. Perhaps you can return on the same crossing as Lord and Lady Griggs so you have some company."

Ned wrinkled his brow. "It was good enough that they took me into their home while we were undertaking this enterprise, but there is no reason why they should wish for me to impose on them any longer once it is over and done with."

"So we shall all go our separate ways," Florence said quietly. "That's too bad."

"Yes. It is."

Ned walked away. He stood with his hands resting on the railings, staring down at the water. Florence joined him. The sea was glossy black with white foam tips. It made her feel slightly unsteady to see the way it surged against the sides of the ship and rolled back.

"It doesn't look entirely real, does it?" she murmured. She reached out for the railings to steady herself, and her left hand brushed against Ned's right. His little finger edged closer to hers then slipped in between so that they were almost holding hands. Over the scent of the salty air, she caught a hint of his cologne and was unnerved by the slight shudder of desire that tickled the length of her spine. She glanced sideways at him and he must have chosen the exact same moment to look at her, because she met his eyes. They stared awkwardly at each other before Ned blinked and looked back at the sea, withdrawing his hands as he did so.

"Shall we go see if the shuffleboard courts are vacant?" Ned asked.

"I think that's a good idea," Florence said, removing her hand and adjusting her gloves.

The atmosphere on the games deck was lively. Groups sat at small tables or in canvas deck chairs, some drinking pots of tea and others having cocktails, even though it was barely three in the afternoon. Florence nodded to a few to whom she had been introduced.

"Life on board ship is very strange. We meet strangers, share dining rooms, bathrooms and play games together for a week and then most likely will never encounter each other again," she mused.

"Perhaps this is what Purgatory will be like," Ned answered. "A sense of lives on hold but with no end to the voyage in sight."

Florence smiled. "There would be worse places to spend eternity than on a ship with every luxury. I'm not in any hurry to be back home."

"You surprise me," Ned said. "I thought you would be glad to be safely out of England and away from the risk of being married. You won't find many peers of the realm in New York."

Florence made a non-committal noise. She might be escaping that worry, but Clayton hadn't called them back without reason. She had no idea what tragedy or scandal would be waiting on her return.

All three shuffleboard courts were busy, but one game looked close to finishing, so they decided to wait. Florence spotted an empty table and they claimed it.

"I think I shall have a cocktail," Florence announced when the white-clad waiter arrived. She studied the menu. "A Sazerac, please."

"Absinthe and whisky in the middle of the afternoon!" Ned remarked.

He ordered a gimlet and they watched the game. Florence drew near to Ned so she could speak confidentially. She indicated towards one of the players: a stout-chested handsome man in his early fifties with an excellent set of whiskers. Florence slid her eyes towards him then back to Ned.

"Now this is interesting. That gentleman is the heir presumptive to a viscountcy. Can you tell me the difference between that and an heir apparent?"

Ned ran a thumb down one of his sideburns. They were not as impressive as the heir presumptive's, but still fine.

"An heir apparent is the heir of the current viscount and is therefore his direct descendant. An heir presumptive will only succeed to the title if the current incumbent has no direct heir. While there is the possibility of a child being born, he is not guaranteed the title."

Florence beamed at him like a proud parent. "Very good. This poor fellow is Mr Colling, the first cousin of the current Viscount Saltburn. Saltburn has four daughters aged between thirty and fifteen but as yet has no son. It's unlikely he will have one now that his wife has reached the change in life; however, that possibility cannot be ignored. She might die. He could remarry a younger wife and she could birth a boy."

"That's a rather tasteless speculation," Ned said darkly.

"Yes. I know," Florence said quietly, feeling suddenly abashed at using the poor man's unfortunate circumstances as a lesson. It was a real person, not a paper doll, whose life was affected. She paused, thinking how fortunate the Griggs were that there was only a fee simple and the sex of Cordelia's child didn't matter.

"Poor man. Imagine living in a state of such uncertainty for that long. Of course, if the viscount's daughters could inherit then the whole matter would have been resolved years ago and he could carry on with his life."

They regarded Mr Colling with interest. The heir presumptive did not appear to be dwelling on his uncertain status as he was laughing and by all appearances enjoying the game. His partner might have had something to do with that. Florence pointed to her discreetly. She was a handsome woman dressed in a black skirt and jacket with a high-necked grey blouse. Rolls of glossy black hair were pinned beneath a large hat with a scarlet ribbon around the brim.

"That woman is a widow named Mrs Carmine. She's been married three times and each husband has been wealthier than the previous one. The first was a captain in the army. The second was an elderly shopkeeper in a small town outside Salem, but by the time he died, he owned an entire department store in Boston. The third was a complete scoundrel by all accounts and nobody cared that he passed away from scarlet fever."

Judging by her scarlet hat ribbon, the wealthy widow was no longer observing deep mourning and appeared to be very much enjoying the company of the heir presumptive. She kept gaily patting his arm and throwing her head back in a tinkling laugh whenever her disc missed a target. Her carefree manner was enviable. The cocktails arrived and Florence sipped hers, making a face at the bitterness. She had better drink it quickly and get it over and done with.

"I wish I could be so carefree when I lose a game," she remarked. "If I missed as many shots as she did, I'm sure I would have thrown the cue overboard. Be warned of that when we finally get our turn."

"I believe she is letting him win on purpose," Ned remarked.

Florence drew her shawl around her shoulders and wrinkled her brow. "How silly that would be. Then she'd have to deliberately lose every game forever. I'm sure she wouldn't do such a thing."

"She might if she has her eye on the title," Ned pointed out.

Florence took another sip of the cocktail, wishing she had asked for a pot of tea. Her head was beginning to feel a little fuzzy.

"I'll admit I don't understand my own sex sometimes. Quite why she would be intent on finding a fourth husband is beyond my comprehension. Widows have a lot more freedom than unmarried women. She is wealthy enough to need no husband to provide for her. In fact, by marrying, she risks losing what she already has. What could another marriage provide that she currently lacks?"

Ned stared at her with an expression of disbelief.

"What did I say?" she demanded.

"Miss Wakechild, it pains me more than I can tell you to realise that you view marriage only as something to be endured. Perhaps she wants love or companionship. Or intimacy." He dropped his head and toyed with his glass.

"Intimacy?"

After one too many glasses of champagne early in the visit, Cordelia had dropped hints to Florence about her husband's ability to miraculously cure her headaches with stimulating massages and Florence had got the impression it had been a body part other than her shoulders which received the attention. Heat rose to Florence's cheeks and neck. The sea was relatively calm, but it felt to Florence like it had swelled and caused the ship to lurch because a feeling greater than nausea passed over her, picked her up and threw her to one side. She gripped the edge of the table, wondering why she was the only one affected.

"Clearly there must be advantages to marriage that I have not properly considered," she replied, not meeting Ned's eyes.

"Miss Wakechild, are you sure you don't want to marry a viscount?" Ned suggested after a moment of silence. "Not necessarily Stuffy Stretford. There are others."

"Stuffy?" Florence almost snorted Sazerac through her nose. "That's so rude and completely inappropriate. You forget yourself, Mr Blake. Why on earth did you call him that?" She couldn't stop herself from laughing, however, and covered her mouth with her hand.

Ned winced. "It's a nickname from his youth."

"Did you know of him back then?" Florence asked. "I didn't think you did."

Ned shook his head firmly. "No, but the nickname followed him into adulthood and gossip has a habit of travelling. Poor chap, it isn't his fault. He suffered dreadful nosebleeds as a youth throughout the summer months and had to stuff his nostrils full of padding. It meant he snored so loudly the entire dormitory was kept awake. Or so I believe," he added. "Schoolboys can be very cruel."

"Imagine having to share a bedroom with him!" Florence exclaimed. "Oh goodness me, that would be insufferable! One would have to draw one's nightgown up as an ear muffler."

Ned was in the process of raising his glass to his lips. He tossed back a larger mouthful of his gimlet than was wise and coughed.

"Oh goodness, I'm sorry. I shouldn't have said that and made you laugh." Florence patted him on the back then rubbed her hand across his shoulder for good measure. His back was broad and the contours of his shoulder blades rolled beneath her palm. She softened her hand so that her touch was more of a stroke than a vigorous rub. "It is funny, though, I—"

"Excuse me, Miss Wakechild, I have to go," Ned said, cutting across Florence in the most abrupt manner.

"Mr Blake, are you alright?" Florence was half out of her seat before he shook his head and motioned for her to sit down. Under any other circumstances, it would be the height of rudeness, but his cheeks had turned red and he looked stricken. Coughing did that to a person, of course.

"I'm feeling at the mercy of the sea once again. I shouldn't have drunk that cocktail. I need to lie down."

"Oh I'm sorry to hear that," Florence said. "Would you like me to accompany you back to your cabin in case you are overcome or get lost?"

Ned raised his brows. "I'm sure I will be able to find my way back to my cabin."

"Will you come back for afternoon tea? Or perhaps join us for dinner?"

His jaw tightened and he swallowed. "I don't know. It's probably best to assume I won't. Good afternoon."

"I shall send Dottie to carry any messages tomorrow," Florence called after him.

He nodded, and walked away stiffly, his gait suggesting he was suffering an attack of nausea. The sea was calm, so she didn't completely believe he was afflicted by seasickness. Something had upset him but she had no idea what. She searched back through the conversation, certain it must have been something she said; however, she was unable to fix on anything. Perhaps she was wrong and it was simply the combination of cocktail and the sea.

She sat back in her chair and watched the widow and her willing quarry, wishing she might be so daring. Her mind filled with speculation about what intimate acts could convince a woman to tie herself to a man, and more importantly, how she would go about experiencing them for herself.

She finished her cocktail thoughtfully then put her empty glass down beside Ned's. There was about a quarter left in the bottom of his, along with one solitary ice cube that had not yet surrendered to the inevitable. Florence dipped a fingertip in and licked it. Lime juice made her tongue spasm. The drink was even more potent and sour than hers had been, but it was delicious. No one was watching so she finished it, then looked at the glass thoughtfully. The mark of her lips overlapped the one Ned had left. A feeling of butterflies filled her stomach.

She stifled a giggle that bubbled up inside her and she walked with determination towards the stairwell. An unfamiliar gentleman, accompanied by his valet, drew aside to let her pass and she thanked them absentmindedly. She was feeling uncharacteristically reckless and should definitely go for a nap until the effects of the cocktails wore off, but as she walked along the deck, humming beneath her breath, it was not her cabin she was heading towards, but Ned's.

Chapter Sixteen

When he reached his cabin, Ned lowered himself into the chair and put his head in his hands. His stomach was churning, though it was nothing to do with the cocktail or the sea.

It had been bad enough tearing into the life of the heir presumptive. Worse had followed as the conversation had turned to matters of sex. Why on earth had he brought Stretford into the conversation and linked him in Florence's mind with lovemaking?

Florence in bed with Stretford was not an image Ned wanted in the slightest. He didn't really want to think of Florence in bed or in the arms, or even in the company, of any man. The only man he could bear to think of her with was himself. He was absolutely thunderstruck at the realisation. He wanted her.

Badly.

He remembered how every part of his body had felt

when they had danced together. He wanted to do that again and more. Listening to her casually talk about raising her nightgown, while at the same time stroking his back, had been almost enough to tip him over the edge into a whirlpool of lust.

He felt unaccountably, intensely angry that Florence viewed marriage as only something to be endured while she was used as a way of increasing her father's standing. Why did the world insist on women remaining ignorant? Delicacy clearly forbade him from suggesting Florence speak with her sister, but given how affectionate and easy Lord and Lady Griggs were with each other in public, it was fair to speculate that their marital life was likely to be highly fulfilling.

A soft knock at his door brought him out of the pit of self-pity he was descending into. He opened it, expecting to see a steward but Florence was standing there. She looked apprehensive. His heart swelled at the thought that she cared enough to see how he was. He smiled.

"Florence. You didn't need to come check on me. I'm fine."

"I didn't." She glanced up and down the passageway. "That is, I hope you are feeling better, but I didn't come here for that reason. Ned, I want you to do something for me."

He spread his hands wide. "Anything."

"I want you to kiss me."

His stomach plummeted. "Anything but that."

"Why not? I'm not so repulsive, am I?" Florence asked. Her face creased and the sight caused Ned actual pain at the thought that he had given her reason to question herself.

"Good grief, not at all. Far from it. Any red-blooded man would leap at the opportunity. Florence, I don't think you understand what you're asking but you need to go."

She ignored him and stepped into the doorway, preventing him from closing it. "Aren't you red-blooded?"

Desire raked nails down Ned's belly. His hands, still spread, closed into fists and he shoved them into his pockets.

"Very much so, but I'm also a man of honour and I intend to remain one. I am concerned about this sudden decision. The cocktail must have affected your sense of restraint."

She raised her head and stared at him with defiance. Her pupils were enlarged, turning her eyes into polished black orbs.

"Well, what if it has?" she cried. "Maybe I should drink them every day."

"Shhh!" Ned drew her inside the room fully and shut the door. It was the wrong thing to do but the alternative was putting her out in the passageway and risking her being seen or heard.

"I want to know why the widow would marry four times," she said in a loud whisper. "I want to feel some excitement."

She clasped her hands to her chest. Ned could almost hear the heart beating beneath her ribs but realised it was his own, the pulse pounding through his ears. The urgent need wasn't only there, but also in his belly and groin and the sight of Florence's bosom lifted by her hands did nothing to diminish it.

Her eyes grew even wider if that was possible and she turned them on him in appeal. "I may never be kissed by someone I like and who likes me. I want a memory to console myself with if I don't get it in my marriage."

Ned folded his arms across his body. "I can't imagine your future husband would be happy knowing you've asked me this. Even less if I actually obliged."

She pouted. "I don't care about my future husband. And nor should you."

Their eyes met and Ned saw desire staring back at him. Naked and honest, it cut through his endurance, and he could feel himself beginning to fold.

"I thought you intended never to marry," he said, clutching at anything to divert her attention from demanding a kiss. "You disapprove of it."

She made a scoffing sound, turned away, and walked to his desk. Ned had a glimmer of hope that he'd succeeded in putting her off, but she turned back with a pencil in her hand, pointing it at him and gesticulating as if he was a schoolboy and she the teacher.

"I disapprove of being used as a commodity. Men don't have that pressure," she said smugly.

"Is that what you think?" Despite himself, Ned couldn't stop the retort bursting out. Why did she always assume she was right?

"Well, isn't it?" Florence rolled her eyes. "That's a man's

answer. You can choose who you ask. All we can do is hope you will or pray that you won't choose us."

Ouch!

"Do you assume that all the viscounts and dukes you are so keen to avoid marrying are desperate to marry you?" Ned snapped.

"Oh!" She blinked and her lips turned down. "Well, there's no need to insult me."

Great steaming bull's turds! Hearing the insult as she would have, Ned winced inwardly, unable to believe the blunder he'd just made.

"I don't mean that at all!" He walked to her. "Imagine being the owner of property that has been in your family for centuries. That has tenants and trade relying on you for their survival. Imagine you have tried everything you can, short of selling off the furniture, to keep it going but the taxes are increasing and the farms don't produce what they used to. Then a wealthy American upstart appears with his gaudily-dressed, outspoken daughter and offers you the girl along with enough money to secure the land and safeguard the welfare of your tenants for at least the next sixty or seventy years."

He stopped for breath, wondering where the words had come from.

"How much obligation do you think you would feel under? How many marriages do you think have been thrust upon sons by their fathers?"

Florence had listened to the tirade open mouthed. The spots high upon her cheeks began to pulse pink, which Ned knew from experience meant she was offended. There was a delicate balance between diverting her attention and causing her to be upset.

"Gaudy and outspoken? Is that really what you think of me? The waistcoat you were wearing when we first met was the most horrible item I've ever seen in all my days! I hope you burned it before leaving Liverpool."

Ned burst out laughing. He hadn't drunk his entire cocktail, but he was feeling exhilarated and a little lightheaded.

"What is so funny?" Florence demanded.

"You," Ned said, trying his best to keep a sober expression. "You're so wonderful when you are indignant."

"Oh go back to your own cabin and … and … oh, I don't know! Practise using a mustard ladle or something!"

This only served to send Ned into further spasms of laughter. "This is my cabin."

"Stop laughing at me," Florence demanded. "You are making me so mad! Why aren't you taking me seriously?"

"Oh I am," Ned assured her, though it was hard to do. "You're too delightful. I've never seen you so passionate. I didn't know you had it in you!"

"I'm not passionate, I'm furious!" Florence swept her hand over her brow, slightly dislodging the straw hat. A carefully pinned lock of hair came loose. Ned's hand twitched to slip it back into place. His pulse was racing. The cabin was too cramped for this. He was too aware of Florence's perfume, the lingering scent of aniseed, and the heat of their bodies.

"It's good to see you have this coin in your purse. Keep it safe and spend it wisely and sparingly," he said quietly.

Her eyes were burning. "Why?"

He swallowed. "Because it makes you the most attractive woman I've ever encountered and if you use it wisely you could achieve great things. If you use it inadvisably, then men will either fall at your feet or forget propriety and kiss you whether you want it or not."

"You're making that up!" she said, giving him a look that sent his blood rushing.

"Not at all. Why if I wasn't trying so hard not to, I'd be kissing you right now!"

He snapped off the words, stepping back against the bunk and wishing he could turn back the clock and unsay them. His heart was hammering in his chest and he realised that he'd walked straight into a trap.

"I don't believe you." Florence licked her lips and smiled triumphantly. "Prove it."

"Don't play games with me," Ned said.

He walked past her, heading for the door to open it and see her out.

"I'm not playing games with you," she said.

Her mouth contorted with misery. Her eyes became pools of longing. It would be so easy to grant her wish and kiss her. Just one step forward and she'd be within the reach of his lips.

He shook his head sadly. "Florence, I think what you really need is a glass of water and possibly an hour sleeping. I don't know what brought this on, but if I did what you ask me, we'd both regret it."

Not as much as he was going to regret not doing it.

She dropped her gaze, giving a little shake her head.

"I think you're right. The closer I get to America, the less I feel like myself. I didn't tell you why my father has summoned us back, did I?"

"No? Do you want to tell me why?" Ned's curiosity piqued.

She looked doubtful, drawing the corner of her bottom lip in with her teeth.

"Talking about problems can help lessen them," Ned said. "Why don't we go for a walk along the lower deck where it will be quieter and you can tell me all about it."

He held an arm out and after a brief hesitation, Florence slipped hers into the crook. With relief, Ned escorted her on deck. He'd really believed for a while that he would have to force her bodily from his cabin. They walked to the stern of the boat. No one else was there, being a covered area and shaded.

"Father wants us home because there is some sort of emergency. I don't know what it is and as I get closer to finding out, the more nervous I feel. It's horrible knowing that something is affecting my life without me being able to do anything about it. I hate feeling helpless."

Ned swallowed, his mouth unexpectedly growing dry. He'd been thinking the same thing earlier. "That's understandable. Anyone would feel the same."

She dipped her head slightly. The brim of her bonnet

tilted so that her eyes were hidden but the tension in her neck and jaw was clear for Ned to see.

"I wonder whether fate led our paths to cross not so that you could masquerade as a viscount but so that you can help me sort out whatever problem my brother has got himself into."

"Your brother? So you do know something?"

"I don't know but I suspect," Florence said darkly. "The rest of us have been in England so I know we're all fine. It could be something to do with the business, but I don't think Daddy would need us all home. So I imagine it's my brother."

She dropped Ned's arm and leaned back against the railings. They were waist height and there was a deck below, but Ned's muscles tensed at the thought that she might plummet backwards. He stood beside her, ready to tug her into his arms if she looked like she might slip. Florence looked up at Ned.

"Be thankful you don't have one. They are more trouble than they are worth."

"What makes you say I have no brother?" he asked, all the nerves in his body standing to attention.

"I just assumed that you didn't, I suppose. Do you?"

Ned turned so that he was looking over the railings onto the deck below. He had walked into this snare without realising, most probably without Florence even realising she was setting one. What did it matter now if he told her a little of his past? He drew in a deep breath and let it out slowly.

"I am the youngest son of four, though only the second to survive infancy. My only remaining brother was my elder by ten years. We quarrelled bitterly for most of our lives. He always disapproved of me. He thought that a good thrashing would see me mend my nature and encouraged my father to beat me on every occasion he could. It didn't work, of course, but the thrashings I endured for the most minor of indiscretions gave me a hatred of seeing unnecessary aggression. That's why I went for Carver Clarke the way I did."

Florence gripped his forearm. "You have no need to justify that. I have taken issue with many of the things you have done, but taking care of Alfie is not one of them. That brute deserved everything and more."

Her sense of outrage swelled his heart. It was obvious that she really cared for Alfie's welfare even though he was a stranger to her, and was of a different race and a lower class. A woman with such a heart was rare and valuable.

"As soon as our father started to fall ill, we knew that eventually we would go our separate ways. On the day following the funeral, I walked out of the house and have not returned since. I am sure I could have entered a profession that Jasper would approve of, and tried to mend the rift, but I didn't want to. If I'm being completely honest, I chose the life I chose knowing he would hate hearing reports of what I was doing. A secret part of me always hoped he would find himself in need of my help, but he never did."

He waited for her to call him petty or vindictive, or any

of the names other members of the family had called him, but she rested her hand on his arm and turned her face to his, her eyes packed with sorrow.

"I'm sorry your brother was so cruel to you. Perhaps one day you'll reconcile."

Ned swallowed, whether from the gentle pressure of her hand on his sleeve or the words, he wasn't quite sure. "That's not going to happen."

"But it could. Don't give up hope."

"It's not a matter of hope." Ned heard the crack in his voice. He gripped the railing with both hands. "My brother died some months ago. I am afraid there is no reconciliation."

Florence didn't speak. She simply slid her hand along his arm until she reached his fist, coiled tightly around the railing. She covered it with hers and held it there until he felt the tension in his fingers loosen. Unconsciously, he leaned in towards her, only realising when she did the same that their upper arms were touching. It would be so easy to slip an arm around her waist. So easy to draw her head onto his shoulder. So easy to kiss her…

A lump began to form in Ned's throat.

"If you discover that you do need my services with regard to your brother, they are at your disposal," Ned said quietly. "Though I imagine you would need to decide which role you would like me to take, as I doubt very much I could pretend to be a viscount and then enter a gambling den to retrieve your family heirlooms."

Florence smiled. "We don't have any family heirlooms worth gambling. That's Daddy's whole point. No jewels."

Her humour and rationality had returned and though their conversation had been about dark matters, Ned felt unburdened.

"Miss Wakechild, you are your father's greatest jewel," he said quietly.

It was a dreadful cliche, but her lips curved into a smile. He did the thing he had sworn he wasn't going to do and kissed her.

It was quick, his lips just grazing hers, but it lit a furnace inside him. It was over in seconds and left him wanting more. He looked down at her, his heart thumping.

She put her hand to his lips.

"Mr Blake…" she began.

She never finished the sentence, because the touch of her fingers on his already sensitive lips was irresistible. He drew her close and kissed her again, more thoroughly. She gave a little moan in the back of her throat which sent Ned's senses spinning. She melted into his arms and he held her tightly, wanting to sear the moment into his memory forever. They stood like that for what seemed like an eternity, until Ned finally broke the kiss and looked into her eyes. He could feel his heart pounding in his chest.

"I thought you weren't going to kiss me," Florence murmured in a husky voice.

Ned smiled, his lips still throbbing from the touch of hers.

"I wasn't going to kiss you in the state you were in. That

would have been for the wrong reasons. This is because I feel close to you and I wanted to. Remember, when you find a husband, that intimacy is more than physical," he said softly, caressing her cheek with his thumb.

"Let me take you back to your cabin. Escort you there, I mean," he clarified hurriedly in case she thought he was intending to enter it with her. He offered his arm again and she took it. They walked in silence to the first-class cabins. His heart and stomach pulsated whenever Florence's arm brushed against his or her perfume wafted to his nostrils.

At her door, Florence gave Ned's hand a gentle squeeze.

"Thank you," she murmured. "For everything you've done, and what you didn't do. I hope I will see you tomorrow. I'll send Dottie with a message."

She closed the door. Ned took a shuddering breath and filled his lungs before they exploded.

Electricity.

The word leapt to his mind. He had no idea how it worked—few did—but he understood it was invisible to the eye yet still gave heat and light. It came from burning coal, but as Ned floated back to his own cabin in a trance, he could well believe that an undiscovered source was desire.

Chapter Seventeen

Dottie arrived at Ned's door a little after ten the following morning bearing a note. Ned had eaten a breakfast of fried kidneys, two boiled eggs, and toast, and drunk two cups of strong tea, so was feeling considerably heartier than any morning previously. His mood sank when he read the note Florence had written.

It was disappointingly brief, apologising for a headache and suggesting they delay any meeting until the late afternoon, then take a brief stroll around the deck or have tea in the saloon.

His jaw clenched. Yesterday's kiss had been a mistake. She'd realised it and now she wanted to keep her distance from him. He was sure of one thing: he wanted to see her again as soon as possible, but clearly she felt otherwise. He'd had no expectation that she wouldn't regret what had passed between them the instant the cocktail left her system, but seeing her words in black and white sent a poisoned dart into his heart.

He scribbled a few lines in reply, informing her that his seasickness had returned and agreeing to the suggestion of delaying until they both felt better. He curbed his urge to write a full page expressing his wishes for her health and much more. He sealed the letter, hoping in vain that she would somehow divine his deep feelings for her, while also fearing it.

He turned his attention to Dottie. Her nose was red and her eyes swollen. She had clearly been crying and was doing her best to suppress it.

"What's wrong, Dottie?" he asked as he handed her the note. "Are you in trouble?"

"Sir! I'm a good girl!" Despite her misery, her eyes shot wide and she stood straighter.

"I don't mean that sort of trouble," Ned clarified hastily. "Though of course if you were, I wouldn't judge you. You wouldn't be the first girl caught out and you certainly won't be the last. Is it to do with your young man or something else?"

"How do you know I've got a young man?" Dottie asked.

She clamped her mouth shut, realising her answer was an admission in itself. Ned smiled encouragingly and she wrinkled her brow.

"He's called Mr Agosti. He's an Italian valet to an English gentleman. I met him on the first evening. He's got lovely brown eyes and such a nice accent. A couple of days ago I gave him something to look after and he has lost it, and whenever I ask him to look, he brushes me off," Dottie said plaintively.

"Is it something valuable?"

"Only to me. Just a brooch but I like it and I don't have very many nice things."

Dottie sniffed and dabbed her eyes with her sleeve.

"Take my handkerchief," Ned offered, indicating the fresh one on the nightstand. "Have you spoken to Miss Wakechild? I'm sure she'll be sympathetic to your predicament."

"She would but that makes it even worse. She advised me that he seemed a bit shifty, but I didn't listen." She blew her nose on the handkerchief.

"You keep that until you're done," Ned said, glancing at it before she could hand it back. "Let me see if I can do something to help sort the matter. You pop along and go about your duties and I'll have a little chat with your young man. Mr Agosti, did you say his name was?"

"That's right. If you can persuade him to spend a few moments looking for it, I would really be most grateful. Thank you, sir."

Dottie left the room slightly happier. Ned took himself off for a walk to the lower deck. At this time of day, most personal servants had an hour of freedom while their employers socialised. He found Mr Agosti easily: a handsome man with soulful eyes, pomaded hair, and an anchor beard. He was sitting at a card table in the servants' saloon engrossed in a game with two other men.

Ned stood by the door and watched him for a few minutes. He was winning and looked to be playing mercilessly. A risky player, well off enough to lose without suffering hardship, Ned surmised.

Sometimes Ned preferred to play a long game and let the subjects come round naturally to the point at which they had no choice but to do what Ned wanted, but today he was full of pent-up frustration that was crying to be released. He wasn't in the mood for subtleties so he walked straight up to Mr Agosti with a smile on his face.

"I believe you have been playing fast and loose with a young lady I know. Miss Evans?"

"Beautiful Dorotea? With her I play slow and tight." Agosti laughed, then scowled. "What is it to you?"

"She works for Miss Wakechild. Miss Evans is distressed; therefore Miss Wakechild might become vexed. And if she becomes vexed, then I surely will."

"And why should I care if any of you do?" Agosti said, leaning back and flipping a card over.

The tendons in Ned's neck grew taut. "Because when I am vexed, I find it hard to sleep so I look around for someone to take my displeasure out on. As I know you are the instrument of that, naturally you will be my victim."

Agosti paled slightly.

"Why don't we bring matters to a quick conclusion. Give me back the brooch Miss Evans gave to you."

"If she wants it, she just has to take a quick trip to my cabin and retrieve it," Agosti said, spreading his hands out, palms up.

Ned's hackles rose. Dottie would be safer walking into a room full of wasps while covered in jam. He reached out before Mr Agosti could react, seized him by the lapels of his jacket, and pulled him to his feet. He had intended to just retrieve the brooch, but now he decided that wasn't enough and Mr Agosti should be squeezed for every penny he had.

"I could take you out with one blow if I choose to." He let go when the valet's eyes filled with fear. "But right now, I don't have the inclination to scuff my knuckles. Why don't we play for it? I have the rest of the day free. The brooch as your stake and five pounds as mine."

"It isn't worth that," Agosti scoffed.

"It is to Miss Evans," Ned said.

"So to Miss Wakechild and therefore to you," Agosti sneered, raising an eyebrow.

Ned didn't bother correcting the assumption. It would have been better that he hadn't invoked Florence at all, but it was too late for that. Now he had to concentrate on winning. He sat down and reached for the deck of cards.

"Gentlemen, who is in?" he asked.

He couldn't spend the day with Florence as he wished, so parting this arrogant fool from his money would be the next best thing.

It had come as something of a relief to Florence when Dottie had returned with a reply from Ned suggesting they did not set a time until she was feeling better – so why she had flung herself onto her bunk with a temper was something she couldn't understand.

She'd scandalised herself with what she had asked Ned to do. She felt embarrassed and ashamed for suggesting something so outrageous. She had never expected Ned to agree, but his honourable refusal to do it made her feel even worse about the situation. She swallowed, remembering his explanation of why the time had been right when he had finally kissed her. He'd been so kind and such a gentleman when she had been shamelessly uninhibited.

She was still dwelling on Ned's absence the following morning. She'd almost poured her coffee into the milk jug instead of her cup and dropped an earring into her pot of cold cream. Dottie had to ask her twice whether she wanted the pearl-tipped hairpins or the blue enamel comb shaped like a butterfly to go with her dress for the Captain's Dinner on the final night of the crossing.

She barely cared, if she was being honest. The dinner was for first-class passengers only and would be a glamorous affair. She would rather have spent the evening sitting quietly alone, or with her family. Or with Ned.

At least Dottie seemed happier than she had done for a while. Since the second morning, she had been drooping and looked like she was crying most of the day, even though she denied it vigorously. Florence assumed she was having a bad time of the month, but now she seemed happier. Her nose was no longer red and she was wearing her pretty cameo brooch at her neck.

Florence didn't insist on her maid wearing an apron or

cap. It made her look too much like the parlourmaid. As far as Florence was concerned, if Dottie was smartly turned out, she could wear a dress of whatever colour she chose as well as a discreet item of jewellery.

"I'm sorry, Dottie. I'm being far too indecisive," she said. She forced her mind onto the outfit, eventually making a decision and pointing to the comb.

"It's good to see you looking happy again. Between my sister and Mr Blake both confining themselves to their cabins for much of the time, it hasn't been a particularly fun voyage."

She stared out of the window.

"Would you like me to take a note to Mr Blake today?" Dottie asked.

Florence avoided Dottie's eyes in the mirror. She hadn't seen Ned since their kiss, and in her mind it had grown to something of far more significance than it should warrant. He had probably forgotten it already and she was avoiding him for no reason. He must have experienced a hundred better kisses.

A thousand.

She closed her eyes, feeling butterflies in her stomach. The warmth of his lips against hers had ignited something inside of her that she had never experienced before—an intense passion that had consumed every inch of her being and left no room for doubt or fear. She hadn't wanted to stop. She wanted to do it again and at the same time she never wanted to do it again in case she found it too irresistible. It was hopeless to imagine a future in which they could be together, but when she had laid her head on the pillow the night before, she'd been beset by dreams of being Mrs Blake and living in a small house somewhere quiet within reach of Cordelia's home.

She realised Dottie was still waiting for an answer to her question.

"No, I think not," she decided. "Perhaps after lunch I shall feel differently but not for now. I will let Mr Blake recover in peace. You may have the next hour to yourself. I'm sure you have things you would like to be doing. If I want you, I will ring down to the servant's saloon."

"Thank you, Miss."

Dottie skipped off. Florence picked up a pot of beeswax and began massaging it into her fingernails. She suspected Dottie had found a young man to spend some time with. It would be nice if Dottie could find somebody to walk out with, although on balance, that would be no good for Florence if Dottie married and left her. Something scratched against her thumb and she realised she had a hangnail. Tutting in annoyance, she looked for her nail file but couldn't find it. She knew Dottie always kept a pair of scissors in the sewing box so opened the box to get them. Her eye fell on something.

A monogrammed handkerchief, neatly folded. She recognised it at once. It belonged to Ned. Florence drew it out, wondering why it was in the sewing box. She held it out and inspected it. It was not torn, and the embroidered monogram did not need touching up, so why did Dottie have it in her possession? She tried to put it out of her mind but could not ignore the horrible suspicion that the young man Dottie was interested in was Ned.

Was that why Dottie had been so keen to take a note?

The thought made her feel sick. It wasn't fair. Why did Dottie think she might aim as high as a viscount?

Because Ned Blake was not an aristocrat of course.

Ned Blake was just a man who was pretending to be one, and Dottie knew that. He was a working man who would be the perfect match for a personal maid. She scrunched the handkerchief tighter.

Florence knew she had no right to interfere in either Dottie or Ned's affairs but she would have no peace until she knew the truth of their feelings towards each other. She wrote a note on the back of a card asking him to join her in her stateroom between the visiting hours of three and four.

At three o'clock prompt, there was a knock on the door. She opened it to see Ned waiting. His eyes widened slightly at seeing her answering the door herself. Presumably he was expecting Dottie to open it. Presumably he was disappointed.

Her stateroom was not as grand as Cordelia's or Twemlow's but she had two comfortable armchairs and a small table. Her book was propped open over the arm of one of her chairs to keep her place, so Ned took the other chair. She noticed his eye slid towards the table. She hadn't ordered any refreshments, nor did she intend to. He placed his hands in his lap.

"This feels like the morning you gave me a dressing down for fighting. Am I in disgrace?"

"Should you be?" Florence asked.

She hated it when people didn't play straight with her so pressed on. "Are you in love with Dottie?"

The look of surprise on his face could not have been anything other than genuine.

"No, I'm not in love with Dottie."

She couldn't explain the relief that flooded through her at his answer, though it was immediately supplanted by a worse thought. "Are you toying with her affections?"

"I'm not toying with anything," Ned said, holding a hand up. "I don't know where this idea has suddenly come from, but it is completely unfounded."

"Is it?" She took his handkerchief out of her bag and passed it to him with a flourish that no magician producing a rabbit could hope to replicate. "Did you give her this?"

"Yes, I did." He held the handkerchief up and examined it. "I see she has not had time to wash it," he remarked in a tone that was completely out of place given the severity of the situation.

"I don't care whether she has laundered it. Why has she got your handkerchief?" Florence snapped. "I knew as soon as I saw it that something must be going on that I didn't know about and I was right."

Ned gave a long-suffering sigh. "I gave it to her because she was crying and I couldn't stand the sight of her sniffing and using her cuff to mop at her eyes."

"Why was she crying?" Florence asked. "What did you do to her?"

Ned rose from his chair. "Miss Wakechild, you are

beginning to offend me! Firstly, you accuse me of toying with Dottie's affections and now you accuse me of making her cry. I did neither."

He began to pace around the cabin. There wasn't really room and he was unable to take long strides. It gave Florence the impression of a big cat kept in a too-small cage at the zoo. He turned and faced her.

"When Dottie came to my room to bring your note she was crying. I gave her a handkerchief. She was anxious about something and I was in the position to resolve it."

"What did you do?" Florence asked suspiciously. Even though she was relieved that her initial suspicions were wrong, she felt put out that Dottie had not come to her for help. What could he do that Florence couldn't?

"I'm not really sure that's any of your business," Ned said stiffly. "You know what importance I set by confidentiality."

She couldn't deny it. "Dottie is my maid. If there is trouble, I should know about it."

"Then I suggest you ask her," Ned said. "Though perhaps don't begin by accusing her of conducting a romance with me."

They stared at each other, tension simmering in the air between them. Ned straightened his collar. "Excuse me, Miss Wakechild. I think I shall take my leave."

Without waiting for her response, he left the room. Florence threw herself back onto her armchair and groaned aloud. What a fool she had made of herself. She had been too quick to jump to conclusions.

Now Ned was rightfully angry.

And annoyingly right.

She should have asked Dottie directly and tried to understand the situation better before accusing Ned of something terrible. She broached the subject the following morning while Dottie was putting the finishing touches to Florence's hair.

"You've been worried since coming on board, I know, and yesterday Mr Blake told me he had to help you. If you're in trouble I want to help too."

Dottie looked mortified. "Mr Blake was such a gentleman. He said he wouldn't tell you."

"He didn't," Florence said hastily. "I found his handkerchief in the sewing basket and asked him why you had it. He still wouldn't tell me anything."

Dottie looked uncertain, so Florence nodded encouragingly.

"I promise there's nothing to be worried about. I won't judge you. You know I try to be fair."

Dottie's lip wobbled. "I did something really foolish. You see I have a brooch that my great aunt Dolly left me in her will. I didn't think it was worth much but then I got talking to one of the valets of a gentleman in second class and he told me it was worth quite a bit and he could get it valued for me, and so I gave it to him, but then he denied all knowledge. Mr Blake found me crying and I didn't want to tell him, honestly, miss, but he has a way about him that just invites you to share confidences, doesn't he?"

The words were a jumble and afterwards Dottie heaved

a sigh of relief, or perhaps it was just to refill her lungs after talking without inhaling for so long.

"Yes, he does," Florence said thoughtfully.

"I don't know what Mr Blake said to him because, lo and behold, he brought it straight back to me yesterday morning and apologised for ever bothering me. Mr Agosti, I mean, not Mr Blake."

"I see." Florence very much did, filing away the miscreant's name in case she needed to take further retribution on Dottie's behalf. She doubted she would need to if Ned had become involved, and she also doubted the brooch had been given straight back willingly. Carver Clarke's ruined face swam before her eyes.

"And you have no idea what Mr Blake said to him? Or did?" she added as an afterthought.

Dottie looked worried. "Did I do the wrong thing? I wasn't going to mention it at all. Mr Blake asked me so nicely, as if he really cared why I was upset, and I didn't want to refuse to speak to him."

"You did nothing wrong in telling him," Florence said quietly. She had made a huge error in her assumptions and how she had handled them. The back of her neck was starting to prickle with embarrassment. Ned had been playing the knight in shining armour for Dottie. She realised she was clenching her jaw and made an effort to loosen it. There was no reason why he shouldn't, but all the same it rankled slightly to think that while she had believed him laid low with seasickness, he had been doing…

Well, that was the trouble, wasn't it. She had no idea

what exactly he had done to retrieve Dottie's brooch. She needed to get to the bottom of the matter, and the sooner the better.

She patted Dottie's hand.

"Dottie, in future don't give away anything important to somebody you have barely met." She bit the inside of her lip. "And make sure you always have your own handkerchief."

"Yes, Miss." Dottie curtsied.

"I think I'll go for a stroll on deck. Please can you fetch my hat and the cape edged with rabbit fur," Florence asked.

Once she was dressed for the breeze, Florence left Dottie casting her expert eyes over the green dress. She did go for a stroll but instead of making her way to the deck, she descended a floor and made her way straight to Ned's cabin.

Chapter Eighteen

"Miss Wakechild, good morning."

Ned didn't look too pleased to see Florence after their quarrel the previous day and the first stirrings of doubt flustered her. His ire had been entirely justified, given what she had accused him of. She was aware that she owed him an apology for her accusation, but that could wait until later. She would reserve her judgement until she had discovered exactly how he had retrieved Dottie's brooch.

He opened the door a little further and gestured down at himself.

"I'm afraid you've surprised me in a state of undress. Please give me a few moments to make myself presentable."

He was dressed in shirtsleeves, with his waistcoat open, as were the top two buttons of his shirt. She couldn't stop looking at the hollow of his throat, which was usually concealed beneath the high collar and necktie, and the curvature of his clavicle. He was unshaven and somehow the stubble that covered his cheeks and chin only made him look more attractive.

She realized that she had been staring for too long, so quickly averted her gaze to the floor. She felt embarrassed by her own reaction, but Ned seemed oblivious to it.

"Don't worry about that," she said briskly, walking into the room. "I need to speak to you now. I don't care what state you're in."

"What did you need to talk about?" he asked, his voice gruff.

"Are you feeling ill again?" She narrowed her eyes. "Or have you been engaging in another fight?"

"Excuse me?" Ned blinked and took a step back. His mouth twisted. "I thought you might have come to apologise for your accusations, but I see I was wrong. You're here with more unfounded accusations."

"I asked Dottie what happened like you suggested," she said sharply. "She told me that you had been assisting her in retrieving her brooch."

"That's right."

"How did you manage it?"

Ned folded his arms. "Does that matter? Dottie has her brooch back and the man in question will think again before he tries to take advantage of young women."

"I want to know." Florence was close to stamping her foot in frustration but fortunately she had enough self-possession left to resist.

"I engaged him at cards. Nothing I haven't done before. I beat him." Ned smirked, causing Florence's blood to thrum through her veins with irritation. She remembered tales he had told her about his previous exploits.

"Did you cheat?"

He raised his brows.

"No, I know you didn't. I retract that. I'm sorry," she said hastily.

"I didn't need to. He wasn't expecting an upright gentleman traveller to be able to spot when he was about to overbid, or be able to bluff so convincingly."

The smirk deepened. It made him look rakish and defiant and very handsome, which was no help at all in quelling Florence's temper.

"Mr Blake, I did not train you so that you could go and swindle people."

"But that's exactly what you did," Ned said calmly.

"No, I didn't." Florence thrust her hands onto her hips, outraged.

"You can't even see it, can you?" Ned shook his head. "You want me to dupe your father into believing I'm something I'm not. What makes that different from what I did with Agosti?"

"Because that was just something you did for your own ends to win at gambling," Florence said indignantly. She almost preferred the thought that he had been in an illicit romance with Dottie to the knowledge that he had been tricking people out of their wages.

"Whereas I'm deceiving your father for honourable reasons?" Ned sneered.

"Yes! No!" Florence took a deep breath. The

conversation was not going in the direction she had expected and she felt like she was floundering in water that was growing ever deeper.

"I mean, it's not the same thing at all. No one is going to be hurt. We're making sure of that."

Ned sniffed. "No one was hurt yesterday. I cleaned the man out, but after hinting at what his intentions were towards Dottie, he deserved to be humiliated so I think I was very restrained."

He ran a hand through his hair before giving Florence a smile that radiated cunning.

"You never told me I had to leave my tools in the box until you allowed me to get them out and use them. Who can blame me for putting them to use when I saw the opportunity?"

Florence sat on the chair at the dressing table. Ned's eyes never left hers. It made her feel uncomfortable to be so scrutinised, but she was determined not to show it. She stared up at him boldly.

"Is that what you plan to do once we part? Get into games with higher stakes and go back to what you were doing before?"

"I don't know. What did you envisage me doing?" Ned leaned against the wall and folded his arms again. "You teach me airs and graces, how to behave, and dress me like a paper doll, then once you've proven your point, you send me back to carry on doing what I was before? Or will you give me a job as a stable boy like Alfie? You'll help me to 'better myself', but then what?"

Florence frowned. "A stable boy! Don't be absurd. You will be able to move in different circles. More doors will open to you. You won't have to be making a living gambling in grimy whorehouses anymore. You won't have to be following girls around to spy for their fathers. You can be respectable."

"Respectable!" Ned spat out a bitter laugh. "You mean conform to the rules that you're asking me to break?"

He made a bow, twirling his hand in an elaborate, mocking flourish that struck her as deeply as a physical slap.

"Shall I get a nice, respectable job in a bank, advising men like Mr Agosti how to best invest the savings they have embezzled from unsuspecting women? Or would you have me become a head waiter at the sort of restaurant you and your elegant, newly rich acquaintances might beg to get a table at?"

Florence's stomach plummeted on hearing the bitterness in his voice. She didn't want Ned to do any of those things, and even though they were all admirable, his tone made them sound like something debased.

"Perhaps I shall open a school and train people to be counterfeit noblemen," he said airily. He smiled at Florence and ran his hands through his hair, giving it a few quick ruffles as he preened.

"I could call it the Wakechild Method."

"You wouldn't dare!" Florence took a step towards him, on the verge of exploding like a firecracker.

Ned laughed, though Florence couldn't detect much humour in it.

"Why wouldn't I? After all, you cannot be the only woman who needs to pretend she has aristocratic associations. I've been an excellent pupil and I'm sure I could be an equally good teacher. Or why create unnecessary competition? Perhaps I shall embark on that myself."

"But it's fraud," Florence snapped. The thought of him using his considerable talents and charms in the service of other women was unbearable. "You could get into a lot of trouble."

"Yes, I believe we discussed that matter a few weeks ago when we started this little escapade. Admittedly, it's warming to know you care what happens to me once we've finished our association."

Of course she did, and the thought that Ned doubted it was dreadful, but even more dreadful were the implications of admitting such a thing to him.

"Why do you assume I care at all?" she snapped.

Ned took a step towards her. His eyes burned. "Because you wouldn't be here demanding answers of me if you didn't, would you?"

Her heart urged her to tell him that she did, very much, but she held her ground.

"That doesn't mean I care about you. It just means that I want to know the truth. In fact, I don't really care right now."

She was beginning to shake and could feel tears rising to

her eyes. She needed to leave before she began to cry. The thought of him seeing her in tears was unbearable.

"For all I care, you can move out of your cabin and take a berth in steerage so you can gamble to your heart's content and drink all you like, and then as soon as we dock in New York, you can get straight on the next ship home!"

Ned's face hardened. "Thank you, Miss Wakechild, I shall give that some consideration."

His voice was icier than the waters which surrounded the ship. It took all the heat from Florence's rage, quenched it, and froze it. A lump began to fill her throat. Before it could work up higher and burst out as a sob, she pushed past him and ran from the cabin. Ignoring the passengers she passed, she ran up onto the deck. With trembling hands, she grasped at the railing, pulling herself up until she could lean over it and gaze out into nothingness.

What an absolute *ass* of a man Ned was!

Justifying his opportunism by suggesting Florence had sanctioned it. Had approved of and encouraged it. Then suggesting that once they had parted, he did what they had been doing but with other women! To suggest there were others like her who could benefit from the deception. It was absolutely out of the question. Quite intolerable to think of. Her situation was entirely different. She was different.

She walked back towards her cabin, shaking and barely noticed the elderly gentleman who drew to one side. She thanked him and carried on but within a few paces the man had caught up with her.

"Miss Wakechild?"

She turned back. She'd encountered him the day before, as she had made her way towards Ned's cabin and he had let her pass then too, but that didn't give him the right to address her by name.

"Yes? Have we been introduced?" Disinclined for niceties, she was brusquer than politeness required.

The man raised his hat. "I'm afraid not but I need to speak to you in any case. My name is Gerald Finch, of the Thirsk Finches. I happened to notice you on the games deck yesterday in the company of a gentleman." He sniffed, as if he was using the term unwillingly."

"Yes. What of it?" Florence asked coldly.

"I don't know how well you know the gentleman, but my valet told me some disturbing news about him a day ago and I feel I must make you aware." He tilted his head to a young man dressed in a black suit who stood at the end of the passageway.

"Go on," she instructed warily.

Mr Finch bristled at being addressed so forwardly. "It seems that the man appeared in the Servants' quarters and proceeded to engage my valet at cards, whereupon…"

Florence turned to look back at the valet. He had dark, slicked back hair and an olive complexion. Her neck prickled as he gave her a smooth smile and an obsequious bow. Dottie had a soft spot for a charmer and the jigsaw in Florence's mind filled another piece.

"Is your valet named Agosti?" Florence interrupted. "If so, I already know Mr Blake was indulging in a game of cards with him, and I know why he was playing. Do *you* know why?"

He ignored her question and blinked. "Really, young lady, is that how you speak to your elders and betters?"

Florence clenched her hands at her side. "When I am accosted without an introduction, I might take the liberty of speaking however I choose."

Until ten minutes previously, she had been furious at Ned. Now she would defend him with her last breath. She straightened her hat and lifted her chin.

"Mr Finch, of Thirsk, wherever that is, there is nothing you can tell me about Mr Blake that could alter my opinion of him. He did my personal maid a kind service for which I am eternally grateful, and which I suspect your valet has not explained. Will you excuse me."

Mr Finch held his hat by the brim, rolling it between his hands. He looked marginally more respectful, but Florence's temper was already at snapping point.

"I meant no offence and I shall certainly take up the matter with Agosti when we are alone. Mr Blake has a familiar face, though I cannot place him. I merely wondered if you could enlighten me. Thirsk is in North Yorkshire, by the by."

Florence swallowed, her mouth unexpectedly dry. Ned was from Yorkshire. He'd mentioned it when they had been talking about archery. It was conceivable that Mr Finch had seen him before, but she was damned if she'd let him know that.

"I do not care whether his face is familiar to you or not,

nor where Thirsk is. If you wish to learn more about him, I suggest you approach him yourself. Good day to you, sir."

She walked off, heading to her cabin but was hailed by Lord Griggs as she entered the passageway. He was dressed in a light fawn-coloured suit with a striped waistcoat that made him look like a travelling fairground barker, and a straw boater with a matching band. Clearly Cordelia had not seen his outfit today or he would not be wearing it.

"My dear Florence, wonderful luck seeing you. I'm going up to the restaurant for a spot of lunch. Will you join me?"

When she hesitated, he took her hand and pressed it in entreaty.

"Your sister is still laid low and I'm in desperate need of some good conversation. She's done little more than groan and pray for deliverance all day."

"I'm not sure how good a conversationalist I'll make, Lord Griggs," Florence said quietly.

"You'll be as diverting as you always are," he replied gallantly. "Whatever is causing your gloom, there's nothing that a spot of asparagus soup and a slice of cold roast beef won't cure."

Her stomach gave a little gurgle that she hoped wasn't audible.

"A little food would be welcome," she admitted.

Noon had long since passed and the restaurant was almost empty. She spotted Mr Finch enter, without Agosti. He gazed over at Florence then took a table at the furthest spot away.

Fortunately, Twemlow was happy talking about his own interests and Florence was required to supply little more than the occasional nod or murmur of agreement. It was just as well because she couldn't stop thinking of the argument with Ned and the strange encounter with Mr Finch. So what if Ned looked familiar? She rather hoped Ned had previously proven to the odious man's wife that he had a penchant for gambling and his wife had scolded him thoroughly.

The righteous indignation that soured her belly was almost enough to put her off her elderflower sorbet and she pushed it around the crystal dish half-heartedly.

"You wouldn't let Mr Blake play with his food in such a manner," Twemlow gently chided her.

She scraped up the last of it before it became too mushy then rested the spoon on the dish.

"When it comes to Mr Blake, I don't know what I should or shouldn't be doing anymore if I'm perfectly honest," she said in a slightly wobbly voice. "I've made an absolutely awful mess of everything by arguing with him and now I don't even know whether he'll carry out the wager."

Twemlow refilled her wineglass. "I'm sure he will. He's a man of his word and I'm sure your little quarrel will soon be forgotten."

Florence gave him a sad smile, unable to explain any of the circumstances leading up to the break between them. How could Ned think she didn't care what would happen to him once they parted? She suspected she would most likely think of him every day for the rest of her life, whether or not she married.

The reason came to her with the force of a hammer striking an anvil. He assumed she had no feelings for him because he had no feelings for her. To him she was just another client, and a particularly taxing one at that. Ned spent his whole life meeting whatever demands his paymasters made. Humouring her was just one of the stranger things he would have had to do in order to earn his living. To him, she was no different from any other woman. The realisation made her knees grow weak.

Even if he had any feelings towards her, her words had been sharp and cutting, and she had said things that she knew she shouldn't have. Now her temper had cooled, she couldn't help but feel a deep regret for the hurt she had caused and the insults she had piled upon Ned.

She sniffed in a most unladylike manner.

"I'm sorry, my lord, but I really must leave. I'm afraid … I'm not … I'm feeling rather indisposed."

The tears which she had been holding in for so long fell at last. She looked around for something to wipe her eyes with and realised she did not have a handkerchief.

The irony struck her all the more cruelly. She fled from the table and did not stop until she reached the sanctuary of her cabin.

Well done, Ned!

He lay on his bed long after Florence had left, breathing deeply to control the lava that was coursing through his veins. Florence was the most infuriating woman he had ever encountered. He scowled, thinking of the bare-faced cheek of the woman to come into his room and, instead of apologising for her appalling insinuations, to actually chastise him further! He had done nothing wrong in his efforts to help Dottie and had been accused of scandalous behaviour. Well, he was done with her.

He took another deep breath, clenched his fists, then loosened them and forced himself to think rationally. He had never failed to complete a commission and he wasn't about to start now. Whatever he might have thrown at Florence regarding his return to England, he would never leave America without fulfilling his obligations to her unless she ended his employment. He'd worked for plenty of people he had not respected or liked. He could certainly be civil in the presence of Miss Wakechild, a woman of whom he had grown extremely fond, until she had so rudely annoyed him.

He'd been in the process of dressing before her interruption, so he returned to the matter of shaving. The water was now barely lukewarm, and childishly he placed that inconvenience at Miss Wakechild's feet too.

There were many ways he could have resolved the matter of Dottie's brooch that didn't involve card games but all of them were flawed. He listed them as he scraped away the stubble.

He could have asked Miss Wakechild to deal with it. He

had no doubt that she would have done so in a most efficient manner, but he had not wanted to break his vow of confidentiality for Dottie.

He could've found Agosti's employer and told him the kind of man his valet was and left the matter in his hands. Of course, that was a threat to the man's employment and livelihood, which Ned considered was going too far. If every man was cast out onto the streets for dark dealing with innocent women, then most offices would be empty, not to mention the Houses of Lords and Commons.

No, there was only one way he could have handled the matter and that was the way he had chosen. Miss Wakechild was simply being overly critical.

As he leaned over the bowl to clean his razor, he caught a glimpse of himself in the mirror. His eyes blazed back at him scornfully. He dropped the razor into the bowl and rubbed his eyes.

Who was he trying to fool?

He'd taken the route he had because he'd wanted to, just as he'd wanted to fight Rafferty at the fair. He'd wanted a distraction from the thoughts of kissing Florence that refused to leave him in peace. He wanted the thrill of a game of cards, and wanted to use his wits as he had done for so long since he had made the decision to live by them. He enjoyed it, that was the problem. He'd always been drawn to games and risks. Why else would he have agreed to the preposterous wager otherwise.

He splashed his hands in the bowl of water then covered his face with them, letting the lukewarm water trickle down his cheeks and jaw. There were too many people in the past who he had caused rifts with, and it pained him deeply to think that Florence would be another. He would have to make peace with her before she grew to despise him.

He spent an hour or two composing letters that he would never send to people he could no longer speak to. When he found himself reaching for the journal in his valise, he knew it was time to leave his cabin before he lost himself in the past, and went in search of a drink. He hesitated before covering the journal and closing the valise. He couldn't dispose of that yet. Perhaps one day he would.

He took the letters he had written and threw them overboard, watching the pages swirl on the breeze before spinning down and being ploughed under the waves by the current caused by the ship. He was ascending the central staircase when he heard his name being called.

"Blake, there you are. I want a word with you."

Ned turned and saw Lord Griggs striding towards him. Ned lifted his hat, a rather daringly fashionable boater that Florence had done her best to persuade him not to buy and was momentarily gratified to see that the baron wore a similar model.

"Lord Griggs. Good afternoon to you."

The baron harrumphed. "Nothing good about it. My wife has spent most of the afternoon trying in vain to stop her sister from weeping, which involved dragging herself from her sofa. Do you have any idea what has caused her decline in temperament? She's usually the most even-tempered creature, but she's been inconsolable. She actually ran from the dinner table before the coffee had arrived!"

Ned looked over the banister to the deck below. The idea of Florence so distressed cut through his sense of indignation at her behaviour. He couldn't suppress the nagging feeling in his stomach that he was not completely the injured party in their argument. Despite what he might have suggested, he had no intention of hiring himself out as a trainer of invented noblemen.

"I'm very much afraid the fault is mine. I acted impulsively and joined a game of cards and did rather well out of it. Miss Wakechild discovered it."

"Was that you?" Lord Griggs looked at him keenly. "My valet told me there's been an almighty furore in the servant's saloon about some banker's manservant losing his shirt to a passenger. Rumours are flying about the identity of the charlatan who is pretending to be a respectable gentleman when he's clearly a rogue."

"I suppose it must have been me," Ned said reluctantly.

"Are you a rogue, Mr Blake?" Lord Griggs gave him a penetrating stare. "Your line of work is unconventional to say the least. I'm wondering if we should have taken references, but I'm just too trusting."

More like too unconcerned, Ned suspected, from what he had learned of the baron's laissez-faire attitude to life.

"I try not to be a rogue, but if you mean am I a crook, no. I had good reasons for wiping out the valet, though as always, confidentiality is important to me. Miss Wakechild will attest to the reasons, if and when she forgives me."

Twemlow sucked his teeth. "Oh no doubt she will eventually. Women don't like to discover things they were never supposed to learn. Makes them feel silly. I suppose she let rip with a few choice phrases, if she's anything like her sister."

"We exchanged words," Ned said warily. He couldn't shake the feeling that Lady Griggs would have a few choice words if she ever learned she was the subject of this conversation. "I regret mine immensely and though it does nothing to mitigate my behaviour, I have been intending to speak to her and beg forgiveness ever since."

Lord Griggs' mouth spread into a wide smile. "There's a wise fellow. Go visit her, grovel, and appear contrite. If you can chance upon a box of peppermint creams or Turkish delight to offer, I find that always speeds up the natural reconciliation. I'll tell Lady Griggs that you will call on Miss Wakechild after dinner to explain yourself. Come to my wife's stateroom and she will be waiting."

"Wouldn't a public room be better?" Ned asked.

Lord Griggs raised his brows in an exaggerated fashion. "Not for an apology, unless you want the world and her maiden aunt to know your business. Don't worry about propriety; my wife will be having a post-dinner lie-down so will be able to chaperone you from the adjoining bedroom. I'll be on deck and if you don't make peace with my womenfolk, I'll throw you overboard myself."

He laughed at the sight of Ned's astonishment then walked off, whistling.

Chapter Nineteen

After a light dinner of curried mutton and a glass of passable Tokay, Ned found Florence sitting in the stateroom with a pot of coffee. Her eyes were slightly pink but other than that she looked perfectly composed, if a little morose. She was reading a book but her glasses had slipped down her nose a little and he suspected it was a show of indifference.

Ned's arrival clearly did nothing to lift her mood because she looked at him, then immediately away.

"May I join you, Miss Wakechild?" Ned asked, hesitating beside the table.

"If you like." She gestured listlessly to the chair. Ned sat, but before he could speak Florence started talking.

"Mr Blake, I'm so sorry I am awful. The things I accused you of are absolutely atrocious. I'm thoroughly ashamed of myself and if you choose to return home immediately, I will not blame you."

Ned sat back in the chair. He had not expected an apology and he felt completely disarmed. A little confused, too, because now he had to suddenly rethink how he intended to speak. Florence obviously felt the silence still signalled anger because she twisted her hands in her lap, screwing up the folds of her skirt.

"I don't deserve your forgiveness," she said in a small voice. "The fault is all mine."

Her mouth wobbled and she gave a little sniff. Ned's stomach twisted in contrition. He wouldn't be able to bear it if she began to cry. The sight of her so distressed and so openly taking the blame was unbearable.

He understood now why he had been so aghast at Florence believing he was in love with Dottie. It wasn't just because the accusation had come out of nowhere and seemed so outlandish, it was because he now realised that he was in love with Florence. He couldn't figure out why he hadn't seen it before but now that the revelation had hit him, he was hopeless to ignore it. He was Adam tasting the fruit of Eden and seeing Eve for the woman she was. And like their fall, the knowledge was a burden and a tragedy he would have to bear for the rest of his living years.

"Florence…" He reached out and touched her briefly on the forearm.

Her eyes flickered towards the open door that led to the bedroom. Ned hastily removed his hand. He dropped his eyes, glad she had issued the reminder before he said something reckless. He smiled gently, the words he needed to say coming easily to his lips.

"We are both at fault. Yours is that you are so certain of yourself that you don't entertain the possibility of an alternative explanation and jump to conclusions."

"Well, the last time I jumped to a conclusion it was that you were going to go fight Mr Rafferty at the fair and I was right," Florence said, jutting her chin out.

"No, the last conclusion you jumped to was that I was in love with your maid," Ned corrected, giving her a stern look.

"Well, the next to last conclusion was correct," she said grudgingly. "Now tell me your fault as you have pointed out mine."

"Mine is that I make unwise decisions and then justify them to myself. I didn't have to take advantage of the valet. I did it because I wanted to. That was an accusation you levelled fairly."

"It was about the only one," Florence said. "You can of course do whatever you want with your talents. Your life is not mine to command. I don't think you should become a waiter or a banker, however. And please don't start fraudulently masquerading as an aristocrat. I'm sure there are many other women, as you say…"

She shuddered then gave a loud sob.

Ned couldn't bear it any longer. He leaned forward and pulled her into a tight embrace.

"There are no other women like you," he murmured, stroking her hair. He wasn't even sure she heard him, but she reached her hands around his back and held him tight.

She sobbed silently as she clung to him, her frame

shaking with the force of her emotions. Ned held on tightly, determined to give whatever solace he could until she was calm again, but his heart was thumping fit to burst and each fresh shake of emotion sent him down a well of misery. He shouldn't be holding her. At any moment, Lady Griggs could walk into the room and see them, but he couldn't bear to let her go.

It was Florence who severed the embrace by loosening her grip on him. Recognising the gesture signalled the end of their closeness, Ned released her. She smiled and dabbed at her eyes.

"I'm afraid I don't have a handkerchief," she mumbled. She raised her eyes to Ned and gave him a faint smile. "After the trouble your previous one caused, I hate to ask but I don't suppose…"

Ned laughed softly at her feeble attempt to lighten the atmosphere. He pulled a fresh one from his pocket, wondering if he should patent a small box to carry multiple of them in for such eventualities. She dabbed discreetly at her eyes then blew her nose thoroughly.

"Miss Wakechild, I really must ask you to pardon my reaction to the talk of what I shall do once we part. My future is playing somewhat on my mind and the thought of this venture coming to an end brings it into sharp relief. The outcome of the situation is beyond my control. It's something I hoped would have been concluded by now. The weight is heavy on me, but it will lessen once I know which path I must walk."

"I understand," Florence said. "I'm not feeling at my

most level-headed and I think that has affected my ability to reason. I do not like this part of me which immediately fears the worst. I know it is there, but when it rears up, I am unable to identify it until too late. I don't know myself very well, I'm afraid."

Ned found himself thinking that she knew herself much better than she gave herself credit for, but it wasn't his place to comment.

"We both said some things that I'm sure we regret. Let's put them behind us."

"Yes, let's do that."

Florence held out her hand. Conscious of her sister's presence next door, Ned took it and lifted it to his lips as quickly as politeness would allow, though he would have gladly held on to it for the rest of the day. When he released it, she placed it in her lap, her fingers curled around the palm and Ned wondered if she was feeling the same tingling sensation that heated his hand.

"It's a fine night. Will you walk on the upper deck with me, Miss Wakechild? I believe we will be able to hear the music from outside and there will be plenty of people around."

The way Florence's eyes slid towards her sister's room then back to his with a gleam.

"That sounds an excellent idea."

Despite the chill, the deck was busy. Children played games, giddy with excitement at being allowed to stay up late. Groups of friends laughed and chatted. Couples strolled arm in arm. Ned pulled Florence as close to his side as he dared.

Lord Griggs was in the company of two elderly men in formal evening wear that was at least two decades out of fashion. He spoke to them then sauntered over to Ned and Florence.

"I trust everything is sorted out and bridges have been mended?"

"Yes, Lord Griggs," Ned said.

"Good. Although it would be in my interest for you to quarrel, my feelings for Lady Griggs prevent me from taking advantage of it."

"Advantage in what way, my lord?" Ned asked.

The baron smiled. "This wager is turning out to be more inconvenient and expensive than I expected. I have a ghastly feeling I'm going to lose it."

"You flatter me, my lord," Ned said.

"No, he doesn't," Florence said, patting his hand. "In appearance, clothing and deportment, you are easily as noble and handsome as any man on this ship, but it is your manner and conduct which truly elevates you."

Lord Griggs made a harrumphing noise. "Once this is over, I expect you'll be looking for further employment? I may have come across something which sounds like the sort of thing you do."

Ned tried to look keen, though the imminent end of his time with Florence was something he was doing his best to avoid thinking of.

"Did you notice that portly fellow in the grey suit

which makes him look like an undertaker? He owns a newspaper and his son has eloped with a Bosnian countess. The chap was last seen setting himself up as an artist in Boston. His father wants the affair to end and the son to return home."

"Returning is one thing, but why should he give her up?" Florence demanded.

Both men appraised her and she returned their gaze unblinkingly.

"Because it's a foolish affair according to his father," Lord Griggs said.

She jutted her chin out. "Well, the father might be wrong. I hope they have already got married; then even if they are forced to return home, they'll get to be together."

"It will be a lot easier to untangle them both if they haven't," Lord Griggs said. He met Ned's eyes.

"I don't suppose you fancy tracking him, Mr Blake? Or are you keen to return to Britain?"

"I have no plans," Ned said, carefully avoiding Florence's eye.

"Excellent. I'll tell him I've found an agent," Lord Griggs said, apparently completely ignoring Ned's answer. The baron turned away and followed his companions into the smoking room.

"Don't worry, he won't have a contract drawn up by the time we dock," Florence said, clearly thinking the same as Ned. She laughed gently and looked up at him. He drank in the warmth of her gaze and smiled tenderly. The moonlight caught the red in her hair, turning it to gold. Ned had never wanted anyone as much as he wanted her, and the thought of losing her was unbearable.

All he could do was play his part and ensure that she was not condemned to a marriage she would find unbearable. If the coin that was currently spinning in the air fell one way, could he dare to hope? No. He wasn't a particularly superstitious man but thinking like that could only doom him.

"Ned, with your permission I would like to persuade the captain to invite you to the formal dinner tomorrow," Florence said. "It's the last night of the voyage so should be something to behold. I'm sure he will agree, if not for me, then for my brother-in-law. He practically curtseys when Lord Griggs passes by."

Ned laughed at the image her words conjured. There was only one night of the voyage left. Any time they were together once they reached New York would be in the act of carrying out the deception and they'd never again get the opportunity to be alone together.

Then they'd be parting.

Even though he knew that it was inevitable, it still felt like a physical pain inside his chest every time he thought about their future apart.

"Very well," he said, taking her hand. "Let's make tomorrow a night to remember."

Florence had to admit that a titled brother-in-law was useful, as a word with Twemlow meant that he put a word in the right ear and an invitation was secured.

Dressed in her green silk with the pearl comb ornamenting her hair, Florence could barely contain her excitement and nerves as the Captain's Dinner drew near. She walked with Cordelia and Twemlow to the restaurant where they had agreed to meet Ned. When she saw him, Florence's breath caught in her throat.

Ned was dressed in a formal evening suit with a crisp white shirt, a high collar, and a bow tie. He completed the look with a black tailcoat, trousers, and patent leather shoes. His hair was smoothed back with pomade and he had a pocket watch tucked into his waistcoat pocket on a faded gold chain that looked old. When he took it out to check the time, Florence saw the case was intricately carved with inlaid stones of a reddish hue that could have been rubies. She didn't know he possessed such a thing and was intrigued, but when he saw them arriving, he slipped it away.

He walked towards them and greeted Lord and Lady Griggs then extended his arm to Florence.

"Miss Wakechild, you are breathtaking. Seeing you approaching, I was at first convinced a siren had climbed from the sea to lure me to my fate."

She had been feeling nervous but the image made her relax.

"You have never heard my singing or you wouldn't say that," she said.

He chuckled. "Will you allow me to escort you into the dining room?"

"With the greatest pleasure, Mr Blake," she murmured, slipping her arm through his.

Florence and Ned were seated with Lord and Lady Griggs and another couple who were older than the baron and baroness. They introduced themselves as the Glenarrises of Scotland, owners of a whisky distillery, which immediately drew Twemlow and Ned's interest. She caught Mr Finch looking at them from across the room, but when she glared, he returned to his conversation.

It was one of the nicest evenings Florence could remember in a long time. For the last night, the chefs had outdone themselves and the food was excellent, from the chilled tomato soup to the lemon soufflés. Even Cordelia managed to try a little of each dish.

The conversation was filled with laughter and comparisons between American, English, and Scottish upbringings. Lord Griggs regaled the table with stories of his youth in a boarding school, which sounded to Florence like something from a medieval history of the monasteries, while the other couple shared tales of their life in Scotland in accents Florence could barely understand.

Throughout the meal, she stole glances at Ned, admiring how effortlessly he mingled with the other diners, looking as at ease as if he had been born to it. Whether he had genuinely been to Scotland to walk the streets of Edinburgh or was making up his experiences, Florence had no idea. She was certain he had never been to an English boarding school, but he apparently was able to sympathise with Twemlow about the trials of washing in icy water, writing out Latin verbs with fingers stiff from the cold, and early morning runs across the moors.

Despite her reluctance to speak with strangers, he gently encouraged Florence to join in, prompting her to share tales of her childhood and anecdotes from her visit to England, as well as books she enjoyed reading. She discovered a kindred spirit in Mr Glenarris when it came to the stories of Alexandre Dumas and became so carried away with the discussion that she almost forgot to eat her game pie until Twemlow pointed out the waiters arriving to collect empty plates. As she devoured the buttery pastry, she caught Ned's eye. He gave her a wink and raised his wineglass to her. They held each other's gaze, a private moment in a room full of others where they might have been the only two there.

As the women rose from the table at the end of the meal, Mrs Glenarris leaned towards Florence and whispered conspiratorially, "I must say, my dear, you and Mr Blake make a lovely couple."

Florence's cheeks flamed. "Thank you, Mrs Glenarris. We are not a couple, however, merely friends travelling together."

Ned looked over at her, his expression unreadable. She wondered what he would think if he suspected she felt the disappointment at that truth so keenly it wanted to make her cry.

Florence didn't know who had administered the task,

but for the dancing, she had a wide variety of partners. Among other men, she danced once with Twemlow, once with Mr Colling – which earned her a couple of hard stares from Mrs Carmine – and once with Captain D'Abney himself.

He was a serious man, his face weathered so much by the elements that his age could have been anything from thirty-five to fifty-five. He was completely bald but scorned a toupee and let his head display its natural state.

"Miss Wakechild, I should admit that I was hesitant in allowing your second-class acquaintance to attend tonight but he is an admirable gentleman."

"I know." Florence beamed with triumph at Ned's success. "He's a man of excellent reputation and family, and would have travelled with us in first class, only he was unable to engage a free cabin. I can give you my assurances that you will not find a more gentlemanly passenger on board the ship than Mr Blake."

"Indeed. I should warn you I have no intention of carrying out any of the other duties which I am authorized to do," Captain D'Abney said.

"Other duties?" Florence wrinkled her brow, having no idea what he meant.

The captain's dark eyes twinkled as he leaned in closer. "A captain may perform the ceremony of marriage."

A host of butterflies erupted inside Florence. She straightened up. "Absolutely not. Mr Blake is a friend of the family, that's all. We will certainly be doing nothing of that kind."

The captain gave her a long look and she feared she had been too vociferous in her denials.

Florence only danced with Ned at the end of the evening. The music was slow and romantic, Ned holding her just close enough to remain proper while still allowing some closeness between them. They didn't speak as they glided around the dance floor, and knowing that their time together was growing short, Florence was content merely to be in his embrace, his scent filling her senses until all else faded away.

When the music ended, Ned stepped back and bowed slightly before taking her arm and escorting her off the dance floor.

"I think now is the time to start the rumours that you are really Viscount Telford," Florence murmured, aware of the covetous eyes that followed them. "I shall drop hints to other ladies in the powder room that you are more than you seem."

"Be careful," Ned cautioned in a whisper. "I don't want to be subject to a campaign to have me married off. The adventurous Mrs Carmine might decide I'm a better bet than the heir presumptive!"

"She'll have to get past me first," Florence exclaimed, appalled at the prospect of the scheming widow adding Ned to her list of conquests.

Ned's eyebrows shot up. Florence held his gaze boldly.

"I haven't gone to all this effort to lose you before we reach New York. Once we have arrived and we are finished fooling my father, you are of course free to do whatever you wish, with whomever you wish to do it with."

Ned surprised her by reaching for her hand again.

"Florence," he murmured in a low voice. "I have no intention of letting anyone – wealthy widow or otherwise – distract me from our purpose. Besides, with you in the room, who else could capture my attention?"

As they reached their destination, he smiled down at her with a look that made Florence's heart skip a beat.

"Thank you, Miss Wakechild. Not just for the dance, but for everything. Whatever happens in New York, I believe I shall always remember this night."

She watched him go with longing, wishing that just once he could have taken her in his arms again and kissed her as he had done before. She made her way back to the powder room, hoping for some solitude but found herself once again in the company of Mrs Glenarris.

"Who exactly is Mr Blake and what does he do?" Mrs Glenarris asked as Florence sat on a stool and dabbed a little cologne behind her ears. "I don't think he ever got round to telling us."

Florence couldn't resist the temptation and leaned close to whisper. "You must keep it in the strictest confidence, but he's actually a viscount."

Mrs Glenarris gave a triumphant laugh. "Ha! I knew it. I said to Euan that there was something special about that young man. A viscount? I'd have said at least an earl, if not a duke! You can't hide breeding."

Florence couldn't wait to get back to her party and tell them of their triumph.

"He's doing his best to hide it. He's trying to avoid his father who wants him to marry a cousin," Florence urged her.

Mrs Glenarris tutted. "Well, that won't do. He's obviously besotted with you."

"Oh please, don't say that."

"I speak my mind," Mrs Glenarris said briskly. "And if I've seen a hundred men in love, I've seen one hundred and one tonight."

Florence leaned against the wall and dropped her head. Mrs Glenarris tutted again sympathetically.

"It's never a smooth path, but if you want each other enough, I'm sure you'll find a way. Good luck, my dear."

She had never felt more like she would need it. The voyage was almost over. The following afternoon she would be back in her homeland, and she would discover what dreadful misfortune had called them back to America.

Chapter Twenty

The *City of Bruges* docked in the Port of New York on a warm but overcast afternoon. The terminus teemed with passengers disembarking. Those returning to their homeland went one way; those visiting went another to show their visas and complete declarations of intent, while a third group who hoped to be allowed to stay were herded in another direction. With Florence being in the first category and Ned being in the second, she was unable to catch a glimpse of him. She tried not to mind. They had a plan arranged to meet the following afternoon for an outing to Central Park, but she would have liked to see him for one last glimpse.

They were all staying in New York for a week. Clayton Wakechild had booked rooms at the Fifth Avenue Hotel, so Florence and Cordelia went straight there while Twemlow vanished off to his New York club. Ned had a room waiting for him at the Astor House, under the name Archibald

Montgomery Telford, a name so outlandish to Florence's ears that she was convinced no one would believe it was real—which Ned had argued was the point, saying if he was to appear in society without having announced his arrival at one of the fashionable hotels, a plausible cover needed to exist.

As they rocked about in the hansom cab, Cordelia coughed discreetly. "Florence, before we arrive at the hotel, I need to discuss something with you."

"The baby?" Florence asked, spinning round from the window she had been staring out. "Is it definite?"

"Not that, it's about Mr Blake. I wish to speak and I'm not sure when I'll have the chance to get you alone. I overheard what Mrs Glenarris said last night and while I'm sure it was extremely flattering to be told a man is in love with you, I worry that you are growing a little too fond of Mr Blake."

"I think it is impossible to get too fond of somebody, surely?" Florence replied thoughtfully. "If they are worth being fond of at all, why ration it?"

Cordelia clicked her tongue, a habit that had irritated Florence since childhood.

"I shall put it bluntly, as you seem determined to be obstinate in your understanding. I worry you are becoming romantically attached to him."

Florence burst out laughing. "Oh my goodness, how ridiculous! You know well enough I have no romantic intentions towards anybody. When have I ever done so?"

"You haven't. Perhaps that's the problem. This is the

first time I've ever seen you spending so much time with someone male. Watching you dance together last night, it was…"

Cordelia gazed out of the window, a wistful expression on her face. "It made me feel almost envious of the days when Twemlow and I were first courting. You seem to breathe life into each other."

"What a lovely thing to say." Florence smiled. The image filled her mind with flowers budding and blooming in spring sunshine and warmth began to spread through her. It had been a lovely moment. She could have danced throughout the night if she'd had the chance.

"Yes, I suppose we do get on very well. It's invigorating having someone I can really talk to. Do you know, I feel as if he is almost a friend. I shouldn't tell you, but I have asked him to call me Florence, and I call him Ned."

Cordelia reached across the seat and took Florence's hand, squeezing her fingers tighter than Florence thought warranted.

"Oh my dear, you do understand he can never be anything more than a friend, and a distant one at that, don't you? Even if you succeed in persuading father that a husband with a title is not the only possibility, he will never agree to you marrying somebody without connections who hires himself out the way Mr Blake does. You might as well marry a greengrocer."

Florence pulled her hand free of her sister's.

"This is exactly why the whole matter of marriage and status offends me. Mr Blake has proven he can be just as gentlemanly as anyone. He is loyal to his friends and kind. He has ambition and is not above working hard. Just look at what a fine man he has become in the past few weeks."

She paused for breath. Cordelia eyed her seriously.

"Do you hear yourself? Is it any wonder I'm concerned when you speak of him in such glowing terms?"

Florence crossed her arms angrily. "So what if I do? Can't I admire someone without you sniffing out gossip? I have no desire to get married and I'm certainly not romantically attached to Mr Blake," she snapped. "He wouldn't want me to be, in any case."

Cordelia's brow knotted. "Are you sure? The more I think about it, the more I think Mrs Glenarris is right. Mr Blake has his eye on you. I'd like to think it was because he is in love with you, but what if he's just after a rich wife?"

"What if he isn't? What if he genuinely loves me? Isn't that a possibility? I'm loveable, aren't I?"

"Of course you are, darling," Cordelia said, attempting to give Florence a hug.

Florence shrugged her off. She pressed her hands together, feeling each fingertip against its opposite. She sat in silence until they arrived at the hotel, barely bidding Cordelia good day as the porters showed them to their accommodation.

The Wakechild party occupied a suite on the tenth floor of the hotel, with a private sitting room, two bathrooms, and an office for Clayton's personal use. A note was waiting for Florence telling her to come to the sitting room at four. She presumed the Griggses would have one also.

She had an hour to spare so instructed Dottie to draw her a bath. The luxury of heated rooms and hot water plumbed straight into the bathroom was something she decided she would never take for granted again. All the same, there was something lacking in the newness of the rooms that made her think kindly of the old solidity of Goreswarth Chase.

She wallowed in the lavender-scented water for almost twenty minutes, hoping it would allow her to release some of the annoyance that had built up inside her.

The bath failed to rid herself of her tension, so she gave up and dressed in a smart outfit of powder-blue skirt and short jacket with a ruffled white blouse beneath it. As she buttoned the cuffs of the sleeves, she realised her hand was trembling with nerves at the thought of what Clayton was about to tell her.

Was the business in ruins? That would be dreadful, though there was a small disloyal part of her that thought that if they no longer had a fortune, then no English lord would want her. If she was suddenly, miraculously, financially unattractive as a bride and her father could no longer make use of her, would Ned want her? She thought enviously of the eloping newspaper heir and his countess. How brave must they be, and how much in love.

She pressed her hand to her belly, feeling it dipping as if she were still on the sea as she imagined a life with Ned. She wouldn't need much: three or four rooms at most. Cordelia and Twemlow might even have a cottage on the estate they could make use of, for example.

Cordelia's warning came back to her. What if Cordelia was correct and he only wanted her as a rich wife? Well, she'd rather know if that was the case. With dreams and possibilities spinning in her head, she made her way into the sitting room.

Her father was already there and had started on the spread of coffee and cakes that were piled high on silver stands. Florence threw herself into her father's arms and hugged him tightly.

"Daddy, it's so lovely to see you. Oh I wish we could have done this in England though. I have so much to tell you. We met the most interesting person on the ship."

"Florence dearest, I'm so sorry we had to spoil your plans by returning, but don't worry, not all the news I have is bleak."

Not all.

So some of it was bleak. Florence pulled away, searching his face for signs of illness or trouble.

"You look well," she said. "Are you really though? Appearances can so easily deceive. Are you ill? We've been so worried ever since we got your letter. What brought you back? Why have you brought us back? You must tell us at once what has happened."

Clayton laughed gently. He patted her cheek as he had done when she had been a young child. "I will as soon as you let me get a word in edgeways."

He motioned to the space on the sofa beside him and Florence sat down, doing her best to curb her curiosity.

"I'm not ill, my pet. Let me set your mind at rest on that

account. I'll wait until your sister is here before I explain everything. Why don't you pour us both some coffee."

Before Florence could oblige, the door opened and in walked Cordelia and Twemlow. Clayton rose to greet them, bowing deeply to Twemlow. Cordelia nodded a little stiffly at Florence, clearly not having forgiven her.

"Lord Griggs, thank you for joining me, I'm honoured as always," Clayton said.

Despite their previous cross words, Cordelia and Florence exchange a surreptitious wink. The Wakechild and Griggs families had been intertwined for years. Twemlow had frequently invited Clayton to call him Griggs, as his closest male friends did, or even Twemlow as his wife and Florence did, but Clayton was absolutely determined never to refer to him as anything other than by his title. Whether through deference or snobbery, Florence was never able to decide, and wasn't sure what the difference was in any case.

"Cordelia, my dear, you're looking well. Have you gained weight?" Clayton asked as he kissed her cheek.

Florence rolled her eyes at Cordelia. Their father's disapproval would doubtless vanish when he discovered the reason.

Instead of sitting back on the sofa, Clayton walked to the window and stood with his back to it. Twemlow and Cordelia took a second sofa and sat side by side, holding hands. Florence sat on the edge of the sofa, too tense to relax, and wishing she had someone to hold her hand. Wishing Ned was there.

The light surrounded Clayton, casting his face into silhouette. He coughed then spoke.

"Your brother has decided to marry."

"Why, that's wonderful!" Florence exclaimed. "Is the wedding to be soon? Is that why we had to curtail the trip?"

"This marriage is far from wonderful!" Clayton walked forward stiffly. His face was grave. "The woman in question is Mrs Ashbourne."

"But she's lovely," Florence said, recognising the bride-to-be's name and confused by her father's reaction.

Clover Ashbourne was a neighbour back in Philadelphia. She was quite plain-faced and smoked cigarettes constantly. She bred haughty cats and played golf and rode a black gelding. There was some part of Florence that hoped to emulate the Ashbourne lifestyle when she was older. She had been very good to the Wakechilds when the tragedy of losing Mrs Wakechild had struck.

"I know she's a little odd but she's very kind."

"I care nothing that she's an unorthodox woman. The fact is that Clover Ashbourne is some years older than your brother," Clayton said.

"Yes, we know that." Cordelia wrinkled her brow. "The age isn't so great. What is she? Perhaps six years older than Ashley."

Clayton clicked his teeth. "Yes. Her first marriage produced no children and now she is close to thirty-five years old. There is no guarantee she will be able to give your brother a son."

"Good God, father!" Florence sat up straight, her face flushing. "Must you treat every woman as livestock?"

Clayton shot her an angry look and even Twemlow looked taken aback at her outburst. "I must until I know that the business my father and I worked so hard to build is in a safe pair of hands."

"Well, there's no reason she won't have a child, and if she doesn't, then Florence can take over the business," Cordelia said. "She's more capable than Ash in any case. If Twemlow can pass his estate to a daughter, you can certainly leave a woman in charge of the factories."

"I'm sure Florence would be excellent," Twemlow added.

"I'm sure she would, but Florence will be marrying Viscount Stretford." Clayton steepled his fingers, reminding Florence where she had that mannerism from.

"Well, I might not," she pointed out. "It hasn't been settled at all. I've only met the viscount that one time and we haven't spoken since."

"The matter has been settled with me," Clayton said. He smiled proudly. "This is the good news I referred to. Viscount Stretford and I have communicated twice by telegram since I was unable to extend my stay in England. We have agreed on a marriage settlement and he is travelling to New York as we speak to complete the formalities."

Florence sat further forward, tilting so that the rear of her skirt was practically all that was on the sofa.

"What formalities? I haven't agreed to it. He hasn't even asked me."

Her heart began to pound. She looked towards Cordelia for support but Clayton walked and stood in front of her, creating a barrier between them.

"I have agreed on your behalf," Clayton said. "I suppose if you want to do things in that way, he can ask you, but I consider it a done deal and so does he. Your engagement will be announced as soon as possible."

"But I don't want to marry him!" She stood quickly. Her head spun and she sat down again, pressing her hand to her stomach to stop the feeling of nausea from growing any stronger.

If Clayton was aware of her distress, he showed no signs of caring.

"But you will. With your brother's ill-advised marriage currently causing me distress and getting tongues wagging back in Philadelphia, this is entirely what we need to still them, or change the subject to something that does us credit, not shame."

Clayton smiled at Florence. "I'm very proud of you. Your conduct was clearly exemplary while you were in Lord Griggs' charge. It was worth the expense of the trip. Lord Stretford will join us at the Faulkner's charity ball tomorrow night. I have tickets for all of us, and not just in the public areas either."

Clayton's excitement was palpable, and even taking the engagement into consideration, it was with good reason. George and Sapphire Faulkner were definitely Old Money, but Florence and Estelle Faulkner had become friends one summer when they were younger. The family owned a large house on the Upper East Side of Manhattan. Normally the chance to visit their beautiful home when it was dressed for an event and see Estelle would have excited Florence more than anything, but now she felt on the verge of tears.

"Promise me we won't have to talk of an engagement tomorrow at the ball," she entreated.

"Of course we won't," Cordelia said, smoothly moving from her sofa to sit beside Florence and flashing their father a look that brooked no argument. "It would be the height of bad manners to commandeer another family's event for our own purpose, and none of us would commit such a faux pas."

"Thank you," Florence whispered, reaching for Cordelia's hand. Their earlier quarrel was forgotten in a show of solidarity.

A cloud of despair settled over her and she barely listened to the rest of the conversation, which involved other people Clayton had seen in England and the successes he'd had in promoting the dyes to cotton manufacturers. As soon as Clayton dismissed them, she rushed back to her own room. Cordelia caught her at the door.

"Florence, are you alright?"

"Of course I'm not alright. Apparently I'm engaged and I didn't even have a say in the matter. Even you got to meet Twemlow half a dozen times before you decided. I feel quite sick."

Cordelia hugged her tightly. "Don't give up hope yet. There's still the wager."

Florence's eyes filled. "What if there is? Daddy won't back down even if Ned fools him completely. It would be too humiliating to end the engagement."

"I suppose so. I'm sorry. I'm sure Mr Blake would have done so well."

If Florence had been undecided whether to go through with the deception, her last lingering shreds of conscience shrivelled like overcooked bacon. How dare her father accept an engagement on her behalf and drop it into a conversation as if he was telling her he'd bought a new tiepin.

"Would have?" she exclaimed. "We're still going to do it. In fact, I'm going to visit Estelle Faulkner first thing tomorrow morning and ask for a ticket for Ned to the ball. We'll do it then."

Her spirits lifted. Securing Ned a ticket to the Faulkner's event would be easy. If Florence hinted at a mysterious guest, Estelle would practically run across town with a ticket. Florence would commandeer the ball for herself, produce Ned in the most public event possible, let him charm and beguile her father as he was sure to do, then reveal the trickery at the very moment Lord Stretford was about to arrive.

It might be humiliating but that could be exactly what Florence needed. Even if her father did not see the error of his snobbish ways, she would gladly use the fact that he had fallen for the deception as blackmail to ensure the engagement ended before it started. Unless Clayton Wakechild wished to become a laughing stock in the society he hoped to enter, he would forget all thoughts of the marriage. She suspected that the thought of Lord Stretford knowing would be enough of a threat in itself.

"Will you tell Mr Blake about the engagement?" Cordelia asked.

Florence shook her head. Why complicate matters? It would ruin a perfect evening. She wouldn't mention Lord Stretford at all. She would get to dance with Ned and spend some time in his company and in his arms, a place she had decided she would happily spend the rest of her life.

After that, who knew what her future would hold.

Chapter Twenty-One

New York proved to be a delightful city and Ned was sorry he didn't have longer to take full advantage of it. The hotel was comfortable and the staff extremely friendly. The food was good, and when he left the hotel the morning after his arrival, the wide streets, thronging with pedestrians and horse-drawn vehicles, reminded Ned in a curious way of Liverpool.

He spent the morning browsing the great department stores – replenishing his stock of handkerchiefs in the process – and bought a newspaper from a young boy in a large floppy hat who stood on the street corner. Over coffee, he read through it with interest, wondering where he might locate a newspaper from England. The *City of Bruges*, along with other ships, would have brought the papers that had been printed on the day it had sailed from Liverpool, so by Ned's reckoning, by this evening he would be able to read about events from the day following his departure.

He didn't imagine that what he was searching for would make any of the columns in the first pages, but it was possible he could learn his destiny from the announcements listing marriages, deaths, and births. Until he was able to do that, he did his best to put any anxiety out of his mind and concentrate on enjoying himself in the city.

He took luncheon in a small Italian restaurant that served an excellent minestrone, reflecting on how glad he was not to be on the sea any longer, then took a horse-drawn trolley to Florence's hotel to meet her as planned. He arrived just as she was exiting the revolving door, with Dottie at her side. Ned's heart lurched at the sight of her. She was a vision of elegance in a form-fitting green dress that he hadn't seen before. The bodice of the jacket was narrow and pointed in darts at the hips that emphasised the ruched layers of the skirt.

Her coppery hair was styled in an intricate array of curls and decorative pins, piled high upon her head beneath a green hat with an array of feathers. The hairstyle was a work of art, complementing her dress perfectly and emphasising the green in her eyes which Ned could pick out even from across the street.

She looked the picture of sophistication and Ned felt quite abashed. He gave his jacket and trousers a quick brush with his hands before striding forward to meet her, then slowed as he realised she was being approached by a middle-aged man. Ned held back, wondering who the man was, alert in case he needed to intervene. Florence answered the man then spoke to Dottie who walked a few paces away and waited with a look of patience on her face that suggested she was well used to waiting for her mistress. Ned wondered if she would have done the same when Ned had accosted Florence outside Lewis' all those weeks ago.

The man spoke again. Florence shook her head and held her hands out in a gesture that implied a lack of knowledge. The man looked disappointed. They spoke for a minute or two longer before the man nodded and held out a small card. Florence hesitated then took it. The man tipped his hat and walked off. Dottie returned and Florence showed her the card. They seemed to be puzzling over it and Ned would have given quite a lot to have been able to read it.

Ned waited a few moments then stuck his hands in his pockets and strolled towards the women, whistling an aria from *The Gondoliers* to alert her to his presence. She turned and gave him a wide smile, the corners of her mouth creasing and forming dimples in her cheeks. She gave the card to Dottie and walked toward Ned, twirling the handle of the green lace parasol that completed her outfit.

"Mr Blake, or should I say Lord Telford, what a coincidence meeting you here!"

Her eyes gleamed and Ned couldn't help but smile in response.

"I saw you were speaking to somebody so didn't want to intrude," Ned explained. "I hope I didn't keep you waiting."

"Not at all." Florence held her hand out and he kissed it, lingering with his lips on the soft leather of her gloves only a breath longer than he should have done. If she noticed, she let it pass unremarked. He said hello to Dottie who smiled back bashfully.

"Shall we walk to the park as it's a fine afternoon?" Florence asked. "Dottie and I went visiting this morning and it took an hour to cross town and I've really had enough of the streetcars."

"I'm yours to command," Ned said. He wondered if she would mention who she had been speaking to, but she just called for Dottie, slipped her arm through Ned's, and led him in the direction of Central Park with Dottie following at a discreet pace behind.

The park was as busy as everywhere in the city appeared to be and Ned was glad of the opportunity to study the map of the sights. They chose a direction and walked along the pathways until they reached the lower Bethesda Terrace. Standing beside the fountain of the Angel of the Waters were a row of open carriages, waiting to take visitors on rides. They were open-topped two- or four-seaters, with the driver sitting on a raised cab at the front. As they watched, a young couple dashed up, laughing in delight. The man picked his companion up by the waist and lifted her into the carriage while she squealed. He climbed beside her and spoke to the driver who touched the horse with the tip of his whip and moved away as the couple snuggled close to each other.

"Shall we do that?" Ned asked. "Take a ride, I mean. The park is so much bigger than I expected and I don't want to miss anything."

"That's a wonderful idea," Florence said. "I have so

much to tell you. We should definitely drive as far as Belvedere Castle. It looks like something my brother-in-law would live in if he kept on altering Goreswarth Chase, and I want to tell you everything I've learned since I met my father again."

Ned eyed the vehicles. "It doesn't look very private," he said. "Are you sure you want to tell me about that there?"

"It isn't as scandalous as I expected it to be." Florence flashed him a grin. "In any case, the drivers are paid well not to listen to whatever goes on in the back. Or to look, for that matter. Dottie, we're going for a drive. You'll be fine waiting here, won't you."

It wasn't really a question because Florence didn't wait for an answer before walking towards the carriages. Ned gave Dottie ten cents and told her to buy an ice cream from the nearby stand, then followed Florence.

The carriage driver welcomed them aboard. The carriage made its way down the winding paths. The soft, leisurely clip-clopping of the horse's hooves against the pavement provided a gentle rhythm as they made their way around the carriage drive. It was soothing and the warm sunshine was a welcome escape from the bustling city streets.

Ned leaned back against the leather seat, feeling relaxed and at peace. The sound of the horse's breathing and the gentle creaking of the carriage added to the serene atmosphere. He took a deep breath, enjoying the moment with Florence by his side. The driver kept his head facing determinedly forward, as Florence had said he would. Presumably one who got a reputation for not being discreet wouldn't stay in business very long. He was sorely tempted to put his arm around Florence as the young lover had done to his lady, but that was a dangerous path to let his mind stray down.

Fortunately, he was prevented from any further musing in that direction because Florence turned to him almost immediately and clutched his hands.

"Daddy is absolutely furious. He gathered us all together within an hour of arriving and told us my brother is going to marry a widow."

"Not the adventuress from the ship?" Ned asked in astonishment. "I thought she was intent on the viscount."

Florence laughed. "No, not Mrs Carmine, but a different one. Its amazes me how many widows there must be out there looking for new husbands."

"Well, women tend to outlive their husbands and must find something to do with their time," Ned said wryly. "Do you need me to intervene? If the widow is an adventuress, I'm sure she could be persuaded to give your brother up if the price is right, or I could pretend to seduce her and then he will see what sort of woman she is."

To his astonishment, Florence shook her head vehemently.

"No, I don't want them breaking up at all. Mrs Ashbourne is a neighbour of ours and she is a perfectly lovely woman. I'll be proud to call her my sister. She's probably richer than Ashley if it comes to it and she's infinitely more sensible."

She slumped back, shaking her head.

"Besides, even if she wasn't, she obviously makes Ashley happy. I don't see why he should be denied the chance of love just because of our father's ridiculous notions. At least one of us should be able to marry for love."

"I'm glad to hear it," Ned said gently.

"And while we're on the subject," Florence said, sitting forward, "you must refuse to help track down the newspaper heir and his countess if Lord Griggs asks you again. I don't approve of their eloping, but clearly they felt they had no choice and I don't think you should play a part in forcing them to part if they really love each other."

"You don't approve?" Ned asked. He'd already made up his mind not to take the commission for that very reason. Florence opposing their romance was unexpected though.

"Running away is a cowardly thing to do," Florence said firmly. "The man clearly had responsibilities and he ran away from them. What sort of man does that?"

Ned swallowed.

"Would you do it if there was a man you loved?"

Florence looked out across the park. Ned held his breath.

"No, I don't think so. I couldn't upset my father that much by causing a scandal."

And yet she was prepared to possibly humiliate him by deceiving him, Ned mused. She was such a contradiction.

They'd reached a wide turning circle at the far end of the long drive. Passengers in some other vehicles were alighting but Ned had paid the driver to take them on a circular route and return to Dottie. As the carriage circumnavigated the circle, Florence gestured to a wide three-storeyed limestone mansion, set back from the park in a raised garden.

"That's the Faulkner mansion."

Ned raised his brows, impressed. Even in Britain, the name Faulkner was well known. The couple travelled widely, collecting works of art and antiquities. The chance to glimpse some of them was irresistible. It was also rumoured that some of the dealings concerning antiquities from Greece and Rome had not been entirely above board.

"I have tickets for us to the ball Sapphire Faulkner is holding tonight," Florence said. "We'll carry out the wager then. I know I said we would have a small introduction over morning coffee or suchlike, but I don't want to wait. I can't wait."

There was an intensity to her voice and Ned noticed she was clutching her parasol, tightly curling and uncurling her fingers around the handle.

"Are you sure?" Ned asked. "Just think of the embarrassment it could potentially cause your father when the truth is revealed."

She didn't answer immediately but her shoulders stiffened and her jaw tensed. She tapped her forefingers together.

"Completely. At the moment, I don't care too much about his embarrassment. I need to show him he's wrong about everything. My future freedom hangs on it, but more than anything, I want to be able to prove to my father that a man such as you is as worthy of affection as anyone with a title and fortune."

"Affection?"

His skin felt electrified, nerves clanging like church bells pealing. His didn't dare to look at her in case his face betrayed the strength of his feeling.

"Yes, affection." She looked away, the brim of her hat tilted in such a way that it obscured the closest side of her face, giving Ned no opportunity to see her expression. Her gloved hand clenched and unclenched on the railing.

"I know I shouldn't speak in such a frank manner, but I feel that you have become a dear friend to me."

He was moved by her words more than he would have expected was possible. Such a simple declaration made his heart swell with love for her in that moment.

"I hope you will never stop speaking frankly, Florence," he said. "It is one of your most admirable qualities." Feeling he was coming perilously close to admitting his love, he added in a light tone, "As long as you don't jump to conclusions too often."

"I'll try not." Florence laughed. She twisted round on the seat, leaning closer to Ned. So close that he would need to move his head less than an inch to meet her lips with his. Their eyes met. Ned's heart spilled open. Whatever she asked, he would do.

"Whatever happens tonight I want to thank you," she said quietly. "The weeks I've spent with you have opened my eyes in ways I never imagined."

To his astonishment, he saw that her lower lids were growing moist. He gave no reply, not knowing exactly how to articulate what the time had meant to him. He was still pondering it when she leaned forward and kissed him. Not on the lips, but on the cheek. Still close enough to ignite a furnace of longing inside him.

She pulled back. "I'm sorry, I shouldn't have done that."

"Don't be. I'm glad you did."

He reached his hand out and cupped the back of her head.

"We shouldn't," she murmured, gazing up at him from beneath her pale lashes.

"We don't have to."

She ran a finger down his cheek. "I want to."

He smiled, then kissed her softly on the lips.

The carriage continued on its way, jogging them gently as it travelled over uneven ground and, true to Florence's prediction, the driver did not so much as turn his head.

By the time they arrived back at the fountain, they were sitting side by side with a fitting gap between them. Dottie was sitting on a bench along with another maid who was presumably waiting for her employers to return from their ride. Ned helped Florence down, smiling up at her. Whether or not Dottie suspected what they'd been doing, there was no proof and it was a memory he'd treasure long after all this was done with.

They began to make their way back towards Florence's hotel. Dressing for a ball would presumably take the rest of the afternoon.

"I'm sure there will be plenty of opportunities for finding a new commission tonight," Florence remarked. "Keep your ears open and I'll do the same. I don't know if you are planning to stay in America once we've finished or if you want to return home straight away."

"I don't know," Ned replied truthfully. He reminded himself to find a source of news from England. If he was a free man, he was tempted to stay in America indefinitely. If he wasn't, then the implications of that would give him lots more to consider regarding Florence.

"I'd like it if you stayed," Florence said. "I should tell you what happened just before you arrived."

Ned slowed in anticipation. "Yes, I saw you talking to someone. I wasn't sure if I should rush across the street and save you from being abducted but you seemed fine."

"It was the strangest conversation. The man approached me and asked if I was the Miss Wakechild who had arrived on the *City of Bruges*. When I refused to confirm it, he told me he is a clerk employed by an attorney who is acting on behalf of an English solicitor. He was looking for the whereabouts of the heir presumptive who was on the ship. He asked again so I thought there was no point in denying it."

Ned's heart sped up. "Really? Why did he come looking for you?"

Florence shrugged, as if being approached by clerks was a perfectly normal turn of events.

"I don't think he's just looking for me. He mentioned that I had been seen in the earl's company and someone had told him we had been dancing together. I assume he's going to try find all the passengers who were at the Captain's Dinner that he can. There must be quite a number of us who are still in the city. I hope he won't have to travel all over the country trying to track them down. It could take months. Maybe you should offer to help as you know what people on board looked like."

"Did he say what he wants?" Ned asked. Something nagged his brain.

Florence grew excited. "It appears Mr Colling's status as heir presumptive has changed and he is now in fact an earl."

"An earl? I thought you told me he was expecting a viscountcy." That was it. She'd said it and he hadn't really noticed.

Florence pursed her lips thoughtfully. "Yes, I did, now you mention it. How strange. I thought he was a viscount but the clerk definitely said he was now an earl."

"Maybe he got it wrong, or maybe you were wrong in the first place," Ned suggested. His heart began to drum.

Florence twirled her parasol nonchalantly. "Either way, it doesn't matter because I didn't know where he was, so I couldn't help. How frustrating for him, to come into his title after all these years and no one can find him to tell him."

"Assuming he wants to be found," Ned pointed out.

"You're right, perhaps he has disappeared intentionally." She gave a light-hearted laugh. "Wouldn't that be funny. Like something from a melodrama. A disappearing nobleman."

Ned gave a thin smile.

"So it appears our friend Mrs Carmine made a good choice after all. I imagine Mrs Carmine will lose no time in becoming the countess of ... of where? Did your attorney say?" he asked casually.

"I don't know," Florence said. "I wonder if he will marry her. Now Mr Colling has his title, there's nothing to say he will still want her. Perhaps he will prefer to consider a more appropriate match."

She sounded so downhearted that Ned was quite startled.

"If he loved her before he had a title, I can think of no reason why he would not continue to do so," he replied, drawing her arm slightly closer beneath his. "A man who finds love without the weight of wealth or status behind him would be an absolute fool to give it up when he was assured it."

Florence smiled up at him. "You sound quite the romantic."

Ned said nothing. He'd never considered himself as a particularly romantic soul but in Florence's company he would quite like to discover the extent of his skills in that regard.

"I suppose Mrs Carmine is not too young and he will need to think of his heirs," he mused.

"Now you sound just like my father!" Florence exclaimed. From her tone, it clearly wasn't a compliment. "He's obsessed with my brother providing an heir for the company. Is that all that matters to men?"

"It's important," Ned pointed out. "Take Mr Colling. He has lived in a state of uncertainty, not knowing if he can continue his life as it is or if he will be elevated to the peerage. Would he want to inflict that curse onto another at his passing?"

"I suppose not," Florence said.

Ned's stomach was rolling and if he'd been alone, he would have leapt onto the nearest omnibus to go in search of the attorney.

"Did he leave his name?" Ned asked, knowing full well that Dottie was in possession of a card.

"Mc or Mac something," Florence said. "I have a card, only I gave it to Dottie."

They both looked ahead to where Dottie was entering the hotel.

"I can bring it tonight," Florence said.

Ned thanked her. They said their goodbyes then parted.

He walked back to his hotel at speed, the exercise not doing any good in shaking off his feeling of turmoil. The attorney might have been looking for Mr Colling, but Ned didn't truly believe that. Lawyers didn't mix up earls and viscounts. If he had said he was looking for an earl, then an earl it would be, and Ned had a growing feeling of certainty that the earl in question was the Earl of Ayesgarth.

In which case he was looking for the man named Benedict Fitton, and Benedict Fitton was currently living under the alias of Ned Blake.

Chapter Twenty-Two

There was no question of arriving at the ball with Florence, as much as Ned would have liked to see her and ask if she had brought the card from the attorney's clerk. His forbearance had been greatly tested ever since Florence lit the fuse that crawled slowly but inescapably towards the bomb beneath Ned, without even realising what she'd done.

Before that, however, came another moment of truth. Would he be able to pass as a viscount convincingly enough to fool Clayton Wakechild? He lingered in the East Vestibule of the Faulkner mansion where guests were arriving on foot, having left their carriages in the outer courtyard and greeting each other with excitement.

He caught a few glances in his direction and stood slightly taller, trying to exude a sense of mysterious confidence and elegance. Deep down, he had no fears of failing to pass for an aristocrat, though he considered it the height of irony that while birth was on his side, he had been exiled from his true social circle for so many years that he had never learned to move within it.

His clothes were probably the finest garments he'd ever worn. The black tailcoat was impeccably tailored to fit his frame and beneath it he wore a crisp white dress shirt with a high collar and a pleated front. A black bow tie – he gave thanks to Lord Griggs' valet who had patiently taught him the technique of tying it – added a touch of sophistication to his ensemble. His trousers were a deep shade of charcoal grey and he carried a black silk top hat in his hand, which he tipped ever so slightly in greeting to the other guests who made their curiosity more obvious. By the time he saw the Griggs party arriving, he was thoroughly enjoying himself.

The instant he saw Florence, his entire body became alert and he had to remind himself to breathe. Her hair looked like amber, with tendrils of curls framing her face and cascading down her neck. She wore delicate gold earrings with green stones that shimmered in the light and a matching necklace. Both called attention to the grace of her neck and decolletage. Her dress was pale green silk with a skirt that flowed like water as she moved, catching the light from the gas lamps in a way that made it look like it glowed from within and possessed more hues than it possibly could have.

She was stunning.

She looked like a goddess walking among men.

She looked terrified.

Ned's belly jerked with a sense of protectiveness. He almost began walking towards her, so great was the urge to shield her from whatever was causing her anxiety, but he stopped himself. He knew the plan. They would find each other inside approximately half an hour into the event, then Lord Griggs would perform the introduction to Mr Wakechild. Curbing his urge to be close to her, Ned followed the throng of guests into the North Hall, showing the stiff gilt-edged invitation to one of the white-gloved footmen.

The Faulkners had spared no expense when it came to decorating for this event. Everywhere Ned looked, there were intricate carvings and ornate furniture that mimicked stately old English houses from centuries gone by. The oil paintings on the walls, the sculptures in discreet alcoves that lined the long hallway, and the gas lamps that glowed from sconces set at intervals of every six feet along the walls spoke of wealth and privilege which most of the viscounts and earls in Britain could only dream of. It was no wonder the British aristocracy were as keen to access this wealth as the Americans were to access their history. Ned thought disdainfully of the echoey rooms and narrow Elizabethan windows of the house he'd grown up in. What would his late father have thought of this splendour?

The receiving line was edging forward rapidly. According to Florence, Sapphire Faulkner liked things to proceed briskly as she viewed the formalities as a waste of dancing time. By the time Ned reached the head of the line, she had presumably greeted all her close friends and the principal visitors. She looked bored and barely glanced at the trailing line of less significant guests who murmured their thanks to her and her husband.

Ned passed into the ballroom. It boasted a large floor wide enough for four sets of couples to dance down. Three large chandeliers hung overhead, casting an inviting glow over everything below them. A full orchestra played at an alcove raised at one end. Currently they were playing an old-fashioned waltz, but as far as Ned could tell, nobody was dancing. Now the formalities had been observed, the guests were free to mingle, and gossiping and eating was the order of the day.

The Faulkners had arranged for ice creams and sherbets to be placed in twisted silver stands that looked like trees, with branches holding the individual bowls. Ned accepted a glass dish of strawberry ice cream from a waiter. A memory echoed. Last time he had been at a ball, he had been the waiter and he'd spent that evening looking for Florence too. It was that night which started the whole madcap scheme.

He finished his ice, handed the bowl to a waiter, then went to find a place to wait for Florence. She joined him within twenty minutes. She stopped dead as she approached him and took a step back. Her eyes grew wide and her cheeks pink.

"Ned! You look..."

He stepped towards her and took her hand, raising it to his lips, remembering that they had been kissing her only a few hours earlier.

"So do you."

They stood opposite each other, neither quite sure about the familiar stranger.

"Are we going ahead?" he asked.

"Of course. Annoyingly, I have to dance with a few people early on. My friend Miss Faulkner apparently got hold of my dance card because she's filled it in. You're on there, though."

She twirled the little paper book that hung from her right wrist on a loop of silken ribbon. Last year, the fashion had been for silver chains, but Ned preferred this less affected decoration. She gave him a warm smile but her brows were furrowed. She was playing with a ring on her finger, rubbing her thumb over the stone in smaller circles around the setting. She probably had no idea she was even doing it, but it was clear to Ned that she was nervous and presumably found the gesture calming.

"Don't worry, I'll remember how to dance," Ned assured her.

The right side of her mouth switched into something that was a bit more of a genuine smile.

"I know you will. You're an excellent partner. I'm sorry, Ned. I should be the one reassuring you, not the other way around. I have absolute faith that you can carry this off perfectly. I just find social engagements this large rather overwhelming. I always have. As they go on, the noises sound more acute, the scents become more overpowering. Everything feels more vibrant."

She looked down at her hands and adjusted the seams of

her gloves, even though the white silk was perfectly smooth from fingertip to elbow.

"I'm here," Ned said. "If for any reason you find you need to leave, or even if you just want to sit and talk quietly to me for a few minutes, just wink at me from across the room, or if we're close enough tell me you've remembered a funny story about my Aunt Agatha's pug."

"Does your Aunt Agatha have a pug?" Florence asked, a little bit of a smile returning to her face. "Do you even have an Aunt Agatha for that matter?"

"Yes, I do, or rather a Great Aunt Agatha. You'd like her, I think. She's rather eccentric and says exactly what comes into her head." Ned paused, thinking of the woman who once stopped an overlong sermon by the Bishop of York simply by coughing in a particularly disapproving tone. It had been on the subject of the Prodigal Son, ironically.

"Anyway, mention the dog and I'll come to your rescue at once," he finished.

"Well, only as soon as it would be polite," Florence said earnestly.

"Of course. I won't run off halfway through a conversation with a railroad heiress and leave her standing at the punch bowl."

Florence gave a small laugh and gave him a frank stare. "I'm not letting any railroad heiresses near you. I'd be far too jealous."

"Would you?" Ned's heart soared.

"Of course. You're the finest-looking man here, and by

far the nicest. I would turn absolutely green if I had to stand and watch you dancing with someone else."

"Ah." He swallowed. He hadn't known exactly what he was hoping she'd say. A full-hearted declaration of love?

Yes, actually. That was exactly what he hoped for, hopeless though it would be.

He made his mind up in that moment to tell her absolutely everything about him. He'd failed to find the answer to the question that plagued him, despite avidly reading the English newspapers which had arrived on the overnight steamship, but with the identity of an attorney within his grasp, the moment of truth would not be too far off.

The receptionist at his hotel had identified a number of attorneys within Manhattan, but he had not been able to say whether any of them had clerks called Mc or Mac something. He needed the card. If he chose to, he'd be able to discover his fate before noon the following day. Now that the knowledge was within reach, he both dreaded and craved the moment of discovery.

Either way, he was tired of hiding the truth from Florence.

"You're very quiet," Florence murmured.

He looked round at her. "Are you sure you wouldn't like to marry a nobleman?" he asked. "Despite, rather than because of, his title. If one was pleasant and you thought you might like him."

"I am absolutely determined. I will fight with my last

breath not to be one of those women who the world can say had her head turned by the thought of a coronet."

She lifted her chin and fixed him with a determined stare. "Don't talk to me of such matters tonight. Let me enjoy myself while I can."

There was a plea at the edge of her voice.

"I'm just thinking," Ned muttered. "You're right. Now is an evening for enjoyment. When we have time to ourselves again, we should talk. There are things I need to tell you, but now isn't the time or place. Tomorrow we'll meet. I don't suppose you brought the card from the attorney's clerk?"

"I'm afraid not. Though I looked at it and the name is Macallister and he has an office on Sixth Avenue." She looked intrigued. "Why does it matter? You can't tease me like that!"

"I'm afraid I must." He gave her a grin. "It'll give you something to speculate about and take your mind off being nervous."

"Oh you very devil! You're teasing me!" She broke into a laugh. "Thank you. I won't be worried now because I shall spend the whole evening imagining all the scandals you've been involved in. Tomorrow we'll meet for morning coffee and you can reveal them all to me."

Ned's throat tightened but he managed a smile anyway.

The orchestra began tuning up. Florence spun around. "Oh bother! I have to go. I'll find you soon. Look out for me when it's the mazurka because that's you."

She swept away. Ned watched as the ballroom

swallowed her. He leaned against the wall. His eyes grew misty. She was so completely sure of her opinions and he loved her for it. He hoped he knew her well enough that when he revealed what he had to, it would not completely ruin the friendship they had formed. At least he could share the truth on his own terms and in his own time.

Florence tried not to glance around her as she danced. Ned would be somewhere in the room and as much as she had joked about heiresses, she couldn't bear the thought of seeing him with another woman. It was hard enough that Estelle Faulkner had drawn her aside as they had reached the head of the receiving line to snatch a couple of words.

"Thank you for the invitation for my friend," she had whispered.

"Thank *you*!" Estelle had hissed back. "I caught a glimpse of him and he's utterly handsome. I'm so intrigued. I can't wait to see what trick you're going to pull off but I bet it'll be wild. Are you planning to elope with him? I put him on your card, though I had to scrub out a Frick boy to do it."

Florence had hushed her, glancing at her father. Estelle had a habit of talking loudly even when she was whispering but it didn't matter as Clayton was distracted with making over-the-top overtures to Sapphire.

"No, I'm not going to elope"—a spasm in her belly made her stiffen—"but you'll see soon enough."

Now she swept back into the ballroom after her chat with Ned, displaying a confidence she didn't feel, and searched out her next partner.

She recognised a few of the names. The Vanderbilt was a surprise. Johnny Clancy, who she had known since childhood, would be easy to dance with, and of course Ned. Lord Stretford was on her card, which slightly marred her pleasure, but he was not until the last dance so she could avoid talking with him for too long afterwards. She just had to hope that her father did not insist on discussing the engagement with him during the evening.

She had the whole evening mapped out in her head.

It would be a simple matter to dance with Ned, contrive to finish near her father, and then let Twemlow take over and introduce him. Then she could leave them to become acquainted while she danced with her next partner, a Granelli, who she hadn't met before. She'd have a quick trip to the powder room then return to Ned and her father to see how they were getting on. She would offer him an invitation to join them for afternoon tea, which her father would readily agree to. It was at the end of the afternoon tea that she would reveal the trick. The roots of her hair tingled. Ned had something to tell her too. She could barely wait to discover what he was going to reveal. Perhaps he had already found another commission which would keep him in the city.

She turned her attention to the room. Twemlow was basking in the adulation of a quartet of elderly belles who were all rapt. No doubt he was making much of his title to them. Cordelia was dancing in the arms of her friend Eli Levitt. Cordelia glowed in a way that she didn't when she was with Twemlow and it made Florence melancholy to see. Mr Levitt was a kind man, not overly burdened with looks but with a dazzling sense of humour and good prospects. If he had not been Jewish, Clayton would surely have blessed the marriage—if Mr Levitt had owned an English country estate and a title, of course.

Until that moment Florence hadn't fully understood what her sister had sacrificed in order to keep her father happy. No doubt her marriage to Twemlow was happy, but it could have been blissful if she had been allowed to choose the man she loved. What right did Florence have to throw a tantrum and demand to be treated differently than Cordelia?

Perhaps she should grow up a little and resign herself to marrying Lord Stretford.

She enjoyed dancing with her varied partners, but it was only when Ned led her onto the dance floor that she truly came alive. When they danced together, it felt like she was returning home where she belonged. Remembering the way Cordelia and Mr Levitt had danced together, she knew that even if she married another man, she would never love him as much as she had grown to love Ned.

They danced past Estelle, who was dancing with a tall striking man with extremely pale hair and skin like skimmed milk.

"From Iceland," Estelle mouthed, raising her eyebrows.

Florence giggled. Estelle had scandalised her mother by

threatening to elope with a Hindu man from the Indian colonies, with black hair and brown skin. Now she had chosen a dance partner who was almost the opposite and Florence wondered if she was doing it deliberately to spite her parents.

They met again on the other side of the dance floor and this time Estelle looked at Ned and then rolled her eyes back, mouthing, "Heavenly."

Again, Florence try not to smile but nodded. Ned was heavenly. Gorgeous, light on his feet, and every inch the born aristocrat.

As the music died away, Ned executed a perfect bow. Florence thought that if there had been a way of recording the scene so that it could be shown again to future generations, she would have done so that everyone could learn to be so graceful. She curtsied. Her heart fluttered with excitement and trepidation.

"Are you ready?" she murmured. "I can see my father standing close by. There's no time like the present."

"Yes of course. I shall regale him by reciting all the introductions I know and impress him with my knowledge of when to use my snail spoons." He winked at her devilishly.

Despite the lump in her throat, a giggle somehow managed to pull its way past the blockage.

"Don't make me laugh," she said. "You're always joking."

She thought about it some more. "Actually, do keep making me laugh. You do it so well. I don't want you to ever stop. I need to laugh." Florence looked away momentarily, checking whether anyone was in earshot to hear them talking so intimately. When she looked back, she was struck by the force of his expression.

"Florence, whatever you do with your life, find a man who makes you laugh. The fellow that knows how to do that will truly understand you."

The prospect of imminent loss was like a fist clawing at her heart. It was Ned who held the invisible threads to her heart, and though he could not be aware of it, he was pulling her towards him more with every kindness, every tease, every touch.

Clayton Wakechild was standing with Twemlow and Cordelia. As Florence and Ned walked up to the group, she noticed Cordelia crossing her fingers briefly. Behind them, fresh couples assembled on the dance floor. A couple of people paused and looked at Florence and Ned. If she achieved nothing else, she would have created the impression that she was a woman capable of attracting a dance partner of his calibre.

As she approached her father, he smiled then looked at Ned and furrowed his brows. Florence hesitated, realising with horror that she had forgotten entirely in which direction the introduction should go. Should she beg Twemlow to introduce her father to the viscount, or the other way around? It was all going to go dreadfully wrong. She was wrong. This sort of thing couldn't be taught. It had to be ingrained from birth.

Fortunately Clayton, unaware that he was about to

break protocol and not understanding the apparent status of his daughter's partner, stepped forward.

"Young man, I don't believe we've had the pleasure of an introduction."

Florence looked at Twemlow as a signal for help. He stepped forward.

"Miss Wakechild, I must say you're looking lovely tonight. Positively the most enchanting creature in the whole of New York City. And I see you have found our good friend, Telford."

He turned to Ned. "Lord Telford, may I introduce Mr Wakechild, the father of our delightful Miss Wakechild."

To Florence's extreme pleasure, her father looked flustered. He tugged surreptitiously at his cufflink then bowed.

"Lord Telford. I am afraid you must pardon my unpardonable rudeness, your lordship. I didn't recognise you. I didn't know you were in town."

Florence could have cheered aloud. Not only did her father apparently accept Ned at face value, but his vanity wouldn't let him admit his ignorance and he was actually pretending to have heard of the viscount. It would be all the more perfect when she revealed the truth.

They had rehearsed Ned's supposed lineage and he knew the details perfectly. She never got the chance to discover how convincing Ned might have been, though, because at that moment Lord Stretford walked past the group. He stopped as if he had seen something outlandish, then came back.

"Good lord! How unexpected seeing you here."

She was about to retort that it wasn't at all unexpected when she realised he was speaking not to her, but to Ned, who was staring back at the viscount with a look of horror on his face. Florence stepped slightly closer to him before she was even aware that she was doing it.

"Lord Stretford, it's good to see you again," Clayton said bowing. "Would you do me the honour of allowing me to present to you Lord Telford."

He looked slightly worried. "Or perhaps you are already acquainted, being as you are countrymen and both viscounts."

Florence closed her eyes, willing herself to be anywhere other than where she was. Clayton had no place making such an introduction. He came across as gauche and incredibly self-important. The only redeeming fact was that he appeared to have accepted Ned's identity without question.

"Nonsense." Lord Stretford clapped his hands together briskly. "I don't know what game you're playing, but calling yourself a viscount indeed!"

Florence's shoulders slumped. How could Stretford have possibly been able to spot the deception on sight? Surely not every aristocrat knew all the existing titles so well as to be able to spot an interloper so easily. Florence looked at her father whose expression had become one of complete confusion.

"You know each other?" Twemlow asked, glancing at Florence and evidently as taken aback by the turn of events.

Florence looked at Ned. His face was a rictus, far beyond what the revelation merited.

"Of course. I was at Rugby with his older brother," Lord Stretford said. Then he did something Florence would never have predicted if she'd been given a year of guesses.

He bowed.

Ned made a growling noise in his throat and glared at the viscount as if he wanted to rip Lord Stretford's tongue out.

"Ned, I don't understand," Florence murmured.

"Ned?" Lord Stretford looked between them. "Miss Wakechild, I don't know who you think this man is, but his name is most certainly not Ned."

"Don't!" Ned stepped towards Lord Stretford.

The command or plea—Florence wasn't sure which—came out like a rifle shot just as the dance ended and the room quietened. There were murmurings from the groups close by and a few turned heads. Florence could feel herself getting hot and agitated. Any second now, her brain would shut down and her body would take over and she would run.

"I don't understand," she repeated. "Please will somebody explain."

"Florence..." Ned's voice was barely audible and Stretford spoke over him, easily drowning him out.

"I don't know what game he's playing, Miss Wakechild, but this man is no viscount. He is the Earl of Ayesgarth, and I'm glad to be one of the first men to offer my sincere congratulations to him on his inheriting the title."

He turned to Ned and bowed again. "My lord, half of England is searching for you at present. Have you not heard the news from Yorkshire? The child has been born. The countess has been blessed with a daughter."

Lord Stretford looked genuinely confused and was speaking without malice. Ned looked at Florence and she stared back. This was all wrong. He wasn't an earl. She looked from man to man, still not comprehending, but one word flashed in her mind.

"Child?"

Her voice was barely audible to her, but Ned flinched.

"Damn you, Stuffy," he muttered. "Miss Wakechild, I'm sorry, I must leave. Excuse me."

He turned on his heel and walked away without a backward glance.

Chapter Twenty-Three

"Florence?" Clayton asked, looking more confused than she'd seen him in years. "Is that man a viscount or an earl? Will someone explain what is going on?"

His raised voice was drawing more attention.

Lord Stretford nodded curtly. "Will you excuse me. I can see I've intruded on a rather awkward situation."

"Lord Stretford, there's no need. Come and dance with Florence," Clayton said. "Florence is so looking forward to the dance. She's talked of little else all day."

Lord Stretford smiled coldly, the act barely reaching his lips, never mind his eyes.

"Permit me to decline. I shall leave you to sort out your family crisis. Good evening to you both."

He turned on his heel and walked away. Clayton looked like he was about to call after him but fortunately Twemlow caught his sleeve and shook his head.

Florence gave a soft moan of mortification. Not only was Ned leaving, but the viscount had openly rejected her.

She couldn't bear the openly curious looks any longer. Picking up the hem of her skirt, she fled into the hallway. She was halfway to the inner garden courtyard when Ned caught up with her, falling in at her side. She sped up.

"Florence, wait!"

Head down, she carried on walking. "Leave me alone! I don't want to talk to you. Thanks to you, my father is embarrassed and we'll be the talk of the party." She gulped down a sob. "You completely humiliated me. How could you do such a thing to me!"

"I have to explain."

"Explain what? If what Lord Stretford said is true, you ran from England because you were about to become a father! What kind of abysmal scoundrel are you to abandon an expectant mother?"

"I didn't know Stretford would be here. I need you to listen," Ned said urgently.

She spun around, blood pounding in her ears and breathing heavily. Aware that there were guests strolling around the courtyard, she lowered her voice to an angry whisper. "And if he hadn't been, then I'd be none the wiser! I don't even know what is true and what isn't but I don't want to talk to you. Stay away from me or I'll scream."

Ned winced and his eyes filled with pain, but he nodded and stepped away. Giving a sob, Florence ran into the powder room and threw herself down on an overstuffed stool.

Too many questions whirled in her head.

What child? What countess? What earl?

Ned had always been cagey about his background and now she realised why. He'd been lying to her since the moment they met. She realised her nose was starting to run and delved into a hidden pocket in her skirt for a handkerchief. Looking at it, she reached a moment of clarity. She hadn't given Ned the chance to explain, just as she hadn't when she had discovered his handkerchief in Dottie's box.

"Always jumping to conclusions," she said quietly.

She leaned her elbows on the dressing table and buried her head in them, unable to see what alternative conclusion she should have jumped to but she owed it to him to let him explain the situation. If she didn't find out everything, it would plague her forever. She tidied her face then went in search of Ned, hoping he had not left already.

He was in the internal courtyard, leaning against the fountain. He looked up as she approached and his face grew serious. "You came back."

"I am determined not to jump to conclusions," Florence said, trying to keep her voice level. "I will give you ten minutes to tell me the truth."

Ned's mouth twitched. "I expect it will take a little longer than that. Can we find somewhere quiet to sit down and I'll explain everything?"

Beneath a magnolia tree in a quiet corner there was an empty love seat – the irony of which was not lost on

Florence – so she sat on it, glad to have something steady beneath her.

Ned remained standing. "I did not run from England because I was in danger of becoming a father. I have never been married, nor as far as I'm aware, have I had the opportunity to father a child. The baby is not mine."

Whatever else he might reveal, the cords that had tightened around Florence's belly loosened at his words.

"You swear that."

Ned dropped onto the bench beside her and looked deep into her eyes.

"I do. The countess that Lord Stretford spoke of is my sister-in-law, the widow of my brother Jasper, the sixth Earl of Ayesgarth."

"Your brother is an earl?" Florence asked.

"My brother *was* an earl." A dark shadow passed over Ned's face. "Jasper fell from his horse and died seven months ago. His widow was newly pregnant at the time, meaning there was uncertainty over the line of succession. If she gave birth to a son, the boy would become the seventh earl. If a child was a girl, or indeed if the pregnancy failed to result in a living child, then the title passed to the next male in line. In this case, his younger brother. In this case me."

While she struggled to take in what he said, they were interrupted by the arrival of Cordelia who swept across the garden towards them in a bustle of russet silk. Florence had never been less pleased to see her sister.

"There you are, Florence!" Cordelia paused and stared at

Ned with a furious expression, completely unaware of what she had interrupted. "For goodness' sake you have to come back, Father is about to pass away from apoplexy!"

Florence leapt to her feet, her entire body flooding with guilt, momentarily disregarding anything Ned had said.

"Has somebody called a doctor?"

Cordelia shook her head. "I don't mean literally but he is about to explode. Florence, how could you humiliate Father in public! The revelation was supposed to be done in private, wasn't it, and I thought Mr Blake was supposed to be a viscount."

"It wasn't supposed to happen that way at all. I didn't know what Lord Stretford was going to reveal," Florence said, glaring at Ned, who bowed his head deferentially to Cordelia.

"I cannot offer enough apologies, Lady Griggs. I was unaware of my new status myself until Lord Stretford revealed it."

"Then it's true? You are an earl?" Cordelia asked, her eyes growing wide.

Ned grimaced. "Unfortunately, yes." He gave a long, drawn-out, world-weary sigh.

"You've been deceiving me all this time?" Florence asked.

"No. Thanks to Lord Stretford, I have—just as you have—learned that the countess has given birth to a daughter. As you will remember from the very similar circumstances of our shipboard acquaintance Mr Colling, that leaves me to now inherit my brother's title."

"Many titles can only pass to a son," Cordelia reminded her. She turned back to Ned. "Who does this make you?"

"Is your name even Edward?" Florence demanded.

"No," Ned said. "Though in my defence I never confirmed it was Edward. My name is Benedict Fitton." Ned spread his hands out and looked pained. "Assuming Lord Stretford's information is correct and I have now inherited the title, I am the seventh Earl of Ayesgarth, of Levisham Hall in Yorkshire. Whether that is the case is something I intend to find out at the earliest opportunity."

"Yes, you should, though there are more important matters now," Cordelia snapped. They both turned to face her. She put her hands on her hips.

"If any of us ever want to hold our head up in society again, you both have to come back inside and do something to rectify the situation. Fortunately, only a few people overheard what actually passed between us, but everyone saw you both rush out and will have noticed Lord Stretford going. The scandal of you leaving would be ruinous and the gossip will be far worse than the truth."

"I don't even know the truth!" Florence snapped. "I don't think I've learned it all."

Ned – Florence couldn't think of him as Benedict – stepped close to Florence's side.

"Miss Wakechild, we need to talk, but can we do it later? I feel deeply for your father and the embarrassment this is causing for your family. I truly would have done anything to prevent it happening. Will you return and dance with me?"

"I'm in no fit state to dance!" Florence put her hands to her cheeks, feeling the heat surging between her fingers. "I must be glowing like the starboard light on a ship. Everyone will look at me."

"You look beautiful," Ned said, his eyes softening in a manner that would have made Florence's insides quiver under any other circumstances.

"And even if you didn't, you need to go back inside," Cordelia prompted.

"You're too brave to run away," Ned said quietly.

Florence's stomach writhed but his words spurred her on. She lifted her head. "I'll do it, but after one dance I'm going to return home."

Cordelia snapped her fan closed. "Thank goodness. Give me five minutes to warn father and explain to Sapphire."

It was five minutes that lasted a century. For the first two, Florence and Ned looked at the ground, avoiding each other. In the third, Florence looked at him out of the corner of her eye. So handsome and noble-looking. What had she missed?

He caught her eye and straightened up.

"You lied to me," Florence whispered, her voice cracking.

Ned bowed his head again. "I know. Try not to hate me for it."

"I can't say yet whether I'll hate you," Florence answered honestly. "The whole thing feels like a bad dream and I'm unable to untangle my thoughts. You had better come and see me tomorrow. I think you owe me an explanation and we both owe one to my father."

"So do I," said Ned. "But before that, let's dance and show your father and everyone here that Florence Wakechild is capable of enchanting an earl."

She walked at his side, back straight and head high. It was only as they approached the room that she ground to a halt.

"I can't go back in there," she said. "Everyone will be looking at me. I've made such a fool of myself. You made a fool of me."

"I regret that more than anything. I can't do much to rectify that, but let me try. I promised you before that I would be with you and I will keep that promise now. Just look into my eyes and forget there is anyone else in the room."

Ned took her hand, closing his fingers around hers. He'd done it countless times before but never had the gesture seemed so heartfelt.

"Mr Blake, take me to dance," she said.

They crossed the threshold. The chatter of conversation grew muted. Cordelia was standing beside Sapphire and Estelle. She winked at Florence.

Sapphire stepped forward and curtsied to Ned, causing murmurs around the room which died down as she raised her voice.

"My sincerest apologies, Lord Fitton. I had no idea that you were attending my little gathering."

Ned bowed then took her hand and kissed it. Sapphire's eyes grew wide.

"The apologies are all mine, Mrs Faulkner. I have only recently come into the title. Confirmation of the fact did not become knowledge until I had embarked on my voyage to visit my good friends the Wakechilds. You know the family, of course?"

He turned and bowed to Clayton and the Griggses. Clayton looked bemused but managed a bow in return.

"I know them very well." Sapphire beamed at Florence. "In fact, Miss Wakechild and my dear Estelle are the closest friends. Perhaps you would permit me to leave a card at your residence, my lord? I would be honoured to invite you here to view our art collection."

"I'd be delighted. The fame of your collection spreads wide."

Ned bowed again, then turned and looked at Florence who had been standing mutely throughout the exchange. She breathed in and out slowly, trying her best to retain her equilibrium.

"Now, Mrs Faulkner, may I beg a favour? This captivating creature is waiting to dance and a gentleman must always oblige."

"Music!" Sapphire clapped her hands. The orchestra began tuning and couples filled the floor. Ned led Florence to the centre.

"Remember, keep looking at me and all will be well," he murmured as he took her in his arms.

She did and it was.

They moved in perfect harmony, as if their bodies had been made for each other. Florence felt herself melting into him with every step, a feeling of pure bliss washing over her that transcended all the shock of the evening. They passed Cordelia and Twemlow who watched them closely. When the dance ended, they stayed in each other's arms, eyes locked together, until the conversations around them died away and her concerns flooded back. Not for the fear of any scandal, but for what she would have to say to her father and family.

"Thank you," Ned murmured.

He escorted her to the edge of the dance floor where her family were waiting. Taking both of her hands in his, he looked deep into her eyes, dipping his head so that she alone could hear his words.

"I will come to you tomorrow morning and explain what I can."

"There's a tea room on the corner of Bryant Park and Sixth Avenue. I'll be waiting at ten," she said, trying to sound calm.

Tomorrow would bring a reckoning that she didn't know how she would endure.

Ned turned away and walked across the room, whereupon he was immediately swallowed up by a throng of women, including some matrons but many closer to Florence's age. She caught a glimpse of him dancing shortly afterwards with a tall beauty Florence didn't recognise and the throb of jealousy in her heart almost made her stagger. There must be ten or twenty young women in search of a husband who would positively devour Ned, many wealthy, most accomplished and clever. And none who had not made it abundantly clear to Ned that the last man on earth they would marry was an earl.

Ned barely slept. He lapsed in and out of consciousness but was already awake when the dawn chorus started its futile attempt to be heard over the sound of early morning delivery carts and horse-drawn trolleys.

He took more care than he felt like doing as he dressed, and once ready, he unlocked his strongbox and affixed his pocket watch by the chain. On the infrequent occasions he wore it, he usually glanced at the garnets on the back but today he opened the cover and read the engraving. It had been a gift from his father on his eighteenth birthday and the message from father to son made his eyes water.

There was one more item, carefully secreted in a velvet bag: the signet ring he'd kept for so long, a bend sinister with a horse rampant and his initials engraved in the centre. Ned hadn't worn it since the day he had walked away from his family. He rolled it between finger and thumb.

It was not too late to run. He could still leave New York and disappear; start a new life with a new identity as he had once thought of doing. There were cousins who could take the title if he never returned to claim it. Even before he slipped the signet ring onto his little finger, he knew he wouldn't do that.

The wager had presumably fallen through, given the dramatic way his identity had been revealed, so he had no further obligation in that regard. The only unresolved business concerned Florence herself and discovering whether she would ever forgive him for what he had kept from her.

He took a streetcar to Bryant Park and found Florence waiting in the tea room with a pot of tea and two cups. She wore a large blue hat with a veil that obscured the upper half of her face, no doubt intentionally. He would have given anything to properly see her. When Ned approached her, she laced her fingers together on top of the table.

"Thank you for coming," Ned said, slipping into the seat opposite her. "It means more than you know that you've given me a chance to explain."

"Thank my curiosity and the fact that I want to sleep easily without being plagued by questions." She cleared her throat. "Were you ever going to tell me the truth?"

"At first, I couldn't imagine a situation where I'd need to. I thought our association would be brief and I'd be able to hide from fate for long enough. Lately, though, I knew I would have to." Ned steepled his fingers. "I wanted to. Do you remember me saying we needed to talk?"

She gave a faint nod. "At the ball, when you asked about the attorney's card."

"This is what I was intending to tell you. I had no idea Lord Stretford would be attending the event, otherwise I would never have accepted the invitation. I certainly had no intention of being unmasked in such a way."

Florence reached up and lifted her veil. To Ned's relief, her eyes had their customary brightness.

"That was my fault. I knew he'd be there, but I didn't want to tell you. That's why you got yourself beaten to a mess on the day of the fair, isn't it? It makes sense now. It was so you didn't have to see Lord Stretford?"

Ned rubbed his hand across his jaw, remembering the pain. "I couldn't think of another alternative. The moment he saw me, he would have recognised me and revealed who I am. As he did last night."

Florence threw out her hands. "But what does that matter? We could have stopped the wager at that point. I would have stopped it if I'd known. I'm sure Lord Griggs will declare the wager void now everyone knows I didn't succeed."

Ned gave a sad smile. "I wanted you to win. Miss Wakechild, it may be some comfort to you to learn that my general antipathy towards the aristocracy has not changed."

"I'm not sure anything you can say to me will comfort me now," Florence snapped. She dropped her head. "You made me feel so stupid. I believed you were exactly who you said you were. When I think of all the things we talked about … I thought you meant them."

"I did mean everything." He reached a hand towards her but when she glared, he withdrew it. "I did not intentionally hurt you. I would never do anything to hurt or upset you if it were within my power to avoid it. If you believe nothing else, believe that."

She looked at him and he held her gaze, willing her to believe him.

"You told me you were beaten by the earl apparent when you were a child," she said. "And that you left home when your father died. Were those lies?"

"It's all true. The disappointment, the arguments, the beatings. Everything." Ned rubbed his eyes. "I just neglected to mention the familial connection."

"Why?"

Ned sighed. "There are so many ways I could answer that. Because until very recently, it hasn't been relevant. I have had nothing to do with my family for years. If my brother had not died, I expect I would have lived and died as Ned Blake without ever setting foot in Yorkshire again. Part of me is still hoping that Stuffy had it wrong. That when I visit the lawyer, he'll tell me that the baby is a boy and I can carry on living as I have been."

"Do you want to? You once told me that you wanted more than two rooms of your own," Florence said. Her lips quirked, showing the first signs of good temper. "I assume you will now."

Ned grinned back cautiously. "There's a gulf between two rooms in a boarding house and fourteen bedrooms."

"Fourteen! My sister has only eight," Florence said, looking at him keenly. "Where do you come from?"

"Yorkshire. You'd like it, I think. It's an oddly shaped bit of property. There are moors in one direction with long beaches and tall cliffs and dales in the other direction with waterfalls." He sat back, momentarily homesick for the wildness. "If I decide to return, that's one of the things that will make it bearable."

"You aren't sure you will? But it's your duty." Florence's brow knotted.

Ned looked down at his cup. "I know. The thought fills me with dread. I was never meant to be the earl, so I was never trained as Jasper was. I don't really know what to do."

Florence smiled. "You'll learn. Besides, you're too brave to run away."

Ned grew warm inside. With Florence looking at him with such confidence, he almost believed he could do anything.

"Maybe I'll come visit you. I'm sure Lord Stretford would be overjoyed to associate with an earl. That is, if he hasn't decided to end our engagement before it is even formally announced."

"Engagement?" Ned stared at her, aghast. The vein in his temple began to pulsate.

"That's why he is in New York. My father told me it had been settled as soon as I arrived at the hotel. They are intending to announce it as soon as possible." She bit her lip and dropped her head. "So, you see, the whole wager was irrelevant after all."

Ned looked at her, feeling sick. "When you kissed me in the carriage, you already knew you weren't free to do so."

Florence looked stricken. "I shouldn't have but it was a moment of weakness. Of selfishness. I told you the truth: I wanted a memory of someone I like kissing me. My father promised me he wouldn't reveal the engagement until after the ball. That's why I didn't tell you Lord Stretford was going to be there."

Ned put his hands to his lips and stared out of the window. His stomach churned as if he were still being tossed across the Atlantic Ocean. Would he have kissed her if he had known? His sense of honour wanted to say he wouldn't. His sense of honesty knew he would have done it like a shot and damn Stretford.

"I don't think I'd want you to visit me in Yorkshire. I'd gladly have Miss Wakechild as a guest, but never Lady Stretford."

"Oh."

He turned around to look at Florence. Her expression was pensive and he wanted to reach out and kiss the lips that she was worrying with her teeth. Rational thought and caution flew out of the window. He reached for her hand and she allowed him to take it.

"Because I would be spending every moment reliving our kiss in my mind and heart, and eating myself alive with regret that you were not free to kiss me again. Because I love you, Florence."

"You love me?"

He'd been hoping that she might return the words, but she just stared at him, eyes wide.

"More than anything. Not only that, but I'm in love with you. I know I shouldn't speak but I can't remain silent. Call it a moment of weakness. Of selfishness. I would never forgive myself if I didn't tell you. Even though everything feels hopeless now."

He sat back, weary beyond measure.

"We've made rather a mess of matters, haven't we?" Florence said quietly, in what Ned considered to be the world's largest understatement.

"I think we have," he agreed.

Florence stood. "I need to go. I have to speak to my father. Somehow I have to explain the whole thing from start to finish. I'll still pay you the fee we agreed," she added. "Come by the hotel later today."

Ned waved a hand. "I won't take it."

She stood hesitantly in the doorway. A waitress approached.

"Can I help you, miss?"

Florence smiled at her. "No, thank you. I'm not sure what help anyone can give me now."

She glanced at Ned then left.

He sat back and drank his tea. It was mediocre at best, but he didn't care. Florence was engaged. Whatever he had hoped might happen was beyond him. He should have told her he loved her as soon as he realised. Told her the truth too. It might not have made a difference but he would never know.

Chapter Twenty-Four

After paying for the tea, Ned presented himself at the door of Sturges-Lake, Shote, and Lake, Attorneys at Law, and asked to speak to Mr Macallister. Shortly after that, he was escorted into an office to speak with Mr Hiram Sturges-Lake himself. The signet ring and watch inscription acted as enough validation of his identity. Within ten minutes, he had been shown a telegram from the firm of solicitors which his family had used for generations. It confirmed that Mary, Dowager Countess of Ayesgarth, had indeed given birth to a daughter and owing to the lack of a son, the title had passed to Ned.

"May I offer you my sincere congratulations, Lord Ayesgarth."

The address was like a punch in the guts. The urge to refuse the title was still there. Could he do it? If his father had officially disowned him, it would never have been an issue. Florence's words came back to him. He was too brave to run away.

Was he?

"It's been quite a quest to locate you, your lordship, if you'll permit me the liberty," Sturges-Lake said with a manner that suggested he didn't much care whether or not Ned was going to permit it. "I believe my associate in Great Britain only discovered you were heading to America thanks to a friend of yours in Liverpool who said you were travelling with a party called Wakechild."

"That would be a Mr Van Hoon?" Ned asked.

When it was confirmed, he shook his head, laughing gently. If he hadn't bumped into Van Hoon on the dockside, his whereabouts would have still been a mystery, buying him more time. Then again, Stretford would still have revealed his identity at the ball.

Stuffy and Florence.

His stomach clenched.

"Do you plan on staying long in New York, my lord?" Sturges-Lake asked. "I'll send a telegram back to our London offices to inform them we have located you but they would appreciate learning when you'll return to Yorkshire."

"I can't answer that at present," Ned replied. "I'm not being contrary, but I have matters to attend to and I don't know how long they will take me. I will contact you again when I have a better idea."

Sturges-Lake didn't enquire what the matters were and Ned wouldn't have told him anyway. Florence had said the engagement hadn't been announced. She was unwilling in any case. Was that tiny flicker of hope enough to become a beacon? Disrupting an engagement was far from the conduct an earl should display, but Ned was going to do his best regardless of propriety.

Florence couldn't exactly remember how she got back to the hotel, but she must have because she found herself back in her bedroom, being addressed by Dottie the moment she walked through the door.

"Your father wants to see you as soon as possible. I told him you had gone to church."

"Dottie, you are worth your weight in gold," Florence said, hugging her maid. "Please tell him I'm back. I'll go freshen up and go straight to see him."

Dottie hurried out. Florence absentmindedly removed her coat and hat, barely seeing herself in the mirror.

Ned loved her, just as she loved him. Her heart soared then plummeted. So what if he did? So what if she did? She was already engaged.

With a sense of dread in her belly, she made her way into her father's office. Clayton was sitting at his desk with a pile of ledgers. He turned and faced her, looking grim-faced.

"Now Florence, I demand that you tell me everything. Who is this man whose appearance made an absolute farce of last night's events and with whom you danced so closely? Is he an earl or a viscount, or perhaps he's the Grand Old Duke of York?"

"He is an earl," Florence said. "I didn't know it when we met. I thought he was just a normal person."

"Indeed?" Clayton looked at her sternly. "Then what is your connection with him?"

Florence sucked her teeth. There was no way to explain how they had met that wouldn't cause her father even more consternation.

"We met in Liverpool at the ball," she said almost truthfully.

A knock at the door interrupted her before she had to go into more detail. The door opened and Cordelia and Twemlow walked in.

"I asked for privacy, Cordelia," Clayton said sharply. It was a measure of his anger that he would ever consider speaking so sharply to his daughter in front of her husband.

Cordelia kissed her father's cheek, ignoring the snappishness as if he hadn't even spoken. "We don't believe Florence should face you alone. The wager was partly our idea too."

"A wager?"

"I hadn't got to that part," Florence said, wincing. "It's the truth though. I bet Twemlow that I could pass a commoner off as a viscount'. He thought I couldn't."

Clayton leaned against the table, his expression one of astonishment. "This is worse than I even realised. Lord Griggs, I can scarcely bring myself to believe that you are involved."

"But that's my point," Florence snapped. "You think that because Twemlow was born into wealth and family, he must be a cut above everyone else. You put him on a pedestal because he was born into wealth and family but he's just a human, with flaws the same as the rest of us. No offence meant, Twemlow," she added.

"None taken," he said with a wave of his hand, looking quite unconcerned at the affront to his character. There was a knock on the door and he strolled off to answer it then left the room.

"But why?" Clayton asked.

"I wanted to show you that your absolute obsession with aristocracy is stupid," Florence said. She put her hands to her head. "I wanted to prove that what you consider good breeding can be taught. We would have waited until you were convinced then revealed the truth."

"Again, I ask why?" Clayton said, a touch more irritability in his voice.

"So you would stop your ridiculous determination to marry me off to anyone with a title."

Clayton glowered. "Well, you've certainly ensured Lord Stretford will not be marrying you. I received an embarrassingly short note this morning telling me that any association I might have believed we had is ended forever. He says he has no intention of being linked to a family that caused such a scene as we did."

Despite her despondency, Florence's heart leapt. "Do you mean that? How wonderful."

"It's not wonderful!" Clayton slapped his hand down

onto the table. Florence flinched. Her father was the mildest-mannered man she had ever encountered, and to see him brought to such a state of violence was alarming. "I shall have to go and plead for him to take you back, and I expect you to come with me and throw the entire weight of your charm into the enterprise. It might not be too late for him to reconsider."

"No, Daddy, I won't," Florence said. She took her father by the hand. "Please don't demean us by chasing after him. Let this be the end of it. He doesn't want me and I certainly don't want him."

Twemlow coughed. "Mr Blake is waiting outside. He has asked to speak to you."

"Bring him in," Clayton ordered. "We'll have the entire set of conspirators."

Twemlow left and returned with Ned at his side. After his declaration previously, Florence couldn't look at him.

"Mr Wakechild, I have the honour of presenting the Earl of Ayesgarth."

"You can stop the charade now," Clayton said coldly. "Florence has told me of your wager."

"It's no charade," Ned said, inclining his head. "I have indeed come into that title within the past week. I only discovered it myself yesterday in the manner you saw."

"So you see, Daddy, I failed," Florence said. "I wanted to take an ordinary man and turn him into a viscount. Instead, I took an earl and failed even to pass him off for more than five minutes."

"You didn't fail," Ned said, moving to stand close to

Florence. "I wasn't an earl when I met you and until I did, I would have been dreadfully ill-prepared for the role."

He turned to Clayton. "I must explain, Mr Wakechild. I broke off from my family years ago and I've been living by own means ever since. For the majority of the last decade, I have been an ordinary man. More than that, I've been bitter and resentful. When I discovered I might be called upon to take the role I thought would never be mine, I became even more so."

He ran his hands through his hair and smiled at Florence, then at the other occupants of the room. Clayton said nothing.

"I've spent the months of my sister-in-law's pregnancy wondering what I would do if the child was a girl. Would I accept my fate or run from it? America is a big place. A man could disappear quite easily. I could become someone else entirely."

"And what are you going to do, if I might be so bold as to ask?" Twemlow asked.

Ned smiled at him. The two men had always appeared to get on well.

"I have reconciled myself with my appointed path. I shall accept my responsibilities. My brother was not the best earl, and though it isn't right to speak ill of the dead, I don't think he will be overly missed. Even his widow has little cause to grieve his passing."

"Are you going to marry her?" Florence asked.

Ned blinked in astonishment. "Good lord, no! I'm not King Henry the eighth marrying his brother's wife. I shall ensure the dowager countess has a generous allowance and shall ensure my niece is well-educated and brought up with all advantages. She is still the daughter of an earl, even though her father is deceased."

Ned sighed wearily. He walked across the room to where a crystal decanter stood with four glasses, gestured to it, and raised an eyebrow at Clayton.

"May I?"

"My lord, allow me." Clayton immediately rushed forward and poured three tumblers of whisky, handing them to each of the men.

"I shall be fascinated to hear about your estate, my lord," he said deferentially.

Florence and Cordelia exchanged a surreptitious smile. Whatever lesson they had hoped Clayton might learn, it appeared he was going to show the same awkward mix of overfamiliarity and reverence with Ned as he did with any other nobleman.

"There will be lots of work to do. Lots of bridges to rebuild, and I'm not just talking metaphorically," Ned continued. "I've heard that the estate has been neglected and the tenants and the businesses that survive on our land treated pitifully."

"So you'll be returning to England?" Florence asked. Her voice sounded unusually quiet to her. "I mean, you won't be taking on any commissions to find runaway heirs for Twemlow's friends?"

"I think I have had quite enough of runaway heirs," Ned said. He gave her a slightly odd look.

"I was always returning to England but now I shall take a first-class cabin. I shall enjoy the peace of being my own man before the hard work begins. I'm afraid my brother squandered a lot of the family wealth and thanks to some careless investments, I imagine there is very little money available."

"Ha! Now I see it," Clayton said, a note of triumph creeping into his voice. "You have your eyes on my daughter's money. Well, if you think you're going to get your hands on it, then you're very much mistaken! Do you think I'll just hand her to anyone with a title?"

All eyes turned on Clayton, everyone else presumably as astonished as Florence at this sudden display of hypocrisy.

"Daddy, that's exactly what you were intending to do!" Florence exclaimed. A horrible thought occurred to her. Cordelia had warned her that Ned might intend to marry her for her fortune. What if the declaration of love had been a ploy all along?

"You don't want to marry me for my money, do you, Lord Ayesgarth?"

Ned looked away, his lips moving soundlessly.

He didn't know about the broken engagement! The shock hit Florence like a slap to the face.

"If I was free to marry, I mean," she said quickly. "Which I am."

He looked round at Florence, hope lighting his eyes. "Are you?"

She nodded and crossed the room to him. "I'm afraid that Lord Stretford has terminated our engagement. Thank goodness it hadn't been announced because the embarrassment would be too much to bear."

"I absolutely cannot have your family embarrassed," Ned said. He reached for her hand. Aware that her family were watching, but not caring in the slightest, Florence allowed him to take it.

"Florence, my darling, I want you *despite* your wealth. I want you for your passion and your ideas and the way you make me feel when we're dancing or talking. And for your expert knowledge in how a nobleman should behave, of course."

She couldn't stop the laugh that bubbled inside her. He made her laugh like no one else. *Find a man who makes you laugh*, he had told her. Well, she had.

"I am an expert in that field as you know."

Ned dropped to his knee.

"You have made it perfectly clear that you don't want to marry an earl. I have made it equally clear that I don't want to be one. Why don't we both resign ourselves to our fates and face the world together? Will you marry me, my darling?"

From the corner of her eye, Florence could see Cordelia grasping Twemlow by the arm and beaming. She laughed and reached for his hand to pull him upright.

"Lord Ayesgarth, Benedict, Ned, my dearest, of course I will."

Ned stood and she wrapped her arms around his neck, ignoring the muffled sounds from the direction of her father. They might be of astonishment or pleasure or rage, but right now, she didn't really care. She would deal with that later, with Ned at her side.

Ned drew her closer until there was not the space for a piece of paper between them. He leaned down, pressing his cheek against hers. As their lips found each other's, she was dimly aware of Twemlow's voice coming from her right.

"So who won the wager? I've a hundred pounds at stake, you know."

"Oh," Florence said, pulling momentarily out of the kiss to gaze up at Ned, who looked back at her with eyes radiating joy and love, "do you know, I rather think I did."

Author's Letter

Some thoughts on Florence

Florence Wakechild speaks forthrightly to the point where she is considered rude. She answers questions literally and takes things at face value. She info dumps about champagne grapes at parties and becomes engrossed with the rules of society to the extent that she decides to systematically apply them to a complete stranger to turn him into a perfect example. She's awkward in social situations, misses social cues, finds large gatherings exhausting and as a child preferred to go off and line up flowers in size order than join in games. She talks about masking (though literally in her case) and she stims.

Today she'd probably use the term 'sensory overload' to articulate how she feels when she's in a crowded, noisy room, but at the time the book is set no one would use that terminology, or diagnose Florence as being on the autistic

Author's Letter

spectrum (the first case was described and recorded in 1799 but the term itself wasn't used until 1911 and the diagnostic criteria weren't standardised until the 1980s).

For many years I didn't understand why some of my feelings, thoughts and behaviours made me stand out as different and why I was never quite able to 'pass' in company other than I was the 'weirdo' or odd one out. I never even considered that I might be autistic (I definitely am not a maths genius or artist and I was articulate rather than the opposite like Dustin Hoffman's character in *Rain Man*). It was only when my own children began their journey towards diagnosis that I (like my husband) began to consider how the criteria related to me. Knowing more about it has helped in so many ways, the most important of which is that I'm kinder to myself when I don't manage to fit in (I'm still the weird one but now I can spot others and gravitate to them where we can be weird together and info dump about our latest obsessions).

I find it fascinating to read books written before the condition was widely understood and spot characters whose behaviour indicates the author was describing Autism (Mr Darcy in *Pride and Prejudice* and Mr Dick in *David Copperfield* being a couple that spring to mind and maybe you have your own thoughts in which case I'd love to hear them).

Writers of TV shows or books sometimes say that the interpretation is up to the reader/viewer and they haven't deliberately written an autistic character but when I wrote Florence I purposefully set out to write her as autistic

Author's Letter

(drawing a number of her traits from my own). I was delighted when the notes came back from the copyeditor asking if she was intended to be on the spectrum. I've written characters previously who show traits, some more than others, and if you've read *Daughter of the Sea*, you'll recognise Effie's son as being on the spectrum in a very different way to Florence. As well as first-hand, I've taught many children over my twenty-plus years as a teacher who have been diagnosed or are waiting on the (shamefully long) list to get their diagnosis and there are so many different ways in which the condition manifests.

If you spot yourself in some of the things Florence does or says and it sparks some curiosity towards your own neuro-behaviour then I wish you all the best in discovering if and where you sit on the spectrum. If you spot a friend or relative then be kind to them and listen when they info dump (it's a love language) but maybe don't try fraudulently creating a peer.

Apologies for all the brackets, by the way, but apparently that's something common to us so we can include as much context as possible.

Acknowledgments

I have absolutely loved writing this book with the characters giving me more fun than I anticipated.

Thank you to my editor Charlotte and the staff at One More Chapter who have been so enthusiastic about it. Thank you to my family who have tolerated my singing of Lerner and Loewe's songs around the house and insisted that Twemlow was a great name for a character (it's a local village and the character bears more than a little resemblance to Matt Berry). Thank you, dear reader, for picking it up and I hope you've enjoyed. I'd love to hear from you via whichever social media platforms are around by now.

ONE MORE CHAPTER

YOUR NUMBER ONE STOP
FOR PAGETURNING BOOKS

The author and One More Chapter would like to thank everyone who contributed to the publication of this story...

Analytics
Abigail Fryer
Maria Osa

Audio
Fionnuala Barrett
Ciara Briggs

Contracts
Georgina Hoffman
Florence Shepherd

Design
Lucy Bennett
Fiona Greenway
Holly Macdonald
Liane Payne
Dean Russell

Digital Sales
Lydia Grainge
Emily Scorer
Georgina Ugen

Editorial
Laura Burge
Arsalan Isa
Charlotte Ledger
Federica Leonardis
Bonnie Macleod
Jennie Rothwell
Kimberley Young

International Sales
Bethan Moore

Marketing & Publicity
Chloe Cummings
Emma Petfield

Operations
Melissa Okusanya
Hannah Stamp

Production
Emily Chan
Denis Manson
Francesca Tuzzeo

Rights
Lana Beckwith
Rachel McCarron
Agnes Rigou
Hany Sheikh Mohamed
Zoe Shine
Aisling Smyth

The HarperCollins Distribution Team

The HarperCollins Finance & Royalties Team

The HarperCollins Legal Team

The HarperCollins Technology Team

Trade Marketing
Ben Hurd
Eleanor Slater

UK Sales
Laura Carpenter
Isabel Coburn
Jay Cochrane
Tom Dunstan
Sabina Lewis
Holly Martin
Erin White
Harriet Williams
Leah Woods

And every other essential link in the chain from delivery drivers to booksellers to librarians and beyond!

One More Chapter is an award-winning global division of HarperCollins.

Sign up to our newsletter to get our latest eBook deals and stay up to date with our weekly Book Club!
<u>Subscribe here.</u>

Meet the team at
<u>www.onemorechapter.com</u>

Follow us!
<u>@OneMoreChapter_</u>
<u>@OneMoreChapter</u>
<u>@onemorechapterhc</u>

Do you write unputdownable fiction? We love to hear from new voices. Find out how to submit your novel at
<u>www.onemorechapter.com/submissions</u>